Almost Unstoppable

R.V. Devlin

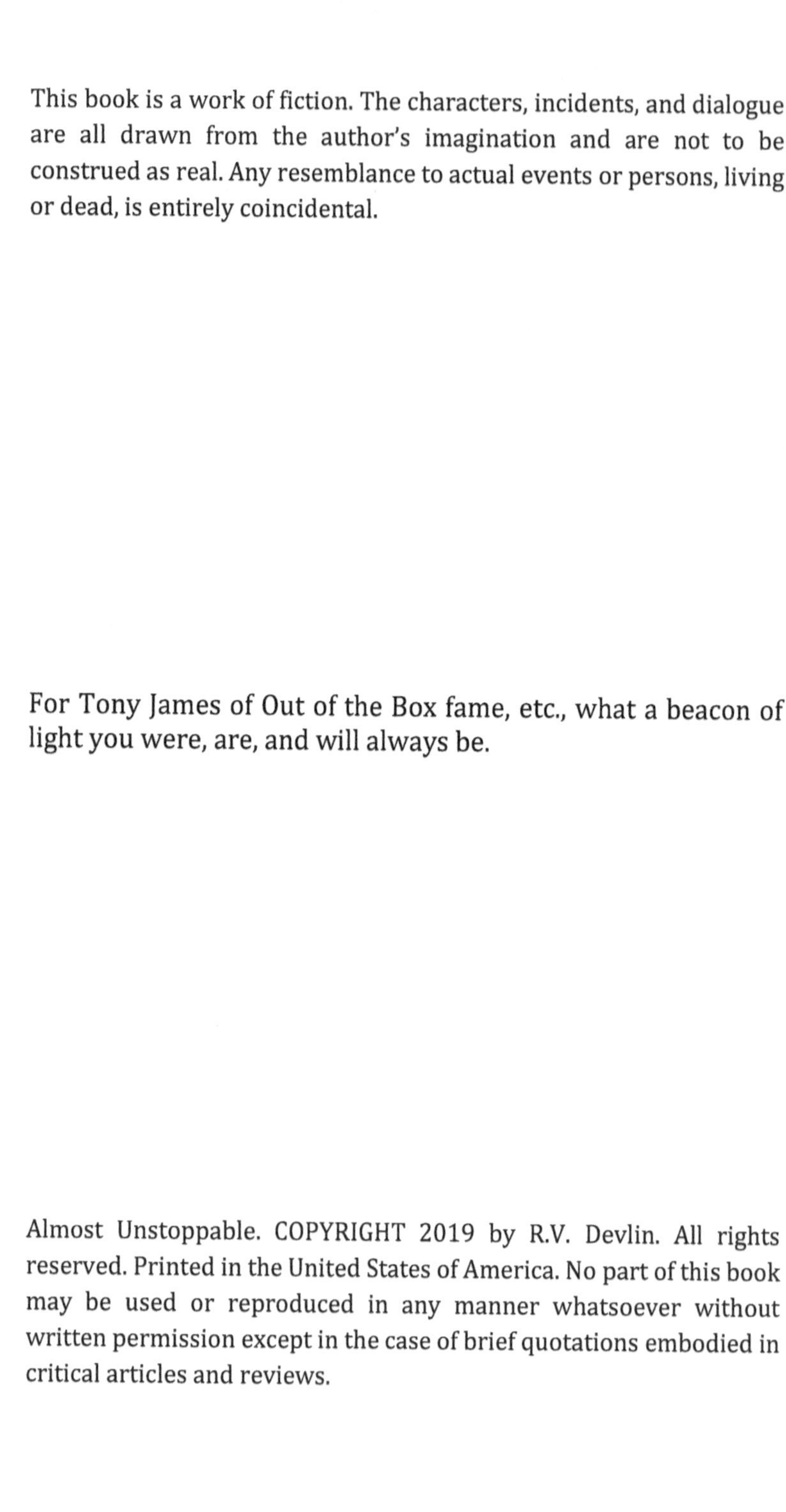

This book is a work of fiction. The characters, incidents, and dialogue are all drawn from the author's imagination and are not to be construed as real. Any resemblance to actual events or persons, living or dead, is entirely coincidental.

For Tony James of Out of the Box fame, etc., what a beacon of light you were, are, and will always be.

Brickenwood

Make Me into a Volkswagen

The anticipation, two boy's desperation at being helpless to defend themselves, the repetitive confusion of it all, shame at being demeaned in front of each other, and a more formative shame at this ritualistic plight in front of our mother. As was the custom in our father's kingdom she'd been sent to our bedroom to tell Benny and me it was haircut time so, to quote him, "we'd best be fixing to shut our yaps." Benny was playing with the galaxy of Kleenex Men he'd invented and I was perusing anything morbid in the encyclopedia when just like that befell that sickening terror. The unabridged truth be told, awaiting his imminent summons I was always a Dead Man Walking once my hair had grown out.

When we got to the kitchen my panic was full throttle. Benny as usual got that defiant bearing, braced to be as non-reactive as possible. By the time our mother had set up the two chairs, one in back for the Master Barber, I'd launched into tears. There was never any money to visit the barbershop so long ago our father had assigned himself that duty. Lucky us. This meant ending up bald an inch around the ears, "white walls," with an inch of hair elsewhere, which for a nine-year-old like Benny, or a ten-year-old like me, wasn't a dream come true. Despite our slight objections, to protest more would've increased daddy's shameless wrath, it was done that way so we'd need a haircut less often. The higher above the ears, the longer before he had to "put up with our belly aching again." Whether, because we were both "accidents," there was also some revenge mixed in, is open to debate.

Our father entered, shirtless and already sweating, over-accentuating the disdainful scowl of someone who maintains, even despite any evidence to the contrary, that he alone is the victim in the scenario.

With nothing safer for us to center on other than our addled mother standing there as toothless as a plant, bedecked in her half apron on which was pictured an idyllic farm scene replete with banjo player and exuberant maiden milking Bessie, once again he was out of control.

"Goddamn it," he raged at me, the vein in his neck bulging so grotesquely that an outsider might've conjectured that he was also passing a cluster of kidney stones. "Why the hell are you crying already? Be a man for Christ's sake, it's just a Goddamn haircut. Sit, you're first."

"I'll go first," Benny said.

"Who elected you the boss?" he spat back and turned to me. "Cheeks to chair, Goddamn it. Stupid cry baby."

I sat. He started cutting. Seconds later I moved a millimeter and he wrenched my hair to yank my head back into place, his jug-handle ears flapping away.

"Ow!"

"Quiet! Stay still, damn it. Again, this crap. A two-year-old can hold still better than you," he barked.

The shock like at every other recurrence so unnerved me that it was impossible to remain inert, perpetuating the chain of torture. Wrench hair, smack, snip hair, an incidental movement, pull hair, smack, "turn your head right," if I didn't heed commands instantly, smack, twist head, and on and on. Even worse, like someone at the guillotine watching the head prior to his plop into the basket, the agony finished for one of us meant the other was next. He would be so traumatized, that he was light years away from being able to function with the alacrity that hysteria entails. There's nothing like witnessing your sweet brother violated before enduring your own. When it was finally over....white walls! White walls!

My name is Davey Thompson and I shall be your narrator for Benny's story...Our story. Much of what's to come I was there for, some Benny recapped shortly after, and some he revealed to me way down the road after a crucial juncture in his life.

White walls freshly sheared, which was only slightly better than if we were sporting matching pink dresses with bonnets, an hour later all eyes were on us as Benny strolled unaffectedly and I lumbered still anguished toward Bucky's unit. As kids in the late 1960's ensconced in a racially integrated housing project called "Brickenwood," there were three fashion statements you always tried to avoid, "white walls," "high waters," and worst of all, "Salvation Army Threads," if you were so Salvation Army that even accessorizing couldn't mask it. The youth who lived nearby respected Benny's daredevil, won't back down exploits enough to not lob a comment, at least in earshot. Their visible consternation just read: "Oh, not again." Aggie Boza was another story. It was hard to decipher when she didn't favor something because she wasn't one for facial expressions. Since the day a year earlier when her family of seven moved into the unit that was two over from ours, and when not at school, she'd stoically spent every waking hour installed on her stoop like the Great Witness to all, button mouth so low on her chinless face, two eyes set too high up and far apart, all as if her nose was perpetually mediating a dispute amongst features. Rumor was, fearing for their safety, her family had requested to be transferred there from Presidential Heights, another of the housing projects that funneled its children to Mt. Pleasant Grammar School. Their transgression, Aggie's older brothers used to pummel snowmen mercilessly until their creators ended up in gangs at their doorstep. Even in the schoolyard while everyone darted about Aggie observed, eyes turning as far sideways as possible before she'd expend energy moving her head. She never joined her fellow first graders in hopscotch or jacks, or for that matter the second graders whom she was in the first grade with the previous year. Or, wore any color other than red. Though no one had better refer to her as "The Almost Human Tomato" in front of Benny. To her had extended his inclination to defend those who couldn't fairly defend themselves. We lived on Princeton Street, at the intersection of Harvard and Yale. The street names I surmise were to inspire us to greater heights. Originally built as transitional housing for those from The Greatest Generation who'd fought in the war, it was now oversaturated with petty criminals flashing their cool, single mothers who'd thought he was cool, dropouts who thought it looked cool at the time, blue collar workers unlikely to improve their lot in life, and families who'd kept alive the art of inbreeding. This last category included the Cubbards, who were once again outside undeterred by armpit stains so enormous that they seemed sprayed on. Five boys and a girl, they had a knack for standing in a group with their mouths equally open breathing and blinking in unison. As Benny passed by unfailingly tall and proud, like he hadn't just received his portion of daddy's smacks during the haircut, he could tell from Walter Cubbard's few insecure steps in his direction that it was his shot to act all brave in front of his brood of remedial readers. "White Walls," Walter chimed, forcing me to pretend like I didn't hear it and Benny to pause and glare. Hadn't Walter learned his lesson the last time? He fought like a boy in a girdle, cast iron flexibility allowing for kicks so high and fast that they untied Benny's shoe.

Any further zingers stayed stored in the Cubbards so we headed off. Seconds later Walter released another "White Walls" and it was grounds to charge. While I trembled in place, Benny zoomed toward them causing all but the oldest two Cubbards to flee. They outweighed him by twenty pounds. A few yards from them, as their fists were raised, Benny slid as if into home plate, got up and trumpeted: "What are ya blind? I'm safe! Whatdaya need glasses, I'm safe I tell ya!" and off he went. Invariably the perception that this one is crazy afforded you a strand of housing project cred. Even so, this shouldn't make it look like he was that punk kid always bent on being the alpha dog. Only those two breaking points when boys had pushed it too far did it turn all punch and kick. And then Benny moved so fast, and with such relaxed fury, that one time the combatant hightailed it while apologizing, and the other he had a certain Cubbard pinned, regarded his bloody nose, and let him quit without even giving him one more for the road.

When we got to Bucky's unit, he was outside throwing a ball into the air and missing it when it came down. Bucky wasn't half the athlete of the other tyke called "Bucky," though twice the student in school. This Bucky would never raise his hand in class to dodge being teased as "Einstein," like any of us barring him were tuned in to who that was. The other Bucky often tossed up his hand to ask that the question be repeated. This Bucky had buckteeth and a gap between the front two good for shooting spurts of water farther than his noodle arm could throw. The other Bucky was spared the gap, but never the rod, so he was destined to stand alone in the corners of high school all Alice Cooper. This Bucky already knew about Chang and Eng Bunker when their fourth-grade teacher, Miss Gregory, tried to peak their curiosity by displaying a poster of those famous 19th century conjoined twins from Siam who spawned the phrase Siamese Twins. Chang and Eng were joined at the chest yet somehow each had found a wife. For Benny's class it was a double anomaly because they'd never seen an Asian before excluding Sulu, so every time Miss Gregory turned toward the poster certain kids slanted the sides of their eyes by pulling them. Though that behavior didn't interest Benny, and even if it had he was already preoccupied with two school tasks. There was the old gum to sneak out of his mouth, and the new gum to deposit inside. He'd learned to do both in a single act of dexterity. Practice makes perfect, even when it's covering your mouth during a fake cough. To cough the teacher's attention in his direction while committing a gum infraction heightened the thrill.

Later that day Charlotte joked that Chang and Eng's wives must have been hit in the head and assumed that they were seeing double to "go for them boys." It cracked her up so much that the dandelion she wore behind her ear fell out. Thus, Benny began his talent for rewriting songs by improvising....

"Stand By Your Man....And His Twin Brother
Give them two arms to cling to
And something warm to come home to
When nights are cold and lonely
Stand by your man....and his twin brother!"

He ran up to Bucky, slid, got up like lightening and contested, "What are ya blind? I'm safe."

"You're out I tell ya. You're out!" Bucky overruled. "So, you'd better play basketball."

"Walter Cubbard goes all 'white walls', so I had to chase that chicken."

With me standing disconsolately nearby, Bucky took one gander at Benny's skull and proclaimed: "Ain't no white walls. It's a whole car. It looks like a Volkswagen Bug and I like'm." He knew that Benny also liked VW bugs. To be liked he liked to like what Benny liked.

"Yeah!! That's me. A Volkswagen."

"Really like a Volkswagen bug. Ain't fibbing," Bucky confirmed as we entered the parlor of his unit.

I didn't want to be there so I sat quietly. I just wanted to commiserate to Benny as I always did about whatever grief our father had cast our way. Suddenly Bucky knocked Benny onto all fours and straddled him like a horse. Benny's first impulse was to buck him off, but he quickly got into the spirit of the moment. Okay, I'll be a horse. He didn't catch on that to Bucky he now actually was a Volkswagen. Just then Bucky's mother moseyed in and they rode right by her screeching "out of the way". They were circling around and around a coffee table like the oval at the Daytona 500, when Benny detected something tailing them. Frightened, he stopped short nearly ejecting the car's driver. Bucky's mother passed by them on all fours chortling as if this was just what she needed. She got up and clapped like a borderline psychotic who at only 25 years old heard languages in her head that she didn't speak, always had on slippers that didn't match, but was otherwise a loving parent.

"Don'tcha think his haircut's like a Volkswagen Bug?" inquired Bucky.

"Sure do," she agreed. "And they got engines in the back where the trunks are supposed to be."

"The engine is in my butt?" Benny blurted then bit his knuckles when he realized he'd let that loose to an adult. That's when it hit him. Bucky's mother does Bucky's snips super good, he thought. And he sure didn't itch to endure more distressing "white walls." Thus, he said: "Can ya really make me into a Volkswagen?"

"Even a mechanic couldn't do that!" I piped in.

"I wanna be a Volkswagen," Benny pressed. "Can ya do it? It's worth having white walls if they're underneath a whole Volkswagen!"

I expected her to utter the obligatory, "I'd have to ask your parents." Instead, with an impromptu look of determination, she promenaded out of the room. Hands raised to our shoulders Benny and I waited for Bucky to spell out what just happened. This was often necessary concerning his mother's behavior. Nothing sprang forth. Zoned in like God had entrusted her with an assignment, she reemerged with an electric razor and scissors. Bucky's mother had attended beauty school before her mind had altered.

"Fix it good," Benny exhorted then sat up tall in a chair, set for a game of calling each other's bluff. She wasn't the bluffing kind though, also proven the morning she'd underscored to Bucky that to limit him missing school she'd curtail the spread of germs by emptying out a closet for her to sneeze in. She did it all right, not a headband or a coaster left inside, and once Bucky returned home from school, she sure had the speed to hit that closet. **Achoo!** Not too wacko to prank him on April Fool's Day!! But on this occasion, she was all business. Far too poor to buy her son toys, she had a secondary interest in this succeeding. She sheared and cut, shaved and sculpted, the hood, the windshield, the trunk, all the while whistling through her missing front tooth, strangely in rhythm with Bucky whistling through his gap. Every so often he added a: "Yeah," or "Go, Ma." She carved, and drew lines and circles until there was no turning back the clock. Without a mirror for Benny to see, he could only hope that he wasn't being transmuted into some type of gargoyle.

"What do ya think, Davey?" he asked me.

"Nice," I answered. Inched into the spirit, I would later call the scene, "certifiably amusing."

When she was done and a mirror produced, despite the lightning bolt shaped crack in it, the reflection of Benny's Volkswagen haircut was the work of a first-rate artist. Even better, by the time Bucky also had a flawless VW Bug sculpted out of the hair on his noggin it was apparent that Bucky's mother had finally found her calling. Toy maker. It was evident even to a kid like Benny who'd made the mistake of sticking a raisin up his nose the previous week, and that raisin had yet to reappear. And the best of the best, the icing on the frosting on the most perfect cake of all time, Bucky and he were anointed kings for a day when they dashed outside and urchins they did and didn't know, did and didn't like, even me though self-consciously, set about riding the VWs and each other in races around a grand oval invented out of shoes and shirts. There must have been fifty races, all while Chuckie, no relation to either Bucky, screamed 'Uuuuuuuu" as everyone cheered.

At one point an Old Guy with his cane hanging off the back of his pants sluggishly tottered by. Benny sprinted up to him feigning terror. "Sir, sir is there sa'em on my head?"

"Think it's a car," the Old Guy replied.

"Get it off. Get it off!" Benny begged, falling to his knees, hands chest level in prayer.

Once his and Bucky's knees were too overtaxed for any additional races, going back inside with Chuckie and me in tow, they high-fived everyone along the way. The other kids remained outside the door clamoring for more, some of who must have contributed to the twenty-one cents Benny had inadvertently earned.

Basking in her otherworldly glory Bucky's mother supplied the three of us some lemonade in the spaghetti sauce jars they'd used since the day she'd thrown all of the drinking glasses at their neighbor's door. Unwritten rule! Opera records should never be played too loudly with an off-key accompaniment, especially in a housing project. We all sat to rest. Bucky's mother picked up the electric razor and approached to shave off Bucky's Volkswagen. Just like that the festivities were over, or so we gathered but the eyes of Bucky's mother began gyrating clockwise like a yoga eye exercise, a sign that the Mad Genius was again inspired.

"Oh boy, there she goes. You numbskulls best hang on to your britches 'cause sa'em is up," Bucky pointed out. "What's up, Mum?"

"Just percolating up here," she replied, pointing at her temple. It was no secret that if the eyes reversed direction the idea percolating had to be actualized.

"Uuuuuuuuu. I like when Bucky's mother goes all brainiac. Uuuuuuuuuuuu!" Chuckie yelped, so excited he got up and attempted the 437th back flip he never quite completed.

"Nice try" she remarked. The eyes stopped, focused like a wax replica of her in one of those museums. Before Benny could ask if she needed an ambulance, the eyes rotated the other way. Bless the beasts and the children she wasn't going to call it a day at one act of brilliance. She switched on that razor, twirled it around like a magic wand and brought it toward Bucky's VW. Sublimely eager to outdo herself, she somehow sculpted a square out of the VW's roof, and four, inch thick peg legs of hair where the VW's sides had been, one attached to each corner of the square. She grabbed a coaster off an end table and placed it on Bucky's head, as confident as Picasso in his prime.

"It's an end table!" Benny and Chuckie shrieked, unison propelling Bucky to the mirror to check it out. "Bucky's head's an end table!"

"Nice head, Mum. Nice head!" Bucky hollered.

"Uuuuuuuuuu! I'm a piece of colored drawing paper," Chuckie ad-libbed when it was his turn to become an end table. "Colored" was the term back then. Too roused, he couldn't sit motionless, forcing her to employ Benny as a head stabilizer. Once done with him she turned to me but again I refused, concerned that altering Daddy's handiwork wouldn't be well received by him. So she pivoted to Benny. Thirty minutes later the three recipients busted out the door screaming, "End Tables!!" and once again it was Let the Games Begin. A throng of youth, with a parade of Cubbards amongst them, gathered to cheer for and bet on the three boys they tried to speed walk across the lot with cups, plates, and even ashtrays with chocolate cigarettes in them balanced on their end tables. Chuckie was never apprised that his cranium gave him an egg-shaped disadvantage. Every time the coaster fell off it was, "Balls!" Somehow, renowned athlete that he was destined to never become, Bucky got the most victories, his prowess saluted by onlookers for weeks to come Kids loved to run around Brickenwood broadcasting whatever was afoot, so soon even Aggie Boza had trudged to the festivities. Even Bucky's mother hatched a rare trip outside, volunteering some sage advice after Benny suffered a series of close defeats. "Don't give up, Benny. Anything truly important is worth working for." Encouraged, he uttered "watch," grabbed Bucky and bent him forward so his torso faced the ground and the top of his end table pointed forward. Benny also bent forward, conjoined his end table to Bucky's and announced: "Siamese Twins joined at the end table!" That was the funniest thing she'd ever heard. From then on, she'd mention it whenever they crossed paths. It always made him proud.

As day became dusk, and kids from only one walk of life had to scatter home to their units, Bucky's mother performed one further act of magic. She pared it all down to crew cuts so that they weren't entirely bald. Nonetheless, crew cuts for white boys like Bucky and Benny in Brickenwood were as pathetic as white walls, but those who'd missed the vehicle and furniture games had at least heard about them so the few jibes that came brought scores of defenders. The whole scene was rendered even more unforgettable when twelve years later Benny resurrected it as a short story that his professor Dr. LaPrade would call the best he'd ever received.

Skeletons in The Closet

All wasn't rosy in my mind though, and not only due to our lacerating father. Robert Kennedy and Martin Luther King Jr. had just been cut down. Both of these tragedies tossed me around, more so because their demise exacerbated my fear that danger was around every corner, a slant that only a non-poisonous insect like me surrounded by so many fly swatters fully understood. I kept reminding Benny, "They had body guards with guns and they're still six feet under. How safe does that leave us?"

"Today we've lost a great man," Miss Gregory announced, ceremoniously starting off Benny's class.

Benny's hands gripped his desk, feet tapping with unease that it might be Carl Yastremski, or "The Boomer," or even one of the Red Sox pinch hitters.

"Mr. Robert F. Kennedy Jr. was assassinated and all of the country is in mourning," Miss Gregory continued. Her words affected Benny about as much as the going price of caviar, the topic switching in his mind to how Chuckie's drawing that hung on the wall of Benny the Volkswagen was a cut above his of Bucky the Volkswagen, and miles better than Bucky's of Chuckie the End Table.

"Were you sad at all during the minute of silence?" I asked him later.

"I was too busy wishing I had the power to hear what's going on in Orlandodo's pea brain."

"But someone died!"

"So?" Benny asked, his questions always so disarmingly unpremeditated. "I didn't know'm. I didn't even know he wanted to be president."

It reminded me of when we were pallbearers at the funeral of a cousin we'd never met. While I unceasingly stared into the open coffin, analyzing the makeup and speculating if that's what the corpse looked like before he was a corpse, Benny managed to have a rip-roaring time with the kids who were still alive. Everything about him made me jealous.

"I didn't spend the whole minute thinking 'pea brain.' I did some deciding too, about which Skelathletes should go on which team for this year's football season" Benny amended. The Skeleton football league was information that only I, in our many pacts of secrecy, would ever hear about.

In fact, nothing unusual of public knowledge had gone down of late around Brickenwood. No one had been caught stealing hubcaps or shimmied down the sewer to mine for mythical alligators and alighted upon Mrs. Stillwell's dead chihuahua. Mrs. Dariteau's 300 pounds hadn't collapsed another lawn chair sending her and her dish of American Chop Suey flying, while Mr. Dariteau, who weighed less than half of her, gleefully finished his before assisting her up. Their love of American Chop Suey and how edible it was for those lacking teeth also hadn't diminished. No one had yet to conjure up a makeshift bowling alley in the cellar, equipped with a bowling ball named "Cuddly." There had been no fights where a mob of fifty were chasing one small fry and his mother stormed outside in his defense with a two feet tall standing ashtray as a weapon. Her proficiency at doing that without dropping the cigarette from her lips was the basis for legend. Yep, nothing unusual had transpired, at least until a moving truck went and another came.

Time moves slowly for children because the world is new to them, especially if their latest neighbors are a circus family whose stage name is "The Tedro Family." With four children and a bunch of small dogs in the act, they performed in carnivals and entertainment parks, often for cash only so they could dwell in government subsidized housing amongst us. The oldest son did some balancing tricks, but specialized in juggling. The balancing fell primarily to a 13-year-old, curvaceous daughter whom I ogled from behind my curtains, 11-year-old Dale and 8-year-old Tino. Feet toward the sky, Tino balanced on top of a standing Dale effortlessly, one hand to head, head to head, hand to hand, you name it, practicing on their lawn cordoned off by six-inch stakes and fishing line, a gaggle of locals gaping. Rui Tedro, their surly, bellicose father, coach, manager, and bully demanded that they avoid us like the lice we were born to circulate. His progeny was more like flesh and blood business assets than children, so he didn't want our slovenliness undermining his plan for circus world domination. Though Tino admired Benny, probably because with his record player humming out of the bedroom window, Benny would dance on the stoop to "The Jackson 5" humbly aware of what a natural he was. That boy could dance.

Benny was also the implicit leader of a select troop of friends, Charlotte, who always wore a shirt underneath her stains, that tough as beef jerky Tomboy who licked everyone other than Benny in the fifty, Chuckie, otherwise known as "Balls," and Brian, who used to misspell his name "Brain" disproving the veracity of his nickname, "Brain." Charlotte and Chuckie were black; Brain and Benny white. They'd scoot around like lunatics playing "Mod Squad" that undercover cop show featuring two white males, a black male, and white female, alternating characters as easily as flipping pancakes. This was all happening while The Equal Rights Amendment was being debated, though they didn't know that. They were just kids zeroed in on the moment they'd invented and keeping hidden how their families behaved behind closed doors. They were unaware that only one of them would live to age forty, and that one would verge on being a goner also.

Their only concern in the outside realm was a pack of six slightly bigger, nattily clad white boys from God Knows where. Dubbed The Raleigh 3 Speed Boys, they'd bike into the schoolyard right up to The Mod Squad, taunt them with "Oreo Kids," cackle through their orthodontic teeth, and retreat. The Mod Squad had no idea that "Oreo Kids" referenced their racial makeup. They presumed that their choice in cookies was being disparaged, a hot tip that The Raleigh 3 Speed Boys had mysteriously gotten. Nuisance Mongers love to stir up trouble where they can't foresee consequences, but The Mod Squad wasn't intimidated, preferring to leg after them with Charlotte shouting "fraidy cats," and Brain firing off, "faggots." The Raleigh 3 Speed Boys weren't clued in that fighting in Brickenwood was a blood sport. If someone had you pinned, the crowd around might go all Roman Coliseum and clamor for memorable damage.

The Mod Squad was sick of it, so they convened to strategize. Joined by their classmate Corey Paskell, (as always, I chose to preserve my status as a non-combatant), they planned an ambush, and most certainly due to numbers and size get themselves slaughtered. Drinking Grape Kool Aid, like Warriors decorated for battle adorned with purple lips, they lay in wait for hours at a time near the dirt path in a stretch of woods that The Raleigh 3 Speed Boys glided through to do their taunting. No luck so they'd always end up back home on our stoop where, as usual, it was never long until Benny began to dance. The rest of the "Oreo" talked sweet revenge, while tuckered out from practice Tino and Dale Tedro gazed longingly out their window at the liberty denied to them. As usual Aggie Boza was on her stoop, an unspoken mascot. It was no longer fodder for gossip that none of us had ever heard her speak.

One day perched on our stoop frustrated in their noble quest to avenge themselves, they were particularly energized. Less easy for Benny in that our father had again "tanned his hide" for next to nothing. Brain had gone home before all of the leftovers were eaten, so that left only four, but now they were armed. Chuckie had lifted someone's brassiere off a clothesline, filled it with a rock, a slingshot at the ready. Benny sang to Chuckie "I got the feelin'. Baby, baby. I got the feelin'," then to Charlotte for, "You don't know what you do to me. People are heavy, down in misery. Hey, yeah, awright. Hey, yeah, good lord." Then to Corey, "I got the feelin', awright." As he finished off the "baby, baby, baby...baby, baby, baby"....in the direction of his most ardent fan Aggie Boza, as her face scrunched its recognition of danger. There was no mistaking that expression. We'd seen it when Tino had fallen off of Dale's head ending up unconscious. It was spotted when some Joe with more gargantuan breasts than Mrs. Dariteau traipsed by without a shirt on. The Raleigh 3 Speed Boys were riding up, spread like the wings of an eagle with the leader scanning leisurely as if he hadn't by then picked the prey. Ominously, not only were they apprised that The Mod Squad ate Oreos, but also where they lived.

As I came to the window to watch from the safety of indoors, they stood over their bikes menacingly, their Second in Command goading Chuckie with, "There's my favorite spear chucker."

"Wish I had one now," Chuckie fired back. "'Cause this woodchuck could chuck wood right in your eyeball and out your ass."

"Make sure you sharpen it first with that Brillo you call hair," their leader added.

"Say that again and I'll smash your mug so far in that it ends up on the back of your head," Benny said. His dancing would elicit miniature grins from Aggie. That really stretched her smile.

"You and what Oreo Army?" their Second in Command asked, before turning to Chuckie. "Spear chucker."

Chuckie took a step toward him. Corey clasped his arm to avert him.

"Fight. Fight. A nigger and a white," another one repeatedly chanted, joined by the others. That didn't impede Charlotte from proving that there's such a force as beginner's luck when she picked up the brassiere and used it to slingshot the gooey fudgesicle that had been adding to the stains on her shirt. It dipped like a curve ball, landing smack on the leader's thigh.

"Fight, fight, a fudgesicle and a white," Benny chanted proudly.

"Ya wanna fight?" asked the leader, smirking confidently.

"Jump off ya bike, Beaver Cleaver," Benny responded. Our father was off working in the boiler room at Serodyn, so Benny was free to guard his territory. Finally, they got off their bikes, as cocky as six Steve McQueens keen to do battle with a bunch of four-eyed Girl Scouts.

"You're a pimple on our beautiful butts," one of them wisecracked to Corey.

"You're a monkey butt," The Second in Command stated to Charlotte.

"You're a pimple on her monkey butt," the leader sniped to Benny.

As The Mod Squad approached them, suddenly the Raleigh 3 Speed Boys looked confused. At first, I thought they were astounded at The Mod Squad's wrong side of the track courage. Then the wind blew by in the shape of Tino and Dale Tedro. Benny hustled to get in his licks, Chuckie his kicks, Charlotte her bites, Corey his chokeholds, but it was hard with full-priced shirts being flung around left and right with privileged boys inside of them. Any point when a member of the Mod Squad went down and was sure to be pummeled, Tino or Dale would bust in to finish the attacker off with world champion punches. Their profession molded them as strong as men. The underlying anger made them stronger.

None unscathed, five of them snatched up their bikes and bolted. I hotfooted outside to revel with the victors, bounding up and down, hands raised as if I too had done battle. With a badge of distinction swelling underneath his eye, Benny dragged the captive onto the stoop and propped him up. "Say you're sorry' every time we go you should, or else," he warned. He strode away five steps and pivoted back like a game of red light. "Say it!"

"I'm sorry. I'm sorry," the leader balled.

He apologized each time one of us paused to, "Say you're sorry" and he did. “Louder,” and he did. I sauntered up ghoulishly close to study his face, curious yet mocking. In his eyes I could see it. He’d landed on another planet, especially when Tino took to balancing on top of Dale’s coconut, toes splayed toward the sky.

----------------------------------+----------------------------------

Days later as Benny entered Corey’s unit, he did his best to conceal his despondency. The dilemma wasn’t the style and violent manner of haircut he’d again gotten, typical of him he’d moved on rapidly, it was that three of his skeletons were missing and the quest to relocate them went unrewarded. Creepy Crawler machines were the rage at the time and Benny only used ours to produce skeletons. You plugged in the miniature oven, poured goop into the mold, and minutes later presto, out came a four-inch long rubber skeleton. Each of his thirty skeletons was concocted of disparate colors, had its own personality, and unique set of skills. Two of the missing, Bony Bones and Butch, were favorites. Worst of all, his all-time favorite, Jump Bones, was also gone. Boy could that one jump.

The plan was to listen to 45’s in Corey’s bedroom, then cruise around with cards in the spokes of their bikes, nude playing cards that Benny had scavenged from a garbage can. Corey had hung out in our bedroom just two days earlier, but for some untold reason it was the first time he’d ever invited someone over. All of the units in Brickenwood were receptacles for third hand furniture, but what was noticeable in this case was how scant it was, as if someone had taken half of the stuff and someone else had kept those spaces empty for years pining for that first someone to return. Benny assumed Corey’s dad had headed for the hills, although it was something you didn’t ask in the projects. There was a saying, “After nosey comes bloody nosey.”

As Corey and Benny ambled through the parlor toward his bedroom, three old women peeked out of the adjacent bedroom. Each sported a duplicate mod multi-colored stripped tunic tank top that emphasized the creased sagginess of their arms. They studied Benny for a couple of seconds, barely waved in unison, and closed their door.

"That's my mother," Corey said.

"Which one?"

"The young one."

All three ladies struck Benny as candidates for the Shawmut Nursing Home so he inquired, "Who are the other two?"

"My grandmother and great grandmother. They wear matching shirts on Wednesdays."

"It's Tuesday."

"They're trying stuff on for tomorrow. My mother works at Silverstein's Department Store. She returns it all after they wear it," Corey confided revealing why he constantly had apparel that he donned only once, a diverse wardrobe that afforded him a player's cool. He was 'all it', as we used to say, and his willingness to the fight alongside of The Mod Squad sealed the deal. He unlatched the closet, slithered inside with the door barely open, and came out with a box of 45's making sure to close the door again.

"I'm Henery the 8th," he announced, inserting that Herman's Hermit's chart topper on the spindle.

"No way, man," Benny disagreed. "I'm Henery the 8th I am I am."

"But I got married to the widow next door!"

"Wrong widow. She was a dog. I married the real widow next door," Benny insisted as the song started up. Corey hadn't shut the warped, splintered closet door tightly so it gradually opened as they sang along, *"I'm Henery the 8th I am. Henery the 8th, I am, I am. I got married to the widow next door. She'd been married seven times before and everyone was an Henery. Couldn't have a Willy or a*

Sam. I'm her 8th old man I'm Henery. Henery the 8th I am, I am. Henery the 8th I am!"

While "Crimson and Clover" played Corey insisted the reason mailmen wouldn't deliver to Old Man Mac's house was that he too often slaughtered and buried them. Benny regaled him with a colorized account of when Brain vaulted behind him off of the one-story roof after they'd collected all of the pinkies from the gutter. That's how he broke his leg with the vast array of unsightly moles on it. Out of the corner of his eye Benny caught a glimpse of objects in the now exposed closet. His heart raced like a Matchbox Indy car around the track regularly constructed of the mottled sheets on his bed. The beige and red of his beloved Jump Bones would've caught his attention from any distance, especially when it was seated up on a shelf next to the other two victims of kidnap. Corey went red and pleaded, "Sorry I done that." He rushed to seal the closet as if that would expunge reality. Benny glared at him, biting his knuckles to compose himself. He retrieved the victims and walked to the door.

"It's okay. Just don't come to my unit again," he warned backing away. On route home, straining to stave off his first taste of betrayal by someone not called "our father," Benny pitied Corey. The agitation in his eyes screamed more than "bagged," the disorientation of someone less self-assured than his persona. Another housing project kid who someday would yearn for relief and end up a heroin addict.

Benny proceeded by Albert, whom he now customarily gave the stone face. That's because I'd recently informed him why four years earlier, I'd blocked him from going into that tent, the one where Albert had schooled me, more than once, in how to play "Doctor." Now 19 years old, no different than his heyday at 15 with me, Albert made up in politeness for what he affably pretended to lack in savviness, his notable gift of chattering with kids appreciated by parents desperate for a hiatus from them. One snapshot intricately examined and they should've realized it was too peculiar how that boy consistently wore collared shirts tucked in too tightly, and pants up laughably high creating a wedgie that emphasized his obscenely round caboose. Yet somehow it was all chocked up to him just being a nice boy who naively wasn't aware that it looked odd. More realistic would've been to perceive of it as three pairs of underpants worn to thicken the appearance of said caboose, something unappealingly he'd exposed when it was my turn to be the doctor and he'd whipped out his "boo boo," which was coincidentally located invisibly on his "pee-pee." It was my Hippocratic duty to lick it all better. Per our bond as perpetual victims of our father, Benny and I decided that abuse would remain confidential also. After all, this wasn't the days of pedophile alerts so who would we inform, our mother?

"My Mama's been hollering for Edna so long that she sended me to get lozenges," Chuckie sprinted up announcing. Typical of mothers in Brickenwood, if they needed to summon a child, they'd bellow out the screen door. She just did it more frequently. "Edna! Edna! Shondreiii, Chuckieeee, Chuckieeee, Edna!!!!" She sure loved her children, and was especially proud of what an honest boy Chuckie was. He was honest. He took credit for too many farts that others would've passed off as *source unknown* to doubt that.

"You know I ain't for tellin' on kids," Benny said. "But Corey can't be part of The Mod Squad."

"Why no?" Chuckie asked with bulging eyes. "We was gonna ask'm to join tomorrow.

A dodo from my class flew by them riding a broomstick, cowlick flying in the wind, unconsumed calories from dinner smeared around his dopey smile. The most witless ragamuffins, the "dodos," seemed to stem from the largest families. Like the lack of smarts had been passed down the line by parents who'd yet to pinpoint what caused pregnancies.

"Corey five finger discounted my stuff," Benny revealed, displaying the skeletons as evidence.

"Balls," Chuckie blurted out. "Did ya beat his ass?"

"Nope. He fought with us so that makes it even steven in my pea brain."

"We gotta go bash his ass."

"He lost friends. That's enough punishment," replied Benny. "And except for my brother I don't want this burning through kid's ear wax."

"That's why ya kisser was all long like a telephone pole when I first saw ya. Hey, let's go spy on somebody. That always gets ya happy!"

Benny just wanted to go home and lick his wounds, the place he usually fled to lick his wounds. Once there he let the kidnap victims leap about while transporting them upstairs to reunite with the others. However, he couldn't shake off the sadness so he decided to head back outside. As he unbolted the door there stood Aggie Boza about to knock, all three feet, six inches, and a hundred plus red clad pounds of her.

"Come on in, Aggie Boza," he announced like Captain von Trapp, almost cracking me up. He'd recently seen "The Sound of Music," an extravaganza that to him was only a step above a visit to the scorching breath of our depressive dentist. As only a bona fide gentleman would, he even walked outside to shepherd her in with, "To what do I owe this visit, Aggie Boza?"

She glanced left, right, at her red shoes, then at the ceiling while shrugging her shoulders.

"Then it is my honorable duty to inquire again," Benny went on. "To what do I owe this visit?"

She shrunk down and rose back up mustering courage. "I dunno," she murmured, dispelling my theory that she was at the level of a Helen Keller before the retooling. Her eyes peering up at him betrayed that she longed to be like Benny as much as I did. We two weren't capable of that. We were destined to self-identify as outcasts even in a room well stocked with misfits, and the awkwardness that I brought to everything, including watching them surreptitiously from the stairs, was proof of that.

"You don't know! That's exactly what I was hoping for," Benny continued. "So, let's figure out a how come, okay? Thinking caps on here comes one. The why of you coming here is hoverin' around and landing right there."

He pointed at her brain. She was on the spot now so she blushed and looked down again.

"We, we need, we need to borrow the ketchup bottle for our meatloaf," she disclosed, covering her mouth like she'd just tattled family secrets.

"That's a great reason. You're fast," he exclaimed then wagged his finger at her. "Did you just make that up?"

To ask Aggie a question was similar to addressing a photo of her. It immobilized her until finally she'd gaze around as if in search. She took her hands out and raised them shoulder high to claim, "I dunno."

"When you find out, would you fill me in?"

"I dunno................maybe, could be."

"So what was this about meatloaf?" he asked before yodeling….."Meatloafffffff! Meatloafffffffff!"

"We, we can borrow the ketchup bottle for our meatloaf?"

"Absolutely, Aggie Boza! I'll go pour all of the ketchup out of the bottle into a Tupperware right now, deposit that properly in the fridge to keep chilled, then I'll bring you the bottle."

"Ah, um, oh, oh thank you, thank you anyway very much thank you," she said, her mouth twisted like a figure eight. "We just, we just need the ketchup bottle with the ketchup."

"Okay, but don'tcha use any of the ketchup, Aggie Boza. Ya promise?"

"I, I, I, I, I dunno."

"You have to promise or I'll be worried about it all day," he exhorted, hands on his hips.

"Ma, Ma, Ma, Maaaa...Maybe," she answered, emitting the first giggle we'd ever heard from her.

"You wanna use the ketchup bottle to flatten out the meatloaf, right? That's what I do."

"Ah, ah, ah, no, no, we want, we want, we want to borrow the ketchup bottle to get some ketchup."

"Oh, you should've said that. Now I get it. You want the ketchup bottle to get ketchup, right?"

"Yep."

"Okay, Aggie Boza. So, I'll pour a couple of ounces of ketchup into a Tupperware for ya. That way your busy schedule won't get all messed up 'cause ya gotta bring the bottle back and also there will be ketchup on hand here in case my mom whips up sa'em best served it. Tell me that doesn't make sense," he embellished, going into the closet. He came out ten seconds later. "Darn, no Tupperware. But hey, I have another idea. You go home and bring back that juicy meatloaf. I'd be happy to pour some ketchup on it."

She gave it some serious consideration while incongruously

tweaking her expression. "I can't. My pop is eating it."

"Without ketchup? Oh my God this is bad. Aggie Boza! It's horrible without ketchup. Rescue mission!" He zipped into the kitchen so preoccupied that he didn't catch me spying and returned with the bottle of ketchup. "Come on, there's ketchup without meatloaf, I mean meatloaf without ketchup," he protested, careening out the door pulling her by the hand while she smiled from ear to ear, leaving me astounded by how gleeful he'd made her and how instinctive that was for him.

Nevertheless, his roller coaster day was destined to go back downhill in the form of a threat, and there was nothing that even his iron will could do about it. You see, an unspeakable injustice had occurred leaving our father with unfinished business. To him nobility necessitated that he regains sovereignty over an unruly mob, so later when Benny and I were in our bedroom hashing over Corey Paskell's pilfering of skeletons, he popped up in the doorway.

"Ya mother complains I'm too rough on ya. She doesn't get that ya like making me mad. But ya think you've seen mad. Next time I say stay still, ya better or ya'll really get it. Go ahead. Just try me," he said, stomping off to leave Benny and me staring at each other.

Ten seconds later, pointing at our haircuts, I commented, "Sure are a lot of skeletons in the closet."

"Huh?"

"These haircuts we get are also skeletons in the closet. Nobody knows how it happens, except Ma."

"What?"

I gladly explained what a skeleton in the closet is, and how our haircuts and his stolen rubber ones fit into that category.

Two TVs And A Pillow

One day in school Benny's class learned about John Paul Jones. After running around with Chuckie announcing to anyone with at least one ear, "I regret that I have but one life to give to my housing project!" Benny barely got home before the deluge erupted. Straight down like missiles, the raindrops crashed into each unit's square of desiccated lawn transforming them into a thousand mini craters, mud, then puddles in which to float toy boats. No one dared to venture outside other than Benny who scampered around wearing only gym shorts and belly flopping in the mud until all that remained visible of him was eyeballs and teeth. As each lightning bolt reached Earthward Benny jumped up to catch it. Thunder meant that he opened his mouth as wide as can be as if he were its source. I burned to release my fifty shackles and team with him. I couldn't. Someone else might be watching.

"You don't care, do you?" I asked, as he came in resembling a rotting tree come blissfully back to life.

"About what?"

"What people think."

"If people leave me and toads alone, I leave them alone," he reminded me. He'd recently spotted Gilly Karolikas lobbing toads skyward so that their demise would be an untoadlike splat on the pavement, like sacrifices to the God of imbecilic children. Benny sprinted, caught the one a foot from oblivion, released it after staring intently into its eyes, and admonished, "Hurt another toad, and you and me have a problem." The toad population stabilized at that instant.

After a bath Benny joined our mother and me in the kitchen to play blackjack, grooving to "Sittin' On the Dock of The Bay" on Benny's transistor radio. Otis Redding was so smooth that even Rui Tedro's monarchical roar next door was distanced by it. Benny had this ability to memorize which of the cards had been used, so toward the end of the deck the pennies flew toward his pot. It wasn't intelligible that he could do that and I couldn't, considering unlike him, I'd proven that a five-year run of all A's in school doesn't make you friends.

"Blackjack!" he reveled, scooping up the pot of pennies. "Guess I'm double lucky today!"

Double because our grandmother on my mother's side had just bought a new used television and donated her old one to us. Our mother peered into the freezer, snapped up the remaining two-stick Popsicle, split it, and distributed it between us. Benny returned his to her automatically, a gesture that never crossed my mind.

"Tonight's 'The Addams Family', he said, vaulting up onto his chair to croon, "And when we get to see'm, their house'll be a museum, and they'll be on a spree'm. The Addam's Family."

As Benny retook his seat the unwelcome creaking of our back door pierced our camaraderie, a Pavlovian eradication of a trio of smiles. Our limbs tightened and breathing constricted. We heard the footsteps on our parlor floor.

"Goddamn it," our father groaned, trudging in wearing his Serodyn soot coated coveralls. He shut off the radio turning angrily to our mother. "I slave all day in that heat to put food on the table and I gotta come home and find some scatterbrain's keys in the door again?"

Her cringing submissiveness fast firing, she replied, "Sorry."

"Does it take any smarts to remember to remove the keys from the door?"

"Maybe I was carrying too many grocery bags," she half-heartedly answered, sheepishly shrinking as so often before. I could never understand given its frequency how she could look surprised at being interrogated.

“Excuses. Excuses. Well, if I gotta treat ya like a child in front of the boys then I gotta. Is there any common sense in lugging so many packages that ya can’t handle the keys?”

“Probably not.”

“Are ya so busy playing cards and eating Popsicles that there’s no leeway to carry less bags at once?”

“No.”

“There’s a right way and a wrong way to do things,” he scolded once again. “Boys, mind what your mother does, do the opposite, and you’ll be better off out there in the rat race.”

She placed the Popsicle along with her lost appetite into the freezer, took her Raggedy Ann pinafore off the wooden peg, slipped it on, and pulled out a pot to whip up dinner. Hiding behind food preparations was one of her frequent sidesteps. However, his maniacal head shaking had begun so it was time once again to assert his birthright to spew at us whatever he thought, whenever he wanted. He stated, “Sometimes I suspect that you couldn’t find your own head if it wasn’t attached to your shoulders.”

Immediately this collided head on in my mind with how again last night the radio in their bedroom had been turned up to insufficiently muffle their love fest. Those grunts, the howling in ecstasy, was it all canned to revolt me further?

“If she couldn’t find her own head, what does that say about you that you married her?” Benny sassed, steeled to pay the price. In one motion the smack to his face flowed onward to the freezer where our father seized the negligibly licked Popsicle on his way out. Benny didn’t emit a sound.

“Sorry,” Our mother whispered.

“I made my own choice,” he replied, pushing through the outside door ahead of me. We sat on the front porch and watched the clothes flutter on the collective clotheslines.

“I could never do what you just did.” I said. “How do you do that knowing he'll strike?”

“She's my mother,” he grumbled, nothing more, nothing less.

Most other women would've swept up the kids and transported them to safety. Not this breed of enabler, one who at age six was deposited in an orphanage by her mother who that night celebrated her 21st birthday at The Crossroads Tavern, toasting her latitude to finally drink legally, so energized that she finished off her pack's twelve remaining Lucky Strikes. For six years our mother prayed to be retrieved from that orphanage where the nuns thumped her for the unthinkable transgressions of being left-handed and tongue-tied. Normal human development probably wasn't facilitated when her mother then told her, “I would've kept you in there until you were eighteen if your father hadn't wanted you.” The mystery father whom she'd never met or seen a photo of, who shortly after disembarking from the landing craft on D-Day had hidden behind a fresh corpse where he shot himself in the foot to take himself out of action, was now back from the Army. At least that is until months later when his newfound guise of “War Hero” catalyzed his insatiable horniness and compelled him to abscond. Thus, her mother vengefully let drop that he actually wasn't her father, a hysterical sub clause to threats of suicide in lost love's wake. Nor were her mother's other four future husbands the father, including the last one, Herb Oppel, whom she met at the Cross Roads Tavern on her 43rd birthday. He was only five years older than our mother. His pickiness had been substantially diminished after, all spruced up in his brother's ill-fitting blue suit on both momentous occasions, he'd had the rare distinction of being twice left at the altar. Like a perverse game show for children where the adults never intend to reveal the answer, her father's identity remained unstated. So, our father became security, of a sort, where only bewildering abandonment had been.

Beholding the "Munsters" or "Lost In Space" on the first television we'd ever owned was like finally merging with the real world of fantasy. The fact that the audio on this fourth-hand Magnavox, vacuum tube Godsend no longer functioned when we received it didn't diminish the buzz for us. Trapped in an unstocked cave for too long without sustenance, one probably would jump at food even if water weren't also on the menu. And there was something more Shakespearean about Fred Gwyn's commitment to his character Herman Munster that the Talkie version wouldn't have exposed. Especially when Benny began improvising his own words to sync with Herman's misadventures. It became life and death stuff, with some housing project gossip thrown in as comic relief. Now Herman could convey his innermost feelings and desires without the censors going all red pen and the sponsors pulling their sugary cereals. My mother loved it and would break up like an innocent schoolgirl. "Oh, stop Benny, stop it, that's too funny. How do you come up with this stuff?" On this stage mesmerizing us with how spontaneously it would pour out of him, united, we were on cloud nine. That lost steam one day when Herman was in hot water and our mother asked, "I wonder what that Munster is really saying?"

There was always this longing that surrounded her, like she craved something more. Now Benny had been clued in, an inside scoop on one way to provide it. The family of stuffed animals he'd bought her with his earnings was no longer sufficient. He'd been reaping up to fifteen cents a day tugging along the gokart he'd constructed out of wheels from a shopping cart, roadside wood, and the rope and seat from a swing. Going garbage can to garbage can he used it to collect bottles, metal, and old newspaper to sell to the dump.

In 1968 a "pre-owned" television rarely could be procured for the five dollars Benny had stashed away, unless it was a wreck. But this one was solid and the single hippie girl mermaid bumper sticker on the side gave it a flare that Benny fancied. Too bad it weighed more than he did. Two galoots, Salvation Army lifers, who saved money on haircuts by monkey greasing their hair back between monthly shampoos, strapped it to his gokart upside down. A mirror hanging for sale apprised him further of their skepticism that he could reach home without an urgent need for medical attention, when they rolled their eyes at each other. The one with the eye patch was less detectable. If God hadn't invented hills, curves, stoplights, and cracks in the road they would've been sorely mistaken. It was more a near death experience than a boy tugging along his little kart. Somehow, he pulled it off.

"Benny, how did you do that?" our mother gushed, elated, tears so big pouring down that you could see them in the dark screens of both TVs.

"I hawked it from the Dariteau's," he kidded.

"No, you didn't."

"Sure, I did."

"No, you didn't," she persisted, laughing.

"Someone had to get revenge for them murdering Mrs. Stillwell's Chihuahua. The revenge of the Chihuahua!" Benny proclaimed, along with a few Chihuahua's barks and sneezes. He hopped to the window, opened it, and craned out to taunt, "Check out those Dariteaus over there searching high and low for their TV. Keep lookin' Dariteaus! Keep lookin'!"

He shot a grin at Aggie Boza, who must've questioned why he was wisecracking to a family that was nowhere in sight. She was cradling the pudgy doll with a red dress on it that he'd also just bought her at Salvation Army. He broad jumped over to turn on our new used TV. It crackled and wailed before words could seep through the dust caked on the speakers. And though only the volume on it worked it teamed up nicely with the Magnavox when he turned that on too. The next minute of me watching Benny all lit up as he watched our mother simultaneously watch and finally hear TV in her own home has revisited me a thousand times since. Transcendent.

"Go put on your good outfit," she instructed him as she floated next door to borrow a camera.

I kept nodding "yes" during the interval they were gone. "Yes," I reveled. "Yes." He couldn't save her, but he sure could present her with what that Munster had to say. When they both reentered Benny stood proudly between those two TVs tricked out in his best duds, a yellow collared shirt and yellow pants he'd so outgrown that they were higher than high waters.

Now say "cheese," she enunciated, effusively.

---------------------------------+----------------------------------

Not long after came another episode that I'll also never forget. I was serving as the non-athlete, statistician wielding a measuring tape to determine the length of Benny's catches. He was simply throwing a pinkie, which is the rubber ball inside of a tennis ball, with his right hand high up against the windowless side of our building, always on an angle to explore how far he could run to one side to catch it leftie. 46 feet and catch. 47 and catch. Dashing right often required an even more gratifying backhand catch. 49 feet should've been taped for posterity in that the full layout dive in the dirt soiled even his lips. A spontaneous flopper, flyer, and fence flipper, a 50-foot catch would've without a doubt been achieved if he hadn't been interrupted.

"Benny, come in here," our mother called from the stoop. That her hesitant voice was less alive than usual, I took as an extension of the inability to uphold her façade of cheerfulness lately.

To get back to the challenge ASAP, Benny hastened inside. He even laid his pinkie near Aggie Boza, a one-woman audience at all of his solo sporting events. If not at school, or fulfilling her latest calling of roaming around to catch butterflies that would be much happier relocated in front of her unit, she without fail toted along the doll he'd gifted her. I followed Benny past our mother. She looked like a hapless, brainwashed accomplice near the scene of the crime.

"Go upstairs. Ah, your father, ah, he's wants to talk to you," she stammered. The safety of debating his edicts had climaxed long ago when she'd said: "Your father is the boss." And he was the ruler of everything, and anyone who didn't "toe the line" "had a screw loose," or "a lack of smmattts," (New England accent for *smarts),* or deserved a "swift kick in the pants."

Benny complied hungering that for the first time our father might've sprung for a surprise, perhaps a stiff, new baseball glove that would require stretching to break it in. By this time, I'd already selected the subject for my 6th grade essay entitling it, "How To Expect The Worst," so only one flight of stairs later I was hyperventilating. Why would our distinguished father be in our room, instead of his? Why, seated on Benny's bed waiting, was there a warm, professional quality to him that we'd never seen? I imagined a civil servant during The Inquisition whose sole duty was to compel non-believers to confess, beneficently mitigating a captive's consternation before attaching him to the Strappato to end his days on Earth employing cattle prods, whips, and boiling oil that he got paid overtime to protract the agony.

"Take a seat," he said to Benny.

Benny sat next to him detecting that this wouldn't be festive. A gust jumped through the open window, dislodging a single plastered hair on our father's head. He produced his discount black comb, steamrollered that hair's flighty insubordination into compliant uniformity, and pocketed the comb. He sent me off with, "hit the road."

"Now and then people have to be taught a lesson. They gotta take their medicine," our father advised. "Believe me the last thing I care to do on my day off is pound some sense into someone. On the other hand, if it's the only way."

"Somebody got a beating?" Benny asked, fingers lacing and unlacing.

"Not yet. Jesus you're slow," he replied, patience replaced by the bitter burden of being pressed, no choice, out of other workable options, to administer 'medicine.' "Your mother says that you've been answering her back lately. Your medicine will make you stop doing that."

"I haven't been doing that," Benny claimed.

"Of course, that's what you'd toss out. Don't' make it worse by lying. Now lower your pants."

"But...."

"Do what I say!" he snapped, grabbing Benny by the arms so forcefully that it left welts. He yanked his pants down and slung him over his knee. The first twenty spanks were rapid fire as if to shock and disable, then an insufferable rhythm took hold. Inhale, smack while exhaling, inhale, smack, inhale, smack while exhaling to create more impact, 177 in total. What out of body experience compelled me to count the hellishness of that rhythm, I'll never know. Unrelenting, each smack blended into the next, seeping into the paint on the walls like an indelible stain.

"Take your medicine," he kept reiterating with the dullness of a deli worker asking, "Who's next?"

When I couldn't stomach it anymore, I ran into the kitchen. Somehow our mother had gotten spaghetti sauce on her chin.

"Aren't you going to do anything?"

"I guess he's getting a spanking," she answered, similar to a robot that needed to be recharged.

"You guess? What more evidence do you need?"

"I'm sure it'll be over soon."

"What did he do?"

"I don't know."

"You want to act like a man so take your medicine like one," we heard. Equally terrified that Benny would be maimed or I would be next, just in time I grabbed a cooking pot to vomit. Only a dry heave came forth. All Benny repeated was "What did I do? I didn't do anything." When it was finally over our father sat him up and seized him by the hair to declare, "Bet ya won't do that again!" He descended the stairs and invaded the kitchen as if nothing had transpired, each step a thud reaffirming for us that grace of any sort would never be a priority. Time to eat some Fritos, habitually rubbing salt off before crunching them for all to hear.

"That was too long," I asserted.

"Mind your own business or you'll be next."

Fatigued from corporal exertion, he shuffled into the parlor ripping open the bag of Fritos on route, a couple falling to the floor for our mother to clean up. Benny had to use the railing to help himself down the stairs. He hobbled into the kitchen eerily passive.

"What did I do?" he asked exhibiting his bum, red turning to purple.

"I don't know," our mother responded, her eyes veering on and off him.

"He said you told him I was being rude. No, I wasn't."

"I'll talk to him about it later," she deflected, resuming her food preparations, the handle on the spaghetti sauce ladle trembling. I knew her well enough to be certain that she'd thought the punishment would've been 10% as severe, and something not physical. She'd miscalculated.

Even though it was worse than the time he pummeled Benny in front of Brain while bellowing, "Now show your friend how tough you are," or planted him on the stoop at age seven in a diaper mocking, "let's show'm the neighborhood's oldest baby," Benny still just wanted to move on. He wanted to live, to create, not worry, so he proceeded outside. I escorted him sure that I was going to puke for real. Aggie was idling on our stoop doll and pinkie in hand. She'd heard the assault piercing our upstairs window, her distraught eyes pleading: "The world is too dangerous." He retrieved the pinkie from her, patted her on the shoulder, and waddled to the side of our building. As I approached, he tried twice to throw and chase. He could barely move.

I approached him, whining, "We have to talk about what happened."

"What's there to discuss?"

"He's crazy."

"I know."

"He's evil."

"We've repeated that a bunch'a times, Davey."

"Didn't it really hurt?"

"You know that answer," he replied, rubbing his behind.

I aided as he agonizingly sectioned himself to lie in the grass. Shade from the building blanketed us. I sat next to him, groping to absorb his fortitude. Despite that, all I kept hearing was the rhythm of those ungodly smacks until I these words sprang forth, "Overall, I'm happy, so that's not gonna change because of him."

It wasn't bluster or image management, it was his truth.

Aggie knelt near him and brought her doll's face forward so that it could kiss him. He picked up that his attempt to play ball again had further traumatized her, so he gently guided her to sit at his side. He propped up on his elbows to catch a load of the Tedro Family rehearsing in their yard.

"That goddamn Mr. Boza has gotta quit slithering too nearby when we're practicing," he mimicked like Rui Tedro and for only us to hear. It was always a gut buster how he could mimic Rui's voice and cadence while playing off of whatever other character he'd recently taught himself. "I know that guy is a jailbird and he'd better not cause no hassles. Got enough stress working with these damn kids o'mine."

This, to me, was a freak show. Not the circus family, but the super-humanness of how Benny became focused on uplifting Aggie and my psyches. Somehow, regulating the pain like it didn't hurt his blackening rump one bit, he imitated Tino Tedro's constipated acrobat frown and did a handstand against the building's side. He stayed up a couple seconds before overdramatizing one of Tino's rare falls, making sure that his face was hidden upon landing to conceal the grimace. A new word for him entered my mind. "Hero." And he was.

He mimicked, "Tino, can't you even balance on Dale's head for one lousy minute. A lousy minute!"

"But, Mr. Tedro, I do declare that sure was a hard fall," Benny twanged like Scarlett O' Hara. "Maybe poor Tino done hurt his young head."

"Hurt his head my tuchus. He'll get over it," Benny's version of

Rui Tedro rebutted.

"What if he hits his head and it alters the shape of it and ya have to spend years balancing his head on Dale's head again?" Scarlett demurred.

"The show must go on, little girl. The show must go on."

Aggie speed clapped in front of her enormous smile. Bless her heart all she perceived was the quintessential performer. Me, I could see that his sketch wasn't pristinely carefree like his recent ones of Fred Munster taking the driver's license road test or Chuckie's mother pre-coronary summoning, "Edna. Ednaaaa!" Today's sketch was still robust and committed, yet punctured with an effort not normally needed.

"You clap so good that you deserve a prize, right?" Benny suggested in his own voice.

Gazing up like there would be skywriting to provide her the answer, she admitted, "I dunno."

He waddled to our milk box where he'd hidden the paddleball that he'd also gotten her at the Salvation Army, so buzzed to finesse her into attempting new things that he didn't care how long she'd have to employ two hands to master it.

As much as he desired to keep his physical condition hush-hush, the next morning in school it was so much worse that he couldn't sit on his wooden chair. He tried and tried, although only insanity could've facilitated such a pain threshold. His fifth teacher Mr. Nunes, whose personality was so rigid that the uppers and lowers never came apart during his rare chuckles, was not pleased.

"Benny, before making you spend an hour in the storage closet, I recommend sitting down for good."

"I'm sorry Mr. Nunes, I can't do it."

"And why not? Have you forgotten where your behind is?"

The class erupted. Humor wasn't Mr. Nunes' intention. A solo raised eyebrow put a clamp on that. Chuckie and Orlando, the latter secretly referred to as Orlandodo, had both been caught with gum in their mouths and were now sporting it on their noses.

"No sir, I just can't."

"I'm about as much of a fan of disobedience as rock and roll, so out into the hallway, young man."

Benny heeded the command, his gait as fluid as the Tin Man in need of oil.

"Rise!" Mr. Nunes instructed. The class stood up at attention near their desks. Midway to the door he straightened his tie out as if neatness was required to chastise a ten-year-old. "I'll return in a minute."

As soon as he was out of sight Chuckie hurried the gum into his mouth, squeezed off a few quick chews, and relocated it back on his nose.

"Okay, young man," Mr. Nunes began to grill at the same instant registering the tear in Benny's eye, a substance never seen outside of our unit. "What's the matter?"

"May I show you why I can't sit?"

"Yes, you may," he responded, inspecting while Benny shyly lowered his pants to uncover his now blackened bum. "What the ba'Jesus?" He receded a bit to gain a better view. "Oh my. I hope you got in a couple licks in too because that's so bad."

"No sir, I didn't."

"Wow. That's worse than bad," he stated distressfully. "Wait here, son."

This wasn't a place or era in which signs of abuse entailed a call to the police, or to the principal who at 66 years of age spanked kids so inured of the process that he tended to lose count. A minute later Mr. Nunes reappeared with a naptime pillow gotten from a kindergarten class.

"Here," he said, his tone modified to "warm and professional," reminiscent of our father before the beating commenced. "Let's see if this'll allow you to sit. If not, you can lie in the corner. I'll put it on your seat for you, so slip back inside when you're good and ready. Okay?"

"Yes, sir. And I'm sorry."

"Why are you sorry?"

"Not sure," Benny answered. What was operating in him was millions of miles from anything he would've ever shared with anyone. He'd rather have told Walter Cubbard that he liked looking at his face. Or Mr. Dariteau, his competition in business, that he yearned to grow up to be just like him, then beg to go for a drive in the dilapidated 1957 Ford station wagon with a capacity exasperatingly bigger than Benny's go kart for hauling recyclables to the dump. Benny would never fess up that his primary feeling was embarrassment. It was the backwash of denigration against which he internally struggled to accept not having the capacity to fight back.

Mr. Nunes circled back inside. Benny wiped his eyes, trying to dry them by blowing upwards. Trudging back in with shoulders high and head up, he sat on what for now we'll name Mr. Nune's Pillow.

Two nights later our father was spread out on the couch viewing a TV news report about Vietnam. The obligatory squint of disapproval detailed that he was again immersed in pipe dreams of how he single-handedly would've won the war if knocking up a girl hadn't precluded him from becoming that fearless soldier.

"Those gooks wouldn't have known what hit hit'm if Ben Thompson was over there," he bloviated, his favorite toot. As Benny labored past, instead of remorse our father's countenance was that of the unbridled satisfaction of someone who'd done what was necessary. With a smirk of unassailable power, he prodded, "Where ya goin'?"

"Into the cellar," Benny responded, fifteen minutes ahead of our prescribed bedtime.

"Nope. Up to bed," he scoffed. "And hey, decided to not run away?"

Stoic, Benny blinked tiredly and mounted the stairs.

"Maybe I'll catch a break and you'll be kidnapped tomorrow. And while they're dragging you away kicking and screaming, do me a favor and find out if they'll take your brat of a brother also," our father added, one of his frequent "jokes" always accompanied by a laugh. That laugh, a mixture of hyena and meat grinder.

Benny did the best he could to pretend that lying down was no sweat, but when it's done one limb per minute the jig is up. I remained so disabled from the assault that I couldn't quash bringing it up, so he cut that off with "Do ya suppose Carl Yaztremski can win another Triple Crown?"

"You look as atrocious as the victims in my History of Torture book," I responded. I'd grown to vicariously require a steady dose of history's real-life suffering, so I'd finagled a book on torture. Then as we prepared for sleep it occurred to me. Benny had been sold out. After ten years of her husband's round-the-clock scrutiny, our mother's mask of dutiful compliance was being superseded by something much darker. She didn't want her husband to catch on that she was declining mentally. Benny's alleged misconduct was the deflection tactic tossed out to put her husband off the scent. It was the first stake in the heart of the tacit alliance between a mother and her sons.

A week later when Benny could sit without the pillow, he returned it to Mr. Nunes, thanking him. Mr. Nunes held it appreciatively and handed it back.

"This is yours," he emphasized. "Keep it. You're a good boy and someday you'll be glad you still have it."

Did Mr. Nunes want him to keep it as a reminder to beware of our father, or to not become like him?

Bowling with One-Eyed Gumby

With cement floors strewn with cracks and mold encrusted beams exposed above, every unit had its own cellar chain-link fenced off from those adjacent to it, so that one could see into the other three cellars in the building. Down there, even the mention of that purported murderer of mailmen, Old Man Mac, was too much to endure amongst all of the daddy long legs, centipedes, and inexplicable creaking noises. Each also had its own internal door which if unlocked led to a long corridor not much broader than a bowling alley that extended along the outside of the cellars. The Spangler, Telson, and Cubbard boys, all impressed by sneaking a smoke in the boy's bathroom and truancy, were the culprits who committed most of the petty offenses around Brickenwood. At age eleven Benny had partaken in his share of mischief, but there wasn't a crime to his name. Not until the TV daily "Bowling for Dollars" had him too envious of those with the dough to bowl.

Brain had moved away to live in a tenement and Charlotte, tuning her in to even the faintest stain on her attire, was now predominantly allied with girls, so the escapades were left up to just Benny and Chuckie. Jointly over the years they'd stumbled upon a motley teenager standing with his snake in what they probably wrongly assumed was the fanny of his gal pal in that patch of woods where years earlier they'd hidden to pounce on the Raleigh 3 Speed Boys. Chuckie had informed Benny that he would never trust anyone who dressed like Santa Clause. Benny instructed him that it wasn't a "doggie dog" world; it was "a dog eat dog world." Chuckie insisted that his sister Edna wasn't pregnant, "she just be big". He was also on hand when the raisin that Benny had inserted up his nose launched out weeks later. They'd earnestly shared a blood brother ceremony, easier for Chuckie who was already bleeding. Such a background motivated these two, equals in their passion for the finer aspects of housing project life, to formulate a plot. And tonight, was the one.

When Benny entered the parlor, our father was napping on the couch as he often did, snoring, mouth agape, drooling, muttering points that affirmed that he was right about whatever, requiring us to be hushed when his bed was empty upstairs. It was like an interminable victim and King's statement combined. See how hard I slave for you, and that's why I can snooze wherever and whenever I choose. Topped by a blonde, pageboy wig, our mother was in the kitchen striving to scrub away her man's railings that she wasn't an adequate housekeeper. I was seated on the parlor floor contemplating a dead black ant under the microscope of my chemistry set, more fascinated by death than entomology. I'd repaid the world a favor that day for all of the abuse by suspending a magnifying glass above insects to harness the sun's rays.

"Where ya goin'?" I whispered to Benny.

"Football game. The Vegetables vs. The No Beefs."

"May I watch?"

Benny nodded as he bounded upstairs. His thirty skeletons had their own league of six teams, five "men" per team, and like the NFL they played an annual season of fourteen games. Proportionately speaking, given their size, a twin bed worked out nicely as a football field. The team names, The Boston Bonesmen, Chicago Corpses, Detroit Deadies, Kansas City No Beefs (to rhyme with the Chiefs), The San Francisco Fossils, and Los Angeles Vegetables, touted the lack of meat on their bones. He memorized each team's win-loss record, and the number of touchdowns and touchdown passes each player had.

The kick off soars high in the air end over end and is caught seven yards deep in the end zone by Jump Bones. Oh no, he's taking it out. He runs forward past his goal line and heads right barely eluding a diving tackle by Professor Hip Bone. He sweeps farther right, stops on a dime, leaving two tacklers to zip by where he would've been, scampers forward, brakes, jukes left, waits for a blocker to pick off Lurch's Twin, and off he advances down the field. He could go all the way. The forty. The fifty.

THE FORTY. OH NO. SKINNY BONES, THE FASTEST PLAYER IN THE HISTORY OF SKELETONS AS A FOUR-INCH TALL RUBBER SPECIES, IS USING HIS UNMATCHABLE SPEED TO TRY TO CUT HIM OFF. THE THIRTY. THE TWENTY. THE TEN. JUMP BONES IS NOT GOING TO MAKE IT. HE STICKS OUT A STIFF ARM, BUT IT'S A FAKE. OH MY GOD. OH MY GOD. CAN YOU BELIEVE IT? HE JUMPED SO HIGH THAT SKINNY BONES TACKLED THE AIR UNDERNEATH HIM. HE LANDS AND PRANCES BACKWARDS INTO THE END ZONE UNTOUCHED. TOUCHDOWN! TOUCHDOWN! WHAT A SKELATHLETE!! TOUCHDOWN! THE AUDIENCE GOES WILD!

It was a grueling back and forth game in which the Vegetables squandered a 17-point lead to the No Beefs wrapping up the contest in a tie. Of course, they all shook phalanges afterwards. Benny's top-secret societies, Skelathetes and Kleenex Men, were far more decorous than the people who inhabited his home life.

Pumped up in the wake of such a nail biter, with me trailing him, Benny floated into the hallway to slide down the stairs on his backside. We could overhear our father in the bathroom making that horrendous daily throat clearing racket when gargling, detonations that alone should've ended him up both divorced and unmarriageable. Benny slid down fast, vaulted up and skated into the parlor. He'd been doing it for years so it was just part of the flow of the day, and he'd continue that until our father, despite Benny's heartbreak, again opened his bag of fiendish urges, this one being to stamp out things that delighted us. He carpeted the stairs. "Quit your bitchin'. Ya gettin' too old for that anyway."

That night Benny invited me to accompany Chuckie and him so I tagged along cautiously, slating that prior to the actual delinquency I'd lower my tail between my legs and slink back to obscurity. We passed a group of kids playing hide and seek, the seeker with his eyes closed standing on a spot of infamy and ever-increasing lore while the others scattered. The spot, a melon-sized bloodstain that everyone swore was shaped like the devil, hadn't yet been entirely washed away. It was also the symbol of my vicarious revenge because that bloodstain came from Albert. This time he'd played

Doctor with a sprout trained to communicate all happenings to his doting parents, who together partook in the beatdown.

The trek to The Wonder Bowl was like a quarter mile into the next riskier stage of Benny's childhood. Midway he hurled into the air the large burlap bag that he'd scavenged behind Arlan's Supermarket, cartwheeling or front flipping before catching it on the way down. Chuckie was also changing, and now every female who'd yet to face the wrath of menopause got him all hot and bothered. Somehow even on such a moonless evening he could make out proportions as easily as a soaring owl sights her nesting owlets.

"Check out that, Carletha. Yeah, boy. She got her an ass like one of them half men, half horses do," he declared, sticking out his tongue with a sharpness that would've caused more harm than pleasure. "And that Cheryl Mears, yeah, she be havin' some ass, too. White girls got asses. My Mama ain't right on that one." Maybe Chuckie was so calm because his assignment was as the decoy, and he didn't have our father to contend with if the caper went south. "Can't wait for junior high 'cause gonna get me some junior high girls. Should get me some now." He'd outgrown "UUUUUUing" and replaced it with endless anatomical chatter. "Cherie Cubbard ain't so ugly like she used ta'be. Gonna get all happy with her, too, ya know it, ya know it, ya know it, ya know, ya know, ya know it." Suddenly he hips pumped the wind as if it too was female. "Check you that one over there with the halter top. Halter my butt! Ain't haltin' me."

I thought, "How could it be? How could Benny also be so calm? We have the same father." I was terrified of what would happen if he got nabbed, yet admired how he relished the anomalies and energy of what went down separate from daddy. What spooked me most was if our father caught him in possession of his forbidden Gumby, who often rode in his pocket for the big adventures, this time the back pants pocket as a rearview lookout. Eyes peeled for cops, we breezed into The Wonder Bowl. Per usual Carl was behind the counter.

"Of course, Carl's here," Benny commented. "He doesn't wanna die, and only two things can kill him. Daylight and smiling."

Benny was acquainted with him because he'd hung out there a lot of late, raring to demonstrate how to really dance after making a strike. Though he'd afforded three games, the remainder of his income went to only three items, Matchbox Cars, 45's, and spirit lifters for our mother. At 25¢ a game and a dime to rent shoes, it was definitely the sport of the privileged elite who had allowances.

"Hey, Carl," Benny saluted to no response.

"Hey, Carl," Chuckie chimed then muttered under his breath, "Where's his fucking head?"

"Where's his fucking head?" Benny parroted instantaneously though not audible enough for Carl to catch. I'd never heard him use that word, but Carl's lack of head size could shock anyone into a state of echolalia. Never had a more colossal body had a smaller head attached, or at least not one with a cigarette behind both ears. Like his head popped out prematurely, then his mother recalled that she had to skedaddle posthaste to Mongolia to retrieve something, tossed a sarong around herself, indulged her phobia of flying by taking a boat, train, bus, then cab, swept up what she needed, stopped off on the way home in Pamplona to waddle with the bulls, so by the hour she finally turned up back home the rest of Carl was so overcooked that it destined him for a life of asking your bowling shoe size. Or something along those lines Benny had weaved shortly after being playground edified about childbirth.

There was the usual assemblage of miscreants, children of third shift workers who only drink it by the quart, third shift workers who only drink it by the quart, those who suit up in their menial labor uniforms when bowling with the shirt on inside out to cloak how life had panned out for them, and the Union Fish Cutter whose job was to only cut off the heads of the fish, never more, never able to expunge that smell to the satisfaction of her fellow bowlers. That

Fish Cutter was our Great Aunt Hildaberto, so we avoided her assiduously even though she'd donated an unfathomably scuffed bureau to our bedroom. And some of the pre-roll and post-spare gesticulating we were unfortunate to be on the scene for could've triggered a lesser boy than Benny to have nightmares. Actually, it did, so I stayed awake until dawn. Especially the ninny who took his dentures out to roll his ball, in to bite the hot dog, out to roll, in to eat a fry. My proclivity for being disturbed by anyone's oddities was on the rise.

Playacting like we were just friendly youngsters strolling along didn't curtail the scowl on the high school hottie behind the snack counter.

"Are you the boy who palmed the salt shaker here last week?" she addressed Benny accusingly.

"No. I, madam, am an absolute gentleman."

"Better not be."

"Told ya girls don't prefer gentlemen," Chuckie quipped.

"I meant the one who took that shaker," she clarified.

"It ain't him," said Chuckie. "Though disgracefully it was me who took them pepper shakers."

He winked, swaggering off like he'd be back later to have his way with her. She even seemed to fall for his charm a bit when she called after us, "Pepper sucks!"

As we glided beyond earshot Chuckie jabbered, "'Pepper sucks.' That ain't funny. That girl is as humorous as dead people."

In my usual deadpan manner, I asked, "What if her name is Pepper?"

Chuckie's eyes bulged. Making a beeline for her, he played along, "Oh, then I gotta go find out."

Benny grabbed him. "Hear ye! Hear ye! We got us a cellar fit for bowling, 'memba?"

"My priorities have changed."

"Let not your priorities change," Benny exhorted in his Bug's Bunny the swashbuckler impersonation.

"Okay," Chuckie replied reluctantly. "But I'm ridin' me some'a'dat later."

With the whole place cased for cops we ambled back to the entrance.

"See ya soon, Carl," Benny stressed to no answer.

"See ya soon, Carl," Chuckie doubled.

"See ya soon, Carl," I tripled, reticent of voice but glad to be one of the boys.

We flocked out back to where a **No Trespassing** sign hung on the mile-high fence. Over Benny's lifeless body "No Trespassing," not when there were bowling pins in that dumpster.

"That fence is huge," I said, envisioning paralysis or worse.

"So?" he replied. No conversation, only one word was necessary to display how constitutionally unalike we were.

As scripted, I hid behind a mailbox across the street to safely watch, wondering if Benny ever wished that he hadn't been blighted with such a dud for a brother. He scaled that fence no sweat. It was there that he'd caught sight of them discarding old pins while cruising by on his bike earlier that day. Chuckie pulled a pinkie from inside his pants and went about bouncing it off the side of the building, posing as an innocent kid. When Benny touched down inside the dumpster, his ankle twisted radically on an object hard and round. Wincing, he reached down and hit upon "Cuddly," or so was inscribed on that ten-pound, speckled ball. He picked her up and rolled her out of the dumpster. Amongst the boxes, food cartons and garbage bags, with the stench making him dizzy, he unearthed one, two, four, and finally ten total pins, all of which he heaved out. He clambered out of the dumpster, and one by one hurled them over the fence into the grass like an Olympic Hammer Thrower while Chuckie scooped them up into the bags. Elevating the fence from the bottom required the two of them. With no room to spare "Cuddly" rolled underneath.

A ball and three pins into one bag, seven pins into the other, and the sportsmen were fully equipped. They hauled them to Chuckie's unit like 1930's hobos with their bindles over their shoulders, eyes on the lookout. I met them at Chuckie's unit where the bowling commenced within minutes in the alley they'd created at the side of his cellar. One particular strike even elicited a strut down both memory and the bowling lane with the final ...."Uuuuuuuuuu!" we ever heard.

Later when Benny unveiled his swollen ankle he lit up with pride.

"Ya know, walking won't be a ball of roses tomorrow," I couldn't resist remarking.

"Sometimes winners just gotta hop on one foot," he shrugged, warming and dazzling me. "Me, I'm only bummed about one thing."

"You, bummed?"

"I wanna go right up to Carl's itsy-bitsy head to get outta him who owned "Cuddly," but then he'd figure us for the ones all over that dumpster."

---------------------------------+-----------------------------------

Our father's "beef" with Gumby had occurred a year earlier just after...... Benny's thirst for harmless mischief had escalated so, with Gumby facing outward in his shirt pocket, he impetuously shimmied up the drainpipe to the second floor of Charlotte's unit to peer into the window for her. This was no Peeping Tom thing that would progress with age to the class of transgressions that end you up in segregation, cordoned off from the inmates who trade cigarettes like cash and lust after the bragging rights associated with sticking a sex offender. Hanging on for dear life, the only person in sight in the room was Charlotte's 18-year-old sister, Shirleen. Few guys have eyeballed their first naked woman while hanging from a drainpipe. Gumby's 20/20 vision caught it all, too. It was back when he still had two functional eyes.

When Benny arrived home The Tedro Family was practicing in front of their unit. Tino had now mastered balancing on Dale's head with one arm, while his other arm was simultaneously extended sideways spinning a hoop on it. Benny noticed Aggie Boza slouching glumly on her stoop, so he detoured to her. Nearby was her paddle with the ball detached from it.

"What's up, Aggie Boza? Ya thinkin' 'bout coming over to borrow the ketchup bottle later?"

She neither responded nor blinked.

"We got some especially good mayo if you need it. It's Helmond's. Ya ever had the Helmond's?"

She sighed and closed her eyes.

"I'm partial to Helmond's on Twinkies and Devil Dogs," he carried on. "Don't'cha suppose they should fill Twinkies with mayo, instead of that sweet stuff?"

Aggie had begun speaking without prompting of late, but exclusively to Benny. She liked to report what she'd observed that day, keeping him abreast of vital intelligence. It was getting colder outside so he buttoned up her coat. It was then he observed that she'd been crying.

"Cold out. Should ya go inside?"

"I breaked my paddleball," she whispered abjectly, pointing at it. Benny sat to await further clarification, which came five minutes later. "I can't do nothing right."

"I do not concur," he replied. It was his current phrase, even for things he completely agreed with.

She began to twist her hair hard so he delicately clasped her hand. Her eyes on the Tedro Family, one note higher she said, "I can't balance on Dale's head."

"Sure ya can. You can do anything. But you, Aggie Boza, got bigger things to do than that."

She pondered then shook her head "no."

"You, and this is the chatter all over town, you, could be a movie star."

"I can't be no that."

"Uh, huh."

"Na, huh."

"Ah, huh."

"Na, huh."

"Flip me one good reason why not."

With a grin she answered, "I dunno." She stared awhile into

space, fingers in motion like typing forty per. “Though I got, ah, I got a secret.”

“Then don’t tell it to anyone.”

She pulled out a frayed handkerchief, scoured its contents, wiped her nose, and pocketed it. “I can tell you if ya wanna me to.”

“Okay, but first let me shield Gumby’s ears so he won’t hear.” He did it then leaned toward her.

Minutes later, once she’d again trailed off to wherever that mind found fresh footing, she tilted toward him to confide, “I’d like to be a movie star.”

Those were the last words he expected to hear. It encouraged him and augmented his curiosity about her long-term potential. “I could go for being a movie star also. Another why as to why we’re buddies, right?”

She nodded. Benny curled his hand around her shoulder as he caught sight of someone galumphing by. It was Walter Cubbard, a colossal rubber snake wrapped around his neck. Walter paused. His jaw dropped at the sight. He chimed, “Benny and Aggie sitting in a tree. K I S S I N G.” If he’d had a permanent thought bubble above his head, it would’ve been empty.

“Don’t force me to get up,” Benny warned.

“My snake can take your Gumby,” Walter retorted.

“Possibly, but you can’t take a hamster so I advise usin’ those pins to make tracks.”

Walter backed away with more, “Benny and Aggie sitting in a tree. K I S S I N G.”

“Shut the fuck up!” Aggie raged, so stunning Benny that he

tumbled off the stoop.

"Well, that wasn't the girl I recall," he praised. "No doubt now that the name Aggie Boza belongs up in lights."

Blushing, she turned to him to explain, "That's what Daddy hollers to Mommy. It really works."

"Yeah, 'cause she's not a Cubbard," he replied, all in one motion scrambling out of the dirt to rush Walter only swiftly enough to let him flee. He veered off to our unit where he about-faced like a robot front, then back, then front, then back ongoing until Aggie yipped merrily.

"You can do anything. You're strong. You're wicked strong, Aggie Boza" he blazoned, raising his two fists high. She copied him, her face scrunching with determination. For a while afterward, every sighting was punctuated with fists upthrust and face scrunching.

When he burst into our room, he sat Gumby up on the mirror above the bureau, its favorite place to take in the goings on. The bureau was constructed of thin faux-wood that if you yanked a drawer out more than half way it would plummet to the floor, precipitating the demise of several Kleenex Men. We were the final resting place for everyone's discarded furniture, clothes, plates, and God-awful knickknacks. Though we did take pride that the formerly white doilies on everything were purchased new as a present for our parent's shotgun wedding.

Dinner was mother's Shepherd's Pie amply critiqued by that prominent food critique, Ben Thompson. "How many times I gotta nag ya to cook the burger less and put in more corn?" That's the bad news. The good news was that with the meal there was no toast for him to complain that she hadn't reached the butter up high enough into the corners, no eggs that were too runny or too close to the bacon, beef goulash without adequate salt, wrong brand of canned green beans, too much sugar in the lemonade, fat not cut sufficiently off the edges of whatever low priced piece of meat, too much fat cut off, mashed potatoes not mashed enough, french fries not french fried enough, baked potato too small for a "growing boy like himself," tomatoes too ripe, cucumbers with the skin still on "like I care about vitamins when I'm salting up a cuke," beef stew low on carrots, goulash that "if I fed it do a dog that dog would bark no more," jello you could use for a building's foundation, and pudding that "needs more skin on top so put it in the fridge earlier."

After dinner Benny escaped outside to work with Aggie. "Ready to learn how to throw and catch?"

"No."

"Good. Let's do it anyway." He led her onto the grass, took the pinkie from his pocket, and thus launched their first of many practice sessions where he tutored her on this and that.

"Benny! Get the hell in here!" our father shouted apoplectically out of our bedroom window. Benny dashed inside knowing that each second of delay could fuel further ire, only to encounter him dangling the now one-eyed Gumby with no respect at all by its semi-detached leg. Gumby had fallen onto the lamp's light bulb, which was turned on. I crept to the top of the stairs to listen.

"How stupid can you be?" our father ranted. "You could've burned down the damn building. You could've ruined this lamp. Thank God I smelled it."

"I'm sorry."

"'Sorry'. Who cares about, 'sorry.' Well outstanding, now you can pay the price because you've ruined your damn toy," he furthered, smacking Benny upside the head when he tried to wrest Gumby away. "Try that again. Be my guest. There are consequences to stupid and I'm the man who'll guarantee you pay'm." Out of nowhere he converted it into a standoff where he, the righteous one, was willing to confront a monster whose crimes were equal to genocide and intentionally spreading an incurable disease.

"But he's my Gumby. I can fix him," pleaded Benny, near to tears.

"Oh, there ya go, cry like a girl. Then later you'll be blubbering that 'I'm mean and heartless' because ya make me so mad. If shit were brains you'd have the biggest pile."

Yes, that rare tear did fall, but not over the familiar debasement. Gumby was going to be murdered.

"Don't even consider getting this burnt thing outta the garbage if ya know what's good for ya. Ya hear me? I'm fit to be tied! Did ya hear me?"

"Yes."

Of his turgid, unyielding assortment, his favorite cliché was "Fit to be tied."

"Here, ya can keep its leg as a reminder," he spat, tearing off the semi-detached leg and flinging it onto the bed. He stomped outside, opened the garbage can, and chucked Gumby inside like a piece of worthless rubber. Off he stormed, the man who in a couple of years would be sworn in as a police officer.

Benny barely slept, fidgeting and sporadically compelled to sit up or pace. Periodically he'd advance into the upstairs hallway, go through the motions in the bathroom, scheming how best to pad outside on a rescue mission.

"If you go down there, he'll really hurt you," I warned, petrified.

"Good. Then he can go smell up the prison where he belongs."

"If he hurts you too bad, it'll kill Ma," I implored. It's what I had to employ to stop him. He would've gone for it. No question.

At that moment I longed for an adult to help us, as if somehow, magically, one would barge in risking our father's wrath to jet us off to safety, or subdue, thump, then bring to fruition Dear Old Dad's favorite cliché by **fitting** him in the same diaper Benny was sentenced to wear on our stoop and **tying** him to the church steeple. While each episode took another layer off of my innately thin skin, Benny, nonetheless, somehow overcame whatever arose superhumanly fast and was back to being a jovial youngster. His arms and legs were their own masters; limbs so unrelenting that if their cohort and occasional ring leader, his mind, if it sulked, or soured, it would discover it wasn't worth being out of the spirit of things because it was being carried along for the next adventure anyway. I knew that Gumby's murder would be different. It would be harder on him.

The next morning, I felt horrible, fever, stomachache, and those wondrous liquidy visits to the bathroom. I never missed school so no one questioned when I couldn't attend. Benny morosely plodded out the door, too depressed to realize that his shirt buttons were lined up wrong, only to run into our father perched on the stoop, a beastly barricade to any visions of saving Gumby. So, when the Garbage Man carted it all away along with another 1% of a child's precious innocence, Benny would have to carry on. And he was loyal. He wouldn't again haul recyclables in order to afford another Gumby. His Gumby was The Gumby.

I wasn't sturdy. Our world was terrifying for me. I assume I've made that evident. What once in a lifetime bravery it must've required for someone as ill-equipped as me to feign an illness and scuttle outside as soon as our father had departed, barely in time to alert the Garbage Man as he disposed of ours in his truck. It took me days to ferret out the old bed sheets and correct pins to patch Gumby up as best as I could. When Benny stepped foot into the bedroom there it was, a yellow box with a red bow on it.

"Did Ma buy this?" he scoffed, unimpressed.

"Open it."

"I don't want another Gumby."

"Open it."

"No. I don't need an impostor."

"Open it or you're as brain dead as our father."

Reluctantly, he wrenched the box open. That expression of incredulity would be on the cover of this book if Chuckie's 4th grade rendering of "Benny the Volkswagen" hadn't inched it out.

"He likes his new name," I said with my trademark stiffness.

"He changed his name?"

"One-Eyed Gumby."

Benny gaped at Gumby for a bit. "Yep. That's you. One-Eyed Gumby." After roosting him above the mirror for a few minutes, Benny hid One-Eyed Gumby away for safekeeping making sure to only socialize with him when our father was gone. Using a blue crayon and a paper bag he rewrote the song "Green-Eyed Lady" into "One-Eyed Gumby" in honor of the only 45 that I'd ever bought him.

"One-Eyed Gumby, lovely Gumby
You're back and having fun.

One-eyed Gumby, ocean Gumby
They can't kill you with a gun.

One-Eyed Gumby, passion's Gumby
no more garbage can, and you still can see.

One-Eyed Gumby, just like it should be
Now he's ready to set other Gumbys free.

Wigs, God, And A Shark Gets Brained

The squally winds outside fluttered the garments on the clotheslines. Through the parlor window, as dusk obscured, we could see Mr. Tangeran taking a break from Sonny, his never silent, pot-bellied son who was fifteen and still in the seventh grade, and from his wife who, only skin and bones though healthy as a horse, had a case of psoriasis that made me wonder if she was flaking away to nothing. Wearing a Red Sox cap and rubber fishing boots, Mr. Tangeran was flying a kite with his adored, five-year-old son, Paulie, at his side. This was the boy on whom all the hopes of medical school or an ambassadorship to a first world nation were pinned. This was the precocious one who revered how his father angled a fishing pole to fly fish shaped kites.

Our "family" was arrayed taking in the news on the single fully functional TV we now had. In a flash the school year and the tedious after school Catechism classes our father dictated that Benny and me tolerate would all end for us. Benny was on the dark blue chair that no longer had stuffing protruding from the arms because a flowered cloth had been sewn over them. Our mother was on one end of the couch crowned by a frosted wig and I was on the other end with an "Oh My God, check out that pelt on her head," hanging on my face. Her wig phase was now fully in bloom. The frosted one looked as natural as if she'd snatched another piece of that flowered cloth and fitted that on instead. Our father was in the recliner confident that only he had the will, only he had the vigor, only he was the marvel who could right the wrong that had occurred on that beach. He was in a particularly rootin'-tootin' mood after fishing that morning into the ocean. His exploits left him less cognizant of three particulars, our mother's increasing stupefaction, my determination to be saved, and how atypically quiet Benny was. It was like Benny was suddenly living in hyper-vision and the rest of us had cooked up for his eyes a farce.

"So, I hauled him onto the beach and it was a damn sand shark" our father declared. "No sand shark is going to take my bait out of the mouth of a striped bass longing to meet me."

Our mother replicated her long-standing role of captivated listener in his tall tales, while nervously twirling hairs on her wig. Her ten wigs, all variations in color and length without a human hair among them, were displayed on her bureau propped on Styrofoam heads on which I'd drawn various ghoulish faces, some smiling.

"Shark," he drawled in John Wayne bravado. "You've messed with the wrong hombre. And we're going to have to duke this one out."

A commercial for Geritol came on, so as if at a church pew I pivoted around to kneel on the chair to pray, not loudly, but still audible. "Hail Mary full of grace, the lord is with thee. Blessed are thou amongst…." and so on. The priest shepherding my confirmation class had taken stock of my yearning to hitch on to something, anything, and had seduced me to pray often or confront damnation. My preternatural sense of timing gave me the idea to do my praying during every television commercial. Our mother also had that innate sense, so what better point to actualize her haunting need to swap wigs a few erratic times per day than during a commercial, a prayer, and the downfall of a sand shark.

"Hey where ya going? This shark's gonna find out the hard way who's the better man and you're leaving the room? So, I danced around him a bit, stared him right in the eye and said, it's you and me brother."

The commercials ended and Walter Cronkite got back to broadcasting the government's hype on how swimmingly Vietnam was progressing, so with my heartfelt prayers finished I sat facing forward again looking like a candidate for an aneurysm after squeezing in five *Hail Marys* and an equal dose of *Our Fathers*. Our mother returned with her red beehive wig on askew. She plopped down as composed as if she'd been tapped to stay behind at an exploding nuclear facility, the assignment to megaphone, "Melt down. Melt down."

"Then boom, I pounced on him before he could attack. Whack.

Whack. Ain't gonna swipe my bait. Whack. Whack, you know you're hankerin' for another. Whack. One less shark fouling up my morning. Whack. Whack. Brained him with my club until he wished he'd been hanging out in a different ocean," he dramatized, gloating like he'd wrestled a great white with his bare hands instead of a beached sand shark as mobile as a sloth heaved into the ocean. "Nobody messes with Ben Thompson!!!"

He often joked "I'm a legend in my own mind."

A glimmer of my contempt relocated my features so I screwed on captivation. Waxing like an ungrateful sinner not impeccably possessed of my duty to venerate thy father and mother, I circled again pre-commercial to mouth another kneeling…."Hail Mary, Full of Grace. The Lord is…"

"What's your take on that?" he nudged our mother. Any more sharks gonna have the cajones to throw down with me?"

"Probably not," she concurred, further misaligning the beehive by feel.

"How about you?" he asked Benny.

"Nope," Benny agreed quietly, to that point the clearest moment of his life. Its starkness reinforced that he didn't belong there. That he was unlike us, maybe even sublimely normal. So, he excused himself, as was the rule, and went outside to settle on the front stoop. The last sound he heard when exiting was the victor's prerogative to belch thoroughly expressed.

His cap now on backwards, Mr Tangeran seemingly struggled to reel in the fish kite. He called out, "We got us a big one here, Paulie."

"Reel him in dad!" Paulie squealed.

"I think he's a keeper, Paulie."

"Reel him in dad!!!"

It was the most beautiful thing Benny had ever seen. Despite that he'd have to share a room with Sonny and his obsession with train sets, and even shuddering that he would abandon our mother and me, he just wanted to forsake his ever-burgeoning role as the valiant one and move in with The Tangerans. At that moment, had a Wizard of Oz tornado spun in, swept him up and landed him as a valued son in a loving and well-adjusted family, I surmise that the past with Ben Thompson, the father who'd never played catch with him, or assisted him with his homework, or assured him that he'd done anything right, would've faded.

Bedtime for Benny

On perpetual rewind in my mind, in contrast to how zombified Benny now appeared in the hallways of school, had been his infectious excitement at the advent of last summer. Especially when he first spotted Gina. Aggie Boza, he and I were lounging on our stoop when an old moving truck rumbled up, sputtered, sprung back to life, advanced two feet, stalled, then chugged into a parking space. Out of it bounced the most beautiful people of the female variety I'd ever seen, ages 30ish, 13, 10, and 3, destined to move into the unit directly across from ours. This gang's carriage and style had a pizzazz that contrasted, **We've been demoted to a housing project**, and they'd definitely never gone all Hamburger Helper without the hamburger when the greenbacks ran out. Yet, they each had a distinct look, as if they'd just crossed paths at the moving company and impulsively decided to move in together. Jean, the mother, was that woman in the streets of London who'd known a Beatle intimately and would never play second fiddle to a man. Her polyethylene dress and go-go boots read that this is what I wear when not in the University library finishing my doctorate. The three-year-old had on the latest fad, culottes, as if she were mocking those checked out, suburban housewives who stayed afloat by donning the latest fad, culottes. The 13-year-old, to my post-pubescent delight, mixed a series of batik fabrics in a mode that accentuated her newfound voluptuousness. Any teenager who masturbated to his poster of Raquel Welch in "20,000 BC" would have covered it with one of her bending over to pick up a moving box. Let it forever be ordained though that Gina was the standout, and the first object of my white-hot readiness for promiscuity. Her bell-bottom jeans with a touch of paint on them, tye-dyed shirt with a thick brown belt around it, and gum wrapper chain bracelets on both wrists, carried her like a virtuoso is by a sudden vision. She was way cooler than someone who thought she was cool. In other words, she was less likely to notice me than a speck of dust floating a block away.

Perhaps they were escaping from something, debt from purchasing that eye-catching wardrobe? More probable they were on assignment sent by Look or Life magazine to garner an impression of who lived in the projects during these days of free love and social upheaval. There was definitely more than met the eye, made more evident when it became public that they were only there for transitional housing until the end of summer.

Benny was beyond confident about why his moves mesmerized others, but to capture Gina, whom he'd yet to meet, viewing him on the sly from her bedroom window later that day while he danced in our room, was a whole other level of power. The power of seduction. The marketing tool that would last for a dozen years of enticing women into approaching him had been triggered.

The next day when Chuckie and Benny were monitoring Old Man Mac's house, plotting to ascertain, after years of debate, if there really were deceased mailmen inside, they saw Gina strolling by shielding herself like an Elizabethan aristocrat with a parasol. His ticker racing, Benny zipped off to saunter thirty feet to her left, slinging a Frisbee forward so that the wind would repel it back to him, feigning too engrossed to notice her. When she saw him, she turned away lickety-split? His peacock feathers floating in motion in our bedroom had done the trick. That was proven when she twirled the open parasol high into the air like a flying saucer, copied his dance moves as best she could, then caught it while skipping away.

By the time he got home Gina's stature as his dream girl was as set in stone as my fantasy that a pandemic would wipe out all males excluding Benny, leaving me strikingly appealing to the fairer sex. Thankfully, our father hadn't returned yet to continue the morning's rant about how he was the only one in the household with any common sense, and our mother was upstairs chasing dust bunnies, so we were at liberty to peak through the parlor curtains for a glimpse of Gina. Two scruffy imps lumbered by hauling a female mannequin. The way one of them used her more than ample knocker as a carry post sealed my imaginings for the evening. The Tedro Family was practicing in shiny costumes, which made the boys look like fairies and their sister the equal of that mannequin. Chuckie and Todd The Toad, no relation to Gilly the Toad Tosser, were throwing a Nerf football back and forth but for once Benny elected to be inside peering out. So, when Gina's mom Jean came out of her door he froze. Would Gina come trailing along behind her? Nope. Just Jean going about another day in her mystery life, walking, walking, hey wait, walking straight up toward our door. What in the name of either one of us would be elated to marry your daughter right now is going on? Was 24 hours in the projects so daunting to Jean that she'd joined the local custom of knock, borrow, and return what you'd borrowed before you get a rep? She had that I'm gonna have a one egg IOU look, so that must be it. She was obviously here to borrow an egg so that Gina could put the final touches on a culinary masterpiece with one hand while painting a portrait without the assistance of numbers with the other.

"Breathe, Benny. Breathe." I prompted, opening the door.

"I can't. I'm in love," he replied, from where he'd moved off to sit on the couch clutching his knees.

"Hi," Jean enunciated with a seasoned matchmaker's silvery timbre. "My daughter Gina would welcome a visit from your brother. Will you inquire if that suits his fancy?"

"Benny is married, so he can't," I ad-libbed, flirtatiously.

She enjoyed that, offering a thumb up. I forgot all about Gina that second and relocated my wellspring of devotion on to her. To this day I don't suppose she's singled out who secretly sent her that box of Goobers.

"Okay, if he suddenly gets divorced and would care to meet my daughter, please advise him to stop by."

As she departed, I charged up to Benny and stared at him from unsettlingly close, a favorite of mine on those rare occasions that I caught him nervous. I teased, "Nervous?"

He slid away from me on the couch fidgeting like I'd never seen him, as the door flung open betokening another cataclysmic mood swing.

"You failed Catechism!" our father yelled, hurrying in to stand over Benny. He shoved the failure note in Benny's face and flung it in the air for dramatic effect. "Failed! All ya had to do was pay attention some, memorize a few basic things, and what maybe take a couple'a damn tests? What the hell's that require? You an idiot?"

You would've thought that Benny had strafed a convent with gunfire. The wrath, automatic as it was unchecked, carried on for a half hour, while I trembled on a chair hoping it wouldn't turn physical. He had to regurgitate it again and again, not to assure that it was understood, but to self-indulgently heighten and prolong the terror. The phrasing told me that it wasn't actually, primarily, about Benny having failed; it was that the King had been ignored. This was personal. It struck at his ego that anyone would dare to not fulfill his assortment of demands.

"It's just silly stuff," Benny said. "Stories about walking on water, and some guy who didn't stay dead. Chuckie makes up better junk than that."

"Who are you to decide?"

"You don't believe in that stuff. You don't go to church."

"Boy, it'll be forever and a day 'til this isn't, 'Do what I say and not what I do.' This isn't a democracy," he spat with eyes even a Superhero would've feared. "So, therefore, I'll fix your wagon. I'm gonna subtract the thing that you most cherish. You'll lose for the whole bleeping summer the thing that will most hurt you and I'll bet you won't disobey again after that. Guess what you're losing."

"I don't know."

"I said guess!"

"My bike?"

Our father whooped wickedly, as if Benny was more likely to lose his life. "Your bike. That's rich," he mocked, erecting a fraudulent smile. "Try say, your freedom."

His eyes squinting, Benny squeezed his chin hard, like that would render what he'd heard fathomable.

"And don't think I care to look atcha during your sentence, making me sick with all the problems ya cause. You get to spend your summer sweating in bed. Now, don't pretend like I'm unreasonable. Ya can sit up, squat, stand up, even jump up and down for all I care, feast your eyes out the window at everyone enjoying the day, just don't get off that bed and make me come in there. And, even better, ya can start right now."

"But..."

"Go ahead, say sa'em else like, please give me a good beating, too," he tossed out as if they were as common as sparrows. It was his favorite phrase, and quite the oxymoron. He was incessantly blabbering about what a good beating everyone needed, Ted Kennedy for Chappaquiddick, Chuckie for getting caught boosting penny candy, half the guys he worked with, not just us. For a while there I detected our mother at the top of the stairs eavesdropping. I knew she'd soon withdraw.

"Why are you still here? You know where your bed is," our father said, twirling his finger around in a bunch of directions before settling on the correct one. Benny's climb upstairs was disembodied, the despair lingering in the hallways for days.

"Appears ya gonna have extra chores this summer," our father prodded me, inferring that Benny had also done me wrong.

"I'd rather do some of Benny's hours for him trapped in bed."

“That’s not going to happen.”

“A whole summer?”

“That’s right,” he exulted, whistling like the day was turning out okay after all. He strutted along the hallway like a professional wrestler who’d just vanquished all of the pretenders who’d absurdly dared to challenge him. Benny was slumped on the bed. “Are your feet touching the ground?”

“No.”

“Don’t let me discover otherwise. And you’ll be excited to know that there are a couple more rules. No using anything electric, including lights. I’ll loan ya a flash light. Ya mother and brother will be told to not visit you. Ever. Hey, wish you’d passed that class now, huh?”

“Yes.”

“Too late. But don’t worry. There’s always next summer to pal around with Aggie Boza,” he rubbed in, not a crumb of concern that being caged for a summer might not be beneficial to a child’s identity formation. Exiting, he closed the door little by little for special effect. Halfway down the hallway he paused, feminized a quarter turn and executed the series of sidesteps needed to reopen the door and peak in. “By the way, that Aggie is retarded, ya know.”

“No, she’s not.”

“Keep looking. It’ll hit ya in the head eventually.”

The first few weeks in bed Benny hoped that this was only a temporary scare tactic to “teach him a lesson”. Listlessly, he’d sit up and play with his skeletons for a while, or listen to his transistor radio when he could get it angled right to pick up a signal. But the blatant injustice, sparks of an underlying fury, and a need to amuse himself to avoid going bonkers, all smashed into each other like three BBs in a box. Throughout the summer that hope waned replaced by the grayness of the limbo all around him. And what a wizard our father became at tiptoeing, pantomiming it even if mother or me was in view as if it were comical, and opening the door quickly to ensure no one was afoot. He relished slipping home during work hours to verify that his edict was being upheld, the bloodlust that he would catch a petty offense written all over his face.

Day became night, and afternoons like dawn. Sleep was in anxious spurts that were never predictable, leaving Benny increasingly discombobulated. His three per day allotment of bathroom visits, and every other day bath were relished like a child's excitement at going to the beach, each respite dragged out for that extra minute. Like a highly decorated soldier nursing his life altering wounds with leaves and mud while encased in isolation in a prison camp, he spoke to himself and invented games to play in his mind. He shared stories with shadows of people he created as hand puppets on the wall, not friends; friends would've rescued him.

The only infusion of solace came at each sighting of Gina in her bedroom, an enchantment for which he endlessly longed. Often, they connected through their separate open windows, her on a chair, him on his bed, gaping at each other with elbows on windowsills arms up to support their chins with hands, whatever playfulness or smiles she would send his way were, even if only momentarily, supplanted by a wistful frown. The same after she'd blast music out of her window and from a distance they boogied. Again, after she'd mooned him, riveting to him not because he'd laid eyes on her little derriere. This was a kindred spirit. Irreverent, joyful, untamable. As if to lessen his plight somewhat, she always departed with a merry, protracted wave that foreshadowed the dynamic flow of comings together and brief separations that would be their union. It was ameliorating for him, until minutes later when that prevalent sentiment, shame, would again slam him far up onto shore leaving him stranded. The dichotomy that was Gina for him, a paragon of optimism and another deflating reminder of what had been ripped from him, instigated him with frequency to clutch on to Mr. Nune's pillow.

One day, as a paroxysmal desperation overtook him, he drew a face on Mr. Nune's pillow. And there he was, his other most loyal companion, with oval eyes, a perma-smile, and freckles. A comrade who he peered at until he laughed, or cried, or an hour had been spent in fleetingly palliative meditation. When it was necessary to stow away that comrade from our father's up-close inspections, incognito simply required that the pillowcase be slipped on. A child's ways of survival aren't conscious choices selected out of a catalogue with trees bearing fruit and the vast open sky on the cover.

There were moments of analysis that were also a deviation for that kid who just liked to have fun. He wasn't a deceiver and didn't intentionally upset the apple cart. This wasn't an eleven-year-old who was way ahead of his sociopathic time scuttling around inscribing 666 on anything or stealing baby turtles from the pet store to fling them through people's windows. The recognition had begun that he was the whipping boy, an object our father could utilize to vent his frustrations at being in a dead-end job, at an age when he should just be settling down, in a housing project that was beneath his pompous sense of superiority, with a wife from such a horrid childhood. But there was even more to our father's story, and all of the monotonous slights he'd thrown at Benny and to a lesser extent me, and like clockwork to our mother.....*Thick skull, shut your pie hole, jello for brains, shut your yap, don't know your ass from your elbow, your mother's child when it comes to having a clue, born to repeat the same blunders again and again, not very swift, on a path to nowhere fast, destined to not notice the obvious, in a dream world, a mistake waiting to happen, something the cat dragged in, half boy-half hopeless, a screw loose, some marbles missing, lead between your ears, soft in the head, a rare case of slow, a menace to all intelligent life on the planet, barely able to tie your own shoes, on a slow train to Dumbville, cruising for a bruising, skirting for a hurtin, pushing your luck, begging for a knuckle sandwich, need some sense pounded into ya, must have been dropped on your head when he was hard at work, selfish, mental midget, spoiled, a day late and a dollar short, switched at birth, daft, whistling to a different tune than the one playing, full of hogwash, full of manure, living on Mars, the Gilligan of Brickenwood, would forget to eat unless reminded* yet *eating him out of house and home, permanently wet behind the ears, nit wit, dim-witted, little girl, cry baby, little baby, big baby, on a fast track to the pokie, need to buckle down our bootstraps, suffering from cobwebs, surprised you can remember your own name....*all of those were more proof of it. Proof that he actually was a sadist, with a bottomless appetite to debase us.

In early August, when our father wasn't around, Benny began standing up on his bed now and then to assert, "You're wicked strong!" Same way he'd encouraged Aggie Boza. It was only once each rising, marked by a forced, heartrending quality of steadfastness that didn't harken of my omnipotent brother. It seemed possessed, as if the past life Benny, or a subsequent incarnation, was crossing time lines to assist him to persevere. I'd even whip into his room to remind him, "You're wicked strong!" and off I'd go before a certain blowhard could snare me. With four days left in his sentence, Benny abruptly discontinued trumpeting that once he'd received the answer to the only words he would ever convey to Gina. They were written one word per page in bold print on pieces of paper that I'd provided him and shown to her like flash cards one by one...**Please Don't Move Away Gina Delillo**

And her flash card response, **I Have To Do What My Mom Says Because I'm Only 10.**

He kept compelling himself to look out the window during their departure, edging up somewhat, not high enough to be seen, before collapsing back down too embarrassed to weep like that in front of her. Slumped on the stoop, my hands on my cheekbones so that I could wipe away promptly, I cried too, viewing her tightly knit family at the packed moving truck waiting for her while she breathlessly leaned out her window hoping to wave goodbye to Benny. I bled for him and for her, empathizing with a selflessness that would become more difficult for me over time. Though I couldn't see Benny's window above me, I deduced from her forlornness that she wasn't receiving the farewell she'd so innocently desired.

"Gina is going now, Benny. So please, please sit up and wave to her. She's in her window," was all I entreated tearfully, once I'd decided to trot upstairs to him.

Around his eyes was swollen, the eyes so red that I wondered if he could see me. The toughest little bugger I've ever met surrendered to his fear of adoring her face-to-face one final, irreversible time. He couldn't bear it, so he haltingly raised his pale hand. Though it shook, even so I saw life in it, like a flower threading its way through a crack in the cement. The wave lasted a few seconds, and if multiplied by how often I've surveyed it in my mind, many times longer. The wail that came out of him as he dropped his hand was something new, a seeming breakthrough in his willingness to not suppress, yet chilling in its desolate rawness.

The morning Benny was to begin at Normandin Junior High, his first day not bed bound, Chuckie was waiting for him outside of our unit with his 'fro' having grown out all summer. Benny was gaunt and jittery, his muscles atrophied. From the window where I gave birth to cataloguing the after-effects of Benny's internment, it was plain that the mini-hug they shared was taxing to him.

"Ready for Normandin?" Benny chirped, bent on coming across as unaffected as possible.

"Ain't gonna be goin' wit' ya 'cause I went all dunce cap again and failed summer school," Chuckie replied, cheerful for someone who had to wallow in grade school for another year.

"Ya leaving me flat?"

"No, I ain't."

"Flatter than a piece of paper with no writing on it."

"I told yo' heinie that I'm gonna be scorin' me some of that art teacher, Miss Flynn, and ain't leavin' Mt. Pleasant till I do."

"Jr. High is gonna suck lemons without ya."

"Cool-city is what you're in for. It's gonna be bangin," Chuckie jived, hitting Benny with a new lingo he'd never heard.

"Bummer, anyway."

"I gotta book 'cause the principal wants to give me a talking to on sa'em."

"See ya after school?"

"Fo-sho."

Chuckie sped off, braked, and reversed his tracks. "Aggie Boza rapped on your door yesterday to go all goodbye and stuff. Yo Papa told her ya was being punished so ya couldn't see'er."

"Where'd she go?"

"They moved to Atlanta as far south as Georgia."

Grimacing, Benny shielded his face with the hand that didn't have a pinkie in it. This alarmed Chuckie so he zipped off adding, "It's hot as cow turds there."

Minutes later Benny stopped staring at Aggie's stoop, squeezing the pinkie so hard that I suspected he'd crush it. I invariably felt less unstable by quantifying things, so it was then that Benny began speaking about 10% as many words as he used to, usually in lines of five words or less, with an even lower percentage of his old zest. It only required one example of his repercussions to identify that he was much more disarranged than even those auspicious numbers demonstrated.

----------------------------------+----------------------------------

Eyes darting about, Benny again felt like a prisoner of war who before being captured had survived the enemies many attacks, but who now forecast that his wounds were most likely fatal. The toxic combination of dread and resignation were all that he could register. He simply couldn't concentrate otherwise. After an interminable summer in prison for the transgression of failing Catechism, the drudgery Ben Thompson forced him to endure in case someday he opted to get hitched in the Catholic Church, he was now doomed as a student. It was even less comprehensible because in his smug, all knowing fashion, like countless things others cared about, our father frequently disparaged religion.

The moment that Benny grasped his fate he was in Mr. Taz's Seventh Grade Math Class, on only his fourth day at Normandin Junior High. Transfixed, he was staring at the boy in the seat next to his nicknamed not lovingly as Richard Slide Rule, Normandin's number one Ban-Aid on the glasses, math nerd. Richard had just sequenced three logical questions that required only a C student's understanding of the first four days of math, and Benny couldn't unravel an iota of the questions or Mr. Taz's responses. He tried to zone in, to snap out it so to speak, even giving himself a boxer's self-punch to the chin to stimulate alertness, but like everything verbalized in the classrooms aside from his seat assignment and some adolescent prattling, it wouldn't sink in. It was as if his brain were fried like the Count of Monte Cristo's had been after a decade of solitary confinement, before Abbe Faria chipped through the stone wall to guide him toward internal liberation. Unfortunately, no savior was coming for Benny. It was as unnerving as someone in a conscious coma desperate to express to his loving, supportive family who'd been holding vigil at his hospital bed, "I'm here. I'm still here." But those muscles that once composed him lay dormant. He gawked at Richard bewilderedly for so long that Richard amassed the nerve to glance back. Being in an intractable fog can come across as mental illness to a nerd preconditioned for logic and conformity.

Benny's next few weeks flailing to repossess his former brain were a peculiar whirlwind. The perpetual urge to sleep, angst about his demise, and flecks of awareness that soon dissipated about the subject at hand, all augmented his sense of doom. Students who unabashedly participated seemed like aliens. They were pubescent talking heads speaking in tongues. They might as well have sold Benny off to a traveling carnival, attached balloons to his ears, and let every local yokel with a quarter and a dream clutch a water pistol at nine paces to shoot streams into his mouth. Be sure to also notify the city's teachers not to fret because the unprecedented outbreak of ADD, with the abundance to plummet thousands of feckless youth into straight Fs across their report card, was all concentrated in poor Benny.

But it wasn't ADD. It was trauma's evil spawn. And heeding that without average effort on his part he'd been selected after grade school to join the one third of students placed into the "college track" courses, this new dysfunctional student named Benny was like a death to him. Or, he was actually the alien, body snatched by creatures from a downwardly mobile planet where everyone flunked out of school. Even the scholastic feats of Orlandodo and the Cubbards left him feeling like an eggplant with arms, as if only programmed to flip the page a beat behind everyone else. His most pressing anxiety that he might now be permanently defective, without a headfirst dive into the low side of the pool to justify it, added to the hopelessness.

To turn to our father for understanding, would've meant being blamed, humiliated without compunction, and maybe another few months in prison. To scream, "I'm brain damaged and you caused it," would've at minimum brought our father's convenient denial that such a cause and effect was the issue, and just as likely his monochromatic viewpoint that such a cause and effect was possible. Benny also wasn't destined to become some altruistic guidance counselor's pet project. No charitable librarian was going to intuit his condition and volunteer to tutor him in private for as long as it would take to land him back on track. It was clear that the only method to survive was to cheat in school until he could somehow again function. For years he would wait for that light at the end of the tunnel to pop up interspersed with fleeting, fruitless attempts to focus, ones that might've been further circumvented by the escalating chaos at home. And thus, he pulled it off. He cheated in every class with a survivor's lack of guilt. It would necessitate every ounce of the highly evolved faculty to live by his wits that his life with Daddy, The Great Enabler, and a bit of poverty also required. There were two irrefutable facts. He knew that he was screwed, and he didn't brief anyone about what was going on with him at school, not even me.

------------------------------+-----------------------------------

It was months into Benny's grade seven. We were divided into two teams, my team, The Skins, and Benny's team, The Shirts, each with eleven players on it. Like in humane basketball five players from each team played at once, so there were players rotating frequently in and out of the game. Unlike humane basketball, in Tackle Basketball the eleventh man on each team was the goalie, the position I received in light of the fact that I would've been flagrantly non-participatory otherwise. My refusal to run with it when the football was thrown to me, or to finish a lap around the track, or to catch a fly ball dreading that it would hit me on the head, were only a sliver of the age inappropriate reasons that I'd failed my only class ever. And thus, Benny and I were classmates, namely his seventh grade and my repeat seventh grade PE. Stationed on a platform underneath the regulation basketball hoop with a overflowing bin of dodge balls at the ready, the goalie's job was to cause the other team interference not by cascading boiling oil onto them, but by hurling dodge balls at them as they dribbled the basketball his way, and at the basketball during its trajectory to the hoop. Shots to the face weren't wholeheartedly discouraged, so an attempted layup could prove lethal.

Prior to becoming a gym teacher Mr. Noor had been a 20-year military man, serving under Patton in World War II, even transfiguring into the personification of Patton indefatigably motivating the troops, undermined somewhat by a wisp of a lisp he'd managed to only partially cure. Half military, half male fashion designer, he preferred to wear a swanky basketball referee's uniform for the games accentuated by what could only be described as a pocketbook that housed a scorecard, mini-pencils, and Ban-Aid brand adhesives. His second favorite motto was, "to be doubly prepared is to never founder," and thus he always wore two whistles around his neck in case a defective pea exploded.

Like Gladiators psyched-up to impose their adolescent will The Skins lined up on one sideline and The Shirts on the other. Their grills ranged from bloodthirsty to my inalienable right to wimpiness. "Ms. Drill Sergeant," otherwise addressed as Mr. Noor to his face at school or when in public walking his Doberman Pincher and Toy Poodle, set up mid-court. The rumor was that the military had made him a bit too heavy in the loafers to find a suitable boyfriend, so he complemented the two sides of himself with contrasting K9 companions.

"Welcome to your first week at Normandin, youurrrr juniorrrrrr higgghhhhhh!!!. Honor it and love it because someday you'll flash back on this as some of the greatest memories of your lives," he saluted. "And, welcome to Tackle Basketball!!! Tackle Basketball, the game where sissies cry and cowards lie down waiting to crawl back to Social Studies class. There are only four rules......

#1. No crying or you get to squat in the coward's corner.

#2. If you're fortunate enough to possess the basketball, you have to dribble it wherever you go.

#3. If you throw an elbow it best not be above the neck or below the waist.

#4. No tackling anyone except the player with the ball.

That's that. You can block, you can pass, you can scream like your hair is on fire. And, did I mention.....**crying.** There are too many reasons to list why rule #1 and my #1 motto are identical. Ready to recite the abridged version of my #1 motto!"

"Yes sir," hailed 22 kids, the one who'd languished for a summer in bed looking like he needed an exorcism.

"I will not cry in gym class, or in life, even if fatigued, bruised, or maimed," Mr. Noor announced.

"I will not cry in gym class, or in life, even if fatigued, bruised, or maimed," we sounded off.

"I can't hear you! I will not cry in gym class, or in life, even if fatigued, bruised, or maimed," he bellowed.

"I will not cry in gym class, or in life, even if fatigued, bruised, or maimed," we screamed back louder.

"Very good. Now, first teams on the floor. Goalies under the basket. Let's get rocking!"

The tougher boys hooted and "sissies" primed to linger behind the basketball pretending to participate. Tackle Basketball, a game that would never be found in any school nowadays that didn't mandate that its students' parents sign a hundred-page liability release form. Nor is there fifty feet of rope attached to the ceiling with only a three-inch thick mat on the floor to break falls. A rope that only the fat boy and I refused to climb.

The tallest boys from each starting team stood center court ready for the jump ball, while the bench players congregated on the sidelines screaming like quashed depression-era alcoholics deprived of their drink at a bare knuckle's boxing match. I perused Benny from my perch as we got underway. He was riveted on the basketball with the concentration of an afflicted soul a couple of notches away from full-blown lunatic.

THE JUMP BALL IS ON HIGH AND ENDS UP IN THE HANDS OF SKIN #1. HE DRIBBLES LEFT, BUT HIS DAVID CASSIDY HAIRCUT AND WHITE HEADBAND GET ALL MESSED UP WHEN BENNY IMMEDIATELY TACKLES HIM.

"YOU UGLY TURD," HE MUMBLES TO BENNY. THE BALL FLIES FREE AND IS RETRIEVED BY SHIRT #1. AS ATHLETIC AS A FIRE HYDRANT, HE BEGINS TO DRIBBLE AND DOWN HE GOES WHEN ONE FOOT TRIPPED OVER THE OTHER. SKIN #2

WRESTLES AWAY THE BALL, PASSES IT TO SKIN #1, WHO PICKS UP SOME BLOCKERS AND DRIBBLES IT DOWN COURT. SKIN #3 KNOCKS BENNY DOWN, WHO'S UP IN A SECOND AND SOARS LIKE A MISSILE IN THE DIRECTION OF THE BALL PLOWING RIGHT OVER SKIN #4 ON THE WAY. SKIN #1 STOPS TO SHOOT, OBLIVIOUS TO THE DODGE BALLS FLYING BY HIS HEAD. THIS IS AN ATHLETE READY TO TAKE ONE FOR THE TEAM. HOLY MOLY, JUST AFTER HE RAISED THE BALL OVERHEAD TO FIRE, BENNY TOOK IT OUT OF HIS HANDS FROM BEHIND AND DRIBBLED THE OTHER WAY.

"OH, THAT BOY HAS SOME DEMON IN HIM!" BAWLS MR. NOOR. "AND THAT'S WHAT LEADS TO VICTORY."

BENNY ADVANCES TO CENTER COURT, BARELY STAYS UP WHEN SKIN #5 WRAPS AROUND HIM THEN SLIDES DOWN ALL THE WAY TO THE FLOOR WITH NOTHING TO SHOW FOR IT OTHER THAN RED MARKS. BLOCKS TO HIS LEFT AND RIGHT CLEAR A PATH TO THE BASKET. HE'S NOW IN SHOOTING RANGE SWEAT BLURRING HIS VISION.

"WHERE'S THE DEFENSE! DEFENSE!" SHOUTS MR. NOOR, HIS TWO WHISTLES FLOPPING BACK AND FORTH ON HIS SHIRT.

BENNY BRACES TO SHOOT, TAKES A NON-BROTHERLY DODGE BALL OFF THE SHOULDER, ANOTHER ONE TO THE HEAD, AND JUST BEFORE HE RELEASES THE BALL IS PUSHED BY SKIN #1 WITH A FEROCITY THAT HURTLES HIM TEN FEET ACROSS THE FLOOR AND DOWN. OH, THE DAMAGE TO NAKED KNOBBY KNEES FROM THAT ONE, RELOCATING HIM AS FAR AWAY FROM THE BASKET NOW AS A THREE POINTER. BENNY IS AS DETERMINED AS SOMEONE WHO'LL END UP IN AN EVEN MORE PICTURESQUE PARADISE THAN THE ONE ADVERTISED IN THE CATECHISM CLASS HE FAILED, IF ONLY HE NOTCHES THE FIRST POINTS. HE ROLLS OVER AND FROM HIS KEISTER SOMEHOW MANAGES TO FAKE A SHOT AS A DESPERATE SKIN #1 FLIES BY HIM GOING FOR THE BLOCK. AS FAST AS YOU CAN REPEAT TACKLE BASKETBALL THREE TIMES THE CROWD SHIFTS FROM FRENZIED TO HELD BREATHS. HE

RELEASES A HIGH ARCING FLOATER TOWARD THE RIM. ONE DODGE BALL MISSES IT. TWO DODGE BALLS, AS BOYS SCRAMBLE UNDER THE BASKET TO REBOUND. THE BASKETBALL HITS THE INSIDE OF THE RIM, WHAT A SHOT BOUNCING HIGH UP ON THE BACKBOARD. IT HITS THE RIM AGAIN AND DEFLECTS OFF TO NEAR WHERE SOMEHOW BENNY HAD RISEN AND FED TO UNDER THE BASKET.

"SO CLOSE. THAT'S HOW YOU DO IT BOYS," MR. NOOR CALLS OUT.

SKIN #1 REBOUNDS THE BALL AND GOES TO DRIBBLE IT. BENNY AGAIN WRENCHES IT OUT OF HIS HANDS, DRIBBLES ONCE, LAYS IT UP, AND SCORES AS ANOTHER DODGE BALL BOUNCES OFF HIS SCALP.

"DAMN TURD," SKIN #1 SNIPES. "YOU'RE NOT SCORING AGAIN."

"LET YOUR PLAY DO THE TALKING, YOU" ADMONISHES MR. NOOR BLOWING A WHISTLE. "TWO TO NOTHING. INBOUND THE BALL. LET'S GO."

AS SKIN #3 TAKES THE BALL OUT OF BOUNDS BENNY DARTS UP COURT, TURNS LIKE HE WAS CREATED IN A LAB, AND CHARGES BACK AT SKIN #1 AS THE BALL IS INBOUNDED TO HIM. SKIN #1 TRIES TO PASS IT BACK TO SKIN #3. BENNY INTERCEPTS IT, SHOOTS, AND SCORES ALL IN ONE MOTION BEFORE EVEN ONE DODGE BALL CAN BE HURLED. HIS TEAM GOES NUTS AS HE HASTENS BACK UP THE COURT.

"HE DOES IT AGAIN," PROCLAIMS MR. NOOR. "THIS ONE IS DESTINED FOR THE TACKLE BASKETBALL HALL OF FAME!"

As Benny bent to tie his shoe Skin #1 slid by and, angling to not be witnessed, stepped on his hand. In a flash Benny lunged upward, dragged him down by the neck, and fired off the best shot of the day square to the jaw. As a dazed Skin #1 scurried to flee Benny frosted that cake with as many as he could ahead of Mr. Noor rushing over to tote him out of bounds by the seat of the pants. Had I left out that Mr. Noor lifted weights three hours a day?

"You, go the principal's office," he directed Skin #1. "Attack Dog, inbounds the ball after you tie your shoe!"

TREE HILL ACRES

Two Rookies in The Burbs

It was like watching a cartoon with two hits of acid careening around in your brain. There Officer Thompson stood in the living room, in full uniform, police academy completed, chest puffed out a la Dudley Do Right, geared up for his first night patrolling the streets.

"Pretty Snazzy, huh?" he boasted.

Still disquietingly sullen, Benny exchanged a glance with me.

"Very nice," our Mother answered, tossing in a couple of torpid gestures to appear animated.

"Bet the criminals won't be out tonight when they hear I'm on the street," he went on. It was even more chilling when he was merry. Guilt should've eradicated such liberties.

"You'll do very well out there," she said. Her wig phase was waning replaced by a series of mindless hobbies, 'hobbies' being a 'suggestion' her husband curatively prescribed to counteract the damage from her childhood. To him he was without question 100% the solution, 0% the cause.

"See boys, told ya your mother has a mind of her own!"

I couldn't stop thinking, "What does a criminal who's never been caught have to do to become a police officer? Answer: "Take a civil service test." Long past my days of praying during commercials, the armor of prayers having spared me few slices, I was now, from A to Z, an aficionado of all things Holocaust. My collection of Holocaust books was well worn, the details of photos of the dead, dying, and emaciated repetitively inspected through my magnifying glass, and specific methods of torture and execution brought up ad nauseam to whomever would listen. This probably augmented my vision that Officer Thompson would get blown away on his first shift out there. Maybe by a deranged taxidermist who'd then stuff him and affix him to a golden pedestal to keep vigil erect like the officer that he so briefly was, his head to be used for games of ring toss by one and all. Benny conjectured that once said taxidermist was caught, found criminally insane at trial, gradually rehabilitated and released, that if he married our mother what a step up in the father category, we'd luck into.

"No one has to lock the doors with me out there," Officer Thompson proclaimed hand on his revolver. With that he mounted his white horse, reminding our mother to lock the door behind him.

The second he was gone, Benny said, "What an asshole."

"Benny!" our mother objected.

"Oh, you know it as much as we do."

The obvious assumption is that Officer Thompson would, using his favorite phrase, "knock some sense" into someone who'd dared to violate his city's ordinances, sending him back to the boiler room at Serodyn. It didn't take us long to catch on that the opposite was going to play out. He would be the most by the book lawman in town. From his first second on the job he was a role model to the older guns, as he would someday be to the younger ones. This fellow who foamed at the mouth if his kids or wife made the slightest slip-up, such as drop their fork or stub their toe, would just uphold the law, rigidly suppressing all emotion and his compulsion to flog all transgressors, murderers and loiterers alike. It wasn't that he was suddenly fair-minded, a series of epiphanies having mended his formerly unexamined ways, it's that he definitely didn't want to end up back at Serodyn, and, let the drum roll begin...It turned him on playing the role of the peerless professional in the eyes of coworkers, the citizenry, and especially members of our extended family. It afforded him status, even more verification that he soared above the ordinary man than he could self-serve himself at home.

He conned everyone on the outside by making it appear as if he was the epitome of self-restraint, genetically one of the good guys despite the philistine bent, and what a blessed wife he must have. This twisted psyche had incongruous compartments underpinned by a veil of saintliness slipped on and off at will. An image managed extolls its virtues to the unwitting.

There was an even more insidious aspect to this dichotomy of self. It wasn't simply a Jekyll and Hyde phenomenon where Officer Thompson seemed normal one minute and transmuted at home the next. It was more misshapen than that. There was a bigger game being played. His thing was beyond perverse. It was a pathological craving to frustrate his wife and kids. He loved to frustrate us as much as another man might enjoy ferrying his family to an uplifting movie. And what more justifiable way to do it than with these haunting words, "People wouldn't believe you anyway if you told them." He'd already written a doomsday manual so that if his domain at home came undone, the world at large would side with that upstanding officer of the law. This pillar of society, who hangs his club at home when not at the shore mirthfully braining fish, couldn't even conceive that the halo above his public persona could be tarnished.

Yet it was strange, there was also an iota of pride that my father, a rookie cop, was wearing that badge.

"I think he's beginning to mellow with age," our mother responded, inciting Benny and me to collapse to the floor in stitches until we coughed. What flashed through my mind was the previous night, me listening outside their bedroom as she tried to muffle her sobs with oldies from their love fest radio.

"Thank God he now has a gun," Benny persisted.

"Until the day he retires he'll wish he could shoot first and not ask questions after," I added.

"That's your father you're talking about."

"Don't remind me," Benny and I cracked in tandem.

On par with a Hummingbird zooming by, it all unfolded so quickly. Benny's ability to function in school had incinerated a year ago, Chuckie was shuffled off to an alternate junior high that specialized in "slow learners," Officer Thompson had donned the uniform of authority, the tumult that is puberty, and now we were transferring moving boxes into a compact, one story house in a suburb with three models from which to choose. Though Chuckie and Benny exchanged a couple of tenuous phone calls they were now on diverging paths. The next time they'd see each other was when Chuckie arrived at high school a year after him. Now tall and lean beneath a foot long fro with a lime green pick in it, Chuckie was parked where all of the black teens congregated. He'd recalibrated his speech to ring more "black," like since conception he'd lived in what some locals referred to as "Coonsville," the area around Kempton Street. With the mullet of someone who hadn't cut his hair in a year, Benny rushed up to him and caught two things on his face. It's great to see you, though not in front of the brothers, leaving Benny awash in betrayal.

Our new house, with a back yard that sloped gently, a screened in patio with bird feeders, and our own little wallpapered bedrooms, was an upgrade worth noting. That might've been easier if not for two buzz kills. 1. The lingering odor of the former owner's tendency to remain cadaverous there for weeks without anyone discovering hadn't yet completely faded. 2. Officer Thompson kept reiterating, "See what I do for you." It was his reminder that the promise of a fresh start in the burbs wasn't genuinely ours to own, just loaned to us by a higher power. Oh, how he slaved for us ingrates, while all other men had careers as The Vice President in charge of Pool Parties and Golf Trips.

Benny, who'd added to his repertoire a standing backflip, now began to refine hurling himself over fences. His favorite was to sprint to our three-foot tall chain-linked fence, like a chasm of heartache to breach, his stomach thrust into the top to flip over upside down landing on his feet on the other side. Here was another dare that I wouldn't attempt. And once it became apparent that his brain without a doubt wasn't going to function again in school, he also perfected the art of cheating. His homework was all copied, tests eyeballed from the person next to him, essays plagiarized. His hand stayed down always, and if called upon by the teacher some lonely or timid student in his camp would somehow prompt him. Officer Thompson's signature was forged on the yellow cards Benny received when failing classes mid-semester, those classes barely raised back up to a passing grade by report card day. He was in an unconventional school of a sort, one where he could've taught a course on covert operations, pulling the wool over the eyes of even the most suspicious teacher. Obviously, some inflexible personality could push that if all that resolve went into cheating, why not put the intelligence it demands into doing your work? Systemized cheating is basically a repetitive process that you can control. To focus at other's pace where one element leads to the next or you fall behind is the opposite.

In the projects we used to walk to school separately, Benny with his friends and me with my fears. We now sat together riding a bus to school from Tree Hill Acres. To me, even before the inevitable occurred, it was a bully's haven, teeming with commentaries about anyone's zits, hair, clothes, speech, way of carrying books, sneezing, sitting, walking, laughing, gazing out the window, and worthiness to be alive. It didn't help that I carried myself, shoulders sloped forward and eyes cast down, with the lack of bravado of someone whose intuition that he'd ceased growing at five feet five inches would prove torturously correct. One day, since we'd been delayed by one of Officer Thompson's rants about how to properly squeeze a tube of toothpaste, we were the last ones to board the bus. Benny had begun to rebound, especially after I'd confronted him about his prolonged slump with, "Remember when say three years ago you vowed, 'Overall, I'm happy so that's not gonna change because of him.'" I was proud of my provocative invitation to restore his indomitableness.

On the bus there were only three seats available, the one near

Ferd, who'd long ago escaped into the complexity of ant farms, near Katey, who must have rated cardboard as a delicacy because she consumed more than her fair share of it, and Jimmy, the only black child in Tree Hill Acres. No one ever sat with him. The first two oddballs reminded me too much of myself so I opted for Jimmy. Benny plunked down near Katey.

"Hi," Benny broke the ice, respectfully curious how the chalk box that was her breakfast tasted. She didn't respond. You'd figure she'd be happier given that her family was now rolling in the dough. The Jart that had impaled her younger brother's skull had brought a doozy of a settlement.

"Good morning," I greeted Jimmy, as formal as an eighty-year-old who'd just learned the basics of English. I tried to hold eye contact with him, akin to how I'd read that Adolph used to.

"Hi," he replied, scared, less of me than his surroundings.

"Hi," mimicked Zeke, the surly ninth grader slouched behind us. The slap on the back of my seat was proceeded by a piercing cackle. "Hi, Jimmy Coon."

Benny's Tackle Basketbrawl hadn't tempered his readiness to defend, so he sprung up to loom over Zeke, glaring with the gritted teeth of Officer Thompson like in order to intimidate he was emulating that ignominious trait.

"Bbbbbenny, sit down," I stammered, eternally programmed to turn tail and run. "He's too big."

"So?" Benny grumbled. Preceding the growth spurt that would shoot him from five to six feet tall, again all he needed was "So?" There are people who stand up to other people no matter what it costs.

Zeke's jaw quivered, straining to appear unfazed.

“Get up,” Benny ordered. “You got something to spout then up.”

“I can’t fight on the bus.”

“Wherever ya start it that’s where I finish it. Up, yellow belly.”

His distaste for any type of harassment was rising, the pace upped when someone suddenly started tucking us in for bed.

“Well Zeke, if you decide you’re starving for a fight this bus ride will be over in a jiffy. And once I cream style corn your face you won’t need that lunch money anymore, will ya?” Richie Mavis stated with languid authority from a few seats back.

Zeke focused straight ahead. He was having an unexpected encounter with his own mediocrity.

“I can fight my own battles,” Benny objected.

“I can see that. Take a load off, Rookie. We’ll powwow later,” Richie replied.

I logged that as the moment, galvanized by a new ally with some backbone, as the Second Coming of Benny the Unstoppable.

Richie took a sip from his Yoo Hoo, yawned, then bellowed, “Nobody goes ‘Jimmy Coon’ again unless Jimmy and whoever this rookie dude is both give ya written permission, and ya lick Jimmy’s shoes, or you’re dead!”

Richie Mavis, the premier little league baseball player the city had ever seen, who’d quit due to boredom and not because his ancient father had to be assisted home drunk at the end of each game that he’d pretend to watch while lusting after the young mothers of the athletically mortal. Richie Mavis who tried out for the varsity football team in the ninth grade not to make the team, cognizant that once his D average became public, he’d be academically disqualified, but just to zigzag through the players again and again during practice dispelling their fond hopes of going pro. They even bowed to him in the hallway until he bowed out of high school. With long, wavy black hair and Paul Newman eyes, his avocation of standing on street corners for passersby to admire sustained him.....for now.

For Benny there would now be a band to belong to, one street wise in the array of shenanigans Officer Thompson boasted that he'd prevented Benny from falling prey to by trucking him out of the projects. Officer Thompson, who out of the blue had decided he needed to connect more with his boys.

Weeks earlier, Benny had just turned thirteen and I was fourteen when it started. Officer Thompson appeared in the doorway after I'd lain down for bed. As natural as an amnesiac might to a boy everyone insists is his, he inquired, “Ready for bed, son?”

“Ah, yeah.”

He tromped over and ham-handedly secured the right side of the sheets more tightly around me. I cringed, grateful that the darkness obscured my reaction and his jowly face. He did the same with the blanket.

“How's that?” he asked, dryly.

“Okay,” I answered, more nauseous than if I were losing my virginity with the oldest woman alive.

He walked around the bed. I shuddered that this was a smoke screen for a pending blitz. Every muscle in my body braced. All he did was arrange the other side of the sheet and blanket around me so that I was as snug as a bug in a rug. Each little contact was so unspeakably repellant that it coursed through me like 1000 volts.

“Your mother and I love you, ya know that?” he said, like he was groping to convince himself.

As much as I tried to answer, my throat was so constricted by disbelief that I couldn't.

"Your mother and I love you, ya know that?"

It felt perilous to not respond, so I forced the air through that allowed me to murmur, "Yes."

"And do you love us?"

Oh please, I thought. Stop. Why wasn't I granted at least a decade of warning to train for this? Then I realized, best to double down on my desire that this end ASAP by going along with the charade.

"Yes."

"Good night."

"Good night."

He accorded me a counterfeit pat on the head and left.

Officer Thompson had randomly decided to tuck us into bed every night. What misconception was that one suffering to assume that it was okay to alter between rabid and familial by breaking out a convention best saved for toddlers? If he was just being task-oriented, advancing his secret desire that as usual in his presence we'd be crawling in our skins, he'd sure fulfilled his goal, always making sure to pat us on the head before departing. We implored our mother to persuade him to spare us the anguish, disclosing candidly that we'd rather be tarred and feathered. Mercifully, just before she'd revert to concealing all displeasure with her marital lot, it was when she was sleepwalking through an unrewarding bout of "sticking up for herself." Thus, she'd mustered up the "gumption" to induce him to scrap giving us those haircuts from hell. With much deference to his over-baked ego, she'd laid out this new predicament for hi by saying, "I, I, I, I, I'm sure they appreciate it, but it's, well, maybe the boys are too old for that sort of connection."

"Oh malarkey. They just like to bellyache," he scoffed.

"Maybe you just don't remember being that age."

"Sure, I do. And I would've died to receive such attention from my father."

She couldn't placate his vision of injustice, though the tucking in part of the nightmare ended. Shortly after, as Benny lay on the floor in his room mellowing out to the Jefferson Airplane on the turntable, Officer Thompson entered and stood over him. Stoned-faced he alleged, "I know you swayed your brother about me not tucking him in also. Not smart."

The silence could be heard it was so oppressive as he glowered downward. He backed away and stopped. "Unless ya wanna testify that it was his idea."

"No," Benny didn't hesitate to say, aware what he was inviting.

Soon Officer Thompson would whisper in passing, "You don't know when you'll get it, but it's coming. A syllable to your mother and it'll go double."

Subsequent to that every crossing of paths for weeks, lamely signaling it was forgiven, all Benny received was a lame smile and insipid jokes. It was like being in the dark tied to a splintery board, knowing that a tarantula was crawling around the room. After eight days of sleep deprivation, in a fit of slumber as restful as being in the cellar when your house is blowing away above you, Benny awoke to the shadow of someone wearing a police hat above him. Just then his mouth was covered and he was pinned down. Smack, smack, smack, smack, wrench head, smack, smack, punch, punch, smack, punch.

Madness.

Benny misled our mother that those welts resulted from an overzealous game of street hockey. He figured that if she hadn't left her man in the wake of being told that "you're almost as intelligent as the Pet Rock ya wasted money on," this wasn't going to incite her to do it. Though, downplaying it like a blip on the radar screen of his Second Coming, he was franker with me exacerbating my paranoia that the best, so to speak, was yet to come.

Back Against the Wall

God, I wanted to feel up Mickey Souza. I wanted to feel her up and down and up and down until the energy from it pranced throughout the universe forever. Halter top, cut-off jeans so snug that her bubble butt was suspended even higher, that bubble butt that would pass through the doorway a second after her as if making its own grand entrance, legs with a fullness of thigh muscle that screamed I can crush you. Do you want me to? You know you do.

An inventory taker by nature, she'd calculated what she had shortly after the seeds sprouted, years before full bloom. Truth be told, she'd been planning on it, by the 5th grade already praying that she would take after her mother's side of the family. This wasn't the ungainly adolescent beset with shame no matter what her assets were. This was the tempered vixen pretending that there wasn't even a thought of casting her spell over the rest the boys. How she would lie on her stomach and let the bubble float up in the air when she laughed. Lounge on her side with that slight extra pressing together of her impeccable B's, so round, so dense that it would entail a half-century and/or five sets of suckling triplets to knock them down for the count. And how aiming to go unnoticed, her eyes would flash at those beauties for a millisecond, verifying that they were creating a lasting enticement for whomever lolled in the grass across from her jawing about, as always, rock and roll. She loved her some David Bowie. Wham, bam, thank you, Mam.

Since the day Benny had linked up with the crew two months earlier, she was almost as fascinated by him as I was. "Boogie Rookie," she'd cheer on as he danced around the bonfire with his oversized sombrero spinning on his noodle, while the rest of Richie's Crew and their girls got stoned and wished that they could dance like that. She found it exotic that he'd relocated there from a housing project, frequently whispering to him, "You're a former pimp, right?" and "Is it true that you already have five bambinos?" and "What's that reform school they named after you?" She often demanded tales from that underworld, so he'd impersonate Chuckie, Rui Tedro, and Aggie Boza for her in their uncut distinctiveness, sprinkling in her chipper voice too, alternating back and forth so flowingly that it seemed like the four of them were having dinner as a group. And when Benny and she were flopped on the ground at the bonfire she'd rest her head on his shoulder, the inference that he's too young so no biggie. He was five months younger than her, but, at the time, three inches shorter.

"Wow, man," she initiated, prompting him to be one of her favorite characters. I was propped nearby against a tree, the only one drinking soda or wearing corduroys, this time dark brown ones.

"Wow, Man" he cooperated, now starring as stoner Cheech to her stoner Chong. "Did ya ever think that twenty years from now the Earth will have almost, give or take one or two hearty souls, all different dogs than the ones alive today?"

"No, man. But it's exceedingly important that everyone does, man. Superduperly important."

"A toast to that rare four-legged friend who reaches twenty years old, man. Bark on!" he reveled, his eyes rolling back and lids closing, playacting too stoned to stay awake. She tapped him on the shoulder startling him back to alertness. They toasted with their plastic cups and used a quart of Budweiser to refill. "Hey man, I got some wisdom for ya that I learned in the mental institution, man."

"Lay it on me, sir. Make me as wise as a loony."

"When your enemy is in a strait jacket, that's the best time to exact revenge, man."

She mulled it over. Gradually she nodded. It was growing on her. The idea was really growing on her. She confided, "I'm itching to get that Flossie back."

"What did she do now, man?"

"Bit me on my big butt."

"That bitch."

"What a big bitch."

"Wow man, that big bitch bit you on your big butt?"

"Yep."

"Wow, man. That really sucks," Benny embroidered, again tipping to the side eyes closing for mock sleep. She tapped him on the shoulder startling him awake. "You, you, you mean that big bitch that bit Bird bit you on your big butt?"

"Not full force, but she tried to," she replied, gripping not to crack up.

"Just as unforgivable, man. First of all, from the notes I've taken over all my years of keeping an eye on things, I find that it's very rare that a dog gets put in a strait jacket," he advised, now also barely able to maintain a straight face. "So, you could be waiting super long for that, man."

"Way out man, you're smart."

"That's why it's best to aspire to be just like me."

"Absolutely."

"Secondly man, Flossie is an old butt biting bitch. You cannot let her dodge what's coming to her by letting her croak first, right?"

"Oh, that bitch. She wouldn't dare!"

"Who knows what that bitch will do."

"I love dogs ya know, especially senior citizen dogs. But, man that bitch has to pony up for what she tried to do to my big butt."

"Hey, then listen up. My advice is that you lace Flossie's Kennel Ration with enough LSD that her tail starts chasing her."

Again, she pondered. That's when they couldn't hang on any longer and fell all over each other laughing. As usual, my admiration for him mixed with jealousy. It also always amazed me how Heath, her slightly older boyfriend, was able to keep his jealousy to himself regardless of whom her eyes were fixed on at the moment. Perhaps he foresaw that to protest would be to lose what he couldn't believe he'd scored.

One day she, Heath, and Benny were meandering home from the bus stop. Conspiratorially she whispered to Heath, while the three of them goofed on their history teacher who was infamous for two things, the first was bow ties as expansive as bat wings, and the second that he couldn't have been more flagrantly unbothered by how inept he was, a one-man testimonial to the ridiculousness of irreversible tenure, so indisputable that even a student who cheated on everything could get the picture. Wearing pink short shorts that she'd sewn a feather on to the right hip, Mickey asked Benny, "You think this feather makes me look unladylike?"

"Take off the shorts. Reattach the feather. Unladylike," Benny answered, titillating her again with his quips.

"Maybe down the line when you reminisce about this special day, you'll recall me wearing this feather," she underscored demurely.

When they got to our house Benny said "bye" and turned into our driveway bouncing a super ball fifty feet up into the air along the way. When he arrived at the gate, he heard someone scurry up behind him. It was Mickey. She pushed him back against the side of the house, stared at him with those black pepper eyes, pressed her perfection against him, and kissed him for so long on the mouth that he almost surpassed the shock enough to kiss back. Every inch of him felt it. The next week of him felt it. In advance of scooting back to Heath, who could only raise his shoulders acquiescently, she purred, "That was your first kiss." They were already home playing badminton before Benny could move on.

In Tree Hill Acres the only material I ever saw anyone read was The Standard Times. Not a single book visible in any house I set foot in. Except one man bucked the trend. Only one scholar was expanding his horizons. Officer Thompson had become a voracious consumer of books on offshore fishing, which is exactly what he perused after he'd snatched me as I passed by and plunked me indelicately onto a chair with nothing more than, "Wait here until that other burden gets here, too." How intently he scoured those pages replete with photos of lures and hands stuck into gills raising the catch of the day, vibrating with what he planned to do, an intersection between recreation and recklessness.

"What did we do?" I stammered.

He took some deep breaths to concoct the impression of being encumbered by my question, while ignoring it. I could hear myself emitting these pitiable gurgling snorts. No pity was coming.

Benny entered blocking what could only be described as a Mickey Souza induced woodie, if the hands in the pockets were any indicator. Without words the angling book went down, Officer Thompson got up, and forcibly lined us up backs against the wall, his expression diabolically transmuted in a second. Our mother was taking a macrame class so freedom ruled. She now kept herself distracted with this most recent series of short-lived hobbies, cake decorating, crocheting, crossword puzzles, movie star biographies, and local talk radio. There was also the declaration of her previously latent entrepreneurship by hosting a Tupperware party.

"Who the hell pissed in the Maxwell House coffee cup? Was it you?" Officer Thompson roared at Benny, saying and spraying. He turned to me. "You?"

"No," I could barely squeeze out. When he'd apprised me in

expectation of Benny's arrival that I'd have to sit there to find out what the "big trouble" was, I couldn't picture that it would involve his favorite perma-stained cup and unclaimed piss.

"No," Benny answered, his woodie deflating faster than a kiddie pool punctured by the local vandal.

"Good. I didn't reckon that either one of you would be man enough to admit it. So, I'm not stopping until one of you does."

Breathing through his nose with the amplification of the morbidly obese, he latched on to Benny by the shirt and smacked him in the face. Then I got mine, setting off my convulsive, girlish weeping. Like a line worker acclimated to repetitive tasks, he secured one object and added a smack to it, then the next one, smack, and so on, only pausing at one point to squirt nasal spray up a hairy nostril like he was also allergic to us. "One of you will confess eventually." Each smack bounced our heads off the wall with no regards to the partially formulated brain they encased. He'd fine-tuned the art of hitting without causing cuts, probably what he ruminated about while again and again practicing his signature to perfection.

"I did it. I did it," I untruthfully confessed to a face so blurred by my tears.

"And ya let ya brother get punished, too? You should be embarrassed. Anyway, when ya ain't in school, you get to spend a month in bed. Got it!"

"Yes," I whined.

"Say you're sorry!"

"I'm sorry." I heard my voice, shrill and beseeching. It was hard to envision that I would someday be a man.

"I don't think he did it," Benny protested, defiantly. "I don't believe it even happened."

"That cup didn't piss in itself."

"Let me see it."

"I wasn't going to keep piss in my favorite cup!"

"So, you hit us without evidence to prove it?"

"I know what I saw. And that's all that matters."

"That cup is black so you can't see through it. How do you know it was piss?"

"I could smell it."

"I don't get close enough to piss to catch how it smells."

"You've never had to change diapers."

"Baby piss and teenager piss smell the same?"

"Piss is piss."

"Then maybe a baby pissed in your cup. Or the neighbor's dog went on the patio to piss in your cup because he's not a fan. Or something turned rancid and smelled like piss. People always moan stuff smells like piss."

"Now you're being ridiculous."

"Unlike beating the two of us to force a confession. Hey, seeing as I didn't do it, then where's my apology?" Benny demanded, his temerity exemplifying my recent realization that there were only two similarities between him and me. We were both partial to Fluffernutter and were each blessed with four functional limbs.

"Call it a reward for whatever I don't catch you doing."

"That's sick," Benny yelled, stomping toward his room with me in pursuit. "Maybe your wife pissed in your cup!"

Suddenly Benny opened his closet door and pulled out a baseball bat. There was no doubt or debate, only a single-minded mania about what had to be done to a cranium using sporting equipment. To forestall him I closed the bedroom door, causing a draft so that the chains fashioned out of beer can tops that draped the length of his ceiling fluttered causing a futuristic glow.

"If he gets it away from you, he'll murder you," I pleaded, dragging my sleeve across to sop up tears and snot.

"It's worth it," Benny blared, aiming for the door.

"You have to get by me first." I must have looked awfully insignificant adjacent to the enormity that was Jimi Hendrix in the glow in the dark velvet poster attached to the back of the door. Especially, because in a tizzy, I'd accidentally hit the wall switch that turned on the black light attached to the ceiling. We stared at each other. It didn't seem like Benny gazing back at me. I couldn't recognize him. He didn't seem real.

"What the hell are you doing in there? You belong in bed!" shouted Officer Thompson, pounding on the door. I used that distraction to charge toward Benny, snatch the bat, chuck it out the window into the bushes, and careen into the hallway to be wrenched by the ear to my room. Mickey Souza and Officer Thompson had both pinned Benny against a wall. It instigated my penchant of scouring for positive/negative correlations.

Around 10pm Benny came to visit me in bed. He was carrying a newspaper that was folded over to the obituary pages. There was a reticence toward me that I'd never seen before, like I should've fought back also. I showed him the cover of Time Magazine with

Charles Manson's mug on it, a madman expression so like Officer Thompson's.

I asked, "Who copied whom?"

Benny glared at it, snatched it from my hand, and took it with him to the cellar. There he ripped the cover off the magazine and attached it to the corner wall above the record player perched up on two milk crates. He sat on the floor and randomly opened the newspaper to the obituaries. A photo of the invitingly determined face of a 13-year-old Puerto Rican girl caught his eye. She'd perished in a fire at her Evergreen Park unit, another of the city's housing projects. She'd raced back into her smoked filled unit four times, flames encircling her, the first three to carry out her younger siblings. The fourth was in search of her mother, who unbeknownst to her had been arrested an hour earlier scoring a dime bag from the undercover officer peddling nearby. Benny liked the name of this girl who like him was from a crappy home. Esterlie. From that night on, time to time, with her Standard Times photo pulled out of his wallet to peer at, he'd fantasize about rescuing Esterlie from kidnappers, murderers, or whoever he visualized her sordid family to be that day; or, if she were still alive, about her being his sweetie. Soon on the top of his school notebook that he pretended to use he'd cryptically printed her name, ***eilretsE***.

He excavated everything else from that area of the cellar, not easy when our parent's sustained pauper's mentality disallowed disposing of anything, a Tonka truck with broken axles, a sheet so stained that there were facsimiles of Mr. Potato Head and Nixon on it, and right there kicked off building a room out of sunken furniture and old blankets draped from the ceiling. This was the place where Benny wouldn't be disturbed, never suspecting that my fixation on all things Benny would impel me to pussyfoot down in the coming years to eavesdrop when friends visited him. There I'd also listen as he talked to himself, and to Mr. Nunes pillow, about the love and equality he aspired to share someday with whomever his future wife turned out to be. He also used his eye for people's idiosyncrasies to voice stories. All that might sound like he was on a malnourished journey to CRAZY, but the sweetness with which he did it would've actually been beautiful to overhear if it didn't beget more sibling comparison. Predictably, I decided that if girls overheard him, they'd deem it alluringly eccentric, but if they caught me comparably engaged, "weird" or "eerie" would be their description when blabbing it to anyone and everyone.

Not long after Benny dreamt of Mr. Nune's pillow. It was now the pillow's turn to convey a story. The face drawn on it had faded somewhat, making it seem wiser. With oceans more aplomb than your run-of-the-mill talking pillow, it delivered one about the blue-blooded woman who, very astutely, came to a decision concerning her otherwise accommodating bulldog. Instead of going all hot under the collar at how bulldogs lie down when being walked, refusing to arise until good and ready, she'd decided to adapt. Super-rich, she hired an assistant to trail behind them in case she needed to go somewhere and the bulldog began running the show. Suddenly, as a realization dawned on it, the pillow changed subjects.

"Hey, what's My Name?" it asked Benny.

"Mr. Nune's pillow."

"No, that's who gave me to you. My name. What's my name?"

"Sorry, I don't know," Benny replied guiltily. "I never named you."

The pillow gathered its thoughts then said, "There aren't many second chances in life, so get to it."

Impulsively, Benny decided, "Okay, I'll call you Romeo."

"Very fitting! Watch out ladies, here I come!!"

Remove the Tarp First

It was slightly after Richie and Benny, the latter purportedly sleeping over at Richie's, hid out in our school until everyone had gone home. Their vital and inalterable mission: to camp there overnight. They raced around those hallways to exhaustion, left cryptic notes in teacher's planners, graded some papers, wolfed down left over Sloppy Joes from that day's menu, used a Bunsen burner for a ceremonial lighting of their joint, substituted a t square to play baseball in the gym, and confiscated every roll of toilet paper available to erect a pyramid in front of the principal's office, all achieved without flipping on a light. And, as usual, they chattered about Led Zeppelin, Grand Funk Rail Road, and their latest addiction, The Who.

It was slightly before Richie's Crew, who Benny had been running with for more than a year, got revenge by commandeering Richie's uncle's car to spin donuts on Mr. Bigos's lawn. Mr. Bigos had made it too public that he couldn't care less that again his psycho dog Flossie had bitten Bird, the crew member who resembled a bird and disillusioned them all when he joined the High School's golf team. That was as smart of Mr. Bigos as if he'd stopped by to ask The Hell's Angels on Acushnet Avenue how often they performed fellatio. Yes, the liberation that came from Officer Thompson working the second shift in the South End while Benny was climbing out his window, falling into the bushes, and tearing off for mischief in the North End.

The small stuff, scaling fences to barrel through people's yards, drinking beer, ringing people's doorbells and scurrying away, drinking Tango, pelting the back of moving cargo trucks with eggs, smoking pot, grabbing the rear bumper of stranger's cars to be perilously tugged along in the snow, smoking hash, inciting the Security Guard at the Industrial Park to chase them, doing PCP, stealthily mounting people's roofs to hang out modifying all communication into whispers and hand signals, dropping acid, and all those hours bumming and whipping around bonfires in the woods indulging the even numbered things listed above. Tolerating me for

Benny's sake, and fostered by Benny's decision to not tip them off that I grooved to Barry Manilow, The Partridge Family, and Neil Sedaka, I was allowed to tag along sometimes. Still I was as likely as Officer Thompson to be invited to be part of their crew.

"Let's go skinny-dipping in Miss Falcon's pool," Richie proposed, blowing smoke rings through which Benny endeavored to pass the light from his flashlight, or the whole flashlight without damaging the rings.

Miss Falcon was Benny's 9th grade Algebra teacher now that he'd gotten through 7th and 8th grade math by whatever means necessary. Along with Richie, Bird, Shawn, Ronnie and Benny, Heath and Billie were there, brothers with long hair so thin and scraggly that it was a break even deal when premature baldness substituted one stumbling block with another, and Manny, who'd gotten fired in his first week working at Chad's Steak House for somehow having sex with the swordfish laying on a slab in the walk-in cooler. What a way to lose your virginity. What a way to squander people's confidence in your ability to keep a secret if you can't even keep your dalliance with a swordfish under wraps. There was Ray, who was as daring as Thor all hyped up on PCP before the codeine in the cough syrup, he took to settle his high down kicked in. Ray actually turned out to be gay, even though for years if a loudmouth at school called him Gay Ray, he'd have an unexpected meeting with the eleven of them. The joke was that we must have been too perturbed about what was shaking politically around the globe to give a hoot about Ray's sexuality. There was Barty and Pike, twins who weren't reunited until they were ten years old because their mother had absconded post-Cesarean section with Barty leaving the father this note, "One for you. One for me. Fair split. We've moved to Neptune." And, Joy to The World, tonight, there was also me, wearing light blue corduroys, and having just indulged more hours of solo scrabble and my study of the gruesome effects of history's deadliest plagues while Three Dog Night's "Joy to the World" spun again and again.

It was a dark night, no stars, as we paraded down Lantern Lane toward Miss Falcon's house, tailor-made for a dozen teens, eleven who were stoned on Boone's Farm and the "oregano" Shawn grew in his vegetable garden. In case fleeing was called for the platform shoes or clogs that usually went with their flared jeans, flannel shirts and t-shirts with logos of rock bands on them, had been temporarily swapped for sneakers. It was the first time I'd noted that Benny always wore garb independent from the rest. Now, no shirt, just farmer jeans and those lean muscled genetics that made me question if we'd undoubtedly spawned from the same two parents. The others smoked cigarettes. He never would. They went sparrow shooting in the woods with their pellet guns. Not a chance and he didn't want to hear about it.

"I can't stop laughing. I can't stop laughing. You mean your cousin's wife is a nutcase who thinks what about her six-month-old baby?" asked Barty and Pike concurrently.

"That her baby is stuck up. Like, fucking has an attitude," said Ray.

Everyone was roaring so uncontrollably that we had to pause, Manny on one knee, Benny jumping on my flimsy back.

"That woman needs Church," Benny piped in. It was his line for everything that month.

"And all she does is eat donuts," continued Ray.

"Another reason she needs church," Benny blurted.

"Got a choir in her mind already," chimed in Billie, barely able to emit the words.

"Our Lady of The Dunkin Munchkins," Benny ad-libbed.

"She needs an exorcism," Heath said.

"I told ya women's lib is fucked up, man. Women should be seen and not heard, so we don't have to hear about what assholes their babies are," blazoned Benny. The hilarity carried on when he inquired, "What's the little issue's name?"

"Wilbert," Ray answered.

"Hey, I met that baby. He is a conceited asshole."

Now everyone fell to the ground, howling feverishly, gasping for air.

"Can ya imagine her psychiatrist as she blabbers on about her six-month-old baby's attitude?" Ray tossed out.

"Like the dude is even listening," said Richie.

"Stuck up, conceited, show off, know it all baby. You know what he could use?" asked Benny.

"He needs Church," the others decreed in unison.

"Nope, a donut," Benny topped, and down they all went again.

"Stuck up, conceited, show off, know it all," Benny listed turning to Ray. "Hey, I like that kind of baby. Ask your cousin if he wants to sell him."

"Rookie, you're the funniest fuck there is. You're fucking wild," Richie said. "But hey, there's a pool that needs conquering so let's put our game faces on."

The mission was at hand so, as usual, I headed back home to the futility of trying to engender safety by posting all A's in school. When they arrived at the house behind Miss Falcon's everyone crawled quietly through its front yard to the back. Benny decided to make it more challenging when he whispered, "Hey, from hereon we gotta bring baby Wilbert with us," freezing them all in muffled laughter. They scaled the stockade fence and landed in Miss

Falcon's unlit back yard. As they crept toward the pool, they could see her in the second-floor kitchen with her friend, Latin teacher Mrs. Siegel, out of earshot referred to as Siegel A. Bird, no relation to the Bird who was about to invade the Falcon's pool, who along with Miss Falcon and Mrs. Siegel was part of the trio tagged, "The Birds of Normandin."

"Wow, this is why Miss Falcon didn't want me to come here to bang her tonight. Because she's boinking Mrs. Siegel, too," Benny said, making them strain not to break out again.

Creeping along, the hellions removed all of their clothes. They could hear the pump flushing the water in the pool and a small dog yapping next door, probably at them.

"The last time birds acted this scandalously they were in a Hitchcock Film," Benny said, causing Richie to crawl on top of him and cover his mouth.

"You funny fuck," Richie whispered.

Suddenly, Ronnie got up and galloped ten feet to dive into the deep end of the pool. It was called a chain reaction rush, when one person did something and the others got a rush from it, now because The Elder Birds of Normandin might hear the splash and be alerted. But there had never been a splash so 10.0 on all of the Olympic diving judge's scorecards as this one. It sounded like zzzzzzzz, which if tested would probably be the pretty standard noise emission when a bantam weight like Ronnie unknowingly dives onto the tarp covering the pool, only to be engulfed by it.

"Fuck, he's in a tarp." Richie exclaimed; his weenie and heinie obscured by the darkness.

Panicked, Ronnie flipped wildly underwater entangling himself more. None of them had any training in nude rescue attempts. Here was a chance to learn by doing.

"Grab the ends. Pull the ends," ordered Richie. All intention of being quiet and not destroying their buzz had gone under with the tarp. While Benny moved off to survey, they grasped the it's edges. Frantically heaving, with the darkness a hindrance, they offset each other by pulling in opposite directions. Decades later Benny assumed that how calm and rational he'd remained was because Officer Thompson had rendered him a seasoned veteran of crisis. He pointed his flashlight to study where Ronnie, now parallel to the pool's floor, was thrashing away. Benny dropped the flashlight in the grass, dove in underneath Ronnie, got turned around so that his feet touched the pool's floor, and thrust himself upward to launch Ronnie and the tarp above the water long enough for the rest of them to adjust. They tugged so forcefully that the tarp, gallons of water, and Ronnie came soaring out. Seconds later, Benny emerged as the house's outside lights were turned on.

"I've called the police. Get out of here," Miss Falcon yelled out the window.

Soaked, luckily Benny happened to be facing away from her as they unrolled Ronnie from the tarp and went to gather him up to escape. He was coughing up too much water to even stand.

"Go. Go," said Richie. "I'll stay with him."

As directed, they put their pants on, threw the rest of their gear over the fence, and scaled it. When they'd finished dressing, not that all of their shirts were facing the right way, they heard the siren coming down Miss Falcon's street. Unless a second cop car came from the back, they were free to flee, though Richie and Ronnie were doomed.

"We have to go back," Benny said.

"What the fuck is wrong with you, Rookie?" Bird yowled, tugging him away from the fence.

"Cops have to chase us or Richie is bagged."

“My ass I'm doing that,” replied Bird, and he fled with Manny, Ray, Mark, Barty and Pike.

Shawn nodded to Benny and was right behind him climbing back over the fence. Next came Billie and Heath. They met Richie on the other side as a cop car pulled up in front of the house. He'd gotten his clothes on and was dressing a still stupefied Ronnie.

“Split the fuck out of here,” insisted Richie.

“Escape over the fence when Ronnie's ready. The chase is on,” overruled Benny, and off he went with the others, darting by the Officers as they got out of their car.

“Halt!” commanded The Younger Officer.

“No,” Benny responded.

The Officers got back into their car in hot pursuit.

“Now,” is all Benny had to shout and the others followed him as he turned into a yard, hurdled that chain-linked fence, the next fence, then a stockade fence into even another yard running full speed through an obstacle course of two For Sale signs, a tricycle, a wheel barrow, and two pink plastic flamingos sticking out of the ground, through the next yard, and out onto another street. As they bolted up that street the cop car came speeding up and another was in sight sending the pursuit again through one yard after the next onto streets, through yards, onto streets again. They'd circled the same territory five times, but these cops had the gift. They were wearing them down, steadily getting closer, and now two other cops on foot were in the game allowing the cars to form a roving perimeter. That's when, while drawing his suspenders up once more, Benny had a last-ditch idea.

“Your house,” he paused to call out to Shaun, pointing them left through a driveway past the Cadillac Fleetwood parked in it, toward a stockade fence with a covered metal garbage can against it. Billie, Heath, then Shaun bolted to that garbage can using it to spring board over the fence, but when Benny hit the top of the can it was already tipping over smashing him into the fence so crushingly that he caromed back into the Cadillac and toppled onto the driveway. He was on his own now, lying dazed propped up against the bumper with the shadow of the fence obscuring him. As one of the cops pelted toward the fence the woman in the house next door called out the window, "They're in my yard," turning the Officer to the left. Benny stayed motionless for a minute, breathing as quietly as his spent lungs would allow. He heard the door to the house open, so it was best to leg it anew. He pushed against the pavement to rise. The bumper's blow to his head had taken his equilibrium and he fell right back over. As he heard heavy footsteps he reclined back and used his feet to shimmy himself underneath the Cadillac before the arrival of a man with an orangutan paunch so pronounced that it carved out its own shadow.

"A bunch of boys ran by and went that way," the woman next door said, again pointing to the left.

"Thanks Judy. These teenagers nowadays. What happened to playing games like horsie that we did when we were young?" he asked while reversing his course back inside.

"It's the hippies. They ruined it all," she remarked, closing her window.

Billie, Heath, and Shawn traversed through a series of back yards to Shawn's house and furtively entered through the cellar, the escalating hyperbole about it all soon to make for many a yarn around bonfires. It had been more than a minute since Benny had breathed, so when he finally had to, he muffled the gasp with his hands. Coated in oil from the driveway, he remained there, muscles releasing tension as the wind accelerated and brushed leaves his way. Soon he felt sleepy and satisfied. His mind began to wander, landing as it often did on Esterlie The Fire Girl whom he'd recently saved from where her evil mother had chained her up inside of a closet. He would've pulled out her photo if it were with him. He also probably would've dozed off if she hadn't crawled under the car, her brown face aglow with love. She moved in to wrap around him, decorous and sedate, her cheek pressed lightly against his. She lay in contact with him purring, the prelude to a kiss.

An hour later Benny got out from underneath the Cadillac, sneaked home yard by yard, tapped on my window for me to open it, and crawled in still a tad woozy. He sat on the floor while I perched on the bed staring at the partially dressed, oily, chlorine mess that was my brother.

"That was A1," he celebrated, and went on to colorize a play by play like a thrill seeker might his jaunt down the rapids.

"How do you always get away?"

"If I killed somebody, they'd catch me."

"You're kind of crazy, you know that?"

"Right, and right now every teenager short of Richie and me are planning for their future."

The wayward son showered, changed clothes, and with me in a living room chair, settled on a side of the couch thrilled again to appear as if nothing had happened, eyebrows raised and conspiratorial smile toward me whenever Officer Thompson turned away. Officer Thompson had arrived from work ten minutes earlier singing, "Mares eat oats, and does eat oats, and little lambs eat ivy." Oh, when happiness at jailing some "no class alchie" or "waste of human space" was expressed through the crooning of a previous generation's novelty songs, it sure warmed my heart. Even the Easter Officer's Thompson face was melting and ears enlarging from the hit of Orange Sunshine resetting buttons in Benny's brain, no matter what, that genius stayed clueless, a testimony also to how survival can manifest acting skills in children. I would marvel at how much Benny again loved being Benny, curious as to what he would've been involved in had he been from that salt of the Earth family. I envisioned him as a pioneer of these modern-day adventurers, with their rock climbing, skydiving, and motocross bikes. Toss in a measure of teenage entrepreneur, too.

Benny's next hang out with the crew he announced that the tag "Rookie" would be no more. He'd earned that right.

Half Empty or Half Full

"It's all about work ethic. If everyone had the work ethic that I have all would be perfect," Officer Thompson stated. More disturbing in that it segued out of berating our mother for ruining our patio barbecue by serving "these damn foot longs that are too big for the buns." That scolding ended with another braying of "Thank God, I'm patient." His only reaction outside of rage if the piddliest misfortune occurred was "Thank God, I'm patient. Ha. Ha. Ha."

"All would be perfect?" Benny questioned.

"Yep," he replied, causing the rest of us in unison to move back like dandelions in the wind. He was unquestionably the hardest working and bravest soldier in the Calvary. The one sent out to locate the lost wagons while Indians lusted after his scalp. He bit off a third of his hot dog leaving his blunt featured carnivorous head speckled with relish.

"Have you ever been confused?" Benny asked.

"Ah, I don't recall being. What's there to be confused about? Ya buckle down your bootstraps and work. Ya pay the bills. Abide by the rules. What a great country, right?"

That left me so inspired that I was ready for a nap. Our mother moved things around, relish and mustard jars, paper napkins that were pinned down by a ketchup bottle so the wind couldn't scatter them, tongs, a frequent distraction technique when concerned something might escalate.

"Have you ever made a mistake?" Benny asked.

"Yeah," he startled us all by conceding. "But I'll bet I could count'm on my hand. Hey, there's a couple of them sitting at this picnic table right now, huh?"

He chortled at his wit like an audience paying top dollar at a laugh fest would've idolized him. I burned to heckle him. I left that to Benny.

"Would it ever be okay for someone to think differently than you?"

A fast forward eclipse came over the power of the sun that was Officer Thompson's self-satisfied expression. He droned, "Okay, I can tell that you're itchin' to ruin everyone's dinner by making trouble. Go ahead. Speak your piece."

"Just wondering."

"Hey, I've done a stellar job providing all the essentials. Food on the table. A roof over our heads. I don't drink. I don't smoke. And I don't run around on your mother. Plenty'a kids long for a father like that, right?"

"If only that were the whole story," Benny said.

"Did any of you see that "Mash" is going to be on another night this year?" our mother tried.

"Hey, and plenty get to see their father beating on their mother. I've never hit your mother, even once. And believe me, she's a peach that one, right hon?"

I could detect from Benny's expression that sanctimonious had finally aligned with delusional when for a second time that year Officer Thompson crowed about his pre-eminent virtue, that utmost sign of Herculean restraint when his buttons were without mercy being pushed. "I've never hit your mother!" It was the epicenter of reminders of our magnificent fortune.

"That's because you'd be extinct if you did."

"What?"

"If you hit her, you'd be pushing up daisies."

"So now you're tough?" he snickered, a schoolyard bully inferring with that twinge of uncertainty that his reign of terror would be over only if and when he decided it was.

"I've always been tough, that's how I've survived you," Benny shot back leading to a brief stare down. He was now as tall as the Officer, but his was recent, bony, vertical growth that had yet to sprout horizontally.

"Okay, now cut it out," our mother intervened. "Let's try to enjoy ourselves."

Benny's loyalty to her knew no bounds. It cut through anything, even the repugnance that he endured when just days prior he popped in at home unexpectedly and found Officer Thompson behind her in the living room giving it to her as if they were actually compatible, him hanging on to her hooters like the handle bars of the "chopper he would treat himself to if he didn't have to fork out so much for us." Later, in a private mother-son moment that didn't warm his heart, she explained to Benny that married couples "share love" sometimes when they least expect it. And that it was normal. And that it had nothing to do with her using sex to mollify, pacify, placate, be conciliatory, and all the other synonyms for scraping to effect peace with someone slated early on for war.

Though as usual never entirely, the tension dissipated over the next few days before the TV Guide slipped out of Benny's hand when, like he had daily, he tossed it across the living room into the magazine basket. Instead, it accidentally hit Officer Thompson on the shoulder as he napped on the couch.

"Sorry, it slipped," Benny explained, nervously.

Benny's mind reflexively screeched, "fight," so he used the handle to close the recliner he was lounged on and rose for action. Now fifty pounds of fat heavier than his Serodyn days, it took Officer

Thompson a second longer to arrive at Benny than in his prime. Perhaps he also wasn't in tune with the physics of all that girth because he had too much momentum. He tripped bending him forward below Benny's punch, and was propelled onto Benny knee first so that they both fell backward onto the recliner. He pushed himself up with one arm while yanking Benny to the floor by the hair with the other. The smacks and punches were old hat, the pain eaten up by an Earthquake of hurt elsewhere. When the barrage ended, he towered over Benny like Cassius Clay over Sonny Liston.

"Looked for a second like you were gonna fight," he gloated traipsing into the kitchen for a root beer.

Unable to breathe, Benny crawled toward his room while the living room spun and seemed to be sliding to the left. He shut the door behind him and collapsed into a ball on the floor, whatever logic he'd made of our life seeping from him with each futile attempt to inhale. That unanticipated second of relief that it would all be over, death by sweet asphyxiation, culminated in a gasp that so overfilled his lungs that it stabbed him, a vibrating rod of agony all the way down to his genitals. The clenching of his fingers flashed in his eyes, rigid and ancient like the arthritis of a senile man. As the pain decreased and his breathing shaped itself into something a human could survive on, he saw a tear hit the floor, an involuntary response he wished he could reverse.

"Cut out the crawling along like an actor, you. Be a man. Ya only got a few loves taps," he heard Officer Thompson chide him from outside the bedroom door, only minutes after a knee had landed flush on his son's manhood. Ten minutes later, as Benny sat up brokenly, he had his first vision of murdering Officer Thompson with his police issued revolver.

To go to sleep is to not know what you'll encounter about yourself in the morning, if you even wake up. That realization didn't undergird my stability. For Benny it meant that his left nut would blow up to twice its usual size, the pain waking him at 6am like a flamethrower expertly aimed.

Davey! Davey!" somehow roused me, cutting &my dream of an aardvark staring quizzically at an anteater. I raced to Benny's room suspecting that misery was for breakfast. And was my appetite ruined when I saw that whopper. He couldn't walk. The pressure of it hanging down was unbearable. I've learned over a lifetime of observing guys, any threat to their balls isn't enthusiastically received, so how he wasn't hysterical I'll never grasp.

"Babe Ruth could've hit this sucker for a homer," he joked.

"I'm gonna call an ambulance," I said, turning and bumping into Officer Thompson, further sandblasting the contents of my stomach when I ended up brushing into his naked Me Maker for the longest second of my life.

"What the hell is he squawking about?" he asked with such potential for compassion. Once he was apprised of the situation and decided that an ambulance was a waste of money, the vindictive casualness began. It upset him that his day off would be ruined having to lug Benny to the hospital, so he took his usual three-act shower.

"Please can we call an ambulance?" I begged.

"And piss away a damn co-payment when I can transport him myself. I'll be ready in a minute," he responded. It was exacerbated by a daymare I suddenly had of his bouts of lividness about this or that child he'd never met who'd been murdered or assaulted in some place he would never be within a 100 miles of, listing with iciness all of the excruciating repercussions that should befall the perpetrators, for how long, the capper being that chair with a hole in the seat so that testicles dangle below for a sound drubbing. He was always disgusted that we weren't as outraged as he was by such crimes against children, condescendingly translating it as him being the only one with a heart. We were flummoxed that in no way he could associate those crimes with our experience at his hands.

"A minute" dragged on to thirty when Officer Thompson re-enacted his usual rendition of gargle, clear throat for all to savor, gargle, clear, gargle, then strolled scratching his gelatinous hindquarters to the kitchen to make some toast with his uncut Me Maker jutting out of the side of those tighty not so whiteys, all the while yelling to "quit over-reacting 'cause that ain't gonna fix anything." Quit over-reacting, sound advice from Officer Thompson, who also decided to save the co-payment for the urologist by enlisting his General Practitioner friend Dr. Green to attend to Benny autonomously, "friend" loosely translated as someone he was acquainted with through the court system. Dr. Green's prescription of ice and painkillers weren't exactly curative. When at last an actual urologist was summoned, he diagnosed that it was too late. Benny's precious left one was destined to dwindle to the size of a sunflower seed. It was time for him to start the psychological process of viewing his bag as half empty or half full, while repressing what caused the injury.

Flip That Triangle Over

Over the next 18 months Benny progressed deep into the 11th grade and me the 12th. Often our father was aloof or boorishly convivial. He'd become somewhat self-restrained, a bit more skilled at knowing what to overlook. The violence no longer progressed beyond perfunctory threats, most of which I managed to avoid with compliance, and by currying favor by doing all of the yard work and car washing days before it was needed. Every day I promptly fetched the mail from its box. He even bought us a gift, which left us more uncomfortable than grateful. Shinier horseshoes than the ones we already tossed wasn't on par with the scores of heartfelt apologies we deserved. Often there was a slow burn of non-verbal animosity from Benny toward him, the unsettling feeling that something larger could erupt at any moment.

How during that time our family managed to co-exist in the same house wasn't the only enigma destabilizing the salvation I longed to unearth by understanding life. I didn't fully comprehend yet that it cannot be understood adequately, and that there's only hope, partial information, habit, intuition, misconceptions, and faith ferrying us along from place to scary place. So, it wasn't decipherable that someone of Benny's oomph had never had a girlfriend, or even a date, and that his only kiss was a heavenly surprise at the lip glossed mouth of Mickey Souza years earlier. "I don't get it," I would muse. "He has personality, vigor, and top ten percentile looks," door openers the lack of which the short, average looking, and uninspired like myself use as excuses to not make anything of ourselves. And other than with our father, he was still ceaselessly positive. All he saw was beauty when that short and ugly cretin who'd won all those days in a row on Jeopardy would celebrate after each victory, embracing and jumping in sync with his short and ugly look-alike family who'd jogged up on stage. With the credits rolling, hands clapping at the behest of the prompter, and closing music playing a la a marching band extolling the victors, they rejoiced, devoid of the self-consciousness that short and ugly should engender. Benny was uplifted by the embodiment of family. I only saw short and ugly.

Benny's hair, now long and heavier than a horse's tail, especially drew the attention of the hippie girls with their hip hugger jeans and undersized flannel shirts that made their breasts strangely hypnotic. He didn't verbalize it, but he wasn't comfortable with girls. He could only hit and run, humor and quandaries he'd conjured up affording him a seduction shelf life of an hour or less before he'd drift off again like the scent of mystique. Primarily, I supposed he was in a phase of detached cool, taking it all in, preparing his next move. Though I didn't know he was in his fifth year of scholastic dysfunction, I pondered if he was embarrassed about something that, bearing in mind his many gifts, I couldn't conceptualize. Especially once he claimed to me that he couldn't care less about losing a nut.

The only hangouts with Richie's Crew anymore were for their jaunts to The Acushnet Concert Hall on Friday nights. The anti-war crowd had naively associated being of age to be in the military with the right to drink, so they'd prevailed upon the state government to revise the drinking age to only eighteen. Now Richie, Bird and Billie could legally suck one down, and whenever the cops weren't monitoring the rest of the crew mooched off their beers. Benny had lost interest in redefining substances and therefore imbibed only a few ounces more than I did, which was nothing.

The Girls at the concert hall also fancied Benny. One evening I'd posted myself in the voyeur's corner of the make out balcony, two future factory workers to my left grinding away any chance that they'd ever have of an original thought, him slipping his grease stained hand up her shirt, me, at the same time, also beholding Benny elevating even the best song to the next level. He was the rock and roll version of Tony in Saturday Night Fever, at his best when flourishing on the dance floor. Like a girl's Stairway to Dance Heaven, giggling, they'd pull him out there with them. Even that made me jealous. Self-sabotaging comparison, the injustice of being born so ordinary, creates lists of slights and inadequacies to validate an impending decline. Short and ordinary was only two steps from crippled in my hierarchy of human worth. I coveted the boundlessness that I'd projected on to him, but instead my blackening mind exchanged whatever potential I had for a modicum of dominion over a chalk-faced, lipless Candy Striper named Lizzy whom I not so secretly hoped would have a late growth spurt so she'd fill out that uniform. Even though Officer Thompson didn't hesitate to refer to her as a "Wallflower," Lizzy's oral willingness to fulfill her role in my nascent comprehension of what a holdover chick was all I needed while waiting for an amenable cutie to come along. I wanted someone more like Jocelyn from Assonet, that one general store town twenty miles away.

The one occasion that Jocelyn's father authorized her to be out so late, he drove her and picked her up from the concert hall. Wearing a maxi dress, white with red stripes, too formal for this den of tube tops, bell-bottoms, fringe-suede jackets, and mini-skirts, she contemplated Benny as intently as millions had the first televised moon walk. As always, he pretended not to notice who was admiring him, all the while enticing, seducing from a distance. From the sidelines I could catch that Jocelyn wasn't one to make the first move, so a mutual attraction had no one to break the ice.

Months later Benny was seated in the classroom for his first day of Driver's Ed at Don's Driving School + Tax Service. From the posters on the wall you'd assume that there was a law that everyone should sit behind the wheel with a whopping toothy grin. He felt nauseous from overhearing the girl behind him whisper too loudly to someone that she adored her guy's body part because it fit perfectly in her mouth. Luckily a more proper farm girl type approached the seat to his left. Before she saw him, he recognized her and turned away. All the same, out of the corner of his eye, the leisurely removal of her peacoat had him. When she slipped the oversized conceal the goods sweatshirt over her head it pulled her t-shirt up too high exposing the roundness of her bra. When she sat his boner was so sky-high that he wished he'd worn looser pants. It rushed so much blood away from his brain that it provoked the temporary insanity that negates all inhibitions, so he opened with, "Do you know where I've seen you before?"

She blushed red delicious. "Acushnet Concert Hall. You

remember me? I didn't even dance."

"The red stripes. I wouldn't forget you," he answered so stoked that he came up with that.

"So why didn't you ask me to dance?" she asked, briefly casting her eyes down.

"I've never asked anyone. Why didn't you ask me?"

"I've never asked anyone."

"Then we have something in common."

"Why don't you ask girls?"

"I don't know. They seem to approach me, so I get to dance plenty."

That was it. An icebreaker, got his foot in the door, an opening salvo, the moment that inflamed him to write **nylecoJ** above ***eilretsE*** on his notebook. They waited quietly for the instructor, aiming to muster up more genius, each grinning like something grand had just hit. He was so plugged in to how kind and unblemished she came across. He finally forced himself to tip toward her again.

"Will you dance with me?" he asked, telling himself to hold the eye contact as long as he could.

"Yes," she responded, biting her knuckle.

Over the next few days he gave himself that little pep talk that a novice might employ to prepare, sensing that she had a miscellany of subjects stored up in need of an ear.

"What are you going to do once you have your license?" he asked, upping the ante at their next class.

"Oh, so much. I've been waiting my whole life for a license because the nearest house is a quarter mile away. Nothing but farms and hicks."

"The squawk on the street is that there's a new fad out there turning downtowns in to ghost towns. It's called cruising the mall."

"Sounds delicious."

"And all that treading up and down aisles again and again gives these American fatties some exercise."

To her Benny was a savvy, streetwise city boy, so accounts of his hijinks and her loneliness intensified the flirtation. She always dressed like she'd just completed her chores, not a spare moment afterward to change.

"So, when are we going to dance together?" he asked the night of their final exam.

"The day I get my license my dad says that I can have his pickup for 24 hours," she replied with such a beautiful smile, one that she composed with her whole face. "May I pick you up for a ride?"

"Sure."

Once the witching hour had arrived, Benny put on his Jordache jeans and funky purple, paisley shirt with the pirate sleeves, as nervous as he was excited. If symbolically he was her gateway to drive through out of sameness and into possibility, she was tenfold that for him. It was simple. She felt obliging and normal. It was one of those pure and impure moments all rolled into one, him lightly parting the curtains to monitor for her arrival, anticipating longingly, me spying on him through the crack in his bedroom door.

When he slid into her truck the love story playing in his mind got a twist straight out of left field. Jocelyn was dressed so like the vixen

Mickey Souza, even her new flicked hairstyle unabashedly advertised that she'd been released from a cage. Halter top, yes. Perky and even a morsel of nip pushing out through the cotton. Low cut jeans so tight that he thought: "Man, her other clothes sure hid that shit." The eight inches between jeans and Halter Top so smooth, firm, and alluring that it gave him the sensation of being vacuumed into her bellybutton. It took every ounce of his concentration to check his enthusiasm, so he forgot to close the passenger seat door.

"You can close the door Benny," she suggested.

"Oh, oh, okay."

As they cruised along, inserting 8 tracks so they could sing along with "Tiny Dancer" and "Hey, Hey, Mama like the way you move, gonna make you sweat, gonna make you groove," he realized that it was the dimness of The Driving School's light that had prevented him from perceiving her flawlessness. No feature or part was exceptional on its own, yet everything was so pleasingly matched. Unexpectedly, she detoured onto a dirt road without the obligatory pretense of, "I'd like to show you something." They bobbed along for a spell, passing little more than abandoned shacks. She pulled over and shut off the car. Without hesitation she dictated, "Pants must stay on, okay?"

To avoid ruining it by muddling words and dispelling her supposition about his readiness to swap spit like teenagers, he nodded. She drew him toward her. Benny had to adapt, rewrite his idyllic vision of a slow, blossoming bond with her by stepping up to the plate and supplying his woman what she longed for. After ten minutes she hesitated to quietly reiterate, "No pants off," to which he mumbled, "Wouldn't want to anyway." That fired her burners even more. At one point he'd forgotten to inhale for so long that she counseled, "Breathe sweet boy." He breathed. She attacked again.

Suffice it to say that the highlights of that coupling, back and forth between the cab of the truck, its bed, and the nearby grass would require an entire novel whose millions of sales to adolescents in need of a nightly joy ride would set its author up in style. She kept directing his hands, while kissing him so perfectly, in so many ways, that if memory served him, he'd have a repertoire like few others. This girl had done this before, in a barn, or a fantasy that she'd replayed so much that it took hold, or a harem in a previous life, somewhere.

She suddenly pulled away to remove her top. That was a jubilant young lady viewing him gape at the most bewitchingly shaped breasts he would ever see not on film at Venus. For a second, he marveled, "It's like a woman. She's only sixteen. Shouldn't it take more years for her nipples to get that hard?" He would've stared forever, but she slowly brought one up to his undernourished mouth and invited, "Kiss". The orgasm in his pants could've launched Hugh Hefner's career.

She laid him in the grass on his side then from behind him stuck her knee up between his legs and reached around to rub with her hand, all while licking his neck. The second orgasm was so intense, that he briefly wondered if he was normal. The joy, the appreciation, the triumph with which she held on to him during each orgasm was her soul speaking its deepest truth at that moment. Desire. Power. No apologies. Number three possessed him for so long that it made him want to be abnormal if that were the repercussion.

It was getting dark when she drove him home. All of that had taken place during the daylight, the place where no one can hide. With the car idling in front of our house, gazing silently at him with penitent eyes, she locked and unlocked her fingers, torn between commitment and the prospect of more.

"We can't do this again," she expressed apologetically, with a certainty that no response could undo. "Because of my fiance'."

"You're engaged?" he heard himself blurt. His hours of ecstasy were unhinged before he could even launch some utopist musings about her.

"For two weeks."

"You're only turning seventeen."

"The wedding is scheduled for my 18th birthday."

He peered through the windshield. The semidarkness made the scenery also seem impermanent. In a hushed, devitalized tone he asked, "Was this our dance?"

"I guess so. I'm so glad that the last one I'll ever have with another boy was with you," she replied, shaking his hand as if he'd done a commendable job of shoveling her walkway.

Recuperating silently, Benny speculated how many other boys this one had corralled while purporting to be stranded on the farm, all while he stood pure and chaste in his vision that someday he was destined to create the opposite of our parent's love fest. The light-bulb moment came that people spin things, words being only words.

He exited the truck, raising his eyebrows at her modestly in protest. She tepidly promised to call him soon. He knew that fortunately she wouldn't. After she drove off, he stood there and summoned up gratitude for the intimacy he'd shared with her. That momentarily overruled his dismay.

Nestled in his bedroom with Pink Floyd massaging his ears, he recalled the pundit on TV who'd stated, "The lamentable loss of innocence can bring someone a more valuable reward, The Loss Of Naivety." That had stuck with him, and now buoyed him for a bit, but the dismay and revulsion won out. Multiply in the coming days he masturbated with imaginings of whom he'd presumed Jocelyn was, sealing the positive part of that memory for eternity and the inside of the sheet to the wall where the wiping off took place. It was logical to forecast in the wake of the first easy notch on his belt that he'd become all, "NEXT!!!" I certainly promoted to him that course of action. But an amalgam of emotions and befuddlement about the whole experience had drained him. He felt antsy and perpetually short-changed. The part where she'd so easily hidden her dalliance from her boyfriend somehow got mixed into the female soup of the ways in which The Great Enabler kept our realm under wraps, and progressively his protracted desolation of a few years earlier reared its ugly head again. This tricky farm girl exacerbated the deep-rooted notion that family means danger, yet a smooshed nut at the knee of an oaf ostensibly was forgotten in no time. So once again, after he'd erased **nylecoJ** from his notebook, the embargo on closeness, and girls, and new friends resurfaced, keeping him often holed up in his cloth room with Romeo the pillow and his obituary photo of The Fire Girl, Esterlie.

------------------------------+-----------------------------------

A month later, still preoccupied by the debacle with Jocelyn, Benny went to close the downstairs cellar door by pushing the wood around the windowpane. He missed and accidentally put his hand through the window leaving a gash in need of stitches on his wrist. Impassively, he let the hand dangle outside and observed the rain drive into the cut like mother nature could cleanse him of man's cruelty. Eels splashed around in a plastic barrel. Bait. Sawdust flecked the vice from the birthday present our mother had just received. A cutting board with her name etched in the handle. Benny didn't pull his arm back in until he heard someone finish descending the stairs. Officer Thompson grabbed his arm and examined it like a rancid piece of meat.

"You'll live," he dismissed disdainfully as I came down the stairs primed for queasiness. "But ya gonna shell out to have this damn window fixed. Ya can drive yourself to the hospital, too. Bring the Blue-cross, Blue-shield card."

The callousness. It echoes. He stomped back toward the stairs as livid as if someone had intentionally broken that glass.

"I'll drive you," I volunteered.

"No, you won't," Benny negated, taking his shirt off and pressing it to his wrist to depress the flow of blood. "He's going to."

"What's that wise guy?" Officer Thompson asked.

"You're going to take me."

"My ass I am."

As I braced myself for more fallout, Benny's eyes grew bigger and more intimidating. Potently, as if he'd been preparing for this since day one, he spat, "Fuck you bitch."

Officer Thompson froze, the muscles in his jaw tightening. He fiddled with his collar for a second, uncertain how to carry on. He opted for, "If I didn't wanna get blood all over me from that stupid cut you wouldn't be saying that."

"Fuck you and every fucking thing you've ever done to us," Benny blazed with an unwavering glare. "Do it!"

"I mean business!"

"Do it!"

"Don't make me!"

"Do it you fucking coward! Or have you noticed I'm not four feet and seventy pounds anymore?

"That day ya tried to fight me didn't turn out so bright for ya," he retorted ineffectually, beads of sweat forming on his oversized forehead......and on mine.

"Just know this you waste of space. I'll keep coming. You win today, I'm back big time tomorrow. This'll never end. Though I'm feeling awfully guilty about speaking so disrespectfully to 'The Head

Honcho,' 'The Top Banana,' 'The King Of The Jungle,' and all of that other shit ya call yourself."

He sucked some blood from his wound and spit it on the wall, for a brief moment demoting him in my mind to only 99% my idol and 1% scary.

"Watch it! This is still my house."

"You and your missing link."

"What?"

"Missing link. Why you think behaving the way that you do is okay."

Officer Thompson walked to the barrel, extracted an eel by the tail, spun it like a lasso over his head while sliding his hand to its neck, stabilized it with his other hand, and snapped its neck. He tossed it backward over his shoulder into the barrel while returning to the stairs.

"Such a tough guy with defenseless creatures."

"Yeah. Yeah. I got you figured out, too boy."

"Let me guess, now you'll call me what, a follower? A long-haired follower who's gonna be scratching for a hand out someday," Benny mocked him, altering his voice to Officer Thompson's lifeless monotone. "'Well, don'tcha turn to me when you need some charity down the road 'cause I slaved too hard for my money.'"

"If the shoe fits, wear it."

"That's why I've cheated in school every single minute of the last five years?" Benny let loose, news to me that made me convulse. "You know everything, dad. So, why is it I wasn't able to function in school, dad? Though I'm sure you'll call it 'plain, old-fashioned laziness.' Well catch this lame brain. It all fell apart after the summer you deposited me in bed. Now comes your follow-up that you're an innocent victim blamed for everything. Well, it doesn't matter anymore because here's the reason you'll chauffeur my ass to the hospital. You, not him. Every fucking thing you've ever done to us I've already typed up. Yes, lucky me, like a trained monkey I've been able to function in typing class. So, listen up. I'll dash off 100 copies of it and deliver them to every cop in this city, one by one. No, no, gotta get it to the neighbors too, and the mayor, the city council, Luigi at Luigi's Pizza, the mailman, even the garbage man with the humongous lump on his chrome dome. I'll score 1000 copies to mail out too. And what the fuck will you do to stop me?"

Benny didn't flinch, standing his ground like that proverbial dog forced to bite his master. The silence and stare down, ten interminable seconds.

"Oh My God," I squealed, knowing that I would never be that impressed again.

"Grit your teeth like you always do you Cro-Magnon. 'Remember how you brainwashed us to think people wouldn't believe it anyway if we told them. Why don't I knock myself out disproving that?"

"You're not as smart as you think," Officer Thompson attempted, for once caught between minimizing repercussions and upholding the pretense that he was still in charge. "I can have you removed from this house for good."

"That won't stop me from circulating the truth. In fact, I left out The Standard Times, the local TV stations, your relatives, and even the fantasy woman in your dreams whom you'd just end up abusing like you do our mother."

His air of invincibility as sustainable as his interior life, Officer Thompson remarked, "You're overestimating how smooth sailing this'll be."

"Shut your trap."

Officer Thompson pivoted to me and looked daggers. I tried not to, but I cast my eyes downward.

"You part of this rigamarole?"

"Ah, ah, no," I slowly looked up to reply. Guilt came over me roused mostly by how patient Benny unfailingly was with me. The previous night when he'd caught me hiding under his bed spying on him, all he'd suggested was, 'Davey, there are better things to do with your time than that.'

"That's 'cause ya swift enough to see that ya brother is unwell," Officer Thompson asserted, his stale eyes brightening with divide and conquer.

"I'm a natural born psycho," Benny sniped, spiced by a mocking smile. The molecules of mistreatment had melded manufacturing quite a meteor.

"Children have to be disciplined or they won't learn."

"Nothing buys you immunity like 'you did it for the children.' Time to ditch that crap because the list I'll publicize isn't ordinary punishment."

"It's your word against mine."

Those five incendiary words, I'm not embarrassed to admit, altered my fantasies from lacing his food with tranquilizers to a substance far more lethal.

"I'm sure you'll dig wallowing in the doubt it creates about you," Benny said.

"But I am part of it now," I unexpectedly heard myself announce. "So, so damn it, drive him to the Goddamn hospital!"

When a triangle is rotated upside down, and suddenly two of its points are on top, the point now on the bottom has a lot of weight to bear.

"You got fifteen seconds to go voom, voom that car or you're done," Benny ordered and began a countdown that I joined. "Fifteen. Fourteen. Thirteen. Twelve. Eleven. Ten. Nine. Eight.......

Like a despot perched on his throne tasting his last fleeting grasp of sovereignty while the castle is being overrun by the masses, Officer Thompson forced us to count down to one before, "I'll meet ya at the car in five. But this ain't over."

"Sure, it is. And after the hospital it's the hardware store. You'll be putting internal locks on both of our bedroom doors."

"That's right," I supported.

Head shaking with unspeakable betrayal, Officer Thompson turned to me. "You're so weak you'd do whatever ya cheater brother says."

"Better than what you spew," I fired back, a brief shiver of mounting possibilities coursing through me.

Officer Thompson climbed the stairs with the tenacity of a man with a dozen arrows sticking in his back. When he got to the top, he stated, "I think you need a psychiatrist. Both of ya!"

"Consider yourself declawed!" Benny yelled back.

As Officer Thompson left, Benny pushed so hard not to smile that it hurt. "Payment due, man. That dude will never touch us again."

"Wow," I praised. "Wow." Unceasingly for months I thought, "Wow."

“And sorry I didn’t come up with this earlier,” he added, on his way up the stairs. “Could’ve saved you and Ma some grief.”

I swaggered into Benny’s cloth room to the photo of Charles Manson, and got within inches to brave one more, “Fuck You.” I was so galvanized that before I joined them at the car, I hit the floor to rip off as many pushups as I could. Seven pushups later and I wasn’t a changed man.

Twitch

"It takes genius to not fail a class for five years the way you did and never get caught," I complimented Benny, sprawled out on patio lounge chairs mixing Pop Tarts with Fresca.

"It's more fun than bobbing for apples," he replied, distractedly.

"Still, with only a sixth-grade education, you took the SAT's and beat 60% of the others. What score would you ring up if you were at the same education level as the rest?"

"Probably better."

"Much."

"Look on the bright side. Just one more year then maybe 'I too can make it in the beauty business.'" That was from his favorite local commercial to mimic.

The sky was gray and discouraging. Unseasonal clouds had racked up, broad and low. In disbelief about all that had proceeded the moment, we shook our heads simultaneously. He added, "Truth is cheating is exhausting. The pressure never ends."

Spring was in full bloom other than twenty feet to our left where Benny's freshly planted vegetable garden had been decimated. Our neighbor's dog had leaped the fence and dug up the unused fishing bait from where Officer Thompson had buried it between the lettuce and tomatoes. If it were my garden, I would've carried on like it was an insurmountable setback. Had it been Officer Thompson's garden and somebody else did that it would've been the "end of the world." Benny just accepted, "innocent mistake,' and resolved to replant it later that day.

"I don't know how well we'd do, but during this summer I can try to catch you up for your senior year," I offered.

"That'd be cool."

"It's the least I can do to thank you."

"For what?"

Instead of answering, for dramatic effect I blew bubbles with the straw in my Fresca. "Remember when he backhanded me for blowing bubbles when he was on the phone?"

"Well he was talking to someone about septic tanks, so you were asking for it."

"I like how close-mouthed he's been these past months since you.... The hesitation in his shit brown eyes."

It turned out that Benny didn't even know what a square root was. Or when to use lie or lay, its or it's, and who's or whose." He thought Egypt was in Asia and that Ben Franklin had been president. Though further behind in formal education than a catatonic in a marathon he was so determined. It had just been too long, so when he lost concentration we'd pause, readjust, then sally forth again.

I was now eighteen and finally unshackled. In hindsight regrettably, to stay near my wallflower's oral penchant for inducing my love, I'd elected to stay put matriculated in the local four-year college. Another reason was I didn't want to get a part-time job to afford my own housing. And I'd never actually been interested in school anyway, excelling merely because it had felt safer. It hit Benny that a year later he'd also be free, a major factor that liberated his brain to function again. When he retook the SAT's his senior year, he got a 1200, surpassing 80%. He even eclipsed Randolph, a student loved by the teachers for his tendency to compliment them, that mastermind in polka dot shirts who'd prematurely begun sculpting the graduation yearbook in their junior year when he'd also kidded, only once, that Benny should be voted, "Most Likely to Kill You." This was before Benny had turned the tables on Officer Thompson. Maybe I hadn't seen the signs as clearly as Randolph.

The Third Coming of Benny the Unstoppable was now at hand. This would be the one that would propel him toward unimaginable heights. His head was up again, eyes wide with curiosity, and his innate wit was alive for all to experience-druggies, jocks, and nerds alike. Richie's Crew was going separate ways, each, other than Benny, to create little and settle into routine more. As for Richie, his premonition, then realization that would smack shortly after he quit school due to an inability to focus almost equal to Benny's former condition, that his star would soon dim and he'd be left lost, would be progressively suppressed with intoxicants. The memories of his ten follower's admiration would soon be the glory days off of which he'd subsist, interspersed with no prospects, no idea of what to do, or even who he was. That was when his second realization came from the tag on his alcoholic mother's post-binge tea bag. "The apple doesn't fall far from the tree." As if they'd never developed, those ties ceased for Benny. Mutual escapism, by definition, isn't about a depth of lifelong connection. The occasional visits to Gabrielle Mindbender's locker to exchange dollars for joints were also no more. There was even an amiable, nondescript sweetheart of a sort whom he didn't even consider deflowering.

"Did neutering our father free you to become a student again?" I inquired, admiringly.

"Definitely." Unlike my paranoia that more arrows would fly, he believed that Officer Thompson couldn't harm us again.

Days before he, One-Eyed Gumby, Romeo the pillow, and Esterlie The Fire Girl would take that bus to his new home in Boston, he and I were sprawled out on the patio again. Out of nowhere, with no apparent provocation, his whole body twitched violently, smashing his head forward. It would've dislocated the jaw of a lesser Thompson like me.

"What the hell was that?" I asked. A cavernous hole ripped in the morsel of serenity Benny had patterned for me.

"I don't know," he replied, a bit dazed. "I get one every so often."

"When did they start?"

"It's no biggie. Until now they've always happened when alone."

"No biggie? It must hurt."

"They'll go away," he said, like it was no more than a hiccup.

He wanted to divert so I tried to quell my tendency to obsess. That's when I thought, or imagined, that I saw something, a flash that ricocheted through my nerves and into my bones. It was like some horrific omen planted in this saga's pivot toward uplifting. Or like Edvard Munch's *the Scream*. As Benny strained to screw on imperviousness again, I ached for that disruptive flash I'd had to dissolve. No humanizing of him was in order, only my perception of him as that self-amused eagle levitating above the ordinary.

He began to bite his thumb as I waited to see what he'd do next. My prediction was that he'd rally his inner troops, eyes toward the future. Instead, I heard a voice short on inflection divulge, "I'm somewhat caught up in school, but I have this nagging suspicion that I don't know anything." There was an unsteadiness there like one of the twenty lights he would use to jump into the unknown, for the moment, was facing in the wrong direction, back to where all of the fumes, and the poison, and the indelible were. He didn't want to recollect. To undergo anything about our past, rancor, or even disappointment, would just impede him.

"Does it seem weird that neither of us have anyone we're close to apart from you, Ma, and me?"

"You, yes. Me, no," I responded. "Well, at least there aren't anchors holding you back."

"Apologies for not including your lady love because you mentioned you only hang on to her for the BJs."

"Accepted."

"By the way, you ever feel guilty about that?"

"Yep. But I can't seem to stop anyway. Once the real thing comes along it won't happen again."

"Good. So why didn't we develop lasting friendships?

"Barring the fact that our relatives are from The Land of The Dreary and Unaccomplished?" This was the moment when I realized that I had a knack for language.

"Yep."

"It's probably harder to connect with people when you come from chaos," I postulated. It gave me a boost playing the wise one with someone I felt inferior to. "I don't know. You must get out of here, brother."

"He goes on and on about how I should go to the local state school like you are," Benny rehashed flicking it away with his hand, the tone less secure than the unconcerned expression he again scraped to attach to it. I detected a yearning for some semblance of a boy sprouts into man family going away celebration, instead of suffering Sergeant Thompson's myopic opinions.

"Vamoose, brother. Hotfoot it to Boston, and don't look back," I advised, pausing dramatically. "But first I need a favor."

"Shoot."

"I gotta know. Did the twitches start when you lost a nut?"

Shyly he replied, "Yeah. At night. In the hospital."

At sundown while our mother was at the sink, scrubbing the plates that had just served one of the same fifteen dinners she'd been preparing for decades, Benny came up to her. On the wall above she'd hung yet another cheaply framed photo of her children in fun moments, temporarily staving off the reality of an emptying nest with picturesque remembrances. A picture is worth a thousand revisionist words.

"You should leave with me. You don't belong here," he said. "Gotta save yourself before it's too late.

She grinned appreciatively, then sighed, washed out and unimaginably resigned to this variant of security. Penitently she responded, "I can't."

"You're not yet 40 years old. We could rent an apartment."

"No, go live. Have your experiences. I'll be fine."

"You can do better," Benny pleaded, wringing his hands. "You could be more."

Her focus reverted to the dishes, blinking rapid fire. She iced over, breathless and glassy-eyed. "Sorry," she peeped. "I just can't."

Months later as she became more depressed again due to Benny's absence, Sergeant Thompson gleaned his opportunity to secure her permanent compliance. He proposed, making sure to posture that it was purely the act of a loving, dedicated husband, to have another child, affixing the possibility that they keep aborting until they hatched a female. For a couple of days, the idea revved her up, a sugary, little girl whom she could protect, train, and raise to never experience what she had in childhood and beyond. But the choleric jealousy of imaginings rose up in her. She could foresee, even taste, an aging Sergeant Thompson fawning over his daughter like she could do no wrong, whatever she did turning without labor into gold. The duality of envying the good treatment of an innocent for whom she'd crave such treatment, put a damper on that idea.

Freedom

Pistah, Loquacia, and Jeff Needs A Lookout

Through a placement service Benny lucked in to a room in a second-floor apartment in Beacon Hill, the two dinky bedrooms facing side by side out on to Pinckney Street. He was all set to embark on his new life at Emerson College, alma mater of his favorite comedian, Steven Wright. "The other day I steamed the map off the globe." When he opened the door lugging the two wilted suitcases purchased long ago by our mother with green stamps, an inexplicable vacuum, like the room urgently needed his presence, sent a swath of air past him. The swath caromed off the wall behind him creating a rebound effect that shot him inside. It was invigorating and only a bit dampened by this observation, "Man, that dude is hairy." With classic moldings and even a lion's paw bathtub, the space had a calming, pliable ambiance. It was neutral territory, a hallelujah workshop where two young men could be themselves.

"How ya doing?" Benny started off, glowing like a man erroneously convicted now standing in front of fifty reporters outside the prison that had just released him. "Looks like I'm your roommate."

"Then God must hate you," over-enunciated Larry Hochman, a product of The Bronx whose father had survived Buchenwald. "Kindly plop down your bags and extend me a token of your good will."

Right then Benny knew that Larry was in a character unreflective of his usual pattern of speech. He was happy to play along. Casually he improvised the thud, hit his knees, and bowed.

"Excellent dramatics!" Larry encouraged, another prototypical first fiddle primed for Benny's predilection for mischief and exploration.

"Hey, and is it okay if I have both beds because sometimes, I like to switch beds in the middle of the night?" Benny asked while standing.

"Superlative far-fetched irreverence!"

"Also, I've brought my inflatable doll with me," Benny continued. "While I'm retrieving the rest of my stuff from the hallway downstairs, would you mind blowing her up?"

"Teamwork, why not? Then I'm going to fuck all of the squeak out of that airhead," Harry quipped. He waved for Benny to stay put for what over years would be the first of a myriad of random interrogations. "But first it's vital that we establish a few specifics, to know if you're a suitable goy for rooming with the perfect Jewish boy. Number one, but not the most important, are you exhilarated beyond belief that above us lives the Frenchman, and below us there's a pimp?"

"It's one of my main reasons for moving in."

"And would you be up for occasionally pounding on the Frenchman's ceiling, especially if we need to alert him that we're about to broadcast out the window whatever spastically comes to mind?"

"That's what I've always done with the French."

"And most importantly, you probably noticed that while I was busy not helping you carry your stuff up the stairs, that I was conversing out the window to the black whore standing outside. Yes, the one who lives with her pimp."

"The pink wig really turned me on."

"She raises the price when she wears it."

"That's pretty standard."

“She and I were chatting about her recent experience of love at first sight. Love at first sight, we should all be so lucky. Anyway, the object of her affection is, oh how do I reveal such prized intelligence? Well, is, You! Are you sensible enough to be aroused by that?”

“I’ll marry her right now if she’s willing to be exclusively my black whore.”

“Ha! That’s so funny that I almost had a URS. Urine Release Session in case you’re not well educated. And, be careful though, that whore can twaddle for hours about how top notch she used to be at Double Dutch and marrying lonely hearts for their money.”

“What did you belch her name is, Loquacia?”

“Loquacia!” Larry shrieked, laughing and falling all over the place. “Nice! That’s her new name all right. Hey, you’ll fit in just fine. I think I’ll even call you ‘Pistah.’ Heschel With the Tiny Peckel will like that name for you.” He picked up a broom pole and pounded on the ceiling. “Frenchman! Frenchman!”

He was five feet, nine inches of muscle, had visions of being in the CIA, and was an MIT biology major who would go on to captain the Rugby team. Wearing stubble even after a shave, he’d been unfailingly misperceived of as a teacher, likewise in high school, toss in junior high also. Thus, the joke that five o’clock shadowed him was that he’d been born clutching an AARP card in one hand and an enema in the other.

All they needed was to get five neutered cats named in order of arrival, FC, (First Cat…missing its tail), SC, (Second Cat…missing an eye), Tripod (minus one leg), and the females, Ralph and Norton, and the place was hopping. Within days Benny had also enrolled in the local karate dojo, an instantaneous second home where he only missed training nine days during his four years of college, holiday closings not included. It wasn’t a shocker that he was gifted at it, with One-Eyed Gumby flexibility that could blast a kick at an opponent's belfry so fast, a monomaniac's willingness to train exhaustively, though he was in no way so one-dimensional, a puzzle solver's mind for figuring out his opponent, and his usual mettle. During the Friday night Kumite sessions where he battled with bigger, more seasoned fighters, no pain or setback could divert him from becoming the first student at that dojo to attain his black belt in only four years. I wondered if that determination was to ensure, maybe subconsciously, that no man could ever rule over him again.

To fund his tuition, rent, the Karate dojo, and an occasional jaunt to a dance club, he needed a job where he could do his homework. Killing two birds with one stone is routine to any whiz at living by his wits, and thus being a Security Guard in a senior housing high rise hanging loose at a desk with virtually no duties other than his homework, was a no brainer. Visualize this moxie. Benny roller-skating, as he now did everywhere, from Beacon Hill along with the traffic down Commonwealth Avenue wearing his First Choice Security Guard uniform, backpack brimming with books, clinging on to bumpers to catch rides, weaving in and out, that wealth of hair creating squiggly lines behind him, off to where the elderly needed his protection from incalculable evil. It was also at that job where he would meet the second of his three closest friends in Boston.

Benny would laugh, "You never foresee that you could be so comfortable with someone who months earlier was a stranger, that you'll help him disrobe and inch himself into the tub." Especially a man 64 years older than him, who rode in a wheelchair fitted with a beer holder on each armrest, and loved to regale Benny with anecdotes about the five times he almost tied the knot, three of those to the same mulatto wedding photographer. A man who was, and will forever be, the second black man to be appointed a cop in New York City. Or, so he claimed. Photos don't lie, but who knows, what fun would it be tooting the seventh or ninth black cop. "I know why those Italians liked to piss off their roofs onto me at night," he recounted. "Must've gotten tired of pissing on each other, and needed to make it more challenging by trying to hit a darker target."

And, he'd crack up. "Smacked one upside the head with my club and he pissed his pants. Finally, I could take my hat off."

Benny confided everything about his present life to him. Jeff had heard of the Frenchman, and of Loquacia after whom he inquired whether she made house calls. In turn Jeff loved to dramatize the legion of characters that populated his 32 years with the NYPD, the descriptions a bit hard to keep up with because his arthritis made the exuberance of his hand gestures land one beat behind their target. Then one day he insouciantly tossed out: "Pretty Benny, I need a favor. I got me a rendezvous. One I'm aiming for every week so I'm needing a lookout." He was as electrified as a virgin, having gotten himself "all spit shined like a real man do." He wheeled down the ramp, peered around as if a conspiracy was brewing, swiveled back to wink at Benny, and continued to the rear of the building. Benny's duty was to ensure that no one tailed Jeff, other than seconds later his own black whore whose booty protruded so far that its shadow resided in a neighboring zip code. Apparently, Benny's job now killed three birds with one stone because Jeff would return, tittering, never neglecting to remark in his raspy, resonant, and forgiving voice: "I got lucky".

Now Benny was on his way, with no doubt that he'd chosen the right school given his affection for harmless eccentrics. His Western Civ teacher got so fired up when re-enacting the charge at Vicksburg, or some poor soul being burned at the stake, that he'd have to hobble into the corner to use his inhaler. His psych professor, the one with the fierce beard with the lint in it from that day's pullover, spilled that he'd forsaken working one on one with patients because he suffered from "babbling burnout." His speech professor spotted Benny's knack for observing rarities and oddities, and encouraged him to compose his speeches along those lines. So Benny selected "My Day At The Food Processor's Convention" which, stimulated by a radio commercial, he'd attended at the Convention Center. There he'd encountered a pear-shaped fellow whose entire career, his calling, was to improve the mouth feel of certain foods. During Benny's speech he gradually transformed into that fellow, excessive usage of the words "you know" and "it's obvious that," while as straight as can be he described the aspects of mouth feel that matter most to such connoisseurs, augmenting it with some occasional chewing and facial expressions of approval or disapproval. It came off so well and farcical, that his professor decided to curtail the day's other presenters since it would be as "unfair as going on after a kid or dog act." All that inspired one of the founding members of the Emerson Comedy Workshop to invite Benny to their school performance. He turned up and was summarily pushed up on stage where, totally unprepared, he lamented about his grievances with the black whore who lived below him, otherwise known as his girlfriend, also sometimes referred to as "Loquacia" because she never stopped nattering especially in her sleep, otherwise known as "Hoops" due to her hatred of all things basketball and fondness for huge plastic, gold painted hoop earrings which she always wore, and of his heavy heart because an earring had accidentally caught on the mirror of a passing truck dragging her mercilessly to the front door of a real jewelry store. And somehow, though Benny improvised it all on the spot and had never done comedy, he was an instant hit.

That evening as Benny lay in bed, he could hear Loquacia on the street below his window serenading, "Talking About Love. Yes, yes, Benny, yes. I'm talking about love!"

Misfits Like Me

"Oh sorry," Benny said, after bumping into someone as they horned into the science classroom for the first time.

"That's okay," that someone replied in the deepest female tone he'd ever heard. "Can't say I don't disappear in these fluorescent lights."

"That's handy," he played along noticing that she was Albino. "So, you know where to hide when the cops are chasing you."

"Haaaaaa! At last someone isn't so put off by the Albina that he won't joke."

"I was serious," he answered, facetiously. "Even though I'm never found guilty of any of the crimes I commit, I always scout out potential hiding places just in case."

"Right on."

They sat next to each other, her hand creating a nervous sweat stain on her notebook. She didn't have a history of much repartee with boys.

"So, hey, clue me in," Benny requested, leaning toward her. "Your accent. Puerto Rican?"

"In a Mexican nightmare."

"Oh, Mexican," Benny responded. "What's your gripe with Puerto Ricans? Maybe I'm Puerto Rican."

"Yeah right. And maybe I'll be the first Albina, Mexican, female, pink-eyed, half blind, addicted to chocolate chip cookie dough, Republican president of these United States."

"I'd vote for ya on the cookie dough alone."

He jotted in his notebook, 'Reasons I'm not guilty of the crimes I've committed.' He raised one eyebrow to inquire, "So hey, I'm more uneducated than most in college. Catch me up. Is there a big difference between Puerto Ricans and Mexicans?"

"It goes something like this. It's Puerto RiCANS! And, it's MexiCAN'TS. Puerto Ricans are the ones who move here whenever they want. Mexican'ts sneak over the border often into the waiting arms of border agents who announce, 'And you wetbacks thought it would be that easy.'"

At that point Mr. Cob intruded carrying a dead baby pig for dissection. Benny and she spent the rest of the class outdoing each other's pretense of fascination at the lesson at hand.

The next class Benny rolled in early so that he could sit next to the Albino girl. He broke the ice with, "I got a follow-up question to our last meeting."

"I called myself an albina instead of albino, and you're itching to learn if female albinos are called albinas in Spanish seeing as you never covered that in your high school Spanish class?"

"No, but now that you brought it up, I'm all ears. Oh hey, we haven't exchanged names. Yours?"

"Alba."

"You're messing with my head."

"Nope. You're sitting next to Alba the Albina Albino. Today everything is coming up roses for you."

"I'm snapping up a lottery ticket right after Mr. Cob jerks the innards out of whatever critter he lugs in today."

"Am I your first?

“It’s likely that you’re everyone’s first Alba the Albina Albino.”

“First albino?”

“Albino, no. Latino, yes.”

“Latino albino or just latino?”

“Just latino.”

“In what white-ass suburb did you learn to crawl? No, scratch that racist remark and hit me with your follow-up to yesterday.”

“Okay. And I’ve actually been curious since I last saw you. Do you favor the dried cookie dough that you have to add water or oven ready in the tube?”

“The tube.”

“Me, too.”

“I’m stuck in Mexico brain where you don’t drink the water or put it into your cookie dough.”

“No living in the past, there Triple A.”

“Triple A! Alba The Albina Albino. Unbeatable!”

At 21 years old Alba Rodriquez had never been asked for a date. She’d never even tasted a crush on a boy because an internal mechanism of futility compelled her to block out that prospect. Though Benny didn’t meet her until junior year, everything that he could invite her to, he did. She was there for his graduation from brown to advanced brown belt, then black belt. She escorted him for Jeff’s 84th birthday party which amounted to the three of them at Burger King amongst the hodgepodge of lonely pensioners nursing a coffee and workless moocher sucking down a 99-cent special.

Leading it all with a single French Fry baton in hand waved like a Conductor, Benny wrangled the entire, unsightly ensemble to sing Happy Birthday. Up against her consternation that her peers would gawk at her, more challenging had been convincing Alba to grace one of his house parties. Finally, she was slated for that weekend.

-------------------------------+----------------------------------

"Heschel With the Tiny Peckel," real name Seymour Aaron Lipschitz, initials creating "SAL" for when he cared to masquerade as Italian, had feelings of inadequacy about everything short of, all elements CPA, and how he loved "DJewing" during the parties at Larry and Benny's pad. They'd stand the couch up on its end to make space, banish the five cats with a total of 19 legs, 9 eyes, and 4 tails onto the roof for their safety, and it was crazy time. Dancing, mild substances, and delectable babes, some of whom Larry handed invitations in the streets to guarantee that they outnumbered the boys, created a sweaty free for all that never failed to unhinge Heschel's comb over. Benny's palate had even opened up a bit with make outs on the roof, but he still wouldn't single one out to stay over.

"Just fuck one," I pushed. "For fun. For no reason other than it feels good."

"I really don't want to," was all he muttered.

Quizzical about his disinterest in sewing his oats I'd recently asked him if being only half full down there interfered with his confidence. He'd replied, "Nope, but I want to have kids someday and if I lose one more that won't happen."

It was the night prior to the party where the boundaries of his unheralded virginity were tested. Larry was asleep in bed. Benny had just skated back from work where Jeff had gifted him his "lost" police badge, number 6299. It was pinned to Benny's shirt with a pride that the badge of another Officer for sure couldn't elicit, tapping on it a couple of times, coincidentally in rhythm with another tapping sound that broke out. Who could be at the door so late? He strained to see through the peephole, so not in the mood for the moment at hand to be interrupted.

"How'd you get into the building?" he asked, having opened the door. The incongruity of Carly's appearance made him wonder if her life had been one long identity crisis. Her turtlenecks and flats never quite matched with her array of fish net stockings and the gobs of makeup an eight-year-old might apply at a slumber party.

"Some French Guy let me in," she gushed in her inimitably overboard style, sauntering in uninvited. "And he told me he'd pay me $40 to coax some badass named Larry to knock off banging on the ceiling and yelling to him out the window."

Carly, a 26 year old former receptionist at a used car dealership who'd christened every model on the lot, who on her 27th birthday decided that she wished to be an actress, who a half year later went to college to major in theater breaking her parent's hearts when she moved out for the first time from their house and into a dormitory, also leaving in the lurch her fiancé, an apprentice plumber in line to take over his dad's one truck business. She had a second dream also, to finance a single boob reconstruction meaning only one boob, the torpedo to be shaped to the near perfection of the other. She'd had an eye for Benny ever since she caught him in an Emerson Comedy Show. She was so juiced up by his ability to associate one obscurely related anomaly, trend, person, place or thing with another that approaching midnight she'd dropped in, her delivery awkward with what she'd been rehearsing for hours, to implore, "I have to suck your dick or I'm going to die!"

"So, would you like to be cremated or buried?" he replied, gently pushing her out the door.

"What's wrong?"

"Oh Shirley..."

"…Carly"

"Oh Carly, how scorchingly messed up do you have to be to blurt that out? You just compelled me to list women in two categories. Clean and Dirty. It's official, women who permit their kids to be abused, and such as you who offer to 'suck' a veritable stranger three quarters her age, will not be listed as Clean."

"Are you playing hard to get?"

"In the realm of possibilities that could be, but time to go."

He gently finessed her out the door and closed it. In disbelief he lay on the floor. Carly remained undeterred, upping the ante by listing through the door all she was willing to do with, to, and for him. The rambling progressed to idyllic visions of what they could build together, pleading, then anger at how he'd led her on by longingly gazing at her at his show. He hadn't noticed her there until toward the end when, to win his heart, she obtrusively took to laughing ahead of his punch lines. The only things that could curb her tirade now were an interruption and/or a consolation prize. Fortunately, the Frenchman put on some cologne to combine both. Unheard by Benny, he'd come into the hallway to invite her to his apartment. She accepted.

Benny called me to discuss the goings on, not nearly as entertained by it as I was. As I was offering my usual advice, but this time with a rare caveat attached, "Just fuck her and focus on the better tit," another knock came on the door. He put down the phone and to vent his frustration shot a sidekick five feet in to the air. It got him ready to reject her again, but when he opened the door it wasn't her. Patricia Appleby, another wannabe actress who he'd recently discovered was on the Emerson cheerleading team when he finally got wind that there was one, stood wearing Eve's smile. He picked up the phone, briefed me that he'd just entered The Outer Limits, and hung up.

"May I come in?" she proposed, coquettishly.

"Okay, but not for long because it's late."

"I was so excited to be invited to tomorrow's party," she exclaimed, too zealously for his liking.

"We're glad that you'll be joining us," Benny pretended, his chivalry an overlay on top of this thought, "Who the hell invited this pin cushion?"

"And should I bring anything?" she brown-nosed, gaping at him as if he were whatever movie star who, for the chance to suck up, she'd cheerfully amputate a toe.

"Beer, wine, munchies, your call."

She deferred to her long-ago suppressed shyness when she stammered, "And, ah, I was also hoping, like, that we could, like, you and me, like, be together, at least for the party. Ah, how's that sound?"

"Boyfriend and girlfriend?"

"Okay!"

She didn't glean that even if he were in partner mode, a girl he'd seen holding hands with three grubby lumps that semester, equaling her present number of hickeys, couldn't best the rest.

"Well," he dodged, leading her to the door. "Thank you for being so forthright. And it's a massive compliment. But I can't consider this right now."

"Why? I'm fantastic. You'll see."

"We've only talked like twice for a combined total of sixty not so memorable seconds," he said, anticipating that Larry would appear cracking up at the prank he'd arranged.

"So? This isn't the 1920's. Women got as equal of a right to ask for what they want as men do," she protested. Forecasting a harangue on how *The Suffragette's suffered for them all*, he nudged her out the door. Shortly after, he overheard her whimper, weep, then wail like the day she didn't place in the top five in a six-person talent contest. She knocked again and in far too many words apologetically apprised him that she'd held out for his advance until she no longer could, finishing with, "And I lost the coin flip and was like, super amped when you didn't pick Carly!"

Double Epiphany. Number one. In league Carly and Patricia had outlined this and a coin flip had determined who got the first shot. Number two. All actresses are nutso, a knowledge fortified when an hour later with the Frenchman having his European way with her, Carly shrieked Benny's name. It woke Larry up and once he'd swallowed the narrative, he laughed so hard that he tumbled off the bed. Baying, "Frenchman! Frenchman!" he sprung up to work the ceiling with the broom pole.

The next night after Benny and Larry came to the vital realization that if they played connect the dots with the innumerable blackheads on Heschel With the Tiny Peckel's face that they could formulate a picture of a CPA sitting at his desk dutifully cooking the books, Larry and Heschel went on the beer run while Benny, Alba, and me set up the party. When I'd met her an hour before she'd seemed nice but, me being me, I couldn't settle in around someone who looked like that. And her eyes skimmed more than once my maroon corduroy pants, like they didn't go well with my top-siders.

"I'm on scholarship for these reasons, minority, Albino, poor, and depression," she confided, stirring the onion dip with one hand and the guacamole dip with the other. "The last one isn't helped by the fact that I have to bunk in the dormitories, which has ended me up with a different roommate every year all three of whom hated me at first sight. My roommate last year immediately changed the subject if I brought up my Albinism, and habitually chattered about the special breast reshaping she's hankering to get."

"No!!!!!! You talking about Carly? You had to board with our most famous 28-year-old sophomore?" yowled Benny, hanging string lights from the ceiling.

"Yeah, you know her?"

"She's as out of her gourd as any girl I've ever met who tells everyone that she wants to boob job only one boob. And I've met a lot of them."

"Mas loca than that. Esa chica always draws below her less sublime spud the scar where her surgery will take place."

"Hey, I didn't see that!"

Alba froze then responded, "No, you didn't!"

"Who wouldn't? Carly's hot," he stated, containing it until they both fell over laughing, gobs of dip from her spoons flung off to replicate a Jackson Pollack on the floor, him wrenching down a row of strip lights that he didn't release in time to salvage his handiwork. "That's some loony shit."

"Crazier than if I wanted to move to the Equator," she commented. "Though I can relate to Carly. I'd like to makeover my outward appeal also."

She and I sure had that in common, but a growth spurt wasn't in the cards for me. As we got back to the preparations, something happened that I inferred he'd never done in front of anyone except me. He twitched. It was a big one. I was already uncomfortable about being scheduled to be the lesser brother around a carefree collection of creative types who I was sure revered Benny almost as much as I did, so this didn't help.

"Twice now I've seen you do that," Alba noted.

"Seen what?" Benny asked.

"I'm smelling a cover-up."

"About what?"

"You got the twitches. I've got the twitches," she pointed out. She fired off a series of them intentionally. "That makes us twitchy friends."

"What?"

"Pretending to not know that you twitched. It's like you're programmed to put on a sunny face. What's up with that?"

"That's how I feel."

"Could be you've got secrets, Bumble Bee," she said, cocking her head to the left. "It takes one to know one."

Benny just shrugged his shoulders and summed up, "Sorry. I wish there were more to disclose."

"Have you seen him twitch before?" she asked me.

The spotlight would never be my magnet, so I assembled this in stages, "Nope............Never."

Later on, as the party began to rage Benny decided that he would abandon the usual fare of dancing with whatever girl asked him. The reason--two slighted actresses ambled in holding hands like former wives at the trial of their bigamist ex-husband. Yes, Carly and Patricia were there to leer at him skeptically. Adaptation in the shape of a human roadblock was now sorely needed so he fastened Alba on one side of him, and Toni, whom he'd just met, on the other side. My sights were set on Carly. Maybe she'd like to avenge Benny's rejection by canoodling with this C student and I sure could use some relief now that Lizzy my three-year holdover chic had flown the coop. Presto. Turned out that the revamped boob was the left one. It was even more ideal than her righty. Left, right, left, right, left. The best of both worlds in that my affinity for such cosmetic artistry had begun.

Before long Alba spotted Benny. He was goggling Toni who had the added perk of the sexiest pillows for lips, so she tossed him a wing woman wink and wandered off. Benny was a kisser. That was his thing. He wasn't hardwired to think with his, shall we say, body part. Nevertheless, enough kissing with Toni could crush any man's willpower, and thus later that evening Benny made us all half proud of him, me, and Larry, and Heschel With the Tiny Peckel, even The Frenchman when Larry bellowed it out the window to him. Half proud because firing his baby bullets onto Toni's leg while searching for her Holy Grail deserves only a muted applause, not the standing ovation we were eager to thunder. Shortly though he was giving it to more than just her leg, two or three times nightly. Why, I would be perplexed, did he bid her adieu a month later, holding her hand while she cried, explaining that he was too busy to be in a relationship, excessively busy in my opinion. Flushed with guilt as if he were abandoning her, he didn't want to spawn for this child of multiple repellant foster homes any more reasons than she'd already had to overprotect her heart.

Amongst it all, Benny patiently tolerated my incessant rehashing of the hell that was our childhood. The twenty-four occasions I visited him at Emerson to stay always for two days, arriving and leaving at the same hour, still all I witnessed in him was self-reliance. The lad who'd never completed a novel now not only read all of the required novels that were part of his BA in English, but also squeezed in 30 minutes a day for Calvino, Malamud, or Kobo Abe. Benny and Larry occasionally even read those books out the window dramatically, cracking each other up, projecting to whomever was passing by, to Loquacia, and her pimp.

Benny Thompson, who rode exuberantly on the back of Jeff's wheelchair like a chariot, vanquishing with Jeff's plastic sword any interloper who dared advance too close to them. No need for fruitless unease about what others, all of those people in a love affair with their judgments, might surmise about him. Just be in the moment, while I'd jealously think, you freak. How can you be so enthusiastic? How can you always find so much humor in everything? It was so beautiful to watch him. The way he organically drew a crowd dancing solo in a club as if he'd given the music permission to own him. Me dancing like Peppermint Patty, with one arm creating a horrifying illusion that it was shorter than the other; that arm flicking forward and flicking forward, no matter what the beat was, or what unattainable girl was donating me a sympathy dance. Flicking forward. It should've been illegal what I was doing out there. It should've been filmed and peddled as a horror "flick."

There he stood alone in the corner of the Karate dojo, the others wise to how quietly formidable he'd become, a bit of an outcast being the only one who didn't speak in male bravado, the only male not interested in standing outside the front door bantering about the tits and ass of passersby. Of course, I counseled him to be careful, not to get hurt, one of a million examples of how handicapped I was becoming in fear of consequences. There, Benny also stood blithely and sensuously in control of the audience, not ashamed to do the funniest comedy routine about losing his virginity on Toni's leg. Who cares? Very little recognition that the universe outside of a child's home was also such a dark place.

And what was this inclination to befriend all of the misfits and mutants, especially now that he was flying free? Now that he could reach the stars unlike his misshapen brother, why was he aligning with and taking care of another oddball? Hadn't Aggie Boza in grade school, Jimmy Coon in junior high, Jeff in his wheelchair, his brother and mother throughout his 20 years, exhausted his desire to salvage those who were doomed or isolated. Now he had to serve up hours that he didn't have, free time that he could've spent with ten Wendys, five Margarets, and perhaps a Toni, time he wasted being a friend to not the girl with the best set of melons, or legs that any ordinary Joe would hunger to wrap around himself, or some pliable Southern vixen raring to join him for any fantasy that involved her bending over. Nope, he was driven to pledge his allegiance to the school's lonely Albino girl. That's not necessary I nagged, scratching to convince him of the pitfalls of such an alliance.

All the same, I admired him for doing it, hanging out in a place where I would've tasted only repugnance. Yes, I fled from those who were even lower on the social scale than I misguidedly perceived myself to be, spooked that they'd imperceptibly smudge their loser germs on to me like I was born without an immune system. In contrast, he hastened to their sides not even securing if there were any malaria nets around to safeguard him. He embraced them with open arms as valuable individuals who simply needed love. I fretted that their mere presence would be "too depressing," my get out of jail free card for everything that I didn't care to deal with. I was honing the putrid art of feeling bad for myself, and about myself, while he found sustenance in advancing other's lives.

Around then I began to conjecture if to a lesser extent, he felt like a misfit too, and thus the gravitational pull.

Dr. LaPrade's Wish

During my second to last visit to Boston, with dusk encroaching and all of us on a blanket in Commonwealth Park, Benny and Alba were lying side by side and facing upward next to where Rose and me lay facing each other. I was wearing what too many would later deride as "Grandpa jeans," which were bought to deter Alba from staring further at my assortment of corduroys. Benny was preparing for that evening's comedy routine entitled, "Why I'm Not Guilty of Any of The Crimes I've Committed," to be performed after we stopped by for an unspecified meeting that Dr. LaPrade had requested with Benny, for some reason to be held at Emerson's tiny performance hall. Rose was my new girlfriend, Rose Bush of the Barnstable Bushes, the polar opposite of a holdover chic. And though facially she looked too much like Harpo Marx, this was the one on whom all hopes of a life worth living were rapidly pressed. She was a freshman, an aspiring pediatric nurse, at my college where I was at long last finishing my bachelors in business administration after five years of incompletes, and dropping in and out, no longer deluded that my cognitive road would've smoothed out if I could've again become a model student. I'd just moved thirty minutes away to Fall River into a modest apartment across the street from the dull as gruel job awaiting me, and for a place to be consistently alone with Rose. It was my first time on my own and not far enough away from Officer Thompson's ostracism that Benny and me weren't achieving the heights that he'd so sagaciously groomed us for. I especially wouldn't miss how he'd begun doing semi-nude sit ups and "calisthenics" in the living room, leading to a two-pound weight loss and a stench that made my eyes water.

"How's my Snuggles?" I whispered to Rose.

"So, so good."

"Wasn't I right that Benny is great?"

"And wicked funny, and very nice, and, and respectful. Holding doors and pulling out chairs. I like when guys do that."

Once I'd converted that compliment from a reason to again feel inadequate into information on how to act, I continued, "Is Snuggles excited to see his show tonight?"

"Super excited, Davey Bear."

Maybe less excited if she knew that my repeated need for reassurance had me fending off the urge to ask her for a fifth time if she'd really never kissed a guy before me. Wouldn't want to be compared to anyone. Wouldn't want to have to worry that he was the conduit of a body fluids transmittable malady now eating away at me. I peeled in on them once I overheard Alba say to Benny, "Your cat Tripod doesn't know how good she has it."

"What?" Benny asked.

"Me. Rather been born with a missing limb than albino."

"No!" Benny exclaimed, putting down his comedy notes to turn to her. Right away, the subject made me queasy. When someone begins with a baby talk foundation to a relationship, everything around it should also be a fantasyland for at least a year, nothing heavy, or the initiator of the baby talk, in this case me, will feel he's not sufficiently in control.

"Especially if it was a leg," Alba amended. "Then I could put on a prosthetic and wear long pants."

"Wow. Sad that you feel that way," Benny replied.

"My family didn't conceal their embarrassment about me," she fretted, unconsciously scratching at her face as if trying to give it color. "Hey, here's one for you. They named me 'Espiritu'. The spirit. The ghost. I'm the one who changed it to Alba. They even trooped ahead of me in public, holding hands as if on route to stage our family portrait."

As we lay there silently the dusk faded into night. I hoped that the subject wouldn't be brought up again in my delicate presence. Quietly I sat up to watch them. Alba's face relaxed and eyes closed as if relieved to have exposed travesties that she'd previously told no one. Benny strained to breath away his contempt for her parents. I saw anger. And then the twitch came. I could tell from her expression that Alba registered it also. I knew he'd work his way through it quickly, and that there would be no more twitches sooner than later, but I didn't want anything to undercut that night's performance.

"You, Jeff, and Larry are the only three from Boston I plan to keep in close contact with," Benny disclosed. "I'm so blessed to have the three of you."

"You're the only friend I have," she admitted, matter-of-factly. "Someday there'll be more."

As we wended our way to Benny's first appointment, Rose and I clasped hands facing each other to spin around like children. Her decency and sinlessness, a virgin who'd know only me in that way, spoke to me of a paradise of simplicity and stress avoidance. Benny was so secure in the expression of their friendship that he reached for Alba's hand. But I could still see that he wasn't right, unstable of step and distracted of speech. His inclination to protect wasn't waning.

At the corner of the park Alba stopped disturbed by something. We followed her lead.

A tall, muscly Russian in his prime was detaining by the arm a mousy, feminine man who was half his size. The Russian wore dark sunglasses, a black leather jacket, and tapered black jeans, all of which smacked of a henchman. The fop wore a white jump suit that would go best in a gay bathhouse. He was trying to pull free. He extricated himself and turned to flee but the Russian lunged forward and grabbed him again, this time by the collar. Unable to loosen that grasp, girlishly he tried to smack the Russian who caught his hand

and wrenched it. The victim yelped and broke into tears as the dreamlike dragging off began.

Benny walked toward them. We followed him. I would've never intervened on my own.

"Let him go," he ordered.

The Russian raised his glasses slowly. He took them off, used his shoulder to close them, and into a pocket they went. His brassy stare announced that compliance wasn't in order. Again, without success the victim strained to release himself.

"Let him go," Benny repeated.

"Why? This is free country. Communist man in free country now free right? So, I do what I want."

"Not to him you won't."

"Mind own business little child."

"He's leaving with us."

"He not girl. Boy protect girl. Boy fight his own fight."

"Thank you for the civics lesson, but you heard me."

"I'm not hurting him. But I one hurt you if not mind your own business."

Benny turned to us to say, "Back up."

"Let's just call the police," I pleaded tremulously, taking steps backward with Rose and Alba.

"With what phone?"

In tears the victim dropped one knee to the ground. The Russian let go of the collar and squared off toward Benny. Benny stepped toward the side of the victim that was away from the Russian creating tactical space. As he cautiously helped him stand the Russian took one step forward and something sounded a piercing alarm in his crotch. Down he went clutching it. After the fact, I was able to register the blur that impacted his balls, and embarrassingly, that as the scumbag was crumbling Rose was moving forward to team with Benny. Rose, not me or Alba. Rose from the exceptional family that I was sure would look down on me as a suitor.

Benny rushed the victim to Alba and returned to stand a foot from his squirming, writhing opponent. He was laser-focused, cut off from non-essential emotions.

"Benny, it's over," I heard Alba say. "It's over Benny. He can't move."

I grabbed Benny's arm and pulled him away. As Alba and Rose led the victim off, the Russian was able to make it to all fours. Benny wrenched free of me, leaped at the Russian, arced a ridge hand to the base of his skull, and equilibrium wouldn't return until we were far off. As Benny walked away with us, I caught his face. The buildup to that second advance had started long before this day had dawned. Unsophisticatedly, I assumed that this not so little episode would get it out of his system.

------------------------------+----------------------------------

At 57 years old Dr. LaPrade had it all. The pipe, the tweed jackets with patches on the elbows, the sleepy sense of humor that telegraphed he'd been teaching Creative Writing for too long, and, of course, tenure. He also owned an East Coast literary magazine so obscure that the only person on the West Coast who subscribed to it was his twin sister, a Creative Writing Professor. "I'd prefer the gallows to withstanding the loosely autobiographical gobbledygook of writers whose protagonists are always writers," he would declaim. "Someone who perches at a typewriter eight hours per day isn't that interesting; excluding me. And, non-sequitur, I fancy myself quite handsome also."

His scintilla of literary success had barely gone regional, yet his gusto for the quest endured. For decades he'd busted a Don Quixote every day at that scuffed and stained mahogany desk fighting the windmill of writer's block, weak ideas, and faulty execution. Nothing could restrict him from broadcasting to all of his Creative Writing classes that he practiced his Pulitzer Prize acceptance speech in case that monumental occasion came, and from bending over backwards to sway Benny's path. He prized effusively and with sugarcoated envy the short stories Benny submitted, whether they were purely fictional or inspired by real events.

"It's inopportune that you long to pursue other interests," Dr. LaPrade grumbled, always fiddling with the patch on his sleeve when divulging his most sobering ruminations. "The natural writer inside of you shouldn't be submerged to go do athletics and to tell jokes. The body's prime is short-lived and punch lines last a second. Great novels last forever. Wouldn't you like some future traveler to peruse yours while her spaceship is on autopilot?"

He even took to teasing Benny with, "Practicing your acceptance speech?" as they passed each other in those less than ivy hallways. He moved with such deliberateness, as if he were addicted to slow motion replays. Then one day with only a month of Benny's senior year remaining, after Benny submitted what Dr. LaPrade deemed the best short story he'd received in his 30 years as a Professor, entitled "Make Me into a Volkswagen," basically the first chapter of this novel after some tweaking by yours truly, the story of an abused kid who clamored for a Volkswagen to be shaved out of the hair on his head, Dr. Laprade even secured for him a full scholarship for Emerson's Master's in Creative Writing. It was Benny's second offer in Boston. The Boston Comedy Club had also solicited him to sign on with their roster of funny men.

Armed with his favorite attribute, persistence, Dr. LaPrade had elected to up his game. He'd sent Benny a written invitation on laced paper to "Attend A Mystery Gathering That Shouldn't Be Missed." It was to be held the following week at Emerson's performance hall. When Benny, Rose, Alba, and I crossed the threshold of that venue we were flabbergasted that an audience of three, two out of place extras who were probably scrounged up, and Dr. Laprade's portly wife, were already spread out and seated. A podium stood center stage with a mic on it. Benny and Alba sat in the center abuzz with what this "mystery" could be. I opted to sit off to the side with Rose to give us privacy. Like he'd had a richly needed release, from the way Benny bantered back and forth with Alba it was as if the confrontation with the Russian had left his mind. Every time that my eyes twisted left to scan Rose, I knew that I'd found my destiny. For her I would work harder. For her I would seek out my best behavior when already underneath life seemed like too much, too difficult, something from which it's easier to withdraw.

"What you think this gathering is for Snuggles?"

She was organizing things in her wallet. "I don't have the slightest, Davey Bear."

Peripherally I caught sight of something in her wallet. It was the 3 by 3-inch photo of my face. I'd formally presented it to her as a token of my eternal commitment and who knows when, she'd folded it to carry in her wallet. She hadn't framed it and hung it longingly in front of her desk at home, but folded it. Right through the nose a crease that from my paranoid slant reduced me to something less than the most important entity in her life. Not her inseparable future, honored and adored, but something that could potentially be discarded.

"You folded the photo I gave you?"

"Yeah because it didn't fit into my wallet."

"I'd never do that to something you gave me. Never."

I'd bring this outrage up multiply over the next few weeks, a moderate bludgeoning of her with guilt. Of course, my amplifying "condition" singed me, once again, with the fear of not saying just the right thing, the ideal words to be perfectly understood in this and all vital matters. So, I worked them out, intricately, with an editor's precision before airing them. She had to taste this from the inarguable point of view I presented, one of heartbreak amidst our unfaltering dedication to each other. She believed that I was hurt, but actually I was threatened.

A rolled-up sign hanging from the ceiling was untied. It unfurled downward to display this, ***"The 2027 Nobel Prize Ceremony."*** Benny wondered if his favorite professor could no longer resist acting out his delusions of grandeur. Then he realized that Dr. LaPrade would turn 104 in 2027 so this had a different angle. Someone whose last name probably began with "La" steadily dimmed the lights. Only a periphery light in the wings prevented arrant darkness. Over the loudspeaker a disguised voice smacking of someone whose last name started in "La" announced, "And now the winner of this year's Nobel Peace Prize for Literature, Mr. Benny Thompson." The stage lights were slowly raised as the trio's applause mounted. I was still too out of sorts, but Benny, Alba and Rose joined in as Dr. LaPrade moseyed on stage wearing a tuxedo befittingly too figure-hugging in the stomach, a product of his second most vital goal, avoiding exercise assiduously. He walked to the podium and picked up the mic. He'd shaved his beard off and wore elevated shoes to look more like an aging Benny.

"Thank You. Thank you. Please take your seats," he projected, despite the fact that they weren't standing. He scanned reverently from seat to seat as if scores of admiring, familiar faces were on hand. He waved at this and that honored phantom. "Instead of listing everyone who supported me in my passage through eight novels and an anthology of essays, I'll condense it down to one towering thank you to you all. Just one special shout out to my writing professor, Dr. LaPrade, who way back when accepted that I wasn't the most educated stripling, patiently guiding me when, for example, I'd used "orientated" instead of oriented, "irregardless" instead of regardless. Thank you, sir, up there in wordsmith heaven for all of your support. With hope and excitement, I've envisaged this day not solely to rejoice, but also for that once in lifetime opportunity to have my voice heard. You see, Dr. LaPrade once said to me, 'Why do people waste a once in a lifetime speech on drivel? Why do they toss around platitudes and clichés when there might be greater lessons to offer?' So with that in mind I offer this..........The threat of nuclear war. The concentration of wealth in too few hands. The political slogans that exaggerate racial divisions and how peachy keen that will all become if this or that phony is vaulted into power. The steady march in the name of progress that hypes too many in the Western World into believing that they can receive everything, from cradle to grave, for free. None of it bodes well for the future. But it'll pale in comparison to the damage from population growth. We've surpassed eight billion souls and nearly 1/2 of the wildlife on the planet has been killed off. Water wars are looming, yes stimulated by the diminishing supply of fresh water. Necessary advances in the prevention of infectious diseases will also exponentially add to the numbers and therefore to the further raping of natural resources and the air we breathe. Let's hope that someone someday wins a Nobel Peace Prize for making real headway in this impending crisis before it's too late. 'Free' and worldwide should be all methods of birth control. Take them out of the hands of the for-profits! And with that thanks again for coming, and for chewing over these unanticipated words."

Off he went to a richly deserved ovation. As Benny clapped, he relished that such a man of letters would move heaven and Earth to incite him.

By and by when they passed each other in the hallway Dr. LaPrade prodded: "Are you planning your speech, yet?"

That stayed with Benny. It unspooled day and night in his mind, including the night senior year ended, a final sunrise before Alba would move to Chicago for a job at a radio station. She and Benny were scheduled to exchange their goodbyes. They'd decided to meet at the Union-Oyster House, established in 1826. With its fabled semi-circle oyster bar and photos hung all about from many generations, it furnished Benny an aliveness to time that he'd never experienced, past, present, and the ominousness that the future can seem. Seated, the whole picture, school ending, and not seeing Alba anymore, all rushed over him in one swoosh of appreciation and trepidation. He also worried that something had befallen her. She was never late.

"You're at the wrong table," he wasn't sure he'd heard whispered. And again, "You're at the wrong table." He looked at the table to his left, the one with the woman with black hair, black eyebrows and lashes, lipstick, subtle bronzing make-up that refined her features into womanhood, lightly tinted glasses, a beautiful flowered dress, and every other move that her and a team of experts could craft to shroud her albinism.

"Incorrect table," Alba prevailed, gesturing for him to join her, smiling ear to ear. On the table was a tube of chocolate chip cookie dough tied with a bow.

"Wow," he mouthed, moving incredulously to her side. Levitating, they each put their elbows on the table and stared at each other, a convergence of straight shooters with no ulterior motives.

"Isn't this where I'm supposed to go, 'so what do you think'? Then you go, 'so beautiful. But to me you were always beautiful.' And I tack on, 'yes, there's nothing wrong with how I looked, but I wasn't content, so for now I'm proceeding differently.' And you reaffirm, 'I got your back no matter what you do.'"

"No, none of that, this is where you're supposed to laugh your butt off because"...out of his backpack he fished a gift-wrapped box and handed it to her. She opened it, a tube of chocolate chip cookie dough. Their crack up turned everyone to them. She opened her arms like a sea bird drying its wings and they held on to each other tightly.

Strolling home after dinner, full of stomach and heart, Benny recounted the narrative of Aggie Boza and how he'd never seen her again.

"And what did you like about her so much?"

He paused, and reminisced, and nodded before sharing, "She was that good egg who if you cared about her would love you and never betray you."

She sighed and gaped upward to note, "What a gift. What a rarity."

Back outside the dormitory, they hugged again. One of those embraces where the participants grieve that life will never be the same.

"I have a favor," she requested deferentially.

"Anything, of course. And no forgetting to call me every week."

She did her utmost to maintain eye contact but twice turned away. Smiling softly, she said, "I'd like for us to ah, ah, I'd like for us to kiss."

He clasped his hands and bit his lip. Inching closer with the sweetest grin he replied, "Okay, but you too do me a favor."

"What's that?" she flirted, inching closer.

"Don't misconstrue the tube of cookie dough in my pocket as anything else," he said, keen to give and receive with utter consciousness.

"I won't tell you if I do," she replied from still closer.

As their lips met, the charge that went through her body made her shiver. When they disengaged, she was backing away. She delayed long enough to exhale, "You," released the eye contact, and vanished inside.

It was my last time in Boston. Benny had requested that I meet him outside her dorm at this hour so I was seated on a wall nearby. He hadn't seen me yet. He looked crestfallen. Though unimaginable to me, I wondered if he was in love with her. A more careful perusal yielded an alternate conclusion. He'd constructed a family of a sort with his three disparate friends, a substitute family, a black, a Jew, and a Hispanic, and in days they'd all be hundreds of miles away; as would I. He'd be on his own again. He'd already had to climb back up the hill too many times. I blocked out that unsettling thought before I headed his way, surefooted that he'd soon be raring to make his mark on the world.

Welcome to Venus

As usual the elevator was out, so with two suitcases in hand Benny had to climb six flights the day he moved into the Washington Jefferson Hotel, a skeevy rooming house, cluster of hermitages, welfare residence of last resort, and fallback position for amorous castoffs in Hell's Kitchen, Manhattan. His Lilliputian room with its concave anciently white twin mattress adjacent to the wall, mini-fridge on the floor with a hot plate on it, and slit for a window facing internally so that day and night were virtually interchangeable, had just housed a cigar smoker. He scrubbed it for hours before doing his best to disinfect himself in the communal shower down the hallway. The smell of dead rat was easily rectifiable, so once he'd emptied that garbage pail down the chute, he cruised outside to survey his new stomping grounds as the sun went on hiatus and the human infestation resurfaced. This was Times Square Circa 1980, the pinnacle for deviants of all sorts.

It was only twenty feet before Benny stepped over his first wino down for the daily count. A swarm of fetid winos had descended, outdoing each other in the under-appreciated art of blubbering and ranting while yanking up their soily pants that again had slipped down. He proceeded right onto Eighth Avenue and nine blocks south to 42nd street. As one of the city's major transportation hubs because so much of the subway intersect there, what was once considered "The Great White Way," now teemed with street toughs, pimps in Super Fly costumes, barely clothed hookers, some gorgeous, some rasping like they'd been freeze-dried then thawed for just one more night of servicing the horny, low level criminals aware that the disheartened police only had eyes for felons, junkies with the shakes peering out of every nook, pushers mumbling to passersby what illicit substances they had hidden between their toes, single room occupancy hotels that rented by the hour and "massage" rooms where so much of the getting happy went on, pornographic magazine stores featuring foot long dildos and rubber vaginas in the windows, X-rated movie houses and peep shows, all interspersed with fancy restaurants where the city's elite dined before strolling uptown a few blocks to take in a Broadway show.

Benny roamed for a while jostled by a surreal mixture of exhilaration and revulsion.

It's hard to imagine him doing what he did next minding that he'd only had sex with one girl when it could've been fifty. Advertised as, "New York's most unique adult theater," Venus's marquise read, "Babette Does the Frat," "Georgie Dreams of Orgy," admission $1.99. On impulse he approached the plexiglass booth in which sagged an old lady with an unlit, half smoked cigarette in her mouth, red lip stick creating inch thick lips above the millimeter worth of razor's edge she was born with, and a black wig apparently worn backwards. He pushed the two dollars under the slot, received a ticket and a penny, and in he ventured.

The entrance was dimly lit with faux-candles. On the bordello maroon walls were too many 1950's black and whites of women in the buff, pudgy by 1980 standards, misaligned as if they'd been flipped on there with adhesive from a distance. A depraved looking codger put coins in the gum ball machine and out rolled a green one. Benny only registered the color once the codger began licking and nibbling on it like he had a penchant for publicly acting out on inanimate objects memories from his sexual prime. Benny thought he heard the man who past him whisper, "Ya workin the aisle?" It was hard to unscramble because his prodigious moustache muffled sound. That moustache ended up in the bathroom that when the door was opened unveiled a hodgepodge of degenerates hanging around in it like a social club.

Benny stopped to scour one of the old photos of a smiling exotic flaunting her straight-shooting Double D's. Seconds later an Old Woman wearing a T-shirt with a picture of Fat Albert on it trudged up to ask, "You thinkin them boobs ain't eye catchin' like that no more, ain't you?"

"Ah, probably aren't."

"Sure, they are," she exclaimed, and raised her shirt to reveal her elephant ear boobs, inciting Benny to rush off up the stairs that led to the theater. Inside the auditorium, a dank, malodorous 150 capacity cavern with gum stuck to the underside of every seat, the first detail he marked was that the screen was too big for the room, as if they wanted the actors to appear even closer to the audience. Babette really was doing the frat. That is if frat boys can be in their mid-thirties and smack of jailhouse snitches. Three non-scholars, the first a young bald male whom the action on screen reflected off of the top of his skull creating the illusion that the orgy was even bigger, the second a transvestite whose falsies seemed a little crushed as if he'd been inclining forward pressing them against somebody's leg performing who knows what, and last but not least a woman who looked as if she fallen off the back of her biker husband's Harley and rolled through the dirt for a few weeks, all three with nervous grins, paraded up and down the aisle like hot dog peddlers in Yankee Stadium. Occasionally, one would lean over and solicit a patron. The audience of sleeping vagrants, businessmen in suits, tourists with street maps protruding from their shirt pockets, and a smiley perv with roaming eyes and a mirror to catch if there was any action behind him watched as Benny, who looked more like a porn star than a peeper, bobbed cautiously down to his seat. Instantly Benny's gaze was diverted from the screen when he peripherally noticed that in the row across the aisle that a Caucasian hooker was sitting back with no shirt on and almost asleep, while a guy on each side of her masturbated with their outside hands using the hand nearest to fondle one of her less than pert boobs. Even her boobs seemed tired of the lifestyle. Boobs that glowed in the dark because she'd tanned the rest of herself into a leathery oak tone, like a backdrop to point all comers, so to speak, where to grope. Benny, the ace at killing two birds with one stone, had never dreamt of her mode of accomplishing two things at once. It prompted him to covertly scan around further only to catch on that most of the guys had their weenies out and were stroking them, like a mushroom patch being pulled. Benny was on another planet.

He took in the flick wondering what brought Babette to the point that she was squatting on one guy's schlong bent slightly forward so that the prong of another guy could thrust in her butt, while she had someone's dong in one hand, a completely shaven guy's foot long in the other causing Benny to realize that he had no idea that a dong, schlong, or prong could be a foot long, then along came an Asian Guy who found refuge in her mouth. Benny questioned if somebody were to have shot her in the thigh, if they would've gotten her medical attention, or just sent in a grip to pull down his zipper and fill in that hole, too. Benny concluded it must've been childhood trauma that caused all access roads to lead to Babette. That's when he heard someone nearby. The Tranie was leaning toward him.

"Blow job?" he offered, flirtatiously.

"Excuse me?" Benny reacted.

"Blow job?"

It so surprised Benny that he covered his mouth with his fist, thumb and index finger on his lips.

"That's right," agreed the Tranie copying Benny but adding in some licks.

"No, I don't do that," Benny blushed.

"No, Goofy Boy. I blow you. Only ten dollars.

"Oh, oh, no thanks. Thanks anyway."

"Why not?"

Benny froze before all he could come up with was, "Because I'm saving for a trip to Europe."

"Fuck Europe, I always end up with the clap there," The Tranie squawked. "Hey, you're so hot that I'll get ya bothered for just $8. Can't pass that up."

"No thanks."

The Tranie scowled over-dramatically, flipped the bangs of his auburn wig as if deflecting an insult, pivoted expediently to sashay away twisting his high-heeled ankle, glowered at Benny as if it were his fault, then recommenced his circuit up and down the aisle with a limp. Five minutes later the biker girl inclined toward Benny, just before scratching her crotch like lately business had brought on some unsolicited guests.

"Blow job?" she asked, her mouth so ravaged by cigarettes that she could color a phallus yellow.

"No, thank you," Benny declined, deciding if he should gallop for the exit and call the fire department or was that smell from her.

Without a plot point to validate it, all of the guys on screen moved away from Babette by ten feet. The rest bowed to the Shaven Guy as he rushed back to her. As he pulled up at the target she bent forward, the compilation of her grin and grimace at what was about to occur unveiling her varied personality. The speed with which he fired his entire foot long into her, a feat that nearly elevated her off the ground like a shirt picked up by the pole of a broom, incited Benny and his lack of porno-worldliness to scream out in shock, "Ahhhh!"

"Hey asshole," someone called out from behind him, "no grunting on Venus when you shoot your load". This while Babette goaded on the jackhammer with, "Yes. Yes. Harder. Yes. Harder."

That night Benny phoned me 2 ½ minutes after 10pm. That would've been preposterously and insufferably cruel of him if it were 12 ½ minutes later in that as part of my limp quest to calm my mind I'd begun hitting the hay at exactly 10:15pm.

"Okay, so you went to a porno house and didn't first cover the seats with plastic and some disinfectant like I would've," I commented, intuiting that even though he'd get a first-rate comedy routine out of it, that somehow this aberration augured nothing favorable. "But, what ultimately matters is, how does it all feel?"

"Having schmoes wanking their willies around me?"

"No, being in the big city."

"It's as if college was a fantasyland where I really didn't have to deal with much. Just do your work and not a lot can go wrong."

"Amorphous."

"What?"

"College has a foundation to it. A structure. Post college usually starts out with little shape or form, and we're either going to do what it takes to seek out interesting lives or not," I expounded as if I had any lasting faith that I could heed my own words.

"Yep," Benny said, capped off by a violent jolting crack like the "huh" of football players colliding.

"What was that?" I asked. There was quiet, as if he'd moved away from the phone to recuperate. I began to sweat, concerned that premature heart attacks ran in the extended family we barely knew. "Are you there?"

"Yeah, yeah, I'm here," he replied, feebly.

"What happened, a meteor?" I inquired with a merriment contrived to not sound stricken. It must be noted, that my acting ability is second to everyone's.

"Nothing," he lied. "I, I, it's okay."

A twitch had nearly taken his head off, though he wouldn't admit that until years later. Unnerved, an exchange that unfolded during our last visit to our illustrious family, days before his move to The Big Apple, replayed in my mind. In it we were distributed as usual in the living room, the place where Sergeant Thompson was happiest watching reruns of Marshall Dillon killing an average of one person per the 635 episodes of "Gunsmoke." It wasn't on so Sergeant Thompson stooped to be amused by Benny's narratives and verve. Still, he couldn't resist.

"I think, actually I'm certain, that instead of all of this kid's stuff that ya do, ya should take the civil service tests for police and fire around here, put in your twenty years, secure the basic pension, then go do whatever ya wanna," he opined with a certainty that only the insane should possess.

"You dig Johnny Carson," Benny replied, as implacably as possible. "He pursued his dream."

"You're no Johnny Carson," he said, dismissively. "That's no insult, ya know 'cause Carson'll always be the best."

"Why thank you that out of the purity of your love you decided to lessen the blow."

I looked at our mother for her to intervene. Her silence was overlaid by the cacophony of breathing of such a disparate group.

"Hey, what I'm suggesting is ya can't be the same hyperactive pip galavanting around forever chasing fantasies," Sergeant Thompson added, folding his arms intransigently.

"So true. Wish I'd thought of that," Benny eventually responded, as if unfazed. The second he stood up his pretense faded and he became inert, afire with an urge to volley back. Twitching barely perceptibly, he forced a step forward. "It's amazing that certain religions preach revere your parents no matter what they say or do."

I used to wonder if the Sergeant was afraid of gray areas, to each his own, nuances, slack, exploration that leads to discoveries, as if anything that couldn't be rigidly controlled or understood was too precarious, or did he just downright see and feel in black and white. What he was incapable of getting was that playfulness and a zest for movement, now reconstituted as stand-up comedy and kickboxing, were what Benny had always done, a refinement of his nature into specific skills and goals. Whatever other motivations lay underneath were secondary.

"He's only 22 years old. Does that mean anything to you?" I said, shagging Benny out of the room. Perhaps I was brasher now since I'd inexplicably landed Rose Bush, not yet fully tuned in to my predisposition for squeezing the juice out of the few good things I'd receive. When I set foot downstairs, Benny was on the floor doing what for him was light stretching.

"If only there were some kind of Hazmat suit that I could wear when I check in here," he said.

"You didn't suppose he was going to change, did you?" I asked, loafing near him. "Shit that sounded like a line from a TV movie."

"No. Hey, it's his loss. I'll never invite him to one of my shows and if I fight PKA it won't be with that one in the audience," he downplayed, still feigning unaffected but I could see it, the tightness in the jaw, the lack of blinking. At that moment I realized that each child, even the most self-engendered, is at minimum further emboldened by the support of his parents.

"What's PKA?"

"Professional Kickboxing Association."

"You're considering that?"

"Yep. Shihan thinks I have the talent."

"Which do you prefer comedy or martial arts?"

"They're equal." He spiraled unhurriedly into a full Chinese split.

"Philosophers question if it's worse to have no calling, a la your older brother, or two that compel you so much that you're unsure which one to afford the lion's share of attention. A conundrum. Anyway, a kickboxing comedian, bet there ain't an overload of them. You brother need a moniker."

"The Fighting Punchliner."

"Serious?"

"No. But I am fond of The King of Comekick."

"Serious?"

"No."

He rolled in one motion out of the split onto his back and maneuvered his foot behind his head easier than I could touch my nose with my finger. Of course, admiringly, it was once again a chance for me to indulge my historically unmatched stockpile of jealousies.

---------------------------------+---------------------------------

Other than joining a kickboxing dojo where he trained every day, Benny spent his first month in New York City roaming around taking it all in. He was drawn to the distinct ethnic neighborhoods, those countries within a country where one element mattered most, family. Benny admiring harmonious families. Now and then he'd also still pull out his now withered obituary photo of Esterlie The Fire Girl. For her he'd recently taken a bullet, still with the child-like imaginings of saving someone long ago deceased. Instead of all this unproductiveness, I'd surmised that per usual he'd dive 100% into his goals, attack like a pack of crazed dogs. It's what I wanted him to do. It's what all those who live vicariously through a sibling crave.

In any event, there was also a need for money so he finally got a job as a bar back at Nino's Rock Club in the village, albeit a more raucous one than he preferred. The noise pollution, smoke, and salary only a few dimes above the minimum wage most surely didn't inspire visions of the middle class, at least until one of those shots where somebody's misfortune is another's potential four aces. He was requested to fill in for an accident-prone bartender who'd broken both arms being mowed over by a bike messenger named Oswaldo Octavio Osmelo. The only obstacle was that the other seven bartenders, four guys and three gals, all tortured artists of one kind or another, each with an affinity for displacing blame and downing shots, had long ago organized a theft ring where in concert they filtered off about 15% of each evening's bar sales. Like all prolonged embezzlement the stealth was systematic, drink orders of two or more rung up as one less with the cash from the extra one slipped into the tip jar. The owner, who berated them as if they were stray cats underneath his most recent Mercedes, felt shielded because one of the bartenders was his nephew whom with scathing devotion, he'd bailed out of jail twice, and another was his cousin whom he'd reluctantly bailed out for indecent exposure. Three arrests between them and trust was in the air. In a velvety utopia where family is invariably more important than the redistribution of wealth, he conjectured that they'd keep their unwavering eyes peeled for him.

Benny simply needed to pay his bills. No interest in abetting their conspiracy. Okay, you do that. You be the one holdout. Just do your job dutifully side by side with seven Shiftys who deem you an infiltrator marching too idealistically down their Easy Street. At closing when they'd divvy up the collective cesspool of tips plus shrinkage, they begrudgingly apportioned Benny what they deemed would've been his share had there been no sticky fingers. They rarely spoke to him, on occasion condescendingly attempting to persuade him that the owner deserved the shrinkage seeing that he was such a gay prick who pricked multi-racial ass in the curtained off, insufficiently sound proofed back of his limo while the driver turned the pages of Sports Illustrated up front. The driver's gag reflex was fully compensated for in the form of random bonuses and a persuasive cut of the blow.

Anyway, it wasn't the theft that outraged Benny as much as the seven of them in cahoots, those without conscience capitalizing in another of life's sordid co-dependencies. Then one day the kingpin, John, an actor and frequent mini-brusher of his beard who bragged that he'd banged over 100 women, a wiseacre that shook vending machines to avoid paying, came up behind him. John reminded him of a grease monkey who if he owned a tire shop would spend the pre-dawn hours around the neighborhood drumming up business with an ice pick.

"Hey Benny Boy, we hear you're a kick boxer. I assume you're aware that WE don't give a fuck," he remarked confidently, accompanied by the guffaw of someone who figures that the numbers are on his side. He moved off toward the employee's bathroom with a strut so engineered that even the most hapless street gang would've rejected him. So, attuned to his momentary dominance that he wasn't cognizant of someone stalking him. As he closed the bathroom door Benny barged in, propelling him backwards and affording Benny space to lock the door behind them. This wasn't destined to be a stalemate amongst two windbags, overflowing with the bravado and face saving of pseudo-combatants who really don't have the nerve to fight.

"There is no 'we' John, when your friends aren't with you," Benny stated, smiling at him so warmly that you'd assume he was going to hand him free tickets.

"Hey, what you doing?"

"Here's where this conflict escalates, John. Will you dare to run your potty mouth now?"

"Ah, ah, will I what?" John muttered marshaling whatever spine he could to unzip his pants as if there were no interference at hand to his much-needed piss.

"You seem terrified, John," Benny said, taking a step forward.

“Ah, no, no problem. I’m no problem,” John responded, now the personification of shrinkage.

Benny threw a distraction punch toward the ceiling. It was like a series of blows because the shadows from all directions imitated it. That further immobilized John, allowing Benny to grab him by the beard and wrench him to his knees.

“You don’t even know what the fuck just happened, John,” Benny asserted, the tone more menacing. “That has to be very disconcerting.”

“Yeah,” he stammered, staring at the floor.

Benny jerked that beard upward so that their eyes met, “Ever going to orchestrate a threat again that involves other thieves?”

“Ah, no,” he bawled, wiping away a tear on his sleeve like a schoolgirl. “Never again.”

“That’s good news. So, I won’t hurt you right now, though I’d take pleasure in that. I’m not proud of it, but it’s the plain truth,” Benny said, never breaking the eye contact. “I’ll clear out now and you’re going to lock yourself in here for 15 minutes then crawl back to work inappropriately late, okay?”

“Whatever you say, sir.”

Benny took a few seconds to bask in the moment before remarking, “Wow. You called me, ‘sir’. That’s so delightful, but from here on ‘Benny’ without the ‘Boy’ will suffice.”

Back behind the bar Benny whispered taunts such as, “Sorry to uproot your confidence, John,” and “Going to tell anyone you shed a tear?” Still none of the other pilferers knew why John was as at ease as someone constipated since birth, or why his routine shtick to charm his way into female patron’s pants wasn’t on tap. Benny had no desire to publicly humiliate him. It was more personal by the mere act of keeping it under wraps. When I heard about it, after my concern that he'd been so quick to be violent again, my second thought was "if only I could be half as alarming to such scum," and not just the co-worker who'd slipped this typed note onto my desk, 'You're Fucking Weird. And ditch the corduroys, too. We're all charting which days you wear which color.'

If only Benny's co-workers could've detected that Benny had suffered an excess of off duty police brutality and deemed it wise to not add their straw onto his back. Maybe they wouldn't have instigated a purging. His stealthy visit to the office magnified the owner's disdain for all but one of his employees when a bold, declarative statement was extended as to why hidden cameras were essential. Days later a band of thieves was parading toward the unemployment line and, with effusive gratitude, the owner phoned Benny to set him up to work for his friend's catering company. Benny was now a waiter/performer like countless others in the city. It was also the advent of a new facet, dark, pulsing visions of revenge. It was a year before the fantasies of crossing paths with John dissipated. They'd been prolonged after he'd met a woman who was taking lessons with a one on one acting teacher, "an exceedingly sweet guy who cares about his students," with very low rates likely to make unsuspecting women more pliable. John sure was an opportunist.

A, B, C, D...

Athena, Bianca, Collette, and Dani in that order.

Finally, ready, Benny did his first open mic at The Comedy Cellar in Greenwich Village, five minutes about a dog named, Smig, the only half Chihuahua, half Great Dane ever conceived. Smig, it goes without saying, was small and big. The subtlety yet flare with which Benny discreetly divulged as if it were an illicit affair that he'd only share with this particular audience, how Smig's parents met, their courtship, and the conception kept the audience "howling." The manager accorded him his first paid slot minutes later, and the pattern of female patrons vying for his attention was off and running. On cloud nine for the moment, he was waiting outside the occupied men's bathroom and a young woman named Athena slinked up wearing a tank top so close-fitting that no one would possibly conclude that this girl could fit into anything less than a C cup.

"Smig is small and big! It's the silliest thing I've ever heard. Yet, I couldn't stop laughing," she blurted with an enthusiasm that cloaked her unexamined need to feel superior to most of what mere humans cook up. It was at that moment when intuition told Benny to skedaddle, but the obstinate anxiety he'd suffered since the minute he'd set foot in town, though consistently covered up, fostered a want for distraction and thus an interest in her sassiness and cleavage. Maybe I would've detected that anxiety had I been willing to visit New York, but I'd written that off as too stressful.

"Most of my stuff is more cerebral," he answered, straining to avert his eyes from the tank top and all it partially concealed.

"No bathroom humor?"

"You putting me on the spot?" he replied, pointing at the bathroom. "I'm not a trained seal."

"You know who you remind me of?" she asked, flitting her eyebrows in her trademark fashion. She raised her arms high into the air, a stretch designed to camouflage a brisk sniff of her pits.

"Who? Size me up."

"That class of gentleman who values the stars and baby's expressions."

"That's me and also why I want to stop being a comedian. Not enough babies come to my shows."

"Then consider me very curious."

"That's subtle."

"Who has time for subtle when a delicacy like you comes along?"

A woman came out of the bathroom and held the door for Athena.

"Are you coming to my show tomorrow?" Athena asked him, tantalizingly, yet with that alpha tone of someone who never under any condition wants to be beholden to anyone. Benny had never been down the path of that self-serving "feminist" who, only when there is nothing to lose by doing so, rabidly judges anyone who doesn't advocate that all women should have careers and not merely be vessels for guy's babies.

"You a comedian?"

"Dancer. Modern."

"As long as you're not a comedian, then why not?"

Later he would be able to recount reams of reasons why not, the least of which was....

"Let's cross dress soon," she threw out one night. It translated like an order and was not long enough into their relationship to warrant spicing things up.

"Once or on a daily basis? Because I without question don't have the money to buy a new wardrobe."

"One-time thing."

"A deviation from the norm? Okay, but no photos and no high heels."

Benny's willingness to attempt anything only excluded necrophilia, KKK rallies, and going home with familial merriment for Sergeant Thompson's birthday, so the night for cross dressing soon came. Of course, he made a bit too beautiful of a woman with his long hair tied up, easily shaved face, tasteful makeup that intimated pure class, and long shapely legs. Standing nearly the same height in her work boots Athena held up her part in the duo, Twiggy cut greased back all mafia, filling out Benny's one and only suit with wide shoulders, two balls of muscle from being the dancer who lifted the smaller ones. Strolling along, they weren't only ogled they were envied. This was that magazine cover couple that didn't have to try hard, a quintessential pairing of masculine, feminine and that touch of androgyny.

"No going all bananas if a mischief maker shouts out how hot I am," Benny stressed. "This dress always draws me attention."

"I'll try, it just upsets me, darling."

"Upsets or threatens?" he replied, halting to scrutinize her. "You're more man than that."

Athena had been a local dance star in her town before realizing she wasn't going to succeed as a big city ballerina, so now she kept the clapping hands dream alive in modern dance. She could be seen on the subway reading pop culture magazines or staring bug-eyed into the anonymity that she so feared. Like the majority of other female modern dancers, she'd dated a series of actors, directors, writers, stagehands, and comedians, all excluding Benny who'd pressured her to drum up some audience for their shows, like she did to them. Her number one issue, the concern that her current man had to listen to ad nauseum, is the disturbing and veritably immoral lack of prospects for modern dancers. "The government should fund it because the arts are important, too." He'd go on to realize that there are thousands like her who go on and on, validating their "need" to dance, indiscriminately comparing themselves to other dancers, mired in their most recent startup dance company's internal politics and gossip, looking down on musical theater dancers as loopy sellouts only interested in flash, powerless to discontinue resurrecting the same melancholy after another show got half the audience than anticipated +/or a mediocre review from a bombastic dance critic who was also once a long-suffering, penniless modern dancer, flocking to New York City from all over the continent bright-eyed and bushy tailed not yet aware of the nonstop frustrations in store for them in a career with promise for only the anointed few.

The next month Athena and Benny were in a Cessna 23 preparing to skydive, his idea.

"Have I told you that I'm afraid of heights?" Benny asked above the din of an open hatch door.

"So why pencil in this teeth-rattling idea, you Dumbalina?"

"To face the fear. Why else? Once I jump there's no choice."

She got within an inch of him and stared.

"Why the space invasion, Athena?"

"Analyzing you from awkwardly close like your brother used to because that is f...ing daft. Jump out and it's a long drop before there's nothing to be afraid of."

"That's the point. Then I majorly have to face the fear."

When she was the unending victim of gossip at her waitress job by a waitress/surrealist painter who was on her ninth therapist and fourth abortion, he penned for her this rendition of Nat King Cole's "Unforgettable" to sing to her nemesis…

"How insane are you? I'd like to know.
Bellevue Hospital, it's time to go.
That's where psychiatrists will prescribe for you.
An anti-psychotic, sedatives + some placebo, too.
Maybe a strait jacket. And a lobotomy for you."

Around that time Benny and Athena visited Rose and me at my apartment in Fall River. Benny looked great, ripped and self-possessed. Still, as hot as she was, especially once she removed her fur-lined puffer jacket, I questioned what he was doing with someone this overt, this geared up to debate. They came across more like friends with benefits than a match. In my life it was the most I would ever feel his equal, such was the power afforded by my love for Rose, what a catch all should deem her, and my view of our indivisible future. She and I could work through any setback, including the recent one where she'd arrived five minutes late. She was quick to appreciate why that was unacceptable. How, if I let it slide, would I know that she wasn't unconscious in a ditch somewhere, her car having careened off the road? Translated, how would I know she wasn't delayed by flirting with another man?

We were seated in the living room, three degrees of physical and emotional separation between Benny and Athena, Rose and me always in contact. I was laying claim, proud that I'd found someone so uncomplicated and easy going. Rose was that choice of babysitter whom everyone felt most comfortable employing. And it didn't seem to alarm her when sometimes I'd sit and get up a few times until I'd sat in a way that felt right.

We were eating pizza from a box while Benny was at this point of a story about his recent visit to our parent's house, "And then, oh, darn, I'm struggling with my impulse control now because this is so rich. Can't stop myself. Trying like no tomorrow but I can't. I have to delay your gratification with descriptions of something barely relevant. The weather! Yes, the weather was unseasonably cooperative and the birds were chirping. Chirp. Chirp. Chirp. You could admire Ferd's father pushing his lawnmower along two houses over while Ferd, listening to Atom Ant on his Suburb Blaster, smashed remote control cars into each other wearing duplicate red headbands on his forehead and spindly right thigh, the mesh tank top, and the lop-sided skate boarder haircut of a thirty-year-old who'd also dressed that way a decade before. In other words, encouraged by his doctor's prescription that he exercises more, Ferd's father had taken to heartily cutting the grass, how do I describe it best? Daily."

"Haaaaaaa!" Athena wailed as laughter more appealingly reserved came from Rose. My response was more distracted because I regretted allowing pizza in the living room. No one, other than me, was paying attention to the potential for irremovable oil stains on the furniture. I calmed down, somewhat, once I'd placed towels on different spots as a preventative measure. Rose always seemed unbothered by such behavior, even condoning it with a smile that at the time I'd misread as like-mindedness. The way that Athena made light of it hinted that it was too heavy for her.

On Rose's suggestion we proceeded outside to the courtyard. Unlike most times, I'd agreed to it because it wasn't too hot for me, or cold, or muggy, or smoky. I was losing steam for the out of doors. It wasn't controllable terrain. Fortunately, there was no one else around in that meeting neighbors was also on my swelling list of potential burdens to steer clear of. Before we headed out, I'd rushed to place a coaster under Athena's glass when she put it on an unprotected side table. And, as I did a few times per day, I straightened the 23 books in my library even if nothing more than the Earth's gravitational pull had shifted them less than a millimeter. This time I'd done it because Athena had rifled through a couple and had put them back incorrectly. The nerve of that girl. Couldn't she tell that it was an organized household?

Benny and I sat away from Rose and Athena. The girl talk was so hijacked, and about dance, that at times I mulled over rescuing Rose from it. Of course, it's easy to predict by now that your narrator was as interested in the arts as he was in playing golf in the midday sun of Arizona.

"I have something to show you," I said, secretively. I pulled out a ring box so only Benny could see and opened it to display the engagement ring. His features shifted toward the center disapprovingly.

"She's nineteen, Davey. Not even done with two years of college. What's the rush?"

"No rush. But she's the one. And I can't do better. I don't want to do better because she's perfect for me."

He looked over to where Athena had gotten up to perform for Rose what we thought would be a phrase of dance. His head shook lightly. I wasn't sure if that was about my decision, Athena's behavior, or both.

"Of course, I'll support whatever you choose. But then at least consider something. You have to stop supervising her. And being so anal. Remember that time we arrived at the mall to meet her for a movie. How you'd been so insulted because she'd already chosen the flavor of popcorn without consulting you first. Maybe stuff like that isn't driving her crazy yet, but it might. And if it does the damage will already be too deep."

I knew he was right. Still I wanted to cull through incident after past incident that he'd witnessed to break down the particulars. After all, how about all the good things I'd done, the surprises sprung for, the many admirable ways that I expressed my affection to her?

Rose's dance went on, and on, and on. To calm myself I watched. It was her entire solo from an upcoming concert that exclusively featured pieces that made political statements. This one required her to dance underneath meat hooks hung from the ceiling. Strips of beef were to be attached to them to bewail the inhumane treatment of livestock.

And thus, got cracking Benny's second intimate relationship. She was the one who coached him on how to please a woman, the intricacies of her erogenous spots all the while misperceiving safety by virtue of how inexperienced he was. She relished how he'd gape at certain parts of her like it was an unsurpassed archaeological discovery. The discrimination with which he'd verbally rhapsodized love and someday creating a family grew to be appealingly counterintuitive to the independence that she'd unendingly professed would never be shackled. Perhaps she, and I for that matter, couldn't detect the chasm between Benny's actual availability to love a woman and the starry-eyed vision he'd created. Twice a week together was his max, even though his ultra-supportive role in her rendering of the modern dancer psychodrama could make it seem as if he were eminently and consciously on board. But what floated her boat most, leaps and bounds more than the eight ex-boyfriends for whom contempt had swollen by the day for letting her dominate them with only token resistance, was that he couldn't be pushed around. It was all too clear so the quest was onto dominate without it rankling him.

She also indulged her unreliable ego by deconstructing the other dancers in this the fifth dance company she'd soon be dismissed from for "being difficult". Benny guided her that maybe this was outmoded behavior in compensation for her younger, more accomplished sister, who also happened to be the WTA's 22nd ranked tennis player. He recognized that even a tinge of being on par with her sister through success in dance appeased somewhat her desire to bolster herself by discrediting others, a trait he was trying to help her beyond. His urge to do that flew out the window one afternoon when they were intertwined just a minute after being intimate.

"If instead of me Renee is given the lead in Alterations in a Mind Game, I'm going to be so pissed," she stated. After the initial shock

Benny tried to open his mind, empathetically endeavoring to feel her concerns as she must feel them. But the title "Alterations in a Mind Game," and his imaginings of the staged pantomime of emotion and forlorn reaching to the sky that it would inarguably require, set him to staving off a giggle. "Alterations in a Mind Game! Oh please" he internally lampooned, "there are people living with quiet dignity in mud huts and your galaxy crumbles if you're not the lead in Alterations in A Mind Game?"

It seemed about a century since he'd first set foot in New York. It was only a year. What sprang forth in him was a rose-colored displacement of blame as to why he was increasingly losing steam as a professional comedian with its arbitrary, fickle audiences that he had to jump through hoops to please in ways that the win/lose nexus of professional kickboxing wouldn't require. That displacement was on to Athena. Overlooking the anxiety that pre-dated her, in his mind it was primarily her who'd been sapping his durability of late. She'd taken his eye off the prize. It culminated in a flash of relief, a cleansing breath precipitated by thoughts of a quick escape when he realized that she could be just a hazy memory not long from now. He knew that before she could attempt again to solidify her role in his life with her last-gasp promises to change, that he could simply flee. It was empowering, as it might be to anyone not yet jaded by a series of breakups and new beginnings. And he decided that it would be easy to do because in some ways, one too many, she reminded him of our father.

The next day from Larry's apartment, hot chocolate in hand to sweeten the distaste for what he had to do, Benny called to tell her that she wasn't the one for him and got off the phone straightaway. Larry had moved to NYC after staying in Boston for an extra year to complete a Master's in molecular biology. What a pity that recruiters from Lehman Brothers swept up MIT brainiacs supplanting dreams of science, entrepreneurship, or the CIA with six figure seductions.

"What's wrong with you?" Larry drilled petulantly.

"What?"

"What is wrong with you???"

"Should I have spent an hour giving her a one-sided version of how she messed up?"

"What type of man doesn't keep his squeeze around until the next one is in place? So vexing."

Benny was much too virtuous for the kind of pretenses that would've kept her legs open. Unlike his older brother, who'd also just hatched the lurid and preposterous scheme to move to Los Angeles in pursuit of my now ex-girlfriend, Rose Bush. You know that it doesn't bode well for your marriage plans when, down on one knee, engagement ring extended toward her, the girl of your dreams breaks down crying and scoots out the door planning to never lay eyes you again. In a flash she'd absconded leaving only a let me down softly hand-written note. Three thousand miles away just to dodge me.

Yep, she dumped me, ridding her of my arbitrary rightness, increasing phobias, flight from freedom, bitter envy, and lack of interest in 99.9 % of the people, places, and things on Earth. Everything had to be my way, well, say, also akin to daddy. Oh, the histrionics a rigid personality can devise, the shortsighted justifications, the use of withdrawal like a hammer to pound at an ingenuous woman's autonomy. Sure, my father and Benny were both alpha males. And, my mother and I weren't exactly go-getters. But the wretched fact is that Athena and I were imponderably more comparable to daddy than Benny was. We cherished unchangeableness like free spirit Benny might cherish the open road.

Still, how naïve of Rose Bush to presume that I'd simply let go. What in her experiences with me led her to conjecture that I wouldn't bend over backwards to unearth her destination? I found out all right. Her new game plan of completing her undergraduate at UCLA minus her one and only albatross might entail a little more gazing over her shoulder. I wasn't going to let that thick chest, those legs strapping enough to squat two of me, a tiny waist curving out like the proverbial hour glass, that jackpot of natural muscle unerringly hidden under the most innocuous dress to lessen my blink of an eye jealousy, just depart clandestinely and let the memory of me fade if ample changes of season really can heal such a wound. This assistant to the assistant human resources manager wasn't going to take that sophomore's virginity, and take it on so many other levels also, and be left with only photos of that bare body in the positions of my choosing. No, she was mine. That neophyte's previous unwillingness to upset the apple cart therein doing whatever I desired in bed had more chapters ahead. All I had to do was excuse my past transgressions with "I was my father's kid" once I accidentally on purpose ran into her at UCLA, fabricate heartfelt and breathtaking assurances that it would now all be different, never sounding desperate, and we'd live happily ever after.

I herein implore my millions and millions of readers to have patience with the previous paragraph's objectification of Rose Bush. I don't want to come across as unlikeable. I just wanted to expose that the magnitude of my hots for her augmented my bounteous love.

The night of his breakup when Benny lay in bed there was a quaint curiosity as to why in the first place he'd gone against intuition, but no wistful need to stay in touch with Athena. A synthesis of reclaimed independence and his recent detachment left him uncomfortable, so he couldn't fall asleep. What compounded it was the advent of a more insidious guilt, because like Toni in college, and more so our mother when she'd refused to move away with him, he felt that he'd abandoned Athena. This was tantamount to doing to them what he would never want done to himself. He couldn't yet perceive that he was a child of abandonment, though by parents who'd been physically present, and that repressed factor was a driving force in his guilt.

For grounding he envisioned something positive, and soothing, his old friend Jeff in Boston, now 88 years old and feeling better than he had in a decade, and how they'd be reunited soon.

He Could Take It

On route to our parent's house for July 4th in a car loaned to him by an adoring student from the weekly karate class he now led, Benny detoured for an unscheduled visit with Jeff at the Old's Folks Home. He jumped around outside the building like a kick boxer ready to tackle the opponent of his dreams, incognizant of the passersby digging through wind cold enough to keep an Eskimo igloo bound. He had metropolitan adventures to relate, a variety of which were about his days exploring neighborhoods that Jeff had once patrolled as a cop. Jeff had a memory for details and by phone sent Benny in search of this particular piece of graffiti shaped like Big Foot swinging a sand wedge, and the blind lady who sang Irish tunes on the corner in Bensonhurst, an all Italian neighborhood. Benny was still bouncing when he approached the Security Guard, a scabby old relic who later let slip out that he hoped to quit working there soon and become a tenant.

"Hi, I'm here to surprise my friend, Jeff Houghtman," Benny stated grinning ear to ear. "I worked this shift here until eighteen months ago. That's when I last saw him. See, even scratched our names onto the inside of the desk."

"He sure boasted about you a lot."

"Cool."

"But sorry, young man, and, well, no ya can't see him no more because, well, ah, it's ah, because Jeff didn't wake up from sleep a couple'a days back."

It was like diving into a hornet's nest, stings high, low, and everywhere in between. The man who confirmed for Benny that his innate joy was a blessing by still being ebullient at such an advanced age, who found felicity in cradling a sensation one more time than society reckons a dirty old man should, and cried watching a puppy out for its first stroll in the vast matrix it would only observe from a dog's POV, had gone away without saying goodbye. He hadn't been a mentor brimming with wisdom guiding Benny to each sign post along the way, just a friend for all times who delighted in who Benny was, that fellow traveler adept at creating harmless memories.

Benny fought to rhythmically regulate his breathing through his nose, like untold days with mouth guard inserted and punches flying at his face had disciplined him. Faint, he outstretched for a wall that wasn't there, tumbling a couple of feet to the left before reaching it and sliding onto the floor. The Security Guard was so rattled that he instinctively reached for his Star War's lunch box, took out a baggie-clad sandwich and murmured, "Peanut butter and jelly?"

"Ah, ah…."

"Maybe you're needing you some fuel. I've read me about blood sugar lately."

Benny couldn't absorb his words, and even if he had, a momentary paralysis would've disallowed any response. After scratching his scalp to spur some alertness, he said a bit too softly, "Ah, sir".

"Whadyasay?"

"Sir, please, I know we've never met and this is so against the rules. But may I go sit in silence outside of Jeff's door?" Benny entreated. He stood up unsteadily ready to accept refusal with grace.

The Security Guard pondered and replied, "Well ah no, sorry, young man, ah, no doin' that 'cause, ah, well, ah, 'cause ya're goin inside." He extracted some keys from a drawer. "Be sure to close the door behind ya so no one sees ya."

"Thank you," Benny said, taking the keys and backing out of the office. To avoid being observed he mounted the seven flights, never feeling the stairs beneath him. The familiar purr of Jeff's door being opened, and a remembrance of Jeff's arthritic hand unlocking it, elicited a smile. He crossed the threshold of the apartment lingeringly, with such reverence, hyper-aware, savoring so it would remain internalized. Nothing had been altered inside Jeff's final home, as if the world were paying homage to a well-lived journey by letting things sit for a bit. Or the management had anticipated that Benny would pop in to pay his respects before out with the old and in with the old.

Benny stared at a framed photo on the end table of Jeff as a young cop, the trademark self-amused grin staring back at him. He meandered around surveying everything, the closets overfilled with threadbare clothes, a wizened old man's final possessions. He even opened the refrigerator to check what was in there on the day that time walked away from Jeff. He pulled out two Schlitz beers, Jeff's favorite, opened them, tapped them together in a toast like they used to, and placed one on the end table near the couch where he'd always sat. He rolled the wheelchair near the couch, fit the other beer into its beer holder, picked up Jeff's cop photo again, kissed it, and placed it on the wheelchair's seat. Plunked down on the couch, he took a sip from his beer as reflections of Jeff emancipated the tears from where they'd wanted to escape since he'd first heard the news.

Days later we were all at the kitchen table on Christmas night with Benny scheduled to drive back to NYC the next day. Our mother had a shiner from where she'd banged into the kitchen cabinet. Eddie, the household cat abandoned by our foreclosed neighbors, was chasing a fly. The obligatory "dumb animal," therefore innocent of all wrongdoing, loved unconditionally by Sergeant Thompson, cute no matter what he did, pissing in every corner of the rug to mark his territory, shattering knickknack gnome, lugging the carcass of his sparrow overkill into their bed, mauling her diaphragm and leaving it like a beached jellyfish on the patio.

I'd moved back from Los Angeles to the same apartment in Fall River, same plain furniture, same 23 books lined up perfectly and as dust free as possible. No one with less than nine screws loose would be thunderstruck that my scheme to hook back Rose Bush didn't end up with us skipping along the decades to our golden anniversary blissfully holding hands and calling each other Snuggles and Davey Bear. The horror when she saw me "accidentally" passing her on UCLA's campus, me donning a look of astonishment about the extraordinary "coincidence" that we were matriculated at the same distant college. What are the odds of that? She was now a junior and I, a counterfeit grad student. The horror couldn't have been worse had I been lobbing hand grenades while calling out, "catch."

"Please, please, I'm begging you to leave me alone. Let me have my life," she implored, straining to not reveal disgust, but the eyes of such an incorruptible creature never lie. Seconds later I somehow managed, I don't know how, to shuffle away abjectly, destined to live my secret obsession in private, a desire to redraft history and blame our demise on her also perpetually festering within me. Though I would, as a distortion in my vision of decorum again took hold, and kindled by writing this chapter, mail her a "the past is the past" letter thirty years later craving that we'd reunite. Lo and behold she didn't respond. She doesn't realize what she's missing. We could share my habit of checking four times before bed that the front door is securely locked. Please keep in mind that FOUR is my magical number.

Each day I lived my obsession about her, skewered by the foreboding that I'd never have an opportunity like that again and that in days to come it would all be settling for pickings not in the ballpark of comparable. I wallowed in "what could have been" simplifications. "She and I would've been an ideal match, if only I'd been more patient." "Her parents must've plotted against me."

"And that's when I knew I could take it," Benny emphasized, capping off a story that Jeff had once told him. Our mother and I laughed because it was damn funny, while Sergeant Thompson deigned to raise his eyebrows like it wasn't half bad. From the stilted cadence of Benny's words, even though the attempt to bring some levity into our mother's bleak existence was so hard-wired, I could detect that he was forcing it. So, when it exploded, the next words that filled the room, it was so out of place I concluded that Sergeant Thompson, salivating, had been storing this one up for a while.

"Speaking of 'taking it'. Ya might not know it, but I was tougher on you 'cause I knew that you could take it," he let loose in an informational tone that masters of the straight face might employ. But he wasn't joking.

Benny gripped up and closed his eyes flipping an emergency switch inside of himself to forestall any reaction. When he opened them all at once he saw everything in the room, the microwave oven, potholders, Eddie licking his paw, a spider climbing up the refrigerator, the other three of us, like a snapshot that if studied could never be as mundane as it appeared. If only he could've achieved the pristine state he aspired to, impenetrable, liberating indifference to that one's onslaughts. He stared at his plate shaking barely perceptibly. Why at that moment did my endless companion and view of life on this planet, those words, "Cumulative Effect," though they had never previously when it came to Benny, flash briefly in my mind? A premonition?

"Is that, like, supposed to be some sort of peace offering?" Benny stammered.

"Just a statement of fact."

"Now? Now, you. The day after I informed you that one of my best friends died. You deploy such a pitiful excuse when you can see that I'm still grieving."

"Are you? People who are grieving deeply don't tell stories about taking someone's hamburger."

"What makes that an absolute. Because you say so?"

"I'm just trying to let you know. No big deal."

"I get the fact that you live in an alternate reality from the rest of us. Even so, are you that monstrously limited?"

"I'm satisfied with who I am," he replied. He picked up the ladle to scoop au gratins. I gestured to Benny that we should head to the cellar. As we picked up our plates we heard, "Can ya say the same about yourself?"

Benny got up with an unsettlingly black look. He walked to tower over Sergeant Thompson. "Ever since I taught your ass that you'd never be violent with us again, all you've been is a three-trick pony. You judge. You give quarter smiles as if you're holding back a judgment. And you stay in a very closed world where no one challenges you."

A collision of grimaces and pouting betrayed that the Sergeant wanted to retaliate. Either he didn't feel safe enough, or couldn't whip up a response that would not illustrate Benny's thesis. Benny stomped off to the cellar after discarding his half full plate into the sink. The three of us who remained idled silently while I watched our mother prematurely wither away. Still she said nothing. Instead, she relocated her peas with a fork.

"In the arena of fatherhood, again you come in last," I retorted brusquely, dumped my half full plate into the sink, and like a hellish ritual followed Benny downstairs making sure to add, "Are you rigging it that we don't visit here again?"

At midnight, when I assumed, we were all in bed, I was lying in my former bedroom calculating how many total hours of sleep our father had cost Benny and me since day one. Though the lights were off, the shades were still up for the assuaging effect of street lamps and stars. Each day of trauma, external and internal, had made unmitigated darkness more terrifying. And thus, even the trance-like silhouette Benny created in the relative obscurity of my doorway was intimidating. The backpack worn conveyed that he was shipping off without any parental goodbyes. His movements were mechanical, as if all the guilelessness that was his genetically was being progressively siphoned off. Though soon I would be misled to suspect otherwise when he reasserted his pattern of filling me in on only the good stuff. His Teflon persona.

"How'd she really get that shiner?" he asked, as quietly deadly as a seasoned assassin who'd sealed all means of escape.

"She alleges smacking into the cabinet," I replied, a rogue impulse to ameliorate Benny's demoralization by awakening Sergeant Thompson with a scalding brew competing with my fear of closed spaces like prison cells and coffins.

"Mmmmm. Fucking better be," he warned, pivoting to leave.

"One second," I said, using a dramatic pause to augment the tension. "You realize that father's statement, 'I was tougher on you 'cause I knew you could take it'. No chance that was a slippery apology or some short walk down a soon-to-be forgotten road of regret."

"I know. I know what his little gambit was about," he stated as he backed away. "It's about mother!"

We both recognized that Sergeant Thompson's statement had been a machination to further muddle our mother's brain. A twisted, circuitous peace offering in the guise of a compliment to her youngest, all designed to diminish her mounting sadness at whatever other abuse she'd endured lately.

As Benny tiptoed off, I sat up. Soon I felt him re-enter my room spectrally. He was much younger and carrying two teams of Skelathletes, The Boston Bonesmen and Detroit Deadies, as curious as to which team would pull out the victory as I was. I saw myself tag after him down the hallway and into our room in Brickenwood where I perched off to the side, a glowing witness to purity. Nothing else mattered, just the Skelathletes, the game, and the inviolable moment at hand.

Fidgeting like a speed baller panic-stricken for a fix, Benny drove the four hours back to New York City not to be seen by our parents for 500+ days, the brain tattoo he'd received replaying in his mind. "I was tougher on you 'cause I knew you could take it." As he entered his apartment, without delay he felt entombed. He snapped up two blankets and skulked upstairs to spend the pre-dawn on the roof shivering under those blankets, holding on for sunrise to bring a fresh start. But the sun came up all steel wool, scraping off more layers of his stability. Time after time Angelica Movie Theatre in The East Village had been a place where he rested and escaped to the otherness of foreign films, so he headed there in the subway, but when his stop came so did the heebie-jeebies about movie theater darkness so he rode by it. Eight hours later he got off that subway car seat to trudge to The Comedy Cellar where he was now a regular, as revved to do his set as he would've been to have his appendix removed sans anesthesia, doctor, and appendicitis.

The MC, with a cigarette in one hand and a double whiskey in the other, warmed up the audience with the scripted to seem impromptu insult humor regurgitated nightly. Benny parked in the corner waiting to go on, morose and a bit unhinged, scraping to psych himself up. He swept the faces in need of entertainment and hoped that there wasn't a heckler there, that half-wit three drinks toward blocking out his frustration by spewing inanities and tittering as if they were witty. He peered at the comedian slouching in the corner chain smoking and saucing himself up to smooth the approach for his set, a huffy misogynist who too often pried Benny about his past, and, though in his forties, too this date couldn't fall asleep without at least masturbating. The brotherhood of comedians, peddling their neuroses like a kind of therapy, while Benny's humor never dredged up his history. He scanned the waitresses balancing their drink trays, fake laughing at a punch line that they'd heard the MC deliver repeatedly, a laugh track prescribed as part of the job description by the craggy, unkempt manager who still longed for the good old days when comedy "broke ground and redefined life." Then Benny bored into himself in the mirror inches to his right for a few minutes, blinking so torpidly that the muscles involved felt overworked.

"And now let's bring up our first comedian. He's been knocking them dead here for months and everybody loves him. A future headliner if ever I've seen one. Benny Thompson!"

Into the Abyss

Bianca

"Mister," Bianca said shyly, behind him on line at Veniero's Bakery. She was wearing a white crop top t-shirt with a picture of a smiling sun on the front and embroidered jeans.

Benny turned and was startled by her bewitching face, bronze skin with aquamarine eyes, and that a woman his age was calling him "Mister."

"Hi," he replied. The lethargy that had hindered him for months instantaneously retreated.

"I was at your show at the Comedy Cellar about two weeks ago. You're the best," she said with a please don't hurt me smile.

"Why, thank you. And what do you do?"

"I, and I know there are a lot of us in this city but, I'm a moderrn dancer," she answered, self-deprecatingly.

"Oh, cool," he responded, stifling all detectable signs to the contrary by fending off a twitch. "Are you with a dance company now?"

"The Kali Dance Company. I've been with them for four years straight out of college."

"There's a deviation. Stability in dance."

"Oh yes, they're like family to me."
"And not one where dancers bail out left and right?"

"Oh no. There sure is turnover but Kali is great. She's like the mother I never had. I was reared Mormon by my father after our mother abruptly left you see, so it was a titanic shakeup venturing here to dance."

Like déjà modern dancer vu that's when intuition recommended that he make a quick exit. But her sweetness, and how 180 degrees the opposite she was from Athena, and those abs so washboard that they reshaped her shirt, made him need to comfort himself in light of a ballooning though unspoken anxiety that left him wanting to keep throwing punches when aggravating opponents were down at the dojo, and at hecklers, subway conductors who grin when closing doors in passenger's faces, and his neighbor in the rooming house who'd ear-splittingly mangled the songs from "Fiddler On The Roof" every night forcing Benny to seek new shelter. So he capitulated to her demureness, and how that went away in bed replaced by elation at causing him pleasure so slowly, mission statement I'm fully here, in every way exposed, as wide open as any man could ever desire with the sinewy flexibility to achieve that, look me in the eye while I do this until you explode, as if she didn't have a record of moving emotionally toward men who after the conquest move emotionally away from women.

I'd painstakingly prepared before Benny knocked on my door four months into their union. The intermittent rain meant that they could be wet, which could escalate to water on the floor, or worse, on the furniture. The throw blankets that were usually put on to protect the couch and chairs on those rare times I had guests, were scrapped for the enveloping plastic covers that I always used if just I, or Helen and I, were there. Runners and mats were strategically placed. Those could also limit scuffs, rug wear and tear, and that demoralizing static electricity sound if Bianca happened to sport nylons. I'd also learned my lesson and no longer served anything that could cause more damage than crumbs. Anything that could clog up drains, like dental floss or paper towels, was removed. Breakables were placed out of harm's way. The window locks were snapped on so no one would raise them high, sit in the windowsill clumsily, lean back, and tumble out the two feet they would plummet before landing on the grass. Even if unharmed, they could inadvertently pull out the screen when flailing during their descent. Multiple other levels of child proofing were employed to guard against incautious adults.

Helen and I had been an item for a few months also while a series of other less than impressive women hadn't taken me up on the offer of a second date, or, in too many cases, a first one. She had an ungifted beautician's version of a Farrah Fawcett haircut and too often wore high-waisted loose pants with anything polyester above it. That eerie hint of facial distortion from the cerebral palsy she'd been afflicted with since birth meant that I'd regressed back to the category of holdover chic. She lounged on the couch sipping a mixture of teas that were prescribed by some overpriced quack to take the edge off of her condition.

Benny and Bianca entered holding hands. There was a stronghold of warmth between them that I hadn't seen with Athena. Once again Benny looked in top form, his declarative level of fitness making him appear taller. Per request they removed their shoes. I wiped them down thoroughly before lining them up with the others near the entrance. The umbrellas were placed in the sink and the two drops of water on the floor pounced upon. I toured them around affording them the rare pleasure of beholding my new purchases, a bedspread with the picture of a lion on it and a poster of the gold medal "Do you believe in miracles?" hockey team. Bianca could've taught him a thing or two on how to pretend to be impressed.

In no time I was such a fan of her unassuming vibe that it didn't fit with the questionable side of her Benny had relayed to me. The scholarly modern dancer type, she could be seen on the subway reading classics and the books nominated for the elite awards. She'd attended a junior ivy league college, Williams, and claimed to have passed on Yale because it was too big for her. Futilely endeavoring to appear unaffected by egomaniacal choreographers who use praise and slights interchangeably, she had a history of exchanging this one exaggeration with other "creative types" also obtainable for a self-affirming one-night stand, "I love what I do so much that I don't care if I'm paid for it." For all the blood, sweat, tears, and bitter pills.

We sat on the couch near our partners. Well he sat. I sat, got up, sat, got up, and finally stayed seated once it felt right. That behavior made me think "sick" to myself, so I had to internalize four times…"Healthy." "Healthy." "Healthy." "Healthy." Please recall that four is my magical number and align that with how often disconcerting words had to be smothered by The Illusory Power of Positive Thinking.

An hour into the conversation Benny said, "'I'm all ears.' I don't think our father knows the word, *listen*. If somebody wanted to tell him something, it's always, 'I'm all ears.'"

"My father never rests. He 'cools his heels,'" Helen let out.

"Oh my, that one gets me," Bianca kept it going. "My father uses that all the time. Especially once he's completed 'the whole kit and caboodle.'"

Everyone laughed.

"Here's one they all use," I said. "If someone isn't doing something quickly enough it's because he's 'taking his own sweet time.'"

"According to my father, I was always 'taking my own sweet time,' especially in the bathroom," Bianca seconded.

"How many times did I hear that one!" Benny tripled. "Especially when I wasn't trying to 'get my two cents in.'"

"Behind closed doors our mother referred to certain women as 'hot to trot,'" Helen switched to.

"'On the prowl,'" Bianca added.

"'Been around the block,'" Benny said.

"'Footloose and fancy free,'" I capped it off.

"My father was always talking about guys with, 'chips on their shoulders,'" Bianca moaned.

"Which could be true even if someone's 'a stick in the mud,'" Benny amended.

"Or tired of this 'dog and pony show,'" I piped in.

"Or from 'my neck of the woods,'" Bianca drawled.

"I think those clichés are part of the pre-television generations," Benny said. "Like a sign of snappiness. The more of those expressions one employed the better their language acumen."

"And how about how our Grandmother sums everything up with little adages." I noted.

"She repeats them again and again," Benny explained. "Relies on them so much that I took her as small-minded."

"A dullard," I said.

"Now I see that if we all stored those little adages in the front of our minds, we'd be better off."

"List one," Helen said.

"Let's see. One of her regulars. 'When somebody shows you who they really are, believe it.'"

"Oh, I like that one," Bianca said.

Benny pointed at her. I took that as an indicator of them being on the same page. But she gripped up, as if Benny had thrown her a zinger stemming from recent tensions.

"Even if someone tries to trick or seduce you, who he really is always shines through eventually," Helen made clear.

"Always," underscored Bianca. Her eyes flashed at Benny. Seemed to me that she was countering by expressing a minor letdown of her own. Beats me at the time what that could've been given his determination to keep up the steadfast front for me.

"But we usually hope that the relationship will go back to how it started," Helen said. "That's the spider web."

It felt like she was talking about me so I clammed up. The next morning after she'd left, and once I'd faced off with all the germs that might've been left behind, I sculpted out how to reincorporate some of our initial newness. A pretense of spontaneity was also scripted for that weekend.

Even if there was a gripe or two, it was refreshing to Bianca that Benny wasn't verbally abusive like her father and a succession of boyfriends had been. She'd tired of striving to change those ex-flames. Used to be that if the appearance of change came her way, temporary as it always was, she would misinterpret it as proof of her worthiness to be loved, further finagling their drive to transform by doing anything sexual on request. All of which just days before she'd somberly confessed to Benny in a diversion tactic disguised as an idealistic passion to bond more intricately through unswerving honesty. Too bad she'd also introduced a pattern long ago in which supernormal sexual skill, aim to please, take care of your man so his eyes don't roam, her simulation of organic commitment, a love so strong that it would elicit even her staunchly Mormon father's approval, stayed the modus operandi only for the first few months of a relationship, to be ousted by random, though never loud or in public, weeping fits with no captions attached other than to blame it on hormones. The use of sex, the boohooing, the scripted recessiveness, in too many ways she reminded him of our mother.

Lying in bed five months into their relationship, the distaste for potentially abandoning Bianca escalating, one of those occurrences from Brickenwood that Benny never forgot began replaying in his mind, causing him to sweat and cover his mouth as if that would temper his breathing. Again it came in slow motion, from onset to conclusion....At age eight, Arthur Telson was the scruffiest of the four Telson boys, the older three having previously donned handcuffs. His scowl was irrepressible, as if he popped out of his mother, registered his odds as the youngest of seven in a three-bedroom crammed with the stuff the neighbors left by the roadside for collection, and scheduled his first smile for his mid-thirties. The same age, Duane Jackson was reserved and more to himself, like he was going to prance through life with only one hangover on his record of self-infliction. Despite that, he'd grown so exasperated by Arthur's bullying that in his first fight he simply overpowered him. Now and then unexpressed genetic strength rewards bravado with a beat down.

Arthur was pinned down, as unable to extricate himself as a newborn. He cried and begged the fifth time Duane punched the right side of his face whipping it violently to the left. All, other than Benny, of the twenty plus kids surrounding them chanted, "Punch him again," as enlivened as stray dogs in a kennel when the food bowls are coming. Duane glanced up at them, cackled, clutched Arthur's chin as gently as fine glass to turn it toward the blue, open sky, and punched it left again. At one point, with the swelling mounting and blood obscuring his voice, Arthur pleaded "But it hurts. It really hurts!" Duane's response, "Why else would I be doing it?" which though in view of the context made sense, had an alluring, salesman quality to it. He was now the Master Of Ceremonies giving the rabble what they wanted and their thumbs were pointing down.

The joyous faces cut through every inch of Benny. He called out, "He's had enough," and started trying to drag Arthur out of harm's way, even though he didn't like him one bit. A 13-year-old, fifth grader happiest in a mob mentality and also wearing plaid pants with the cuffs cut off unevenly, threw Benny back and barked, "Mind your own Business." Benny's eyes canvassed for his friends. None were there so despite the familiar powerlessness, he charged forward again anyway. As he grabbed at Duane, all he heard was "fuck off Thompson" and was launched a few feet onto his back. Fortunately, someone must have knocked on their door because the Telson boys and their interchangeable parts, The Spanglers, came charging up scattering the kids. A Telson wearing only boxer shorts and black socks yanked Duane off, smacked him twice and sent him off with a kick in the pants. They formed an impassable periphery around Arthur, while Kenny distributed milk bottles as weapons. They picked Arthur up, but put him down when they realized that he was barely conscious. A Spangler clumped over to Benny to stress, "scram." That's when Benny spotted the Louisville Slugger so he also high-tailed it.

With Bianca asleep nearby this memory of Arthur replayed again, creeping up from under the covers, up his leg, then torso, into his brain like an infection. It so overtook him that he crawled away from it and ended up falling onto the floor.

"What's going on?" Bianca asked, putting on a night-light and opening one eye.

"Sorry," he replied. He didn't want to be a burden.

"You know I must have eight hours sleep," she whined oh so sweetly, flicked off the light, and rolled back over. Not a word inquiring if he was okay, just an anal need to be rested up for rehearsal for an arcane dance troupe that she'd also recently determined was beneath her.

As he got up it came again, *"But it hurts. It really hurts!" and Duane's response, "Why else would I be doing it?"* He immediately had to settle back on the floor, similar to that squally Tuesday when he'd been concussed at the dojo by a savage kick and some unknowable wherewithal informed him to get down before his rubber legs succumbed toppling him face first. There he was, certain that the room was spinning but it was too dark to be sure, the words replaying like an indoctrination tape, *"But it hurts. It really hurts!" "Why else would I be doing it?" "But it hurts. It really hurts!"*

"Why else would I be doing it?" "But it hurts. It really hurts!" "I was tougher on you 'cause I knew you could take it."

He speculated if this episode was attached to it having been his final show as a comedian, as if a sense of loss had elicited an unrelated panic. He'd enjoyed writing comedy and had a blast during the shows, but everything else, traveling to club dates, all the judgment and repetitive praise, the misapprehension that the lifestyle might be, at least partially, the fuel for his present disinterest in searching out real love, and uncertainty as to why he was so often secretly doleful in a way that no amount of busyness could rectify, all combined with a burgeoning drive to be away from people more, so unlike the easygoing nomad from eons ago. Though his last stand up bit about a guy with six personalities, all who were bisexual, and how Benny alternated between all six voices mannerisms included, maneuvering to seduce this and that couple in the room for a ménage a huit, was his best ever.

Minutes later a similar feeling of impotence cropped up with the recollection of our mother's insistence that her shiner had been self-induced. As it moved toward anger, his nostrils flared. Itching to walk out on Bianca right now and never look back, an opposing urge pressured him to crawl around the bed and kneel next to where she slept. He could hear the trim rasp of her breathing, which soothed him somewhat each time the impulse to grab her by the hair and drag her off the bed rose up. His right hand was shaking so he balled it into a fist, a weapon he promptly realized so he opened it super widely to receive the full load of shame such new impulses induced in him. He lay back on the floor beside the bed and allowed the black coffee darkness of the room to envelope him. A faint temptation to kiss her nipples once more prior to hitting the road dissolved into those durations when, as a boy, he'd lay in the dark engulfed in the self-satisfaction of being. It was the first glimpse that there was some degree of lost self he'd pined to recapture.

The next day when he briefed Bianca about what had knocked him to the floor, she pretended to care. It was all show. She just wanted him to be fun, both of them to be amazed by the sexual voraciousness she was planning to reinstitute, and for her to get a grip on her chagrin that she could no longer boast that her boyfriend was a popular comedian. An initial attraction by two people who weren't presently capable of a sustainable partnership had metastasized into something that poured salt on Benny's ever-increasing inner wound. So, he would again opt for the illusory remedy of a spell on one's own, but not until he'd urged Hector, of "Hector's One Man, One Van Moving Service" to cut out making sexual innuendo about Bianca in Spanish to his assistant the day they all relocated her from one ratty sublet to another. She favored her pale-eyed, Irish mother more than her Peruvian father. Hector didn't yet know that her last name was Vasquez and she was 100% fluent.

"What are you going to do about it?" Hector pushed back, his sham confidence as secure as the safety pin fastening where his increasing girth had snapped off some buttons.

"Don't talk tough, Hector. You can never predict what skills somebody else might have," Benny replied as unflappable as a wishing well before the pebbles are dropped in. He had a thing to prove about how women should be treated. Hector chortled, a tempered charade for the benefit of his whipping boy employee while making sure to not escalate.

Not long after Benny was lolling in one of the five black felt beanbag chairs spread out in a square getting to know his downstairs neighbor Roise Guce (name too unsettlingly similar to Rose Bush). To avoid her trying to draw him back in, Benny hadn't informed Bianca of his move to Long Island City. Larry, Roise, and Roise's aging bloodhound and I occupied the other beanbags, the bloodhound sitting up more like King Tut than the others. Crates with thousands of albums, a stereo on cinder blocks, a war chest with two padlocks on it, and a wicker chair land-mined with so many protruding breaks in it that it was only good for causing puncture wounds, rounded out the décor. The bachelor pad of an anachronistic former hippie for whom this number of possessions was another tainted concession to his parent's materialistic wishes that had also included him becoming a dentist.

Yes, I'd at last made an appearance in New York. Helen had sent me a Dear John letter once I'd mentioned Rose Bush too often, so thus came my first trip to the big city and I hated it. All of those rancorous, frustrated people milling about, competing to be the coolest. Still I'd set foot there to make it official. Etch it in stone. Like I could actually adhere to it, finally announce that I was 100% positioned to mentally let go of Rose Bush. Though I wasn't yet ready to publicize my unparalleled seduction of stenographer Petra whom I'd confound over years into believing that she was heaps sicker than she was, empirically proven to need me to steer her clear of germs, pollution, food poisoning, stress, stress, stress, and so much more.

"So, I told her, you're not the kind of woman I'd want to anesthetize before the pants fly off," said Roise, stoically.

"I'll bet you said that to all of your young female patients," commented Benny.

"Only if they're anesthetized."

Larry and Benny fell off laughing leaving Roise with the bulging eyes of someone affecting surprise that they'd deemed that humorous. As they calmed down the bloodhound howled like a teakettle setting them off once more.

"In the pantheon of fucked up Jews like me, you take the babka!" spouted Larry.

"You gotta be a Jew to be a fucked-up Jew," Roise said.

"There goes my theory that it takes one to know one."

"Nonetheless, they shouldn't have revoked my license to practice the art of dentistry just because I was overly flirtatious. Oh, fuck them. I like being a mailman better anyway. And my therapist sure prefers my mailman problems over my dentist problems."

"So then has he lowered the price?" asked Benny.

"My brother doesn't charge me."

Benny and Larry rolled around aflame again, now accompanied by the bloodhound's howl. Though the legitimate reason remained unpublicized, Roise had lost his license to practice dentistry after only a year, a license garnered at age 41. The good news was that he couldn't do much harm by returning to postal work, other than discarding all of the Sears Catalogues meant for delivery, an overreaction to a beef with them that dated back to childhood. Grudges were his specialty, compounded by an underlying fury at having been born with his eyes almost parallel to his nostrils.

Unbeknownst to me it was the first time Benny had been gleeful in weeks. I chalked up the hint of sorrow to his split with Bianca, and because Romeo the pillow had been swiped during his move, the latter a biting loss even though for years it hadn't served in the role of sounding board. No doubt the porter from his recent sublet had taken it. That shifty bag of fake smiles and greetings with ten kids by nine barely distinguishable women, none of who would've married him anyway so as to not lose their entitlements, secreted off one of Benny's moving boxes when eyes were averted. Romeo was in it. The next day Benny visited that porter and non-violently asked for it. Liars' expressions unveil their guilt for the brief second that someone of Benny's background can't miss. Though he couldn't prove it, so he'd let the porter squirm at the deadly eye contact before walking off.

--------------------------------+--------------------------------

Benny's daily four-mile run completed, a more arduous, coerced trek than it ever used to be, he and I proceeded into Manhattan for training for his first professional bout as a kick boxer. As we rambled along the East Village the neighborhood spandex-clad juggler on a unicycle zoomed past, whistle in his mouth blowing maniacally his

God given right of way. Two shirtless alkies, one white, one black, with shopping carts full of returnable bottles, argued over who'd first gotten to a garbage can replete with bounty, the obligatory racial slurs bandied about indiscriminately. A Hispanic Guy wearing a Yankees cap backwards rested against a wall gawking at the booties that passed by. Benny barely registered any of this. His attention was on a snappy dresser wearing only silver-sequined shorts and an American flag who was installed on a wall singing, "Boogie, Oogie, Oogie" while dancing The Freak, rock star tongue sticking out obscenely. Benny pulled up to watch becoming his private audience, all the smiles, and winks addressed lasciviously in Benny's direction. As Benny moved on with me a step behind, his eyes peripherally caught sight of a tag flyer affixed to a bus stop "Hector's One Man, One Van Moving Service" in bold letters. Reflexively, he'd yanked down the flyer of his one-time nemesis, crumpled it into a ball to deposit in his pocket, and off we went.

Benny sensed someone running up and turned. It was Hector, as out of control as an epileptic mid-seizure. With the element of surprise gone Hector pulled up a few feet away and snorted, his brain so programmed with macho that he blindly resumed the offensive. To rush someone of Benny's skill with your hands wide open at shoulder height half presuming that you're going grab and maul is highly recommended in the guidebook on self-mutilation. For Benny it was like being advanced a one-hour warning that a waddling toddler with poopie pants had him in his sights, it was that laughably slow. Right jab, left power punch, punctuated by a roundhouse kick that missed because the target was crumbling, and one second in all of time had ticked off. Dazed, with his right eyebrow split end to end and blood tinting his already red face, all Hector could do was hurl his cap at his conqueror. Benny caught it, chucked it in an alky's cart, instinctively looked back to make sure I was safe, and walked off with me catching up.

"Fucked him up, didn't I?" he said, all business.

"Jesus Benny, that's the third time that's happened in close to as many years," I groaned, not yet filled in on what had preceded it.

I was both impressed and unnerved.

"Slime that throws its weight around. Sorry if I don't feel guilty about it."

"I'm not asking that brother, just afraid of manslaughter," I moaned. My accumulating condition now came with such an omnipresent fear of tragic consequences that I drove as if a driving instructor were in the passenger seat.

"He rushed me. Now I can defend myself and that's all I did."

The words, "Now I can defend myself," stayed with me. It was a glimmer that he wasn't as beyond our past as I'd thought. But this wasn't the time for analysis so I put my hand on his shoulder to say, "How's that line go, 'maybe he'll think twice before he does that again.'"

At Benny's apartment, before we ate or showered, not having warned me and conscious that our mother would be at work, he dialed the telephone, seemingly as disconnected from this prophetic day's fisticuffs as a sociopath might be.

"Hello," answered Sergeant Thompson grouchily, as usual overburdened when no one was around to handle such lower echelon tasks as the phone.

"When I was there last my mother had a black eye," Benny stated mechanically. "It won't turn out well if you did that to her."

"What?"

"You heard me."

"It wasn't me. You see how clumsy your mother is."

"Pray I don't find out otherwise," Benny hissed, hanging up.

He sat down and stared at the wall expressionlessly. It was as if I weren't there. I drifted off to my room early to give him space, knowing that someday I'd ask him how he'd spent the next hour.

He closed the curtains and lied down, trying to sooth himself by riveting on the thin, insistent beam of light that came through the curtains from a street lamp. With one eye closed he continued, inch by inch rotating his face far away while keeping the other eye on that point, like a dexterity game that required such implacable concentration that the mind could have space for nothing else. Soon another nauseating twinge of pity arose for Sergeant Thompson, pity for those limitless limitations. It slow burned then fired up a pain in his heart so unfathomable, so unwanted, that posthaste he was back in kill mode. That morphed back to his urge to shield the defenseless, not just The Fire Girl and our mother, visions of vanquishing scoundrels filling him. And that is when it hit, the memory of little Arthur Telson getting his beating and Benny powerless to stop it, again replaying from start to finish, as luridly stark as when it occurred.

Collette And the Crackhead

The night of the crime the sugary mist didn't sweeten the countenances on the not so United Nations of passersby on the street. A taxi cruised by slowly with three white guys in it wearing the generic getup common in Midwest towns known best for their meat factories, so obvious that only the bushy-tailed ones lodging in The Youth Hostel couldn't easily detect that they were cops. The last of history's lime green, sky blue, and peach three-piece suits passed by lustfully sported by three Dominican jerry-curled immigrants, like a scream that they too needed some "Night Fever."

Wearing his cater waiter's tuxedo in the wake of a grueling twelve-hour job, Benny detoured outside the bodega on 102nd street and Amsterdam to buy some milk through the plastic window used after 11pm. You didn't remain open late around there in 1983 without at least two "primos" standing guard brandishing flamethrowers. You also didn't hang on a street corner for more than a minute unless it was your corner, or park your car on the street even if the car radio was welded into the dashboard.

"Hey you, how many Spics does it take to crack open a crackhead's head?" The Short One jabbered. His ferret face was a series of discordant scrunches awaiting a response. His gang of Hispanic Crack Dealers stood nearby with mugs both menacing and hungry.

"I don't know," Benny replied, assuming that there was still too much action on the street for a straight-out mugging. Regardless, he set his feet, shifting from tired to cocked and ready.

"Go ask him," The Short One instructed pointing north a block to the black guy wearing only grungy black shorts who was getting up from the sidewalk, broken coke bottle at his feet and a hole in his skull. "Fuck he's standing."

The Short One, in a bright yellow jacket like he'd not read the manual: "A Criminal's Guide to Attire," zoomed back to the black guy, his gang swarming behind him. The black guy tried to bolt by running into the street, the ravages of his chosen habits having taken the teamwork out of his limbs. From such a distance Benny determined that The Short One must have trained somewhat as a boxer before peer pressure propelled him on a powdery path. The chest punch that he threw looked devastating, a shock to the heart that rendered all other muscles useless. The black guy collapsed so fast it was as if a little demolition dynamite had been employed. The rest of the gang halted, prattled to each other in Spanish, and fled east on 104th street.

On his back, the black guy now blended into the pavement in the middle of Amsterdam Avenue. Soon the streetlight would change and all the cars lined up three blocks south would fly forward. Benny left his milk and ran uptown, looked back to verify that the cars hadn't started rolling, and dashed to where the black guy had sat up. Most of it was pouring down his chest, but there was also a water pistol squirt of blood shooting from what hadn't been a punch. There he was, the cocaine high and the high that must be derived from the pointy metal of a knife that pierced his heart all interwoven. Unaware that he would soon be a chalk outline he labored to get up, the will to live more involuntary, more cellular, than conscious.

"Stay down," Benny said, putting his foot on the black guy's thigh to subdue him. "Stay down.

Benny took off his tuxedo jacket so that his white shirt would alert coming cars, dropped it on the soggy ground, and waved his arms. He turned back to where the black guy had surrendered and was now resting back on his elbows looking straight up at him. Those eyes. The fear. The confusion. They seemed like one mammoth eye or fifty assorted eyes reaching in vain to comprehend, with a little, "If only I could turn back the clock" thrown in.

Multiple cars drove cautiously past Benny, some drivers rubbernecking like a dying black guy on the pavement of New York City circa 1983 was a novelty. One of the co-eds hanging out of the top of a limo, her perfectly hair sprayed curls sagging a bit with rain, drunkenly spilled her mixed cocktail on the black guy in passing while calling out to Benny, "you're hot!" As the undercover taxi pulled up a minute later the black guy lay back on the pavement. Close enough to see a last breath go in and out, Benny withdrew so they could take over.

At home he took off his tuxedo jacket that he'd retrieved from the ground. An end of a lifeline of blood had trickled along the street and amassed inside his coat to create a candy cane patch on his white shirt. When he saw it, he ripped off the shirt so fast that buttons chased each other across the floor. If he'd briefed me on this, or of the experiences with Arthur Telson both then and now, I might've been listening more intently for the cumulative effect in not just me, but also him.

------------------------------+----------------------------------

Benny and Collette were sitting in the office of the Winston PR agency on Park Avenue, founded and administered by Collette's cousin Bennett Winston right after he'd graduated from Harvard two years earlier. On the walls were a youth worth of photos of Bennett, his parents and friends, often with their arms around each other. He moved through calls and eloquently instructed his ten employees devoid of self-consciousness, all the while sucking on a lollipop.

Collette was the modern dancer who'd impressed Benny the most. She was grounded, on the level, and undisturbed by the much exertion for few rewards that most modern dancers bemoan. To have a physical avocation, one where she could explore and max out the prime of her body before venturing on to her intellectual and more lucrative vocation, to her was a privilege. A bonanza bestowed on her by a bountiful youth and a grand plan that tempered all trepidation. Her timeline was set in stone. Four more years of dance, retire on her 30th birthday bidding farewell to a well-lived youth, complete her MBA along the way, then use daddy's connections to make her business career fly.

"I don't get it," Benny had whispered to her. "How can he be such a leader at only 23 years old?"

"By the time Bennett was a teenager he'd been surrounded by business and professionals so much that it's second nature to him. His parents are also fabulous and encouraging. Benny, he was very lucky," she'd replied all motherly. She'd been the pursuer months earlier at a black-tie affair at the Algonquin Hotel where she was a guest and Benny was a cater waiter, his charm and wonderment still peeking through sufficiently to dazzle her, initially.

Unable any longer to uplift himself with recollections of the powerhouse he'd also once been, Benny slumped down there, gawking, trying to quell his jealousy. Bennett's aplomb felt hallucinatory, or like it was staged for the maximum, comparative effect. The feeding tube of Benny's love of martial arts and the company of such a dignified woman had barely gotten him through his first professional fight two nights back. With a victory he'd been counting on some elation, or at least satisfaction, not just the numbness of this thought as his trainer picked him up in raptures, "Please, put me down." Now as they waited for Bennett to rejoin them it all seemed so long ago, the training, the temporary salvation that can be derived from the preparation for a single event, the idiosyncratic impression that it's successful culmination would once again, across the board, stoke his fire.

Though Collette would save herself shortly after by parting graciously, Benny never forgot Bennett Winston. He often imagined that 13-year-old Bennett, his age-appropriate concerns so pure. It's was as if 13-year-old Bennett had been operating with a brain unhampered to investigate all of the nuances of a map opening up to his potential; not short-circuited. Benny and Bennett, two origins poles apart.

Dani

"What is wrong with you, Benny?" Dani asked accusingly. She was his fourth modern dancer girlfriend, and the second who would never have the pleasure of meeting me. Plonked on the paisley love seat that the former tenant had left behind in her apartment, she scowled at him when no reply came. Photos hung everywhere of her in all of the dance companies that at first, she'd been thrilled to join, a shrine to the view of her inglorious career through which she wanted beholders to be awed. You'd suppose from the all too posed smile that her artistic life had been a cut above nirvana. There was even a photo of her in a dance piece with her beagle, Windblown, who now lay in the corner licking his *doghood*.

"I don't know," he answered, not shocked that it had devolved into this. He'd been on the floor staring at the ceiling for an hour, with only one thought penetrating, "Wow, I'm a wreck."

"Why are you in this relationship?" she demanded to know in a staccato, spaghetti Western way poorly crafted to make him more compliant.

"What can I say? I like being with you. Mostly," he replied with a softness designed to defuse her need to escalate.

Her alarm was quickly glossed over as if ego pricked her with dreaded comparison; him composed, her seething. To gather herself, she skulked to the window and looked out. Minutes later she returned even more riled up.

"You're not really here. You're not really anywhere. You barely work. You've stopped training and even exercising. I don't want to be somebody's misery loves company, especially when I'm not sure there's a future for me in dance," she stated, her voice rising to the point where she might broadcast anew that, "Maybe I should wish that some rich guy would come along, marry me, and knock me up".

"I'm sorry. The last thing I aim to do is cause you unhappiness," he said, detached.

"Don't apologize again," she shrieked, as shrill as a faulty brake. "What are you going to do about it, Goddamn it? I don't want to waste my life!"

"Going ballistic isn't going to help."

It started with two tumbleweeds on the move in a windstorm. How they, like confused, shapeless wanderers in search of anything that might reorient them, had unexpectedly crashed into each other on that gloomy, mirthless day some months back, as unconscious of the effects from their childhoods as are most people. Seduction, once again Benny and Dani had mustered the robustness to dust off their representatives, those glowing images of themselves. Then came reality in the exhausting wake of unsustainable newness. And finally, repetitively, mercifully, another bollixed relationship of two people without deep roots disintegrates. It's difficult to connect with dysfunction.

"I'm aware that I'm not at my best," Benny admitted, the murky separation between him and all else mounting. "I'm not sure why."

"We never have sex," she claimed. "I'm tired of buying batteries for my damn vibrator."

"It's not never, it's just..." He covered his mouth at a revelation, profound because it was so simple and obvious. "Wow."

"Wow, what?"

He scrutinized her for a few seconds, got up, and grabbed his sneakers from where they'd been left by the door.

"What are you doing?" she asked, swiftly panicked. "Stop it. Why are you collecting your stuff?"

"I knew I wasn't ready. So sorry I got us into this, Dani. Please forgive me."

"Benny, stop it. You're scaring me. I'm not looking to break up. Not now. Not when I'm so confused about dance, and my family, and everything."

He paused to emphasize, "'Misery loves company.'"

"I shouldn't have said that."

"You're right. You deserve better. Please, forget me. Again, I'm so sorry."

"But you can't just split. You know that I love you."

"We've never said love to each other," he replied, quietly. "And this is probably not the moment to start."

Now came the silence in which a fresh storm can build, frightened eyes flickering, muscles clenched rigidly. He could foresee that the impetuousness that can reveal true character was about to explode.

"Okay. Toodle-oo," she yowled as he hustled to exit before she could fire off what at minimum wouldn't be beneficial. "Then take your one nut, get out of here, and stop wasting women's time!"

The same two tumbleweeds, the kind who've mislaid the drive for their individual goals in the bedlam of not being able to pinpoint what's wrong with their minds, again and again smashing into one another, until, poof, the wind propels them on separate paths, the aftertaste of a low blow in his mouth. The tug-of-war between sympathy and repugnance that ensued in Benny was won by the latter, a deathblow, the casket sealed without a tear to be shed by anyone but her.

"Such a fetching display of self-control. Good for you," he said while walking out. He closed the door and stood there appalled. This wouldn't be a demise that would render him all guilt-ridden that he'd abandoned her. As much as he implored himself to amicably leave her to her suffering, he reopened the door anyway. "Hey Dani, payment due, so it's time to be forthright. You're an angry, envious bulimic who cleans up so well after herself that you thought no one, including me, knew about those fingers down the throat. So why not at least be kind to someone who meant you no harm?"

He closed the door for good.

"You one-nutted freak!"

He stood in place for a bit, arranging himself as if he were a child's puzzle. It wasn't anger he bore, just fatigue and an opaque ambivalence as to why again, as he often had, he felt sympathy for her. Sympathy and empathy were his nature calling out, entreating him to keep dominion over his house of cards. He forced creaky steps. Outside on the building's stairs, the moon was so full that it seemed to laugh with him about how all of his four New York girlfriends had been modern dancers. Coincidence? Definitely. That's just who he'd happened to meet. He looked in the Moon's eyes and perceived its wisdom. "No more Modern Dancers for you."

He headed toward the subway, five blocks in which he was blanketed in a fine though not cleansing mist. Trudging along, he intuited that someone was tailing him so again and again he looked back only to find his forlorn shadow in pursuit. Each time the shadow was varying lengths and angles, like too many enemies to vanquish or with whom he could aspire to share a truce. Finally, drooped in a corner of the subway car, there was a brief respite, relief that he wouldn't have to simulate normalcy around Dani anymore. Suddenly another panic took hold. It came so unannounced, so filled with rusty nails and broken glass, that it strong-armed him to rise onto feet that felt screwed on backwards and grasp the subway pole, toiling to not look demented as little twitches erupted again. Focus. Focus on the kook positioned diagonally across the aisle with the baby iguana on top of his head. How often had he seen that in a subway car? As frequently as an octogenarian nun putting on her mascara, and that would be once.

As he labored home from the subway, he stopped to gaze at the handset of a pay telephone dangling impotently off the hook, swinging in the wind, there to hypnotize him for reprogramming if only he would put in a quarter and sit down to stare at it. He refused to ask himself as he had frequently of late why he was so boggled, only to receive the same unintelligible disconnect, a black hole where questions go in and the answer always comes out sounding like a test of the Emergency Broadcast System. It reminded him of the cheater years in public school, stretching to concentrate on why he couldn't concentrate. In spite of that, he was subsisting off of vague expectations that it would all go away soon, like an innocuous smiley face rash, and then he'd be flying again. As if replacement parents were going to magically materialize and bust a tag team against the enemy within. One that now provoked him to lash out in public concerning incidents he couldn't have been more patient about not long ago.

Benny couldn't unravel why the memory of Arthur Telson begging for mercy often reappeared when least expected. The eyes pleading, "I'm scared. I'm alone. Save me." The beseeching eyes of someone who wants to be safe, yet has no capacity to bring that about. And how when Benny took off his tuxedo that unforgettable night some months before the eyes of the crackhead also peered up for help. Him without a shirt on and Benny imploring, *"Stay down. Stay down."* Yet, full-length memories of our father's excess of violations never came. Perhaps that was a subconscious, threadbare desperation to block those out. And there they were again, Arthur and the crackhead, pleading, wailing. Benny ordered himself to regain his composure right here, right now. A sub-clause attached itself to that. It was a reminder of what his Abnormal Psychology Professor had once stated, "Schizophrenia often comes to full fruition around age 25." The age Benny had recently turned.

When he arrived home, Roise was dawdling on their stoop shooting spitballs for a distance through a straw as if that were run of the mill middle-aged behavior. Somehow, so against the grain, a memory of Aggie Boza perching on stoops briefly washed over Benny. Characters on stoops, time was he fancied that.

"Hey Benny," greeted Roise. "Man, am I pissed off."

"Why?" Benny answered, cobbling together lucidity.

"Plugged away at convincing the stupid government to forgive my school loans now that they took away my dentist license, and they were all 'fuck no'. $55,000 and I haven't sent payments in a year so I gotta sell some stuff or the stupid government will mess up my credit rating, too. Care to check out what I'm peddling?"

Benny would never catch wind of how Roise came to own a Samurai sword. He also wasn't sure why he was spending money that he barely had on it.

What I heard from Benny, the retirement out of comedy and working only the minimum number of catering jobs to pay the bills while he trained to rise to the top of his sport, all projected like a natural transition, an organic paring from two life callings down to one. While I was meandering progressively downhill here in Fall River for four years toiling away miserably at the same menial, gossipy office job, I pictured him still in love with life. From my moat of avoidance, same apartment, same 23 books perfectly aligned, I'd visualize Benny training unflaggingly for his second professional fight, sublimely focused, defying gravity. I repeatedly beheld the videotape of his first fight, all 44 seconds of it, me yelling, "Do it, boy. Do it!" The audience screamed when it climaxed with an axe kick. Yep, I was unenlightened that his connection to other people was shrinking as fast as mine.

Should'a Done What I Said

Gray and gaunt, Benny looked as worn down as the excess of transplants who'd blown into Manhattan with their pie in the sky ambitions that ended them up all those years later with only one possession of value, a rent-controlled lease for an apartment that they spend too much time in while never really seeing it anymore. That interchangeable assemblage of curmudgeons, one hit wonders, pseudo-realists, goodbye girls, borderline agoraphobics, and perma-temps, all exchanging the same lukewarm "hellos" with the other relative failures and local doormen, infinitely upset that dreams deferred became dreams relinquished when it was seemingly too late to start something new. Yet Benny hadn't actually flopped. The stoutness to pursue what he'd been succeeding at had incrementally dissipated.

"You've lost weight," our mother observed after some small talk, her malaise mingling with gratitude that he'd finally returned 18 months after the previous falling out. I also hadn't seen Benny in a year and still wouldn't in that Petra and I were on the road to her parent's 50th in Delaware, me, of course, reluctantly. Another note on us love birds... my co-dependency with Petra, whose sensitivities to laundry detergent, cigarette smoke, cats, and innumerable chemicals and smells were exacerbated by how I overdramatized my susceptibility to the same stuff. Add in my others, cold, heat, humidity, the sun, kids, old people, dogs, spontaneity, neighbor noise, street noise, bright light, shrill sounds, fear of stoves, anything "depressing" which is a mega-list unto itself, and we weren't likely to go backpacking around South America on under $20 a day.

"I hadn't noticed," Benny fibbed. Reflecting the old days, he wished he had anything resembling a fun anecdote to share after dinner. There was no light in his eyes that our mother could misinterpret as by some freak of nature this one had emerged unscathed.

The grunt Sergeant Thompson emitted struggling to get up from the couch sounded like he had a medley of hernias. He plugged in the lights on the same faded silver Christmas tree that had inspired festiveness for decades and waddled back as if he'd require weeks to recuperate from the exertion. He'd never informed our mother that Benny phoned him about her shiner, and his manner of masquerading like that call never occurred was to be conspicuously smiley.

"Was it hard to give up being a comedian?" she asked.

"Not so much. To be good at something and delight in doing it, aren't the same."

The long silence that ensued was colored by the brush strokes of Sergeant Thompson's overly pensive nods, as if he so concurred with Benny that every five seconds, he had to affirm that. So, it was unexpected when he released, "Aren't most comedians troubled?"

"Some," Benny conceded, reluctantly, not in shape for the poorly cloaked cloud his elder was raring to spread. "I really wanted to focus on martial arts."

"Hold your horses. I wasn't referencing you with that question. Why'd you assumed that?" Sergeant Thompson maneuvered, barely shaking his head as if someone in the room must be mildly paranoid. "Anyway, seeing as you brought it up. So, whatever became of your martial arts?"

"I did it for eight years and am taking a break. And, I had one professional fight as a kick boxer."

"You?"

"Yeah."

"And?"

"And what?"

"The result?"

"It was a quick knockout."

"And that took care of that idea, right?"

"I added some imperfection to the record of a dude who was 9-0. Why does that surprise you?"

Sergeant Thompson reassembled an air of deliberation before, "What makes ya think it surprises me?"

"Your tone."

"What tone? Hey honey, did it sound like I put forth that question with a tone?"

Her seconds of conjuring up the most palliative lie were ended with, "Sorry my mind was elsewhere, so I didn't hear."

"And you asked, 'That took care of that idea, right?'" Benny said.

"That didn't imply that ya lost, just that there must be some reason ya didn't stick with it. But hey, so ya won your first fight. Good for you. That had to've felt good," The Sergeant said, even flourishing a momentary thumbs up. He was fully immersed in a one-man good cop, bad cop strategy designed to break down his son so he added. "But ya sure don't seem happy about it."

"I am. I plan to go back and kick plenty more ass when I'm ready."

Sergeant Thompson picked up and began cutting slices off of a Granny Smith which he engulfed with two chews. He perused the TV Guide like he actually wasn't timing his next two questions, "So, ah, when will ya start again?"

"To be determined."

Sergeant Thompson scratched his chin as if debating if he should ask what he would, "Ah, ya mean when you're not depressed anymore?"

"What?"

"Well, obviously you're depressed. All my years on the job and I saw plenty of it."

"When was the fight?" our mother tried to shift gears, wiggling to stave off the inevitable. That would be like a zebra hoping that the lion whose teeth are in his neck might suddenly decide he's not hungry.

"Nine months ago."

"That's a coon's age," Sergeant Thompson commented. "I'm starting to worry a bit here that there are already two things that ya haven't stuck with. Everybody has to buckle down their bootstraps and stick with something eventually."

Benny gleaned that "I'm starting to worry" was the fatherly performance The Sergeant had to erect in front of our mother, while concurrently sticking in the knife. He just looked at his hands, the fists, the blades, and ridges, like he'd never seen them, even the back side for spinning back fists, weapons that had assisted his feet to undress a clown who'd jived before the bell rang, "Ain't never gonna lose, especially to no white boy." Then he looked at his bare feet. Hands and feet that not so long ago executed with lethal cohesiveness, now felt as if they'd been loaned to him like mismatched gloves and socks.

A pressed urgent need to get it off his chest, Sergeant Thompson declared, "Ya know what? I think life would'a turned out better for ya if you'd just done what I said and gone to the local state college."

All of the brain tattoos Benny had received couldn't add up to this one, a catalytic event that eradicated what little self-governance still remained. He simultaneously shut down and wanted to strike, barely able to respond, "Oh, you had to say that, didn't you?"

Our mother got up, froze for a few seconds, and flumped down again, like a bloodied survivor who'd crawled through the broken windshield of the car wreck.

"I'm entitled to my opinion. Or at least you should'a taken the civil service test for the police or fire department like I also intelligently advised."

"You.....are...subhuman," Benny over-enunciated, in an attempt to steady himself.

"Hey, don't take your problems out on me. I passed down the best advice I could. Just what a parent is supposed to do."

"And the unmatched eloquence with which you do it. In England they call it, Officer Class."

"Lots of people have had it worse than you did."

"That doesn't make how I had it any better." He looked for our mother to throw in with her son, finally, after all that had been endured.

As constitutionally disinclined to conflict as she was, she couldn't just go mute and fade out this time, so she turned to her man, oh so deferentially and said in the low, meticulous voice of someone now more seasoned, even noxiously sophisticated, in self-preservation through neutrality, "It's best I don't take sides, ah, though, but Benny probably had to do what he chose to do." She thought further, or enacted the lack of motion thought entails, swallowed, then switched to Benny to say, "And he is entitled to his opinion."

This is the moment that Benny's improbable hope capitulated to the seismic reality that families cannot always be kept intact, the intersection between futility and the barrenness that is hobbling off to begin life as a veritable orphan. He got up, walked to his room and closed the door from the outside as if he'd gone inside it. He edged back a few feet to enter our parent's bedroom, reached under their bed to where a strong box was stored, then along the sideboard to where he'd discovered the key hidden long ago, and secreted them into his room. He stuffed them into his backpack, put on his shoes, came back down the hallway, and stopped near our mother, never to set foot in that house again.

"Stay in the middle of the road, lady and a car will plow you over sooner or later," he stated, waved mockingly, and left those dismantlers of innocence, with their diffused accountability and calcified roles, to the squalid silence of wondering if time alone would smooth things over. It was the last day that any vestige of her youthful beauty would shine through. And as an inexperienced author I've neglected to mention that she'd been quite a looker, so many lustful eyes turning her way that she must've registered other options were out there.

Bordering on delirium, instead of retreating by bus back to NYC, Benny hitchhiked to Brickenwood arriving as the sun went down. He sat on the bench near our former unit, scanning, an occasional twitch interfering with an unkind exhaustion. The Dariteaus were loafing on their stoop. Having not laid eyes on him in thirteen years, they didn't recognize him. Breathing like a trained yogi until it calmed him a bit, Benny sat there, and sat, and sat, despite the cold.

Eight hours later he fell asleep for the two hours before dawn reminded him that waking up doesn't change anything. The sun emerged early as if shining a spotlight on to an infiltrator. Overfed and lethargic passersby who'd eyeballed him the previous night began glaring at him. Why is this long hair waif still around looking strung out like the plethora of local junkies that preceded him? He knew that the police would ultimately be called, so he had to disappear soon. That strong box contained Sergeant Thompson's first gun, a revolver moth-balled for a semi-automatic long ago. As it was time to go the door to our former unit opened. Out scampered an 8-year-old girl behind her 7-year-old brother. She jumped off the stoop playfully chasing him. They returned to receive kisses and lunch boxes from their beaming mother.

They glided to school wondrously animated, him bouncing, her skipping, unsuspecting that with makeshift subtlety a troubled stranger was tailing them. The exuberance of how unfettered they were infused Benny briefly with fresh air, and more jealousy. From a distance he also got to watch Mr. Nunes at school, now gray and disguised underneath an oversized moustache and sideburns, organizing the lines of children to go inside to learn practical things that barely scratch the surface of the maze that is life. Benny even looked to the spot where Aggie Boza would laze scanning the shifting geometry of children at play. He'd always longed to see who she'd become in the present, sprinkled he hoped with adorable vestiges of who she'd once been.

Once all of the kids had filed inside, he walked to the school, touched its side, and continued south. Again, saturated with too much mental debris to cull out what is what, he slogged a mile to County Street. He broke off to stare at the spinning barber pole of Mel's Barbershop. Impulsively, he went in. Barely a hundred square feet, the walls surrounding the one chair were adorned with photos of customers, wilted and yellowing, crying children with their snips partially done, whole broods of lookalike boys surrounding their father all with one style of haircut and a collective soul Benny coveted.

"What'll it be?" Mel started off, looking up six inches at Benny through thick glasses.

"Shave it off."

"Altogether? I charge by the inch, so you'll sure be adding to my great grandkid's college fund."

"For real?"

"Of course, plus there is a fee for preventing me from enjoying my soap opera," Mel kidded, pointing at the thirteen-inch TV now shut off on a shelf in the corner.

"That seems reasonable," Benny replied, concurrently relieved to joke for a second yet aware that his hands were trembling.

"You got hair any woman would be proud of. Mind if I donate it to the cancer wing's wig shop?" Mel asked leading Benny into the chair.

"Cool. Maybe it'll live on well beyond my time."

"You're bringing up mortality to an 81-year-old man? Why not make light of arthritis and incontinence, too?"

"Sorry."

"You'll be around way longer than that wig."

"One never knows."

Disquieted, Mel draped Benny with a barber's cape and switched the attachment on his electric razor. "I'm going for 100 years of tolerating what they call 'progress', plus 250,000."

"250,000 what?"

"Haircuts. Snips. You're number 247,113 in my 55 years in his little shop."

"You've counted? Nice."

"It takes considerable mathematical intelligence to add one after each that I complete."

"Sweeten the pot. Tell me you've been married to the same woman for fifty-five years also."

"Nope. Sixty. Everybody needs a best friend, young man. I'm presently auctioning off snip number 250,000 for The American Cancer Society. My best friend is carrying a bit of that around with her. The bidding is at $1,220 if you're of the mind to up the ante. You are Mr. Money Bags, right?"

Mel shaved his head and backed away to gander at it. Benny marveled at how at peace the man seemed, despite the challenge at hand. Mel drew the cape off of him like Zorro creating a funneling motion that gathered Benny's locks into a single pile.

"Thanks," Benny said, pulling out his wallet.

"My pleasure," Mel answered guiding the wallet back from where it came. He gathered up the rope of hair from the floor, joined Benny at the door and whipped him playfully with it. "They're mad at you for cutting them off."

"Then they shouldn't have ridden me in here."

"Sergeant Thompson's kid, right?"

"How'd you guess?"

"There's a resemblance. Though he reckons it's silly that I count my number of haircuts."

"That's no bombshell."

Benny lumbered south, in passage examining remnants of his youth that he'd barely noticed back then, his High School, Buttonwood Park Zoo, even the beach where he'd learned to barely swim. As it got dark again, he realized that he hadn't eaten in 24 hours and that it was best to fuel his mission. Three hot dogs and a coke were the antithesis of this athlete's former diet, but expediency rules when retribution is your footpath. He stopped near the South End Police Station hours before Sergeant Thompson's shift would end. On such a moonless evening, reconnoitering from the bushes behind the station near an SUV with fishing license tags in the window, Benny's ire intensified.

As he surveilled Sergeant Thompson exiting his police car at midnight, daily log in hand, it was hard to conceive that this pathologically impenitent character was our father. It couldn't be real. He watched him advance toward the station, casually raising the revolver and taking aim, amused that the death would be by the Sergeant's own gun. Though sweeping deliverance wouldn't derive from pulling the trigger, he savored every last second until the Sergeant entered the station, an endearing insight into how swiftly a bad seed can be buried never to sprout again. Before restoring the revolver into the back pack, he blew the imaginary smoke away from the muzzle. Eyes zoomed in on the station house door, he watched as Sergeant Thompson reemerged minus his daily log and tromped to his SUV. As he put the key into the door Benny stepped out of the bushes so startling him that he drew his gun for the first time in his career.

Benny remarked, involuntarily, "I'd like that."

"What the hell!"

"Scared you?"

"Are you outta your mind in the bushes like that?" Sergeant Thompson chastised, holstering his gun. "Do ya realize that ya could'a been killed? And when the hell did ya shave your head?"

"I'd never been to Mel's Barbershop. Quite a jokester."

"What is going on, Goddamn it?"

Benny let the silence speak volumes before he continued. "I have a question for you."

"What? Now? This is crazy."

Gruesomely, Benny tilted in to inquire, "Do you know that you attacked me the day before my nut exploded and that's what damaged it? Your knee?"

Sergeant Thompson screwed on the frown of a man so, so wounded by the astronomical untruth in the air.

"The predictable pantomime."

"Your claim's not true," he protested, wagging his finger.

"Yes, it is."

"If it's true, why didn'tcha say it back then?"

"Afraid you'd allege I was lying."

"Maybe not. But you are lying now."

Benny glowered at him then asked, "Would mother think that if I told her?"

He'd never seen Sergeant Thompson so dumbfounded, disabled even. Too enervated to take solace in that, Benny began his departure.

"Yeah, I tossed ya a few love taps, but that tough luck must've happened another way. And the urologist couldn't state for sure what caused it."

"By the time you finally called him," Benny stopped to scoff. "You don't remember me crawling out of the living room after the incident with the TV Guide? Sure, you do, but you'll just deny it anyway."

Sergeant Thompson stood there defiantly, hands on hips. Benny returned to within inches of him, instigating steps backward.

"Don't worry, I won't tell her. She's as responsible for it all as you are, so you deserve each other. And neither of you will ever see me again. One more note that should make you ecstatic. I have your old gun in my backpack. Try trailing me to get it, see how that pans out for you."

Benny faded into the emptiness that only hermits embrace.

Another Skeleton in The Closet

“Somebody’s looking a bit defective,” Roise uttered when Benny passed where he was loitering on the stoop. In the twilight Benny paralleled a kid’s stick figure drawing, with just a week’s growth of hair.

“Good eye,” Benny replied, keys in hand to open the door, not stopping on his way into the building.

“You look like one of those crazies who just killed somebody.”

“Or more than one.”

“No, no, I get it. The effort to look as substandard as I do, proves you admire me,” Roise called after him as Benny closed the door. “Consider me fully complimented!”

Noting that he’d left an open package of now moldy cheese on top of the refrigerator, the unsourced smell of Gouda was finally uncovered. Benny foot flipped his sandals into the corner. On the stove was a pot of Campbell’s Salisbury Steak Soup that he’d forgotten to heat up days before. Flies not all of the same wing had fully colonized the four open bags of garbage in the kitchen. Dirty underwear and socks hung like points on a map to nowhere. He didn’t want to remove the dead mouse from under the sink because he wasn’t sure if it was his friend Bobo, the nightly foraging visitor that abandoned its visits around the time the corpse turned up.

He trudged into the bathroom, took off his clothes and stood facing the mirror to see half the muscle he once had following a winter of almost never being outside during the daylight. Yet the weight loss was so extreme that all that was left was muscle and bone. In the living room he began the ritual of pacing, lying down for hours, more pacing then another decision to return to work before he was out-and-out broke. Becoming odd, rudderless, veritably incapacitated, likely to lurk in the doorways of abandoned buildings at night, fragmented emotions about one’s discarded mother causing further unsteadiness, was a gradual exercise. Daddy's latest offensive had incited the hemorrhaging of whatever was left of Benny's camouflage of invincibility.

Sleep only came in disorienting spurts, a minute's worth feeling like hours, or hours as if it never happened, always with the prospect that a memory would impel him to jump to his feet. Now the memories became primarily of our parents' failings. The time he'd cuffed Benny upside the head for not returning the nail clipper "to its rightful place." Those days forced to sit on a wooden chair in the cellar, facing a corner for this or that petty infraction. Often in bed now he'd have that old sensation of being imprisoned there, so he'd lie on the floor. Or he'd wake up panicked that a shadow in police attire was looming over him, forcing him to stay out until the wee hours roaming until exhaustion. His yesteryear of self-reliance was now his undoing. He couldn't even conceptualize where or how to ask for help.

Now penniless, Benny signed up last minute to work a cater waiter job the next day in Connecticut. As a financial holdover, he called me for a $1,000 loan. The wherewithal to minimize my actual net worth was as cultivated as a glutton's expertise at locating the nearest all you can eat buffet, so Benny couldn't have determined that I had much money. At any rate, it was unthinkable to loan out 2% of the $50,000 I'd saved by doing as little socially as the Amish. What if somehow, I lost the other $49,000 and I was stuck foraging for grubs with madmen who might rape me senseless? I wanted to squirrel away every iota of security that I could. So, yes, I alleged that I was broke, supposing that he'd soften his stance on our parents and scrounge some money out of them. Though in my indefensible defense, I would've dipped into my fiscal lifeline if I'd been informed about his actual mental state.

Therefore, he phoned Larry to roll the dice at 20% of the sum he'd ventured with me.

"Larry, it's Benny."

"Pistah!!"

"Sorry to bother you about this, but, ah, I haven't been doing well lately I figure you've noticed, and, ah, I'm broke. May I borrow $200?"

"Of course, I'll bring it by tomorrow," Larry replied automatically.

"I really appreciate it."

"Hey, what are friends for?"

For Benny the impression that someone cared outstripped money. When the phone rang later Benny even tried to be playful again by answering, "Poverty Central."

"Pistah, hey, I got bad news. I'm sorry, but you know my fiance right and how she is?" Larry asked.

"Yep, is she okay?"

"Yeah, but not with me loaning money. She's firm that we can't do it with our plan to have sucklings in the next few years. She insists that when you loan money once, they keep asking."

Benny hung up without responding, staggered by the ease with which Larry's desire to avoid conflict on the home front devalued their long union. Again "family" seemed more dangerous than war and earthquakes combined, any projection about future relationships relegated to a masochistic desire to be betrayed. It was 7pm, so to guarantee that he'd go to work 13 hours later he put on his cater waiter tuxedo and sat waiting on the couch in the fading light. Temporarily pacified by a one-pointed task, and relieved once all external light had given over to darkness, he listened to the ticking of the wall clock.

As full blown delirium began to envelope him his face lit up and eyes expanded with the image of someone entering. She stood over him, the thin strength of her shoulders, her oval black eyes a beacon of her fierce loyalty. She was here to shield him, even more equal to any challenge that might beset them than he'd originally thought. He swallowed and squinted, struggling to center his attention on her. But he couldn't. As impactful of a force as Esterlie The Fire Girl had been, she was no longer real. She wasn't real. She wasn't real like Romeo the pillow had been so ire enveloped him and he was now finally, justifiably, right after this cater waiter job, bent on avenging that loss during another visit to the porter who'd stolen once of his moving boxes.

------------------------------+----------------------------------

As a drummer Jesse Lee had toured with two big name rock bands whose original drummers had died of an overdose. At 31, black with dreads, as mild-eyed as such a pockmarked face can support, it was now or never that had him strike out on his own as a singer/songwriter, relinquishing his sticks for an acoustic guitar. A foreman at the spiritual assembly line, endlessly erecting a morally and psychologically better self, he'd enjoyed working with Benny the two times that they'd done cater waiter jobs together. He appreciated that Benny had worked undistracted and left the grousing to those who believed they deserved the marquise position at least side by side with De Niro and Streep, if not above. All in their waiter tuxedos, Jesse waited outside of Benny's apartment in the back of a souped-up Grand Am with two actor/waiters in the front seat. The wooden emphasis that one of them had put on how sparkling he'd been as an extra on General Hospital still hung in the air.

The order of events to each individual's slide to the bottom varies, but advancing there is without exception an ever less convincing patchwork self, trumped up to feign normalcy. Benny was so past that point that his entrance into the car was like an ambush. A corpse in a loose-fitting tuxedo had decided to come back to life to serve six tables at the wedding of a property manager named Abe and Lola the x-ray tech.

"Hey Benny. Good to see you," Jesse greeted.

"Is it okay if the door stays open for a minute before we get going?" Benny appealed, sheepishly.

"No. We have to push off or we'll be late," the driver barked like the request had issued from a pampered child.

"Don't be absurd," The Soap Star seconded.

Absurd was the misjudgment that Benny could ride 90 minutes in a steamy car, glue on a smile, and function.

"Patience gentlemen," Jesse said, swiveling back to Benny. "Is it okay if we drive now?"

Reluctantly, Benny closed the door, twitching so hard that Jesse put his hand on his shoulder. The car rocketed off like its driver had to emphasize his point again. Benny swayed back and forth, hands on his knees.

"It's okay. I know it's hot in here," Jesse said. "So, haven't seen you lately. I'm dying to know. How'd your first fight go?"

"I won," Benny murmured. Itchy and overmatched, misperceiving that the driver was pumping the brakes unnecessarily, Benny inclined a bit out the window. He was so feeble that the wind felt Tsunami, so he retreated back inside.

"Did you see that Jack Benny died?" Jesse asked.

Benny nodded, rocking, twitching, rocking.

"Did you like him?"

Benny's eyes squinted.

"Those old comedians all had a gimmick."

Benny did his utmost to remain still, but the pretense was like trying to conceal a third eye under a monocle. He began to rock again, augmented by a prolonged uncontrollable shaking of his head.

"What the fuck is wrong with you?" the driver pounced.

"Hey, it's okay. He's just not feeling well. He'll be better once we've arrived at work," Jesse took over, knowing it wasn't true.

"Damn, if he's meaning to act creepy, he's succeeding."

"How about some music?" Jesse suggested. "Hey Benny, what sort of music are you down for?"

Benny didn't reply. Feeling like he was suffocating, he kept rocking and twitching, one hand on the door handle as they sped along The West Side Highway. The sound of the latch being undone shot through the car, the speed of the pavement passing by below them lightening its blackness. Something in Jesse's history had him ready so he grabbed on to Benny just as he leaned out in search of air and yanked him down onto the car's floor. Keeping Benny pinned, he kicked the door so hard that it rebounded and closed.

"What the fuck?" the driver shrieked. "He opened the fucking door!"

"We have to take him back to his apartment," Jesse stated, as clinically calm as a 911 operator.

"Fat chance," the Soap Star overruled. "That would make us late for work."

"Then pull off at the next ramp," Jesse demanded, keyed into Benny's manic breathing.

And that's exactly what they did. Still more burdened than

compassionate, the heartless thespians stranded them in Fort Washington and sped off to net their $14 an hour. Jesse led Benny, who was bent toward the ground with his hands clasped so hard that they were turning blue, onto a dirt hill to make him sit.

"Listen Benny, listen," Jesse implored while Benny looked around frantically, amped to break free. "Benny, listen. Listen, Benny. Something big is going on and we need to get you back home. Benny, you have to listen. I have to wave down a cab, so can you hold out here for a minute?"

Benny, arms wrapped around them, buried his sallow face in his knees.

"Benny listen, can you do that? Just say you can and I won't be gone very long. Okay? Okay? Benny, listen. Is it okay if I hail a cab?"

A single minute nod signaled time to go and Jesse dashed off with one eye on Benny. When he returned with the cab, he aided Benny to stand. "You have to promise that you're not going to jump out. Can you do that? Benny, Benny, I need you to answer. Can you do that?"

"Don't know," he whispered.

"Then I'm going to hang on to you. It's a five-alarm fire now and it'll require the whole battalion to put this one out." He clutched Benny so uncompromisingly all the way back that his hands hurt the next day.

Employing evocative questions and compassionate affirmations, for the next nine hours, while Benny paced back and forth haphazardly gesticulating and spouting occasional references to the abuse he'd endured, Jesse doused the flames of Benny's inferno. Certain as he was that Benny would refuse to go to the psych ward, he advocated that anyway. His steely confidence that he could wear Benny down to the point that he would eventually sleep was only mired by Benny's visits to the bathroom. With the door locked he could do permanent harm. The click of that bathroom lock closing reverberated like a starting gun in the race to furtively extract another number from Benny's phone book and dash off that call to first our mother, then me, Larry, and lastly Alba about one of those events that no one can anticipate and only the practiced can roll with coolheaded. Our mother fatalistically, yet bearing raisins to prepare bread pudding, with a game plan to swap a half-century of servility for a newfound aptness at giving firm parental commands, presented herself as Jesse's replacement toward 10pm. When a savior is swapped for a major source of the damage it's probably not going to go well.

No faculty light years beyond our mother's previous matrix of inabilities could've shaved an infinitesimal layer off of Benny's contempt. The antibodies to her feckless apologies and half-witted explanations had built such potency that any further inoculation would've merely resulted in the waste of a needle and some cotton swabs. So, when Jesse reported the next morning all that was in the closet recently denuded of its far-flung contents was Benny, emaciated and ghostly, wearing only shorts, eyes wider than a Tarsier's, Samurai sword in hand, revolver laying nearby. Another skeleton in the closet. Benny's interminable progress into the closet, like the march at Rattan but interspersed with raving tirades and clothes shredded by the sword, ultimately had behooved our mother to call Jesse petitioning for further assistance. As if he'd trained for decades, Jesse sat to take stock of the situation, while she was in the chair across from him petrified. He knew that to alert the mental health authorities would also summon the police, and potentially time in prison for an illegal handgun.

"You let it all happen. You. You were the fucking adult and let that one do whatever he wanted!" Benny hammered at our mother, who looked like she was strapped into an electric chair with the full current flowing.

"I did the best I could," she pleaded, about as primed for crisis management as she was for the presidency of anything.

"How, by cutting coupons and cleaning up after that pig? Much of it happened right in front of you."

"Oh, it's coming out now," announced Jesse. "Express what you have to, Benny. It needs to be released."

"Jesse, I have only one nut because of that piece of shit. He put me to bed for an entire summer. Thumped on us like it was a sport," Benny raged. He turned to our mother. "Did you think it was all just an ordinary American family?"

"But you never said it affected you so much," she responded.

"What the hell! Lame ass, damage control bullshit!"

"Mrs. Thompson," Jesse noted, a stalwart who both assuaged and could blast holes through nonsense. "With all due respect. It sounds pretty extreme. He shouldn't have had to ask for your protection."

"You're right."

"And another piece of advice. Start owning up to your part in your son's childhood. We can either pretend like a dominant male has free reign or not."

"All you ever do is protect your pitiful self!" Benny derided.

"Okay, let's approach this differently," Jesse proposed. "Is it okay if I ask your mother a question?"

"First whip out your flimflam detector."

Jesse deliberated before asking, "Mrs. Thompson, if you were back then who you wish you could be right now, would you have done anything differently?"

She burst into mascara dissolving tears. "Oh My God, what have

I done? I so wish I'd done better. I'm going to do better."

"Thank you for the sudden act of contrition," Benny mocked.

He went on for another hour about her complicity in his undoing, more than once pointing the tip of the sword at her like a spotlight on a criminal. He hadn't eaten anything and had drunk very little for 36 hours. It's at that point where everything formerly recognizable of personality and comportment was gone. Sponged out. Made nothing. All foundation eradicated, oblivion's storm was destined to blow across the East Coast. Even the thought of temporary relief or of finessing Benny toward composure, would've been ridiculous. Jesse's mediation was so imperturbably artful, yet pitted up against an impenetrable madness he was just biding his time. He'd been down this road once before.

"Benny, please just put down the sword and we can find you some help," our mother tried, her cuticles now gnawed to the hurting point.

"You need the help. I need the fuck out of here."

"Where will you go?"

"Mrs. Thompson. Not so literal please."

"I don't give a turd anymore about your creepy childhood. Giving license to that savage to torture us!" Benny vented, his eyes now on the gun.

"Should your mother leave and it'll be just us?" Jesse asked, ready to dive toward the gun.

"Time to lay down my burden lady. And once I'm just ashes go rent yourself a spine!"

"Mrs. Thompson, I'm afraid that you should......"

Suddenly Benny gasped, his mouth so open it would've been comical if it were intentional. The gasping grew louder and louder until he fell over onto his side, his legs and arms up raised like he was going into cardiac arrest.

"Aaahhahah! Aaaahhahah! What the! What the…Oh My……Oh My….Ahhhhhhhhhhhhhhh!"

"Benny, what happened?" Jesse asked.

"Oh my Ggggaaawww….What the…What theee…"

His eyes darted around the room so fast that he appeared to be convulsing.

"Please tell us what's going on," our mother beseeched.

"Be quiet please," Jesse ordered her with no leeway for his usual politeness.

"What the hell was that? What was that? Ahhhhhhhhhhh!" Benny yelled. It echoed. And echoed. And echoed.

"What, Benny? What?" Jesse asked, eyes wide with newfound possibility.

"I, I, I heard something," Benny said, sitting up fast, redder than if it were a 50 below, sweat beading on his forehead.

"What did you hear?"

"I, I, I………………I, I, I…"

"Now. Find a notebook and a pen!" Jesse directed our mother. "It's happening!"

"What is?"

"Just do it!" he said. Savoring it like a revered ritual, he knelt next to the closet to softly continue, "What did you hear, my friend? Was it valuable?"

"What the...what was that?" Benny said, more beyond than to Jesse.

"What Benny? What was it?"

Benny tried to speak but nothing came out.

"Will this someday be your foremost memory?"

Bewildered, not certain if he should be aghast or encouraged, Benny stared off into space. Our mother handed Jesse the notebook.

"It just, it just, it just...it came in here," Benny warbled, becoming more intrigued, his tone and volume softening. He pointed at his right ear like a tot not yet blessed with speech.

"That's a good place, right? So, what was it?"

"It.........it..........where did it come from?"

"What? What did you hear?"

"It, it, oh my...........it.............itttttt............it."

"What Benny?"

Benny discontinued all motion, no blinking or breathing. His eyes shot upward and froze again. Ten seconds passed before one mammoth breath led to the eyes firing left to again freeze. His aspect incrementally relaxed, breathing ensued, and his eyes closed, still wound so tight it was as if he were thawing out.

"It...............................it....................it..."

"What Benny?" Jesse encouraged nimbly, gingerly. "Let us know, Benny. What was it?"

Barely audibly, Benny inclined to relay, "It.........It........'It doesn't have to be this way.'"

The words so impacted Jesse that everything in him raised up. He said tenderly, "Nice. Great start. That's what you heard?"

"Yeah," he peeped, again pointing at his ear.

"'Life doesn't have to be this way.' That's cool, right?"

"I don't know. I don't...what the...."

Jesse leaned forward and put his hand on Benny's shoulder. His eyes glowed with the All Mighty as he incited, "My friend, he wants you to know it doesn't have to be this way. That's good, right?"

"What? What? Who?"

Jesse raised his hands diagonally toward the ceiling to expound, "God. Or the Earth. Whoever spoke to you imparted that, 'it absolutely does not have to be this way.'"

Benny contemplated this.

"He wants me to share with you how life can be with the right thought and the right effort. May we do that?" Jesse asked. "Hey, Benny. Let's do it, man. The hour is here. Shall we do that?"

Jesse's smile was an invitation into the next dimension of reality. He held out quietly. The gun and sword were surrendered and curiosity beckoned Benny forward. Not long after he was sitting on the floor with notebook and pen in hand, looking up at his first mentor, a man from Atlanta who was six years older than him.

"You going to write it down?" Jesse asked.

"Okay."

"Here we go. Ready?"

"Yep," Benny said, that single tear accentuating the moment.

"Establish what your principles are," Jesse dictated, affording Benny intervals to jot down and savor those uncontaminated words. "Learn how to embody them." The phrase flowed through Benny's veins, like a starter kit toward huge reward. "Then go for yours."

To himself Benny embellished that last line as, "Not until then do you go for yours." "Establish what your principles are. Learn how to embody them. Then go for yours." Thus, Benny had the divine principle that would guide the rest of his days. The half hour of notes Jesse furnished before deciding it was sufficient for the day combined the practical with the celestial, reality checks with soul-speak, perfect words to wade into the realm of higher consciousness. He climaxed with, "necessity is the mother of introspection." Jesse had been reborn four years earlier, and that doesn't infer in the religious sense. He knew that the entrails could incrementally fade away and that a sustainable vision could sprout. His rebirth mentor was a 71-year-old former drug addict who'd ripened into a devotee of all things Rumi, whose rebirth mentor had been enslaved as a prostitute when she was 13 in Sri Lanka, and so on, and so on.

"And your doubt may become a good quality if you train it. It must become knowing, it must become critical. Ask it, whenever it wants to ruin something for you, why something is ugly, demands proofs from it, test it, and you will find it perplexed and embarrassed perhaps, or perhaps rebellious. But don't give in, insist on arguments and act this way, watchful and consistent, every single time, and the day will come when from a destroyer it will become one of your best workers-perhaps the cleverest of all that are building at your life."

That passage from Rainier Maria Rilke's "Letters To A Young Poet" is what hours later, hunkered down in a corner, Benny pored over repeatedly, while Jesse conferred with our mother. Jesse counseled that she returns home to be replaced by none other than me. Pacified by his assurance that the time for her involvement would alight soon, she reluctantly agreed.

"Just keep preparing for what you'll have the fortune to participate in. Benny is your son. He's ready," he said, raising his eyebrows to continue, "You can't teach readiness."

"He doesn't open up much about what's going on inside."

"Do you mean the boy you once knew, or the man we'll soon get to know?"

Larry hesitantly declined Jesse's phone request for help with nothing more than "I can't," but Alba, who'd mystifyingly put her blossoming life in Chicago on hold, turned up within eight hours, unbothered that her bed would be the floor. She came to be that other unswerving saint, the one with the prescience to not have been fooled about the extra tonnage that, in times gone by, Benny tried to bear lightly. I was also in a bus that way doubting "I would be able to handle it," bedeviled by his collapse that I had no idea was coming.

The first words I thought upon seeing him were "Concentration Camp," the crevices under the eyes, hands as stable as quicksand as, riveted, he raised and lowered his Rilke. He had all the hallmarks of a survivor who'd been led feebly beyond the barbed wire and gun turrets into welcoming arms, a cherubic voice whispering into his ear, "It's over. It's finally over. You're free." His depth of focus was only occasionally interfered with by twitches, the urge to pace back and forth for a bit, or a sudden irate tightening that he patiently unraveled.

To witness that he actually was also damaged goods not so

unlike me left me shaken, unceremoniously uprooted from The Land of Delusion and cannonballed across flak-ridden skies into the kind of Goddamn fucking, miserable bubble bursting reality I wasn't suited for. How could it be? Benny? Throughout my life I hadn't written a journal about myself, night after night I'd written about him. It delineated my half-sighted analysis of his omnipotence, a cast iron resilience that could only spell success. For a minute there I vacillated between dismay and betrayal. I couldn't comprehend how to perceive of him as both this and my idol. It played with my need for order like a tornado with a small town. It reminded me of the afternoon an ivory-white pigeon got hit by a car and kept spinning around on the ground with its broken wing dragging behind it.

His insubordination in my fairy tale even disgusted me a bit, but not for long. He wouldn't remain demystified in my mind. It was transparent upon taking the measure of this ghoulish caricature of my brother that he was beginning to take possession of his destiny. A tragically indispensable tipping point would now allow him to set in motion the process of cutting and pasting. The glorious parts that had always been Benny would now certainly amalgamate with the fruits of new knowledge and consciousness, and come as humanly possible to wiping out the demons that had temporarily waylaid him. All of the injured innocence would now pour out like juices from a wound freshly disinfected. It was time for him to wander curiously onto a long road of epiphanies, fresh eyes essential to glean the expanse of possibilities.

Every day Jesse visited Benny as calm as a leaf in a picture frame. His selflessness astounded me, all discourse substantiated by the wisdom of the ages that also assisted him during his resurrection. That old saying, "If you're ready for a teacher, one will be sent." What a talent. What a man.

"Who Are You?" Jesse probed Benny one day.

"Thought I knew," Benny admitted, a mini-grin breaking through like a logo for this retooling. "Now I know that I didn't."

"Good. Then you can decide who you're going to become. I don't mean some contrivance that won't hold up over time. Something sturdy because, and this is important, it's already broken. All children of violence are already broken. There is no magical real self that you're going to rediscover and he'll do all the labor for you. The masks, the resentment, all have to be exchanged for conscious choices."

It felt for a second there as if we were all going to levitate. Even me.

There was no greater sponge than Benny. He wrote the quotes of renowned sages all over his walls as round-the-clock reminders. Pages and pages of notes were reviewed aloud daily, always with that astonishment about how lacking in introspection he once was. In states of release and euphoria, he could really face the fear now. Alba and I would lounge off to the side, taking it all in, her inspired to introduce it into her own life, me more clinically impressed. Our job once Jesse had left for the day was to ensure that Benny was eating and sleeping, and to discuss whatever he'd initiate, whenever he wanted, even in the middle of the night if he became overwhelmed. It made me feel vaguely substantial all while concealing, how this albino increasingly gave me the creeps the longer she wasn't in proximity to her stylist and the makeup that did its magic. Pitiful me, I only stayed for the first week, shamelessly excusing my compulsion to retreat home with hyperbole about how lethal my girlfriend Petra's numerous allergies had turned. My tireless support was now needed elsewhere. Though I did visit the rental office to pay for his next month's rent. And despite all of his present and coming efforts by phone to ferry me along for this transformative ride, still the one-of-a-kind cesspool I was digging for myself, was easier to me. I didn't really want the level of power that the old Benny had, never mind that which this new Benny was gaining. It brings with it a warehouse of responsibilities. Much easier to progressively become a shut in.

After two weeks Jesse breezed in with a dozen carnations and a card in a sealed envelope intended for Benny and our mother to open together. His aspect was that of unassailable joy as he lazed between Benny and Alba on the couch, turning to Benny to say, "What a rare opportunity you provided me these past two weeks. I'm so grateful for what we've shared. Just please know that what we've set in motion here will require years to complete. I remain vigilant and I'm four years into my crossing."

"I know that I'm just raw clay now."

"Good. That so encourages me on our last day together. The next chapter of your odyssey is here. In no time, because Alba scoots tomorrow also, it'll be just you and your mom."

Benny's eyes grew wide. It was beyond conception. He goggled at a pen like he'd never seen one. "That should be interesting."
"Do you trust me, Benny?"

"To the max"

"She's who you should be with. And there'll be a clinical psychologist that she's paying for. The two of you will reunite at your first session with him tomorrow."

"Wow."

"One piece of advice, my friend. Clean slate. In many ways she was just a child also."

Alba dropped her head on Jesse's shoulder. They rested for a stretch, equally grateful for that which over these fertile few days they'd concertedly reimagined.

"Hey Jesse," Alba said.

"Yeah, my love."

"Did Benny ever tell you about Aggie Boza? She lived in the projects near him."

"No, though that name alone makes me curious."

The memory swelling his smile, Benny asked, "You ever met somebody, a bit of an outcast, who is so distinctly who she is that you must take notice?"

"Why are we gabbing about me now?" Alba kidded, causing a chuckle.

"That was Aggie Boza. I really loved her."

Jesse nodded his head slowly like he was envisioning her. "Aggie Boza. Hmmmmm. You say her name was…is Aggie Boza. Nice." He got up casually. "I think she'd care to join us now." Relishing the opening, he closed the shades to darken the room, and settled between them again. His speech became even more soft and fluid. "Creative visualization. Knowing that all is attainable and that limitations are almost always mental, we'll invite and invoke the presence of Aggie Boza now. The words she once spoke, the smiles she so often shared, and the lessons without intending to that she imparted."

------------------------------------+----------------------------------

"Welcome," Dr. Braiman said. "Take a seat."

Benny joined our mother on the couch across from where he sat in his lounge chair. A veteran of an incalculable number of couch confessions, Dr. Braiman's mien was that of a healer whose empathy had mushroomed in his thirty years of practice, like a man who no longer sweated. His eyebrows were so dense that in a less austere moment he would prove to Benny how easily they could substitute as pencil holders.

"Well Benny, I've heard your mother's version of your family history. She's depicted the cruelty that you were forced to endure, and her role in it. She also informed me that you've struggled with disturbing memories. So, let's start by noting that, it's my first time meeting you. Whether you also struggle with a genetic condition will probably unfold in our work together. What I can postulate is that I wouldn't be surprised if you suffer from a measure of PTSD. People can function seemingly fine for decades in the wake of such trauma, but it can hang around inside of them until it runs the show. Did you understand all of that?"

"Sure did."

"Now before we get underway, I have one question for you. Is there anything that you'd like to express to your mother?"

Looking at the floor, Benny thought about it. Only time lapsed photography could've captured the pace with which his smile grew. He turned to her forgivingly, raising his shoulders to voice, "Here we are."

It was minutes before the next words filled the air.

When they got home Benny's first act was to open Jesse's envelope. Inside it was a hand-crafted card with glitter and a drawing of Benny hand in hand with a woman, inscribed, "You are love, Benny. Be love. I love you. Alba loves you. Your mother loves you. And by and by you'll break the chain and be love for the family that you create. Your friend, Jesse Lee."

Below it was a list of twenty books for Benny to study. He handed her the card, which she read tearfully.

"I'll never, ever forget that man," she said.

"Jesse and Lee. Two first names I'll select for my ankle-biters. So, hey, is it okay if we shop for these books today?"

"Sure. As Jesse said, this is your time. And I have $10,000 that I've saved. This isn't about getting back to work right away, right?"

"Okay. But hey, that one let you keep money?"

"I've been saving a penny here and a nickel there for twenty years. It adds up."

"Escape money?"

"I'm not sure why I did it.""

"Does he know you have it?"

"No."

"Good. And did you ever pinch a dollar from his wallet to sweeten the pot when he was snoring on the couch?"

She became pink with embarrassment, adding, "Maybe not when he was on the couch."

"Good girl."

As they rested quietly, like a symphony building to a crescendo, the first giggle led to an all-out explosive burst. Not because a few dollars had been pilfered, just a ringing of the bells that yes, those years with Ben Thompson, Officer Thompson, and Sergeant Thompson had been insane. They whooped until they couldn't breathe. Whatever doubt there could've been about this alliance disappeared when, after more minutes of lush, appreciative silence, Benny reiterated, "Here we are," the mantra for all to come.

"Here we are," she responded proudly.

It took three books stores to track down all twenty books, but nothing less than the Holy Grail was inside of them so they persisted. While our mother rustled up some BLTs, Benny shaped the books into four letters on the floor, to be configured like that when one wasn't being studied during the eleven more weeks, she would remain with him.

LOVE

I was certain that our mother's involvement would be a nightmare. Instead, she became an equally fascinated study partner. Fancy those two staying up to all hours revisiting their favorite passages aloud, entertained like delinquents who'd burnt a doobie. Even when Sergeant Thompson insisted that she return home, she didn't relent, punctuating the miraculous job she'd done of reinserting herself as worthy of Benny's love. Sadly though, she still didn't permanently bid Sergeant Thompson farewell. And when he dished out his unsolicited opinion that her youngest son was biologically defective, his own worst enemy, once it was relayed to Benny it elicited something unforeseen and irrevocable. The indifference Benny had once aspired to.

One night, Benny and she had just finished a passage about acceptance when Benny surprised her with, "How about if we use that money to purchase a prosthetic testicle."

"Like I said, whatever you want."

Subsequent to our mother's departure, aside from working twice a week at a local restaurant to survive and returning to the karate dojo, Benny persisted with his psycho-spiritual studies for a year. His evolving usage of such language was a beacon of independence. Even his daydreaming aided in formulating a clear, future-oriented image of himself. An innate emotional intelligence that he had little idea existed, not long ago buried under a dominant trait of blind perseverance, was unearthed to never be recessive again. The Fourth Coming of Benny.

Real Freedom

The Gardens of Eden

A wedding band, five members so in sync in their jaded, pungent fatigue, lingered off to the side until the wedding finished so that they could kick off their play list. The singer whose hair was dyed orangutan orange played at being cheerful whenever a guest passed by, a mirth face designed to keep the band booking gigs. The twelve tuxedo-clad cater waiters stood in the backdrop, there to work the reception. Benny had been amongst such a troop many times in the past, signed on to serve appetizer, main course, then dessert, with some intermittent refilling of the water cups, curious as to how each couple's love had ignited, and why it had swelled to this sacred point.

It wasn't a particularly unusual wedding, just the traditional, All-American affair with a beyond cute flower girl, along with as much of whatever the bride requested as could be logically afforded. And what this bride fancied was that every girl that she'd played with on her high school and college basketball teams would be her bride's maids, not choosing one over the other to be the Maid Of Honor, instead conferring that distinction on her impending husband's closest friend, a woman living in Chicago whom she'd met only the day before when they picked her up at the Boise Airport. 35 of those 37 former teammates were able to be there, a few who couldn't afford it flying in at the expense of the bride's parents. Surveying all of those bride's maids energized and indivisible made the groom want to cry with joy. He admired their unity, and how when one of them joked the others would laugh merrily, an egoless reflection of what he envisaged marriage and family should be.

With a canopy over a mini-stage, the couple stood on each side of the non-denominational pastor, a man also in his late twenties. The groom gazed lovingly at his soon-to-be wife, upward also because she was an inch taller than him. Twice he decided to look down just to have the pleasure of peering up at her afresh. The Maid of Honor winged the bride, a woman who'd recently rooted out the self-acceptance to switch back from hair dye and concealing make-up to au natural. At the groom's side was his best man, a short stack gauchely self-conscious about his role in the affair, yet still sprung enough to lust after bridesmaids who assembled near the one and only groomsman, a Black Man with dreads who looked as joyous as the groom that it had all culminated in this. The remainder of the 125 guests, all situated facing the stage, were primarily the bride's extended family. To Benny there was so much about this bride that was like no other. What she exuded was all that he strived to be in both temperament and outlook. Despite how far he'd risen, he still couldn't fathom that she'd chosen him as her husband.

Eden Culpepper is her name. Eden grew gardens in her hats.

Years earlier Benny was home when suddenly he was awash in trepidation, so unlike the calm that had become the norm after the recent completion of his year of psycho-spiritual study. "What if there are more essential elements of personal development that were missed, and I have no idea what they are?" he thought, the jitters about being at a permanent deficit even causing a half-hearted twitch. The most terrifying projection was that his advancement wouldn't come forth to others. As invigorating as it had been, he worried that it would collapse relationally. A brief revisit to the days of pacing back and forth afforded some relief, while accepting that there was no quick result coming to this unnerving question so go slowly, be patient.

Over the next few days the riddle of how many internal pitfalls still awaited him was quaintly discomforting, though not destabilizing. The mindfulness with which he monitored himself and others had transfigured, the assimilation of traits that he wisely coveted in others taking precedence. And what he most valued was the aptitude of well-adjusted people to truly and expressively treasure what they have, to laugh, and smile, and enjoy whatever there is like he'd so uninhibitedly done as a child.

As he entered the Oyama Karate dojo for the annual Christmas party he was soothed by how it had been refashioned for the affair. All of the framed photos of black belt warriors had stencils of Santa hats on them and the punched fists presented bouquets of flowers. It was the one occasion per year when testosterone didn't rule, ousted from that 90% male environment by the comportment that the inclusion of all those spouses and girlfriends demanded. One of the few female students, a 25 year old yellow belt who hit as hard as her lingering displeasure that she'd never made the starting team often hit her, a former college basketball player at Boise State, brought another member of that team, the starting center, a woman of such eye-appeal it's as if God had finally figured out the correct amount of mini-freckles to compliment sandy blonde hair that thick. The center looked like a sculptor's size-enhanced idealized replica of herself. She was dressed in a white blouse and wrangler jeans, one of those women who never operate in the language of primping, teasing, tweezing, dying, or augmenting. She was who she was and had no plans to alter that. All the same, she resembled many women in one aspect. From a distance she loved watching Benny dance.

Benny hadn't danced in forever, apart from the sensuous wiggling of him and his shadow atop his bed the day our mother had left him to study on his own. Unsurprisingly, he still had it and there was never anyone he'd relished having contemplate him more than her. "Mutual mesmerism" is how he later described it. Like Zulus on an expedition to Sweden, amidst an open field gaping at their first snowfall as it nonchalantly floated down to them. When the dance was over, he instructed himself to look directly at her, popped in some "if you snooze, you lose," and ambled over. No more sitting back for them to approach him like the old days, and all of the insecure posturing that had entailed. When he got to her, the warmth of her smile foretold: "I will, without a doubt and until the end be a great daughter, friend, wife, and mother."

"You're going to invite me to dance, aren't you?" she asked with the twinkle of a woman overjoyed to be out of her element. At that moment Benny pegged whom he was dealing with, that child of imbedded morality who'll kick you to the curb if the quality of your character isn't stellar. She'd just vocalize, "You've had your chance," and walk away.

"I sure am."

"You're very brave, most guys who can't dunk a basketball shy away from me. Sorry for assuming that you don't have that kind of hops."

"I can touch the rim."

"And how many tries did that take?"

"Hundreds."

"Fantastic. No quitters allowed."

"It's like bench pressing 250 pounds. Squeezed it off once and there was no upside from there."

"Me, too."

"250?"

"Touching the rim."

"Now I'm ultra-fired up to dance with you," Benny joked. The room silenced amongst all of the noise, only the words of the marriage proposal that he was bristling to voice right there, reciting luminously in his mind.

"I dance like a white, suburban basketball player," she confessed, twisting her lips so far to the left that she got even more gorgeous. "I'd rather report that you MIGHT find it frightening, but I'm more certain than that."

To see her was like gazing at what Benny had no idea would be his quintessential woman. Not a hint of a mask and sincere to the core, including about her dancing skills which evoked more of someone ready to rebound than rhythmic, all elbows and knees wielded to clear the lane. Recruited by fifty schools, she'd been a starter for four years at Boise State, all-American her senior year. The cleanliness and basic good manners of her hometown compelled her to stay local. That changed when Columbia University tendered her a full scholarship toward a Doctorate In Math along with a paid position as an assistant basketball coach. When the dance ended, she shook his hand formally, equivalent to a post-game gesture.

"Thank you," Benny said, diffidently. "So, may I ask you something?"

"Sure."

"What's the most important thing to you?" he asked, convinced that she had the inner strength for such a provocative question.

"For me, that's easy. My family. And you?"

The brief delay in replying wasn't uncertainty, it's that he wanted to express this while looking right into her eyes. "For me it's the family I'm going to create someday."

"That's hot," she commented, attempting a single pirouette that ended somewhere around 320 degrees. "And how about your family of origin?"

"Probably unlike yours, though my mother, brother and I are very close. And I'm sure that they'll adore you if I have the good fortune to marry you."

It was two weeks later, after they'd spent nearly every unscheduled minute together without even a kiss that Eden's secret finally came out. Her flair for cutting the top off the six top hats that she'd dug up in her outings to used clothing stores, lowering it by four inches, sewing it back inside just where it would rest on the top of her head, then lining it so that plants could exist up there, wasn't a family tradition. It was her thing, a flare she probably wouldn't have been comfortable displaying in her hometown. The herbs and wispy plants that grew in her hats before being replanted in the bigger garden on her roof always flourished. Rain or shine, if it was growing season, they could be seen swaying in the wind above her head every Sunday as she went about her day. She didn't mind that the local Hispanic girls called her, "La Gringa Loca" and "La Chia Pet".

"Here's a freebie," she'd tell them handing out tomatoes.

"Did this start in your hat?" they'd respond.

"No better soil anywhere."

"You some loca ass white girl, but my mother loves your tomatoes."

----------------------------------+----------------------------------

Held in Eden's hometown of Boise, only 5 of the 125 wedding guests were from Benny's side. 120+5=Family. Eden had imagined that she'd marry someone from a wellspring of family and friends like her, and that his and her side, four generations deep, would blend into an even more expanding wealth of connection and support. Though she was blessed, love wasn't a choice with which she argued. She didn't care if anyone questioned, and a couple of noisy Nellies did, why only his mother, brother serving as best man, Jesse Lee as groomsman, Alba as The Maid of Honor, and grandmother on my mother's side were able to show up. Certainly, some NYC acquaintances would've attended if proximity were on their side.

"Do you Eden Culpepper take," asked The Pastor, a malleable type joyful at being interrupted at such a juncture.

"Oh My God. Oh my God," Benny gasped. Tears rained and his

legs became so wobbly that he took a knee.

Eden jumped up and down clapping. She turned to her mother, “That’s the most beautiful thing I’ve ever seen, Mom.

“He loves you, Edie.”

“I love him too, Mom. So, so, much.”

“Yes, you do. Now maybe you should marry him Edie. I have wedding cake on the brain, dear.”

The entire gathering broke out cheering while Benny knelt there, mouth covered, gazing at Eden. Alba let fly the most deafening whistle an albino had probably ever emitted at a formal gathering. Eden aided Benny back up, making sure to stick her tongue out at him a bit.

“Thank you,” he said. It was at that moment that he was emancipated of the guilt that he’d suffered about marrying this Earthy, unbleached daughter of privilege. His previous concept had been that he owed compensation for all that this new chance at life had gifted him, so he should be that martyr who showers his undying love on a woman ill-equipped alone to struggle with the ravages of her childhood. His pot-holed road had been too treacherous to now sacrifice himself in the cause of someone else’s salvation, and soon he’d even advise those looking for love to, “Seek the healthy.”

“I love you,” Eden underscored backing up to her spot.

“We love you, Benny,” cried out Jesse, tearfully.

“Yes, we do,” our mother seconded. That motivated even me to mull over a shout out, but I suddenly recaptured my dread of PDA, Public Displays of Anything! Though I was so happy for Benny. Regrettably, and this truly, and cross my heart earnestly did make me feel guilty and selfish, the hours to come of drooping at the table of honor, with this towering cohesive clan smiling with their perfect teeth all looking at my thinning hair, I'd long ago determined would be as enjoyable as being a hockey goalie, slap shots flying at me from every angle, wearing only my Fruit of The Looms.

As the nuptials continued Benny's eyes lingered on Mr. and Mrs. Culpepper. The Culpeppers of Boise, Idaho, whose love like Eden's he'd also ached for.

Even prior to meeting them, ambling to the porch of their nine room, split level house, with Eden immersed in watching him look around, his eyes like that of an Extraterrestrial recently landed, he'd hungered to be part of this uncomplicated family. The mountains that surrounded the house with its one thin road leading in and out also excited him that at least this capital city in America still had such bucolic openness only fifteen-minute drive from the downtown. It was as if the deer and her offspring who peered at them from a stone's throw away were placed there to heighten the perception that he'd touched down on less malignant terrain. There was even an RV in the driveway stenciled with, "Culpepper Caravan."

"I'm impressed that until now you've never tried to have sex with me," Eden whispered sensuously, leading him in the door. Those were the last words he'd expected. The innuendo lingered, yet in a heartbeat it became more evident why she was who she was when he saw her parents hand in hand, smiles as inviting as an untouched stream, under a jumbo sign they'd hung.....

Welcome Benny....
and thanks for bringing Eden, too!

Benny thought, "If either one of this couple has a double life, or a dark secret from their past that if exposed would bring down the house, or a fetish that requires a whip, it would mean that no marriage is safe." Family photos were tastefully spread on the living room walls, a compilation of mutual serenity. Eden was an only child, but there had been three pugs that had gone to the doghouse in the sky, ski trips to 9 states, and 26 more framed photos, one from each of her birthday parties. Benny's rapture barely allowed him to notice the gourmet kitchen with an expansive island, the floor to ceiling stone fireplace, media room, double oven, enormous game room, Cherry wood floors and cabinets, granite, marble and travertine that were all in view.

"It's such a pleasure to meet you, Benny," greeted Mrs. Culpepper who'd spent 28 of the last 33 years in her dream job, kindergarten teacher. She'd taken five years off before returning to work with the tallest kindergartener she'd ever had, Eden Epiphany Culpepper.

"Hi, Benny. We're so glad that you were able to make it out here," added Mr. Culpepper, a former college swimmer turned pediatrician. This was the moment Benny turned sure that he'd made the right choice. He knew of the dogmatic theory that modern couples MUST rehash their individual pasts together, each partner serving as a conduit to work through and overcome the other's issues resulting from the past; that it is ESSENTIAL to deepen their bond. To him it was Western exaggeration and would've been a mistake in this case. Living in the present their relationship was thriving. Living in the present they were equals. The potential pitfalls if he divulged his former quagmire to her now, and then she passed it on to her family now, weren't worth the risk. And she would've done that. And it would've worried them. And they would've told others in their conservative sphere. And on, and on, and on the bygone days could've led to future disapproval. Divulging, if ever, would at minimum be kept on hold.

"It's an honor to be here," Benny answered.

"Oh My Gosh. That's so nice. Bless Your Heart," Mrs. Culpepper gushed.

Instantaneously Benny could project how so much of the New York City crowd would recoil at her All-American chatter. He liked it.

"An honor? Why's that?" Mr. Culpepper asked.

"Because I'm with Eden," Benny replied, looking at her for a second, again that uneasiness that he didn't deserve her passing through him. "And I get to meet the family she loves so much."

"Oh," said Mrs. Culpepper, and she went over to hug Eden. "That's so sweet."

Mr. Culpepper opened his arms and Eden jumped into them. He still maintained most of the swimmer's strength, twirling her around like she was half that size while inviting, "Benny, feel free to be comfortable here and to have a dandy time."

"And to know that whomever our daughter loves, we love. Because Eden would only select a gentleman," Mrs. Culpepper added, her eyes brightening as if she foresaw a harmonious future.

"I need my camera to capture your first meeting," Eden said going into her bag. She extracted an open notebook, handed it to Benny jovially with "Here hold this" then dug for the camera. On the notebook in bold letters was written, **"It's so rare nowadays that a guy dates a girl for months without trying to fiddle with her sticks!"**

Benny often confided to me on the phone about Eden. How she could express so much with so few words, like only artless femininity can. How they'd lain in hugs every night for weeks teasing, inflamed by each other's breathing, without even a kiss. How they'd begun pressing and grinding even harder, until with their lips an inch apart, they'd stare transfixed into each other's eyes. The first kiss, without any motion to heighten sensation, just lips connected for ten minutes while tears welled up. How each time they'd go a bit further with a brief caress of this or a single button undone. How homogeneous they were in the longing for a vast love, an unbreakable bond, yet she seemed ten years wiser than him. Her essence alone was inspiring.

While she adjusted the camera, she looked at him for that extra second interpretable only to him, a woman has desires also. Something radiant coursed through his veins. Once all of the settling in was completed, and the ladies went off for girl talk, Benny and Mr. Culpepper wandered out onto the porch. The bird feeders everywhere had attracted two red finches. Their new pug puppy was jumping an inch off the ground to capture their attention. Athletic, he wasn't.

"We'd be lost without a pug," Mr. Culpepper said. "Never trust a person who doesn't love kids and pugs."

"Now there's a bumper sticker," Benny noted.

"Hey, so you're from New England. Patriots?"

"That's my team."

"Mine, too. I went to college in Boston," Mr. Culpepper continued, natural at finding two-sided interests to start the conversational ball rolling.

Benny already had an astonishing urge to call him "Dad," a term he'd dumped in the 7th grade.

As they sat Eden came outside to announce, "Hey Benny, we're going to whip up dinner and I'm not telling my daddy what. It'll be…" She tilted in to whisper to him. "Let's not have it be much longer before we're united in every respect." She pulled away to finish more inclusively, "Good idea?"

"Wooo, that was different than I expected," Benny warbled.

She bounded back inside. She'd decided that later that evening, as they lay side by side in the guest apartment her parents had built on top of the three-car garage intending in due course that their daughter would return home for good, that she'd quietly invite, "It's time, Benny." When she did, he happened to be recalling this one of Jesse Lee's offerings, "Float over the rocky rapids and into the sun-drenched tomorrows." She moved toward him for the embrace that would seal their destiny.

----------------------------------+----------------------------------

"Do you Eden take Benny to be your lawfully wedded husband, to have and to hold, from this day forward, in sickness and in health, for as long as you both shall live?"

"I sure do."

"And do you Benny take Eden to be your lawfully wedded wife, to have and to hold, from this day forward, in sickness and in health, for as long as you both shall live?"

"I sure do."

"You may kiss the bride."

A+ and The Torso

I can no longer merely scrape to fit us a bit here and a bit there into Benny's magical journey. It's just not fair to the reader. Unveiling the wonderment that is the other male members of Benny's family of origin merits so much more attention. Wink. Wink. Wink. Especially considering that at ages 50 and 30 respectively, Lieutenant Thompson and his extraordinary oldest son decided to authorize our penises to run our lives.

After 30 years of dominating our mother, impulsively Lieutenant Thompson deduced that she was an evil woman. Only a minute before he'd come to that undeniable conclusion, she'd arrived home from grocery shopping. She put the key into the living room door lock, picked up bags from where she'd laid them on the porch, opened the door, and again absentmindedly left her key in it. As he walked down the hallway yawning like a foghorn, she realized her slip-up and before he could discover it rushed back in terror to retrieve the key. He saw her alarm, and once the millisecond battle between compassion and the high of potentially uncovering evidence usable to demean her shifted toward the latter, he sped to the door to investigate why she was out of sorts.

When he got to the door, with her key already secreted away, he sensed that the villainy must be outside. He opened the door and craned his bloated mug out while she quivered like a parole violator in a lineup. The new neighbor two doors up the cross street, a splotchy faced Milk of Magnesia swigging, bald, old, dyspeptic guy with legs the color of White Out, who played croquet on his lawn four hours a day, noticed him and waved. Instantaneously, as fast as Miss Arlene the Psychic once she'd discerned that her new client is loaded, Lieutenant Thompson knew the irrefutable truth. Every ounce of his unbridled perspicacity, all of his years of crime fighting, especially those six years as a detective donning mismatched sports jackets and "slacks" a person with fashion sense would only wear on Halloween, even his intuition that never in his "mind" failed to illustrate his omniscience, all worked in tandem. So, with the confidence of The Dallas Cowboys about to play against a Pee Wee team, he stated, "I don't fool so easily, ya know."

How indisputable could it be that Mr. Croquet's wave wasn't intended for him, but instead for his Secret Lover, that tart otherwise known as Lieutenant Thompson's wife.

Oh yes, she was fully transgressive now putting out unlike any hussy with hot flashes has ever done before. And what further proof would he need other than how nervous she was, as if he hadn't set eyes on that anxiety a thousand times over 30+ years when he was, without compunction or dramatic pauses that would allow his victim to breath, blowing this or that out of proportion. On the spot he'd tried, convicted, and sentenced her to an old age of futilely endeavoring to persuade him that it was only the misdemeanor of leaving the key in the door, with additional sanctions deserved for groping to cover up that abomination. But we've all calculated by now that Ben Thompson is never wrong. Therefore, after an hour of ranting, he sealed the future with this, "Remember that book we read in high school, 'The Scarlett Letter', I think Charles Dickens wrote it. Well, the Adulteress had to wear a big letter A on her dress or her forehead, whatever. Right under my roof with the neighbor, you deserve an A+!"

Lieutenant Thompson's all pervasive **30+ year** effort to recalibrate her had all come to this. As Benny and I hoped it would, our mother's artful participation in Benny's rebirth didn't catapult her to her own irrepressible renaissance. The familiarity of her suffering, the vastness of the unknown that could be out there if she absconded, and the miscalculation that her minutely germinating unwillingness to tolerate every speck of The Lieutenant's nonsense might finally help temper him someday, were like three sets of reigns all pulling her in different directions ending her up in the same place. And thus, even this incident didn't send her packing.

How this little tale of love gone wrong applies to Daddy's Me Maker I'll wrap up soon. First, I'll detail how my No Babies Maker (babies are too stressful) sent me astray. Six years into sharing allergies and phobias living with Petra, whom I secretly named "No

Boobala" for obvious reasons, I not so briefly dated Helen again. Please recall that she'd dumped me the last time. A pallid, over-teased, excessively tweezed woman with cerebral palsy, nine years older than me, and with boobs shaped like barely nutritious bananas had branded me as not in her league. How's that for something to fast-fire my neurosis.

If only when I'd laid eyes on her anew all those years later, she wasn't now the foundation for the most eye-popping boob job I'd ever seen, I probably could've avoided that debauchment again. Forty-year-old women with c.p. and not yet beyond the Farrah Fawcett snip, even those with a siren's set, can find the pickings pretty slim so lo and behold she regarded me in a new, reality-distorting light. And I made that easier for her by matter-of-factly professing that I had a dream job in marketing; salary, benes, and a ladder I was half way up and casually ascending. What a contrast to someone who was actually unemployed for more than a year and as cautiously as possible eating away at my savings.

Anyway, Helen's minuscule waist and her newly reconstructed set (that is why I secretly named her Boobala), what better way for me to not grapple with reality than that? Every time I climbed on board, all I would think is, "Oh, the torso." Sticking straight up like hypnotic mounds of compensation for all that I'd decided that I couldn't achieve on account of the hand I'd been dealt. And now that they'd just engineered Phentolamine to increase blood flow to my No Babies Maker, I'd pound every ounce of her dumping me way back when right out of her. And I was good at it, pumping away feverishly as if success in such affairs would afford me a modicum of self-esteem. It got so exciting for a delusional while there that I ended up guiltily abandoning No Boobala for a love den, meaning an identical claustrophobic apartment in the same monochromatic complex. You'd assume I'd exhibit the self-restraint to not get my jollies with Boobala near where No-Boobala still lived, but it was the easiest choice for me to move only a hundred yards away, Phentolamine in my most secure pocket so as to not mislay it. It also crossed my mind to have the decency to not use Boobala. But I couldn't resist given my history of subsisting off of a single obsession? The Holocaust, my ex-Rose Bush, and now Boobala's torso.

Oh Phentolamine, if only daddy had also discovered it. Maybe he wouldn't have displaced the frustration on to our poor mother that, due to obesity, his Me-Maker no longer functioned.

"You just couldn't live without it, could ya?" Lieutenant Thompson lambasted. "As soon as I had my problem you were shacking up with another guy, weren't ya?"

"No, I was afraid that you'd make such a big deal out of me leaving the key in the door," our mother disagreed, somehow despite **30+years** of him proving that the greatest indicator of future behavior is past behavior, in disbelief that hell had gotten hotter.

"Key, my ass."

"I've never met that neighbor. Go ask him."

"Yeah, right. And I'm the Queen of England."

"But what proof do you have?"

"I don't need proof. I just know, so you can whitewash until the cows come home."

Benny and I conjectured if Lieutenant Thompson accused our mother of sexing up Mr. Croquet to keep her so on pins and needles defending what she hadn't done, that she'd otherwise regress back to the unadulterated compliance that a master deserves. Nice try fella because once her **30+ years** of obsequiousness had turned 31, he was now overestimating how incapacitated she'd remained. He didn't know that for a year she'd been expecting an apology for the false accusation and so much more.

"If circumstances don't change, I'm going to move out," she stated with uncharacteristic petulance, in the driveway just after he got out of his truck.

"I admit occasionally I'm not very patient. I'll plan to do better," he responded, connecting that if she couldn't hold notifying him until he'd come inside, that she must be serious.

His unanticipated droplet of confession threw her off. Undeterred, she rallied in her resolution to unleash her entire rehearsed ultimatum.

"And you have to apologize for accusing me of cheating."

He broke out his oh so pained expression. "I can't do that. I've done my best to forgive, but there's no reason to apologize."

Each looked away. She felt like they'd never met before and hated him upon first sight.

"You're sick that's why," she blurted out with a propped up, super-charged determination while out of the corner of her eye noticing that bird turd had just landed on his windshield.

"Say what you're gonna, but at least I've never cheated. And God knows I've had my chances," he replied, mechanically obstinate. He'd fallen out for years or decades with his parents and all six of his siblings, all with infallible rationales. His two sons shunned him. That was, so obviously, their fault. His rare new "friendships" never lasted. Their fault. Rumor had it that his ideal friend, the one who'd agree with whatever he came up with, would require cloning.

That night when he was snoring mouth agape in his bed, the drool pooling on the pillow, a double funeral on the horizon, a human shadow loomed over him. The point of the knife wasn't steady in the shadow, like another Thompson tipping point had hardened the knife holder's otherwise gentle nature. One way or another this was the last day that he'd have a wife.

A Double Funeral

Benny heard it. “Oh, my word! I was so in love with that guy sitting over there,” shot too loudly from behind him at the Broadway Diner on 101st street. He didn’t want to turn around to see what nutty as a fruitcake New Yorker was chattering with what other nutty as a fruitcake New Yorker. He was at peace eating his Sunday ritual of lightly cooked pancakes after exchanging the usual banalities with Derek, the prototypical middle-aged Greek Diner owner who opened his one and only place in his twenties destined to age there ungracefully till kingdom come, chain smoking and abusing whatever Mexican Dish Washer was hired on under the table for inhumanely less than the minimum wage. Benny sliced off some pancake and raised it to his mouth just when she plopped into the other seat at his booth announcing, “I was so in love with you.”

“Now you tell me,” he kidded reflexively.

“You taught kickboxing at my gym downtown what was it say six years ago?” she exclaimed with ardent enthusiasm. Yes, it had been that long and despite her beauty, long black hair and green, see-into-your-soul eyes, he didn’t recall her.

“Thanks for remembering me,” he answered, wishing it were only him, his three remaining silver dollars, his rumination on the human tendency to be dualistic, and the glass of water that he’d vigorously wiped off with a napkin after as usual the waitress had delivered it to him with her fingers all over the mouth, spreading diner germs with the same consciousness that drove her to shave her eyebrows and draw them back on with what seemed like Crayola shade charcoal.

“I’d observe from the doorway. You were so captivating as a teacher. You were serious, but so playful and witty.”

“Until the day the owner padlocked the door and took off without paying the employees or paying back any of the gym memberships,” Benny quipped as if it weren’t a deplorable fact.

"I should've asked you out," she said, like she'd for too long wanted to confide that.

Benny put his fork down with that bite of pancake still on it. He had the inkling that fate was about to bestow upon him one of those moments that make us all wish for immortality. At the same time, he stroked his wedding ring to prompt her not push this too far. She used her right hand, the one that didn't bear a wedding ring to clutch Benny's hand across the table. With a memory lane smile and a superior ability to on command turn off the excess of eagerness, she squeezed his hand tightly. To the hilt, this was momentous to her. Yet it was innocent. Passive. Harmless. Just the scent of an overpowering desire from long ago waltzing in the air.

Benny couldn't wait to see what she'd do next, exhilarated that the scenario felt both unscripted and practiced. And though he was dazzlingly in love with Eden, there was a taste that these two would've had something solid also if they were single and met now. Like a reunion of former lovers who must accept morally that their undying affection can't be rekindled, they gazed at each other. It was as if he was fulfilling some mystical unfinished business that he didn't know that he'd had, a farewell to the sweet, post-adolescent love he might've delighted in had he been capable of it. And just like that she released his hand, got up, and sashayed to the door. She looked back and lit up like it had turned out better than she could've imagined. Backing up, she nodded and was gone.

Days later he was sightseeing in Central Park, for all was now new to him even if he'd frequented it in the past. Suddenly, there it was, a memory. He sat on the bench and allowed it to wash over him. Like a grainy silent film, he recalled his admirer watching from outside the classroom of that gym back when she'd had a buzz cut dyed blonde. He'd suspected she was waiting for someone who wasn't as messed up as he pretended not to be.

"It's unbelievable. The images that people can create about themselves, that other people grasp on to, can appear to tell the whole story," he noted to himself. "She simply had no idea about me."

When Benny got home the phone was ringing. It was late and Eden was lingering in the bathroom performing the scented grooming that sends a signal.

"Hi. This is Mum," our mother said with a forced poise. "Sad news. My mother passed away today."

"Oh, I'm so sorry." Benny responded, also registering that this news didn't immediately dampen his urge to get with Eden. "How are you?"

"Okay. Very sad though. Do you have the time to come here?"

"I'll be there tomorrow. Fine if Eden tags along?"

"She's your wife, so, of course."

Months earlier our mother had put down the knife and finally left Lieutenant Thompson. Word is he predicted to everyone that "she'll be back." So, when she petitioned for divorce not only his ego was tested, but his omniscience. His first response was to call her, leaving no recorded proof that would sully the waning years of his career, and admonished her that if she tried to "Steal his house in the divorce, the house that he'd slaved for while she spent her days watching 'The Price Is Right' and lusting after neighbors, that I'll burn it down with you in it." Now 51 years old she moved alone into an apartment for the first time.

As for me planning to attend my grandmother's funeral, yeah right. My now stock phrases, "I just can't handle it" and "Too depressing," plus some embroidering of "my bout of the flu" and certainly our mother would be relegated to her role as The Great Enabler, this time enabling her oldest son. I'm still having my jollies with "The Torso." I even hang out with an immigrant girl from Thailand, a mail order bride who hasn't caught on that I long to finagle her away from her overly trusting husband. Yet the one of my mother's parents whom she'd met had died and all I'd planned to do was mail her the lowest priced condolence. Am I now inexcusably unlikeable? I hope not. Perhaps these disgraces were more a reflection of a collapse during such a childhood than an innate character flaw. If someone as strong as Benny could be knocked down to the canvass until the count of nine, what would such a childhood portend for the likes of me?

Eden and Benny arrived at our mother's tenement apartment at sunset. His first thought upon entering was, "Wow, she got old." She greeted them with a sober smile, as if she'd caused Benny so much grief in the past that she refused to burden him with freshly ignited displays of emotion. She had on an apron, the festive one with Santas on it that she'd worn every year at Christmas. Benny noted how out of place that the knickknacks and embroidered wall hangings from Tree Hill Acres seemed, disheartened that she'd transferred any of those proletariat adornments to this oasis half way across town. Why not burn it all along with any photo of our pear-shaped tormentor and start anew?

Seated in the rocking chair in the corner was, me. I penciled cooperation into my schedule once Benny had promised to lead me there, and to the wake, by the ear, if I didn't show up early to both. By the ear, like our father used to. As I approached them, the figure of capacitation that they cut holding hands, their individual choice of style artistically meshed, I felt as unworthy as ever. Even under such circumstances my first compulsion was to compare myself.

"Hey brother," I greeted.

"I'm glad you came early."

"Hey Eden."

Looking down at me, she put her hand on my shoulder and responded, "I'm sorry for your loss, Davey."

Of course, she could only perceive of a death in the family as a genuine loss shared by all. I could tell Benny hadn't dispelled that myth so I ducked my head and said like a sidebar to my pain, "Well, we always tried to get her to be consistent with her diabetes medication."

With our mother in the kitchen cleaning up an hour later, Benny, Eden, and I idled at the table discussing his current favorite topic, how many people don't differentiate between the words "want" and "need." Same for "want" and "expect." One of his favorite things about Eden was that resident in her was a fascination with psychology akin to that of people formerly more messed up than she would ever be.

"Put out a blast, baby. If people just quit assuming they need all they want, they'd view what they have far more clearly," he said to Eden, his voice lowered so that our mother wouldn't come up against playfulness at such an hour.

"But I need a Mercedes convertible, a mink stole, and that trip to everywhere," she whispered back.

"Well, of course, you do. But I think a pet llama would be excessive."

Our mother reentered. She retrieved a plate as the phone began to ring. My knee-jerk assumption was that someone was calling to express condolences. Startled, our mother turned, accidentally flipping a fork that suspended in the air. When it landed on the floor it clanged a kind of warning shot.

"Hello" our mother began, the weariness seeping through from having been bedside for her mother's last breaths. As she listened her placid anticipation rigidified as only exposure to the surreal can cause. "Oh, my condolences to you also. In what funeral home will he be?" When the surreal multiplied, stuttering ensued out of panic. "But, ah, that's, but, but, that's the same funeral home my mother is in."

I inclined drawn to the mystery, rattled enough that the fat guy dust that our father used to raise up when he plopped onto the couch appeared before my eyes. Eden grabbed Benny's hand, the tension even gripping her.

"Did he know that's the funeral home my mother is in?" our mother asked, timidly. The answer so weakened her knees that she had to sit. "Okay. Goodbye. See you tomorrow."

When she hung up, her code red attempt to move her mouth from slack-jawed to words took a whole minute. "That was your father's sister, Joanne. He claims he did it because it would be more convenient for those who choose to attend both funerals to just have to shift across the hallway."

"I don't understand. Across the hallway to what?" Benny asked.

"His father. He died this morning of a heart attack."

"He's going to be in the same funeral home as your mother?"

"I can't believe it," she bemoaned.

"No, no, no, no," I heard come from me.

"That's crazy," Benny exclaimed.

"Why's that problematic?" Eden asked.

"Irreconcilable differences" was all Benny had informed her about our parent's split. He leaned in to reveal, "Just because he was a police officer didn't qualify him as a passable hubby. But we'll get into that after the double funeral."

Eden had never met or spoken to our father and I'm not sure how Benny had excused that. His lack of attendance at their wedding was chocked up to "unavailable."

---------------------------------+---------------------------------

Grandpa Thompson looked like a silent screen movie star laid to rest at the Nobrega Funeral Home. Not claiming he'd ever been that handsome when he was alive, but death makeup can be a lively art. Hung on the casket was a wilted photo of him as a boy mounted on a Shetland pony, the one brought to the grade school so every kid in his 3rd grade depression era class would pose for the same mandatory carefree photo. In it he wore a provincial smile that gradually was supplanted over the years by the scowl of a truck driver sick of loading and unloading other people's wares. His showing didn't start for an hour so no one was in that room, with the exception of Benny who'd wandered over from the other room where our grandmother lay. Staring at him he waited for even a remote sense of loss, but it was like sludge was clogging up his pathways. This was the man who'd trained our father with his own torrential violence. He'd also for Christmas given Benny and me the same skin-drying brand of soap on a rope six years in a row. Buying wholesale and storing it all in the attic was one key to enriching his bank account.

"It's starting," Eden reported coming up behind Benny.

They walked hand in hand to the foyer where I was standing at the twin funeral attendee books that were two feet apart on lighted podiums. They joined me there and were decent enough to not point out that the knees and seat of the black corduroys I'd donned were worn so thin that they looked partially gray. While perusing our grandmother's attendee book to remind ourselves of the names of relatives we'd forgotten, Benny's eyes flashed back to where Mr. Norbrega still stood in the doorway maintaining a circumspect, overly put on, half smile. Benny and I recalled how back in high school this same frozen man had lifelessly professed that "over my dead body, would even a million dead bodies lined up at our door get me to be the fourth generation operating the family business." The guarantee of financial security can snatch away one's former illusion.

Inside the other showing room thirty mourners sat quietly. Our mother's Aunt Gerlie was there minus the four fingers that repercussions from a three pack a day habit had reaped. The good news was that she was now smoking only one cigarette per day in a combined act of self-control and regimentation heretofore not seen by mankind. Every hour she lit, savored one puff then snuffed out her daily cigarette until the timer re-energized her again for that. There was our mother's Uncle Moe who definitely wasn't a hoarder, despite the fact that the one residual pathway in his apartment was an inch wider than him. Also, in reluctant attendance was Uncle Moe's steadily unemployed son Danny who only ate waffles, Hersey's kisses, and Flintstones Chewables, and thus that ashen color.

Eden took her seat preventing Danny from further ogling her, while Benny and I knelt at the pew in front of our grandmother's casket. Laying there after an adulthood of rummage sales, piecework in a series of dying factories, and child abandonment, she looked more like she'd smoked herself to death than someone whose peek habit was only half of her sister Gerlie's. The relatives and friends, all as stylish as your less than average Elk's Club member, now relocated their gawking toward Benny. This was the boy who'd ventured off "in search of greener pastures" while they stayed local eating buttered spaghetti and fried anything, clueless as to why they required a grunting, eye bulging, five second push using two hands and a hideous wiggle just to get up.

Benny and I joined the far end of the receiving line of Uncle Moe, Aunt Gerlie, and Aunt Hildaberto, who'd just buzzed in from work after aiming to cover the smell with some Yardley Daylight Encounter that she'd won at bingo. She'd cut fish for forty years and still hadn't lopped off that hair sticking out of the mole on her cheek. Benny used to call it "the one constant in an ever-changing world." Next stood our grandmother's fourth husband Herb who was ten years younger than her and only five older than our mother. It was in his fifties that he'd left off circling the local ponds to catch tadpoles, his only exercise. He really gained weight then, even though he didn't fancy buttered spaghetti. If there were a Guinness

Book Of World Records for the "Ability to Forget He Told You That Story Before," he would've without question been the winner. Next on line came our mother, Benny, then me.

"How are you holding up?" Benny asked her.

"I'm okay," she replied, but we could see that she was barely above water.

Benny and I did the best we could to project the dourness of the bereaved when each person conveyed: "Sorry for your loss." It occupied us so we didn't catch Lieutenant Thompson parading in with the air of accomplishment that overblowing his career exploits had accorded him. This was the most erudite, successful man in a room filled with "barely tolerable in-laws and slackers." The frayed dark green sports jacket and navy-blue slacks as usual displayed a trendsetter's prowess at mismatching. His hair had turned white, like a surrender flag raised to put you off guard.

He suddenly trumped up a solemn, caring countenance and headed forward, a sight specific contrivance within a larger masquerade. He knelt next to the coffin of the woman whom since their first encounter he'd deemed "sa'em the cat dragged in," and crossed himself like Jesus was his lord and savior. Unconsciously, he did a minor rendition of that throat clearing his progeny used to suffer even when a testicle was blown up to the size of a baseball, as if compelled to spit out the last remnants of the formerly "uneducable halfwit" now all stiff in front of him like sweet justice. Our grandmother was another reason he was devoid of any culpability. His wife had been too damaged by "that one" to unerringly embrace how good she had it in marriage.

"How are you holding up now?" Benny asked our mother.

"Okay. Anyway, we knew that boil would be here."

"'That boil.' Good girl."

Once she'd turned forward, we analyzed her peripherally. She closed her eyes into a squint, more aghast than okay.

Lieutenant Thompson must have been counting back to zero from fifteen because fifteen seconds later he got up, crossed himself like Jesus was his lord and savior, and rotated toward the receiving line. Benny and I are certain to this day that another cover-up occurred at that moment, all of the post-marriage contempt and malice that puss exposed lasting no longer than two frames of subliminally suggestive film during a movie. Lieutenant Thompson walked to Aunt Gerlie, the one he'd privately disparaged as, "The Wallflower That Some Loser Must Have Accidentally Fallen Into," describing her love life and that she'd devolved into the single mother of a "male mutant midget more monkey than man." I could barely hear that stifling drone. It still made me queasy and irritable. I wished that a beverage vendor would whimsically come in lugging a cooler full of Gatorade that could wash away the hunch that there was more on The Lieutenant's mind than just offering condolences and enduring the iota of heartache from his own loss.

Though not a cinch I tried to chock up my hunch as just The Lieutenant seeing, without ample warning to rehearse, his ex-wife for the first time since the split. He waddled along the line, avoiding eye contact as he passed by our mother and Herb to approach Benny and me.

"I see the hair grew back," he said to Benny, the predictable opening quarry.

"Yep," Benny replied, reminding himself to not look away.

"Still doing that martial arts like ya used' ta?

"Just karate. No PKA for now."

"Sorry about your loss," he uttered, robotically.

"You, too."

"What timing, huh?"

"When it rains, it pours."

He nodded solemnly to me, repeated the condolence, then walked past our mother and Herb again to the other mourners, shook a couple of hands, got a pat on the shoulder from Danny for whom he'd gotten the drunk and disorderly charges dropped. Unexpectedly he returned to Herb and stared at him blankly before whispering into the ear of our mother not closest to Benny. Off he went with those eyes ablaze capped off with "peace be with you." Our mother looked toward the ceiling, received no help from God, and fainted to the floor.

It wasn't long before our mother, having refused medical attention and to retreat home, was sitting in a corner between Eden and me. Most of all, and more than ever, once our mother had reasonably recovered, Benny just wanted to focus on Eden from a distance. How unassumingly she'd conducted herself from the second they'd arrived, the sincerity with which she'd volunteered to do anything called for during their visit, her decorum and timing, could've been a case study in social skill. Out of the corner of his eye Benny spotted The Lieutenant's youngest sister seated amongst the mourners crying profusely. He was slow to apprehend why because she'd only met our grandmother twice. He walked over to her and sat, not impressed by her gray jogging suit, the sweatband now wrapped around her wrist. Her facial skin had the saggy exhaustion of someone who'd lost and gained 50 pounds during every presidential election cycle since puberty.

"My daddy is gone. My daddy is gone," she wailed.

"Should I bring over my father?" he offered, the words "my father" seeming as foreign to him as that tribe he'd recently studied who suck ants out of the ground for sustenance.

"Yes, please," she mumbled. "But he probably won't talk to me."

"What? Of course, he will," he said, rising to go retrieve him. Outside the other parlor he lingered in the doorway to permit Lieutenant Thompson the sacred space to kneel at his father's casket. When he stood, Benny couldn't interpret his little smile. Was it a cherished memory or relief that his father was finally as mobile as a rock?

"Your sister is over there very upset."

"Which one?" he responded with abrupt tension.

"Lauren."

"I'm not speaking to her."

"But she's…"

"She's been causing problems so she can just stew in it."

"But she's your.....her father just…" Benny stammered. He recalled whom he was dealing with and returned to Aunt Lauren. She was biting on her rhinestone glasses and tapping her Puma Easy Riders on the floor.

"I'm so sorry," he said, noticing the half eaten Big Mac in her purse. "You're right. He's living out some grudge against you. Probably the tenth time you've been on his hit list, so don't be distressed."

"True but, why now? Why now?"

"For the same reason as usual," he replied, putting his hand on her shoulder. "He's a cave man. You know that. Forget him and go to your other siblings when they turn up. Okay?"

While she mulled it over, he noticed her sister Joanne had slipped in. Once Benny had sent Joanne to Lauren, he stood off in a corner again eyes on Eden with our mother, wondering what would be her assessment of this cast of characters. As one they'd been fascinated of late about how, for the most part, people are a reflection of those with whom they associate. "Show me who your friends are, and I'll tell you who you are." He situated himself quietly next to Herb who'd remained stoically grieving throughout the wake, not the sort to cry in public. I joined them sitting on the other side of Benny. We both detected Herb's anger.

"I never get mad, right?" Herb asked insecurely. It was the case. In general, he was a passive, elementary man who'd wanted little more than to take a ride every day with his wife.

"Not that I've seen," Benny responded.

"Right now, I'm mad," Herb struggled to admit, as lacking in composure as we'd ever seen.

"At your wife's funeral? Why now?"

"Your mother fainted for a reason that you won't like," he replied, his eyes glancing toward the ceiling for too long before settling on Benny and me. "Darn it, I just have to blab. I'm so teed off. I overheard your father say the reason her mother died was because your mother, it's just so disgusting, was having sex with me. That's just not right saying stuff like that at a funeral."

Benny's eyes rocketed toward the target. As Herb and I reached in vain to grab him, he was already climbing over chairs in the direction of the other parlor unable to register the shrieks and moans it provoked.

"You got two seconds to get ready," he warned towering over him as I entered the room. Lieutenant Thompson shrunk in his seat so two seconds later the chair was yanked so hostilely that he crashed to the floor. He got up and careened toward the casket, hunted by his son and the punch that sent him sprawling over the corpse. He crumbled to the floor again. I was paralyzed by the speed of it all. Benny upthrusted a flexed foot as high as his training allowed in order to stomp. Next came my favorite act of love ever. I'm not one for gratuitous soapy stuff, but this one downright impressed me.

Eden tackled Benny just before he could do severe, richly deserved damage. She used her Goddess legs and a chokehold to pin him long enough for the Lieutenant to somewhat gain his senses and sit up. Possessed, Benny kept repeating, "He said to my mother…He said to my mother," not even able to formulate a sentence. Lieutenant Thompson, with an expression more of terror than his ingrained rage, looked toward him. But that rage was there also as he shifted to all fours in preparation to stand, or attack, or stand and attack. I could hear people behind me weeping and protesting. None of this registered to Eden who hung on with all of her might as Benny, turned away from us all, gradually calmed down. The Lieutenant's speed increased, probably to flee. Benny was now exposed, defenseless. My self-preservation clashed with the many tentacles of brotherly bond. Gears ground against the depressed brakes. All of the habitual neutering stop signs couldn't deter me from stepping my left foot forward, right, left, and boom, a kick to the chin. Lieutenant Thompson's head fired back into the casket stand and he collapsed onto the floor still conscious but not thriving.

The power I felt jostled with terror, as Danny and Uncle Moe pulled me away. Unsure if I was being attacked, I called out, "Benny!"

In a second, he bent Eden's finger enough to release the chokehold, twisted, spun and was standing free. Eden rose behind him and grabbed his collar to impede him as he surveyed the situation. He registered that I was okay and ordered Lieutenant Thompson to, "Get out!" as our Mother entered the room. She pointed and announced what happened, leaving her ex-husband on an island that even his sisters wouldn't back. He got up, red-faced and wheezing. Aunts Gerlie and Hildaberto moved toward him to resume the assault, only to be pulled back by Herb. Danny then made his move but was restrained by Mr. Norbrega. All eyes on him, Lieutenant Thompson hobbled out with the photo of his father mounted on the pony stuck to his back, never more to be seen by any of my mother's side of the family.

Mr. Norbrega looked so galvanized that he was likely to brighten up his lackluster future by getting veneers on his beige teeth. Off and on for some time I'd wish that either my or Benny's foot had pleasantly rearranged cartilage and bone. It was the only fisticuffs of my life. I couldn't believe I'd done it. To this day it's my crowning achievement.

Benny's year of intense study, and the years since when he'd been on such a glowing path, even his love for Eden, couldn't deter the old Benny from resurfacing when pushed too far. It seems that our sordid histories are continuously inside most of us conspiring to re-launch us down past roads.

Later, lying facing each other in bed, Benny kept apologizing to Eden contrite with shame.

"Don't apologize. She's your mother and you came to her defense. He would've taken it further if you hadn't," she supported, kissing him on the cheek. "I'm proud of you."

Benny stayed silent for a bit, beyond drained, yet grateful for her endorsement.

"Though it's now time to fill me in about your past, young man."

"Oh boy. You want your eyes opened that much?"

"It won't change my love for you. Let it out. And not just what would be less challenging to hear."

"Soon. Maybe tomorrow. I'll just say something else equally important for now, okay?"

She rose up formally. He followed her lead, looking into her eyes to continue, "There are some aspects, maybe a lot, that I'm still not versed in about love and family. Please trust that I plan to learn and be good at them."

"You're great already," she replied, wrapping around him. They remained that way, unwound and triumphant. There was a requited admiration between these two that never fawned or fizzled out. Each could share in the other's successes and joys without envy.

"Hey Benny."

"Yeah, Eden."

"Let's go really whip his tail."

He knew she was kidding. He smiled anyway.

"We gotta whup'm, Benny. Me and you, shoulder to shoulder. We'll thump his arse until he wishes he didn't have one. What do you say?"

"Let's compare planners to see when we're both available for that."

In Remembrance of Dr. LaPrade's Wish

Freshly promoted Police Captain Ben Thompson didn't approve of how Teddy cut his grass. After all, the pimply, rat-tail haired, Pac Man obsessed fourteen-year-old whom he'd taken under his paternal wing after the boy was nabbed twice siphoning the neighborhood's gas tanks to fill his mother's minivan, should undoubtedly show appreciation by making doubly sure nothing unsightly stuck up between the fence. Thus, Ben Thompson, after thorough deliberation, fostered his self-worth with, "Even my good for nothing sons could do a better job."

"Fuck you," Teddy fired back, and never returned, going on to brag to neighbors he'd previously siphoned about his foul tongue with that "dumb cop."

Breathing like he hadn't exercised since he'd graduated from the police academy, two weeks after his falling out with Teddy, Captain Thompson carried that lawn mower up the cellar stairs one step at a time. He'd show them. He didn't need help or human company anymore, and how would he have time for it anyway now that he was constructing the list of all the people who'd unjustifiably abandoned him, wishing them no success, no happiness, and gobs of suffering that he could privately celebrate. The day had dawned to go it alone, as all noble survivors eventually must. Beyond everything he was still the formidable man that he'd always been, discounting a freshly minted interest in baking muffins, so why shouldn't he cut the lawn he'd toiled so hard to buy? Only one impediment though, when he got to the top of the stairs somehow the door had mysteriously closed. It was probably caused by the wind gusting through the front screen door. Or had it been Teddy? So he pressed that mower tightly against the wall while freeing a hand to open the door, leaning backwards a bit to create the space to turn the doorknob. But he must have tipped back too far. Or, had Teddy gone all "Psycho," and without warning opened the door to push him down? Either way when the one sister whom at the moment Captain Thompson was speaking to discovered him at the bottom of the stairs, he'd been flat-lined for two days.

Certainly, there was an investigation done. Teddy? His fingerprints were everywhere, especially on the lawn mower. "Of course, they were" he testified, "I'd been there a shit load of times." Given his recent boasting he'd definitely had a motive timorous neighbor reluctantly acknowledged. Say it isn't so Teddy! My heart is so broken here at the loss of my sweet Daddy. But there was no proof, and thus no felony, and no arrest, until Teddy was popped a month later for again siphoning.

That sister who'd found The Captain laid out in a pool of his own lawn mower gas, Lauren, the one whom he wasn't speaking to at the funeral, had the misguided idea of asking Benny and me to eulogize at the wake. First, she called me. Of course, it's not hard to predict that I intended to be a no show. Then she tried Benny, but he was at work dealing with....

D'artagnan was the Three Musketeers sidekick before they got their AARP cards and learned to settle disputes verbally. Magically D'artagnan, still dressing in 17th century britches, floppy sword-fighting hat, and pointy beard, was also seated on the subway platform bench centuries later singing The Beatles "I Am the Walrus" while strumming on the sticker collector that also served as his guitar. Benny stood admiring him from a professional distance, a bit separated from the rest of the audience of vagrants, welfare teens pushing babies in state subsidized carriages, and a freshly released "celly" still wearing his pants so intentionally low that God revenged this unsightliness with skid marks too visible on his BVDs. Next to D'artagnan sat a young, Hasidic Gentleman in full religious attire, including the slightly less floppy black hat. They looked so alike that Benny wished he had a camera with him. Though plainly, wearing his uniform, he wasn't supposed to be taking photos of the citizenry.

Benny used to say, "You must switch from a camera to a video camera when a third New York character merges with the scene," which is what he thought as soon as Mr. B.S. approached. Mr. B.S., who was revered back then as Mr. Bull Shit and would go on to be dubbed Mr. Breathe Strip, was for decades infamous between 100th and 110th street on Broadway. Enigmatically, he had no imitators, so he was the only crackpot along there who walked to tongue dangling exhaustion an oversized poodle while wearing his own self-generated version of the not yet invented Breathe Right Strip on his nose. Though selfishly the poodle wasn't also provided a Breathe Strip to wear, Mr. B. S. always came out of nowhere to impose his rambling political views on beleaguered passersby.

On the platform, unaccompanied by poodle though breathing better than the rest, he randomly blazoned: "We finance Israel because the Jews dominate all of our media and Wall Street. If the Muslims did, it would be Fuck Israel!" His 1st amendment right entitled even him to opine though it didn't thrill the Hasidic Gent who began vigorously arguing back and forth with him.

Amused, endeavoring to not be jaded after such a short period on the job yet also ready to react, Benny surveyed while it went on well past the ten-second window in which anyone sane should realize that Mr. B.S. was dealing with anywhere between 14-23 cards. Mr. B.S. was sweating so hoggishly that it loosened one side of his Breath Strip. It became unattached and hung like a long snot from his left nostril, matching not so alluringly with the long snot slithering out of his right one. They fluttered in tandem, energized by the wind from each diatribe meant to talk over his combatant. The Hasidic Gent stood up irately, flicking his pointer finger menacingly. They were on the path to fisticuffs so Benny advanced, then hesitated when D'artagnan broke off at "Walrus," stood up, confided wisdom to The Hasidic Gent, got back a contrite nod in agreement, put his arm around him, bit by bit finessed him into the train still whispering words only he and Benny could hear, "Why argue with crazy?" then waved to him as the train pulled away.

Once the audience including Mr. B.S., began to applaud D'artagnan, not for his music but for his ability to defuse, Benny decided to join in. D'artagnan smiled at him bashfully. He looked at Benny's badge and said, "Why Thank You, Officer Thompson." Inside Benny's jacket he also wore his friend Jeff's former badge,

#6299.

"We could all learn a trick or two from you," Benny praised.

"Thanks for granting me license to practice my conflict resolution skills."

"Where'd you learn those?"

"Acquiring my otherwise unused Master's Degree."

"Hands off that guitar," Benny ordered as Mr. B.S.picked it up. Mr. B.S. put the guitar down gently, tried in vain to reattach his breathe strip, and withdrew gibbering about how they put mind control drugs in the drinking water so that the masses won't seek revolution.

"Nice peripheral vision," D'artagnan commented.

And that is what brought about Benny's second and final lasting friendship in New York City. As the crowd dispersed, D'artagnan sat, picked up his guitar, and recommenced at "Walrus. Goo. Goo. G'joob. Goo. Goo. Goo. G'joob."

Benny did his job while enjoying the show, relieved that this his seventh month of being a police officer in New York City wouldn't extend beyond a year. He was thrilled that Eden had secured a professor post at Boise State, and that they'd be relocating to her hometown where he'd already applied for and been hired by that city's police department. He forecasted that God would continue getting moody, shaking the Earth so that most of the crazies would roll to either NYC or LA, and was ready for the open spaces and simplicity of somewhere else. The irony of becoming a police officer didn't elude him in that years earlier our father pushed for that when, at the time, it in no way fit into who Benny was. The choice was now part of a master plan with multiple components. He'd also been accepted to Boise State to set about the eight to ten-year process part time of earning a doctorate in clinical psychology with the intention upon its completion of retiring from police work, the life of action he still needed replaced once he'd further mellowed by one of intellect. Most rich of all was the re-emergence of kill two birds with one stone. Without neglecting his duties, on par with his days as a Security Guard, he squeezed in some study on the job.

When he got home, he saw the message on his answering machine, that chance to eulogize. Our father was dead. Inert. For the next couple of days Benny alternated between relief and his prevailing indifference. About eulogizing, I vociferously advised him to follow my lead and to instead stay holed up grieving for months, but he surprisingly accepted the invitation. And he insisted that I be there.

The turn-out was sparse two days later at The Nobrega Funeral Home, so recalling Captain Thompson's claim that he'd been popular with his fellow officers, it was noted that there also wasn't a wet eye in the place. Maybe because Ben Thompson, Phentolamine now in his medicine cabinet, had just faced disciplinary charges for sexual advances on a female officer. Maybe because everyone, each in his or her own time, also had realized too late that yes, he had a missing link. The good news was that he couldn't cause any more grief now, other than he'd willed everything to "The Fish & Game Society." Fortunately, by law, his pension automatically transferred to our mother.

They say that everyone becomes equal in the casket, but as Benny knelt studying that cadaver, he could still see it. It was as if the mortician had made him up with some sinister effects, face scrunched disapprovingly, head slanted upward a bit in presumed superiority even when the accompanying depletion of adenosine triphosphate in the muscle fibers had set in. Unpredictably, though I couldn't tell from where I was seated, Benny had a different experience than anticipated.

He reached up and put his hand on Captain Thompson's shoulder. He needed for unknowable reasons to connect with what he'd been incited to flee from long ago. Pulsing in his mind was

Eden's heartfelt condolence that morning, "Sorry there won't be a chance for forgiveness while you're both still alive." As his hand rested there, a bit disembodied, he stared at it reminded that it was less thick fingered than our father's. Still staring as he removed it, transfixed, he was aware that in his youthful lust our father had unintentionally created that hand. Benny raised it to wipe off and taste the tear that welled up in just one eye. One eye only, like there was emotional ambivalence where he hadn't conceived there could be.

As planned, before he got up, he wanted to go on a journey, a rose-colored revisualization of his 13th birthday pre-dawn fishing outing with our father, rising at 3am to trek to the shores of Cape Cod to cast their luck into the ocean's diminishing bounty. Unlike what really happened, these imaginings had none of our father's histrionics when something Benny had eaten played havoc and he was desperate for a bathroom where none was nearby. Only a father and his son casting and reeling them in, the stars fading and dawn creating a luscious shine on the water as if all were still possible. Reeling them in like Mr. Tangeran had so supportively coached Paulie to reel in that fish kite all those years ago. Reeling them in so that there would be anecdotes to recount to future generations, lessons to impart that came from good and basic elements.

Benny suddenly was so sapped that he shuffled as slowly as the inconsolably grieving to sit near Eden. That didn't diminish his resolve. He'd never been so determined. His wife had granted him fervid consent, so he was at liberty to deliver his eulogy. Mr. Norbrega, The Funeral Director, signaled him and up he walked to the podium, looking for a second into the eyes of every person whom he knew, heightening the suspense.

"Back in the day my college professor, Dr. LaPrade, griped, 'Why do people waste a once in a lifetime speech on drivel? Why do they toss around platitudes and clichés when there might be greater lessons to offer?' That stuck with me." He delayed until he could continue unreservedly, proceeding with eyes on Eden. "My wife,

Eden Epiphany Culpepper Thompson, who didn't know I was going to reference her today, is a reflection of the family she's from. Families built around class, integrity, and hard work. Their sincerity and understated confidence prevail above all else. You just want to soak it all in when you're near folks like them. Children need and deserve such an upbringing. Davey, my brother whom I love, you deserved such a childhood."

His eyes made the rounds as he continued.

"Conversely, some parents, and for that matter husbands, should be held up as examples of what not to be. This so-called man resting here before us, sadly, behind closed doors he was petty, abusive, and violent. He put us through endless fear and degradation, leaving Davey and me unprepared to function as adults. He always warned us of the consequences if ever we were to tell anyone of this, and boasted that people outside the home wouldn't believe it anyway. Well, believe it."

"So yes, teach your children strength and how to compete. Do not spoil them or be unsafely permissive. But never forget that they are fragile flowers and you are the deep roots out of which they grow." He dropped his head, deciding if he wanted to cap this off. He raised it up and smiled sadly. "Something else I've also never told anyone." He looked at Eden. "Though life has now turned out splendidly for me, I've always wished that I could've had a healthy relationship with my father." He turned to me. "I'll always wish I could have that."

"Thank you all for listening."

He approached the casket, bowed to our father, gently pulled down the lid, and glided out tall and expressionless. My and Eden's glow as we escorted him out the door, combined with that of the pearly white of the newly veneered smile that Mr. Norbrega could not suppress, could've lighted the place if all switches had been shut off.

The Same for Me

Alba, who long ago referred to herself as "Alba the Albina Albino," had the month of August free because her new husband had gone to China on family business. Benny and Eden were free then also. Her new teaching position didn't start until September and training for the Boise Police Department in October. Thus, a road trip was proposed, heightened by the excitement of all this newness. Alba flew to Boise to join them where together they packed, The "Culpepper Caravan." This was to be that interval of allied reflection and the projection of timelines; decisions such as when to have children, how to invest their money, and five years beyond his first professional fight should Benny forge a belated last hurrah comeback to have one more PKA fight slated for the next summer, challenging with his new job and return to college.

They set off southeast, pulling off at scheduled destinations and inspired by unplanned ones, only dining at the oldest non-franchise restaurants in town. Progressing they picked up D'Artagnan from where he had just completed a yoga certification in Boulder, and then headed northeast for 2000 miles to have dinner with Jesse Lee, my mother, and me at Pa Raffa's, our favor ite restaurant in New Bedford. Also, there was my mother's new boyfriend, Chris Hooperman, a jolly, well-mannered antithesis to our father who was four years her junior. He dressed in combination wear equally suitable for the office and the golf course, and had been her lawyer in the successful battle for the division of assets during her divorce. She looked like a different person, glowing in a sweater dress that showed off what her gym membership had done for her physique.

I, of course, couldn't resist my impulse to have a go at impressing Boobala back into the sack by inviting her to a gathering of such fecund minds; the implication being that I was actually a happening guy reemerging from a social lull. A year before, she'd dumped me again upon discovering that my purported dream job didn't exist, not in the least impressed that I'd joined the interminably syphoning culture of freeloaders who use the government as a conduit to other people's money. Now, upon recognizing my voice, she had the prudence to smash the phone down. It was useless. So, while everyone else was toiling away, having families, and aspiring to build a life, after a night of feeling inadequate listening to such restaurant table themes as "The Power of Excuses" and "The Addiction to Self-pity," disgraces I was the poster boy for, I went back to fifteen hours per day of television and random, highly unlikely musings about writing this book.

During the dinner, while feigning fascination as adroitly as a gigolo versed in *listen, empathize then pounce,* my mind primarily replayed four things…

1. "Hope nobody minds that, to conceal my thinning hair, I didn't remove my Red Sox baseball cap."

2. "If I throw caution to the wind and decide to take it off, this hideaway on the Boulevard that has been serving up martinis and "authentic Italian" for 30 years is dimly-lit enough that if I just lean away from the overhead light I should be obscured sufficiently."

3. "Appear genuinely miffed at yourself and they'll believe that you misplaced your wallet so that you don't have to put in part for the antipasto, macaroni and meatballs, and linguica pizza which you probably didn't savor your fair share of anyway due to how fast and how much D'Artagnan eats."

4. "Benny has built at himself so deftly, so free of artifice, that now I have even more reason to be jealous." And I pondered once again, though not for too long because it would've been "too depressing," what percentage was nature, and what was nurture, in how unsatisfactorily I'd turned out. Guess we'll never know.

As the Culpepper Caravan rolled down the East Coast Benny was surprised that the others, all with appreciable fanfare, insisted that they go to Cloudland Canyon State Park, in Rising Fawn, Georgia. Benny had never heard of it.

"You've never heard of it?" D'Artagnan needled. "What are you from the projects or something?

"Has anybody heard of it who wasn't seeking out somewhere remote to bury a body?"

"What?" Alba persisted. "Everybody dreams of going there."

Skeptically, Benny pivoted to Eden who confirmed, "Oh yeah, my parents told me it's breathtaking."

When they arrived at 10am the trees wore the light green leaves of summer, rustled by a gentle breeze. The clouds obscured the sun so it was pleasurable to hike. Following a two-mile expedition along Sitton Gulch Creek chattering to intrepid birds and examining the wild flowers, they rested a bit in the grass. D'Artagnan, who'd shaved off all the trappings of that incarnation in favor of a proper cut with no moustache, serenaded them with old Dixie tunes on his harmonica.

"What do you say we parade to the bottom?" Eden suggested to Benny while making circles out of her fingers and placing them to her eyes to indicate down the slope. "There's a surprise for you down there."

"A surprise! What the heck could there be in this place?"

"Stated in cliché'd fashion, that's for us to know, and you to find out."

"Hey, is this a setup? That's why you guys brought me here?"

They journeyed along the rim trail to the canyon floor, en route riding each other piggyback. Benny scanned high and low, persons and plant life for clues, occasionally over-exaggerating that chin scratch that indicates curiosity. He imagined it would be Alba announcing that she was pregnant, or that Eden had won the lottery, or D'Artagnan had decided to move to Boise to also become a cop.

He asked, "Considering my recent mastery of ESP, must I still pretend to not know what's in store for me?"

At the bottom they sat on the ground, across from where stood a plump woman around age thirty wearing a Forest Ranger uniform.

"Hello," Benny greeted her.

"Hello, sir. Nice day, huh?" she responded, quaintly.

They laid their blanket open onto the ground lying down four across, peering up as the two waterfalls cascaded over layers of sandstone into the pools below. On the right outside of the group Benny reached to clasp Eden's hand. With each holding of her hand he felt renewed, ready for everything, too steady to be undone by even the most puzzling occurrences that beset people and relationships.

"Here we are," Benny announced, letting go of his curiosity to revel in the shared experience.

"Here we are," Eden seconded, with a smile of good-natured conspiracy.

"Here we are," Alba tripled, reaching for Eden's hand, squeezing tight like this is going to be a five-star shocker.

"Here we are," D'Artagnan quadrupled, inspired when Alba clasped hands with him also.

They were like youth in summer camp gazing up, worry, and the future, and time, of no concern.

"The road to wisdom is paved with assuming you know what you're doing along the way," Benny noted.

"So true," Alba agreed.

"Now ya tell me," D'Artagnan chimed in, making them chuckle.

"Hey D'Arty, isn't it ludicrous how teens and those not much beyond, no matter what generation they hail from, assume they'll never want a quieter life someday?" Benny asked.

"Man, I'm slowing down so fast it's scary."

"I'm so slowing that all I want to do is add to my collections of Scratch 'n Sniff stickers and Wacky Wall Walkers," Benny quipped.

"And some Jazzercise."

"That goes without saying."

A hawk floated above them, gliding with the wind currents, occasionally doing a single flap of his wings to relocate himself.

"That dude's smooth," Benny said.

"He'd play sax if he were incarnated as one of us," Eden replied.

"Hey Benny."

"Yeah, Alba."

"I need a king-sized favor."

"You've already borrowed and not returned my lace fingerless Madonna gloves, so what now?"

"Stay looking up because something is going to happen. No sitting up."

"Done deal," Benny cooperated casually, as if this didn't put him again on sweet edge.

Alba gave the thumbs up. The Forest Ranger crept toward them tentatively. She ended up outside of Benny and laid down in alignment. They all stayed like that listening for each other's breathing, trembling terrifically. The Ranger clasped Benny's outside hand.

He heard his own gasp for air. “This is a bit out of the blue.”

The hawk drifted away as if to afford them privacy. At least 1000 people were born before The Ranger opened with, “I wonder what became of The Tedro Family.”

“No! Oh my God! Oh My God! No!” Benny shrieked as his breathing accelerated. “Oh My God! I can’t believe it. This is amazing. May I please sit up and see you? Oh My God!”

“Permission granted,” Alba replied with a giggle.

The Ranger and Benny sat up in unison, rotating toward each other, her bashfully, him exuberantly. She began to cry. Benny couldn’t stop with the “Oh My God!”

“Hi Benny,” she said. As of old, she covered her mouth like she’d revealed a secret.

He leaned back to get a better view. Like a kaleidoscope the pictures switched back and forth between the present and various past sightings of her.

“Oh My God. This is the best surprise ever,” he proclaimed. He got up and moved off ten feet to do a back flip in place. He sat near her, the tears welling up. “Oh, wow. You’re Aggie Boza, right?”

She hadn’t forgotten how to take too long to reply, this time aflame with joy. “Yep.”

The others sat up and positioned themselves to see. They luxuriated in every word and wiped away the tears with their sleeves. For comedic effect D’Artagnan used Alba’s sleeve. Benny and Aggie took ahold of each other. With eyes dripping, Benny whispered, “At first I didn’t recognize you.”

"Maybe if was wearing all red," she whispered back.

"That would've done it." He released her to ask, "How are you?"

"Very well, Benny. It's great to see you again."

"Oh My God!"

Eden, Alba, and D'Artagnan shifted to wrap around Benny, their arms spread to encompass Aggie. They were so relieved that they'd located her by "whatever means necessary" and put their plan into action.

"A classic denouement," said D'Artagnan.

Eden whispered into Benny's ear, "We just wanted to bring you in contact with someone who long ago, way before me, appreciated what a wonderful person you are."

"Thank you," he replied, kissing her. He turned to Aggie and put his hand on her shoulder. "Is it okay if I introduce you to this clan after I tell you something? I've always wanted to share this with your ever since you moved out of Brickenwood.

"I tried to see you before we left, but your father said I couldn't."

"I know that. I appreciated you trying. But now we're here. Reunited in Georgia of all places. So, I just want you to know that, down deep, in my soul, my heart, my mind, you've been with me all along."

She covered her face and let the emotion pour out. Under there could be heard, "The same for me.

Chuckie's drawing of Benny the Volkswagen

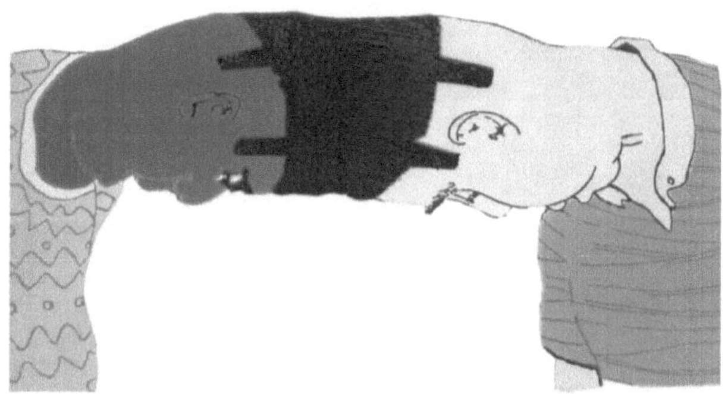

Chuckie's drawing of Siamese Twins Joined at the End Table

About the Author: Raised in New Bedford, Ma., he graduated with a BFA in creative writing from Emerson College in Boston. As an entrepreneur he was the owner of multiple successful businesses in New York City, before turning his focus full-time to fiction writing. He's also a long-time angel investor and martial artist. Married and the proud father of identical twin daughters Dolores and Julieta, he recently became a new member of the 100 club, meaning he's been in 52 countries and 48 states. With such an eclectic and far flung history, his eyes are now on that other 100 club....... years!

Acknowledgments. I'd like to thank Mario Cabrera for his enthusiastic insights about the first drafts and for that amazing stretch of time. I'd also like to thank Lovely Farofaldino, Dolores Devlin, Teri Richardson, Claudia Fucigna, Leyden Guce, Carole Ashley, and my editor, Juliann Garey, for all of their wisdom throughout the writing process.

www.ingramcontent.com/pod-product-compliance
Lightning Source LLC
Chambersburg PA
CBHW031119210626
46816CB00016B/1717

* 9 7 8 1 7 3 3 8 0 4 9 3 6 *